Anne Shorrock was born in Dublin, Ireland. She is married with a daughter and stepdaughter, and two grandchildren. She now lives with her husband in Cyprus. She is the author of the children's book *The Secret Adventures of Amelia and Rainbow*.

'Not to us O Lord, not to us, but to Your Name goes all the glory for Your unfailing Love and Faithfulness.' Psalm 115:1

Anne Shorrock

FOUR GOOD MEN BUT...

AUSTIN MACAULEY PUBLISHERS™

LONDON • CAMBRIDGE • NEW YORK • SHARJAH

A CIP catalogue record for this title is available from the British Library.

ISBN 9781528914185 (Paperback)
ISBN 9781528914192 (Kindle e-book)
ISBN 9781528960816 (ePub e-book)

www.austinmacauley.com

First Published (2019)
Austin Macauley Publishers Ltd
25 Canada Square
Canary Wharf
London
E14 5LQ

Thank you to my wonderful daughter, Rachel, who is always an inspiration to me.

Thank you to my husband, Ian, who is and always has been the wind beneath my sails.

A very special thank you to my friend Colin Pearce for his continual support and encouragement and belief in me. Thanks, Colin.

Prologue

The light was overwhelming, the beauty indescribable, colours, more vivid than any sunset or rainbow he had ever seen. He looked around all he could see was exquisite beauty. Fields upon fields of wild flowers. Meadows filled with daisies and buttercups, and other flowers he had never seen or even imagined in all his life. The sky was an intense blue and through the fields ran a river, gently flowing over rocks and stones. It was an extraordinary sight to behold. And the fragrance, it filled his nostrils, making him practically lightheaded.

Everything he remembered, everything he enjoyed through his life paled in comparison to this amazing sight. "Oh, if this is a dream," he said, "I don't want to wake up." Then he felt the peace, it was tangible, he'd never felt anything like it. Extraordinary beauty, all around him and inside he felt a bubble of laughter that he couldn't control, it was the most wonderful feeling he had ever experienced.

He saw the people. They came over a hill. He saw the colours emanating from them. It was as if they had mini rainbows flowing through their bodies. A wonderful light seemed to be shining from every pore. The people were smiling and laughing. They chatted as they walked towards him. He turned to see where they were going so he could follow. As he turned, he saw a beautiful gate—it looked like it was made of pearls. He couldn't see beyond the gate, only the intense light coming from behind it. He was so happy, *maybe I'm in Heaven*, he thought. Then he looked down to see if his own body showed the same colours and light. He was still in his pyjamas. There was nothing at all coming from his body. He felt devastated, what was going on?

He was grey, just dull grey. He felt a tap on his shoulder, he turned, expecting to be woken up, but instead there was a large black man standing beside him.

"Hi," the man said, "my name is Mick, do you know where we are? Isn't it breathtaking? I just want to sit and enjoy the beauty and never leave this place. But you and I seem to be the only ones without the 'rainbow effect'."

"My name is Derek," he answered, "yes, it is beautiful, but why have we not got the colours and light coming through like everyone else. It makes me feel very dull and dreary," he laughed.

"Well, thank goodness there is someone else that is normal," said Mick. "I was beginning to think I was the only 'grey' one around."

They both looked across and saw two more 'grey' men coming their way. They introduced themselves. One man was called Paul and the other was Harold.

"So what do you think is going on?" Paul asked. "The last thing I remember is working on my laptop at my desk—it was the middle of the day???"

"I remember going upstairs for a lie down." Harold told them. "I was feeling a bit under the weather, but I can't remember actually getting into bed??"

"Well, I remember getting into bed," Derek replied. "Maybe we are all asleep and visiting each other in our dreams?"

"You are probably right," said Mick, "I remember sitting at my table eating a meal. I bet I dozed off."

"Mmmm," Harold looked confused. "How come we are all in each other's dreams? Have any of you ever experienced anything like this before?"

Paul looked shocked, "What if we are dead?" He practically shouted.

"No time to answer that," said Harold, something is happening.

A light shone all around them. It consumed everything. The people, the fields, the flowers, everywhere they looked it was awash with light. But it wasn't like any light they had seen before, it was extreme, it should have blinded them, but it didn't. Inside the light there was a beauty and as they looked into this beauty, they were left speechless, breathless!!

One by one the people with the 'rainbow effect' floated towards the beautiful gates. The four men could see the looks on their faces as they rose. Joy, pure joy, it was the only word to describe it. Their whole bodies looked as if they were on fire but with a fire that doesn't burn.

Then the light dimmed and they were left alone. It seemed as if all the lights of the universe had just gone out. The emptiness and the hollow feeling that each of them experienced was so harrowing that none of them spoke for what seemed like hours, though in fact it was just minutes. The beauty that had surrounded them earlier paled.

"Please let this, be a dream," Mick whispered in desperation. "If we are dead, I think the others have just entered paradise. Where does that leave us??"

"No," whispered Derek, though he didn't feel very confident. "I've tried to live a good life. I didn't purposely hurt anyone. I never stole from anyone and I looked after the people who worked for me. Maybe I could have done more, but I did my best. Surely, if there is a God, He won't condemn me for just doing my best?"

They all agreed they had been good people, well, fairly good. They hadn't deliberately hurt anyone. They all believed in God, and though they hadn't attended church every Sunday, they were all churchgoers.

"What if it wasn't enough," Paul said. "Maybe we should have done more when we were alive and now we are paying the price."

"Who said we're dead!" shouted Harold. "I thought we all agreed that this could be a dream and any minute we will wake…please!!!"

Then the brightness came again. They were terrified now. Each one was reminded of what Paul had said… "What if how they had lived their lives wasn't enough? What would happen to them now, if that was the case?"

If this is a dream, thought Paul, *I'm going to change my ways when I wake up. I'll take more time with my family. I'll play with the kids and let someone else look after the business. Please let me be dreaming.*

A Voice came through the brightness!!!!

The Voice was soft yet strong. It sounded like rushing water. The Voice seemed to cleanse as it spoke, it was the only way they could describe it afterwards. The four men fell to their knees, it wasn't a conscious decision. They couldn't stand when the Voice spoke, the only reaction was to fall on their knees in awe.

"I have called you together to ask you a few questions."

One by one they were called out.

Chapter 1
(Derek)

Derek, a good man, he was a gentleman in both nature and reality. Derek lived on his father's estate, in a twelve-bedroom house with acres and acres of land. He built cottages for his many workers who were scattered throughout the estate. There were four in a row about a mile from the house. These were for the chauffer, butler, housekeeper and gardener and their families. Derek was very thoughtful—he surmised that if the people worked in and around the house, it was right that they should live close by.

Further away from the house there were other cottages. These were for the farm workers. They tilled the land and looked after the livestock. Again, Derek placed them close to their place of work. Always thoughtful of others, he watched the families grow up and every Christmas and Easter, he would get outside caterers in and hold a banquet for all his staff and their families.

No one could quite understand why Derek, who was such a good 'catch' and was very personable, had never married. He was tall, quite well-built with dark hair, now going grey at the temples. He kept himself fit and his clothes were of the highest quality. He was quiet spoken, but had an air of authority that encouraged others to turn to him if they needed any help. He loved the outdoors and was often seen riding his black horse through the fields. Every once in a while, he would call in to the smaller cottages on his farm to check that all was okay with them. He made sure they wanted for nothing. His workers loved him.

He had many women through his life. Most of them would have married him without a doubt, had he asked. But every time the relationship got serious, Derek would back away, and then shortly after, it would fizzle out and die.

Marianne knew this. She really loved Derek, not for his money. She was a very successful interior decorator to the rich and famous. That's how she met him. Yes, she really loved this handsome, lovely man who seemed to have a place in his heart for everyone he met. Rich or poor, it didn't seem to matter to Derek. He treated them all the same. She also knew that if he guessed how much she cared for him, he would back away. So she kept the relationship light, sometimes turning him down when he asked her to dinner, even if it meant she sat alone in her own house. At least this way, she had some control. Her relationship with Derek meant so much to her, she was happy to have a little of him. She had seen what had happened to others who demanded more than he was prepared to give.

She dreamed one day he would turn around and realise that he loved her. She knew it was too late for a family of her own, she had chosen her career over everything else. Now thinking of what could have been gave her a little twist of regret. Although if Derek ever decided that they should marry, she would be able to share the joy of his employees' families. She had always attended the banquets and the fun, and laughter they had at these never left her.

Ah well, maybe one day he will open his eyes and see what's before him, she thought.

She understood why he would never commit to a relationship.

His parents had had him late in life. They were both in their 40s, professional business people. As well as inheriting the money from his father, Derek's dad was extremely successful in everything he undertook. Derek's mum worked alongside him and neither of them wanted children. Derek was a complete surprise and in a way, a bit of a nuisance.

He was brought up by a nanny until he was seven years old and then sent off to boarding school. His parents had him home during the first few years for holidays, but it was lonely for him as they worked constantly. They gave him 'things' to play with to keep him occupied and out of the way. Eventually, he stopped going home at all. At first, he just stayed at the school. There were other students whose parents were abroad, also staying for the holidays. Unfortunately, a few weeks into the holiday, they would join their families and he would be left alone.

Sometimes parents of his friends took him for a few weeks each year. They felt sorry for the boy who had everything, but actually had nothing. Derek got to see what normal families were like.

Then when he was in his 20s, he was informed that his parents had been killed in a car crash. He was totally shocked, though he didn't have much of a relationship with them, they were still his parents and they were all the family he had. So he finished university and took over the farm. He didn't want to be a big business man like his father. He preferred to stay closer to home and enjoy the company of his workers. *What's the point to all of this?* he thought. His parents gave their whole lives to making money, and for what? One minute they were laughing and enjoying their wealth, and the next, they were dead.

He vowed he would never marry or have children. 'What if he turned out like his parents?' It was one thing if one of your parents weren't interested in the children, maybe you'd take after the other. But both of them being like this, he didn't hold out any hope that he would make a good father. 'Better not to ever take the chance!!'

He lived with this fear, fear of being a failure as a father and a husband.

Then one morning Marianne received a phone call, the call everyone dreads. "We're very sorry, Marianne," his estate manager told her, "the housekeeper found Derek dead this morning, he was still in bed. It seems he had a massive heart attack during the night and died." She couldn't take it in. He had been so healthy. He was in his late 50s but he exercised regularly, ate well and he was far from being overweight. What would she do now? What was the point to all this? Where could she go? She could have met someone else by now if she hadn't held on to the notion that he might change and want her. She knew the root cause of his inability to commit to a relationship, but that didn't help her now. She needed to organise Derek's funeral. The workers offered to help in any way they could. Marianne realised just how loved this man was. What a waste!!!!

Chapter 2
(Harold)

Harold was in his late 60s. He was a farmer. His father was a farmer before him as was his grandfather. It ran in the family. He never wanted to do anything else, he loved the land. He felt comfortable on his farm, everything was familiar and that's the way he liked it.

He married Patricia (he called her Trish) when they were in their early 20s. She was the love of his life. Childhood sweethearts, now after all these years she still brought a twinkle to his eye. They had four children, three boys and a girl. Jenny was their youngest. Trish finally had her daughter after three boys. She was nearly giving up hope of having a girl and then came Jenny.

Harold doted on Jenny, but he loved his boys. When they were young, he always took them fishing. They went swimming in the river and he took the time to show them the workings of the farm. He would take them out on the tractor. It was wonderful to see the look on their faces, the first time they got to drive it. He took so much pleasure in showing the lads how the farm worked and they in turn seemed to enjoy doing their daily chores. James, Joe and Jason (they had a thing for J's in the family). They were some of the happiest memories Harold had. Then one by one as they grew older, they left the farm and went off to college to study business, agriculture and science.

Harold was extremely proud of his boys and what they achieved, but it was hard to talk to them now. They were all so clever and if he was honest, Harold felt a bit intimidated by them. They each came back from college with their ideas on how the farm should run. "Don't do it this way dad, do it this way. You're losing so much money, why not try this idea?" They nearly drove him mad with their high and mighty ideas. He was a farmer, he farmed the land. That's what it's there for!!!

James wanted to sell off some fields to a property developer to build one-story offices. Joe wanted to plant different types of produce which would bring a higher yield. Jason only wanted to research the soil conditions to enhance the crops.

Harold felt overwhelmed, and though he loved his sons dearly, they were a constant irritation to him. He never really showed this outwardly, but inside he would get very stressed when they came out with their different ideas.

"When I'm dead and gone, you three can work the farm the way you see fit. While I'm alive, I'll do it my way." The boys followed different career paths after that, and though they came to visit and enjoyed the company of their parents, there was always an uneasy feeling as if in one way they had betrayed their father, who had given each of them a love of the land. On the other hand, they couldn't offer anything new because their dad couldn't see beyond what he knew.

If he was honest, Harold had to admit that he was struggling. The farm work was hard and without his boys around to help him, it wasn't fun anymore. Trish tried to talk to him. "Why not give some of their ideas a try at least?" But he couldn't take the chance. What if he put all his money into their ideas and it failed?? They could lose the farm and all he had worked for all his life. He just couldn't do it. He was too afraid!!!

So he struggled, he and Trish never went on holidays. He could never afford to take her to fancy restaurants, not that she pined after these things. Trish loved her family and now she had grandchildren to enjoy, she was quite content. But Harold, well it would have been so good to take her away and let her be pampered. The truth was, though they weren't by any means poor, he couldn't actually afford to take her on a cruise or a similar holiday, and Harold being Harold thought nothing else was good enough.

The boys and their families came over for Sunday lunch. Jenny was there with her fiancé, David. He was a good guy, they all liked him and Harold was pleased that Jenny had met a good man who would look after her. That Sunday was one of the best days Harold could remember for a long time. Jenny was getting married the following Saturday and the whole conversation was about the wedding and their honeymoon. Nothing was mentioned about the farm and everyone was in high spirits. It was a great day.

The following Saturday came and Harold proudly walked Jenny down the aisle. His eyes welled up when he handed her over to David. She was his baby girl, the last of his children now making a life of her own.

It will be quiet without our Jenny, he thought, *and a little bit sadder. Maybe I should think of retiring, but what would happen to the farm?*

Three months later, Harold was still working the farm. The boys were following their own careers. James was in real estate. Joe was working for a multimillion corporation, testing which types of soil produce the best crops. Jason worked with him, mainly finding areas throughout the third world, where they could introduce crops that would make those countries self-sufficient. Jenny was already pregnant on their first child. She was so like Trish, a real homemaker. Harold was very proud of his family.

One evening he came in from the fields. He and Trish sat down to their evening meal.

"I'm feeling a bit funny," he told her. "I think I will have a lie down, if you don't mind."

An hour later, when Trish had put all the dishes away and tidied the house, she went to see if Harold would like anything. She found him lying on the floor—he was dead!!

Chapter 3
(Paul)

Paul was brought up on a rough housing estate with his two sisters and one brother. His parents had very little money and they often did without to ensure the kids had enough to eat. Paul's dad was in and out of work most of his life. Paul hated the fact that they were so poor. He was constantly put down in school because of the poverty of his family. He hated school he was told by his teachers that he would never amount to anything. He was called stupid and dumb. Most of his teachers ignored him. If he didn't want to learn, then they weren't going to waste their energy on him. There was one teacher who saw some potential in him. She helped him with his reading and writing and with his maths. She explained to him that no matter what he did after leaving school, he would always need these subjects. So Paul learned the basics of reading, writing and maths, just enough to get him by.

He couldn't wait to leave. He hung on until he was sixteen and could legally leave full-time education. He left without any qualifications. Everyone believed he would fail in life. He was known as a dropout.

He was determined to show them how wrong they were. He had a real love of cars, anything that drove really. His first job was washing cars for a huge leasing firm. He worked very hard and was promoted to the office. They soon saw that he had a natural talent for selling, so promoted him again, this time to their sales team. He worked all the hours he could and in no time was the number one sales person in the team.

Having worked in the same firm for four and a half years, though earning great money, he objected always having to answer to someone. He decided to start his own business. He started a small brokerage from his spare bedroom. By this time he had met Elizabeth.

He and Elizabeth were married within two years of meeting. Elizabeth became pregnant almost immediately and she gave birth to Aaron. Paul was so proud of his son, he vowed that Aaron would want for nothing. This meant that Paul had to work even longer hours to bring in the money, but he believed it was worth it. Then Elizabeth fell pregnant again and they had Celia. She was so beautiful she looked like a little angel. Instead of Paul cutting down on his hours to spend time with his family, he worked harder, always wanting the best for his wife and children.

His business was growing rapidly. He decided to rent an office and ran the business from there.

They had a good life. Plenty of money to do the things they enjoyed, but not always the time to enjoy themselves. Elizabeth understood that Paul had to work long hours to make a go of his business. She never complained, after all, she had her two children to look after and was able to be a 'stay at home mum'. What had she to complain about?

Gradually, the business built up. Paul was extremely successful at what he did and he expanded the company from a 'one man band' to having twenty people working for him. The money was rolling in. He had his beautiful car, a beautiful house in a very elite neighbourhood and he had a beautiful wife to go with it. He often thought of the people who said he would never do anything with his life, it made him smile!!

He started buying real estate. He bought his first house, had people refurbish it to his taste. He sold it at a profit of over 20%. He bought another then another. He appointed one of his men to run the car brokerage side while he concentrated on the houses. By the time he was forty, he owned twenty houses. He let them out to tenants and was on his way to making his second million.

Elizabeth dropped and picked the children up from school. The after school activities took up so much time, life was frantic. She didn't want a nanny. She didn't want to miss out on anything they did. She was very grateful that she could spend so much time with them.

Paul, on the other hand, was working day and night. No amount of money seemed to satisfy him. He bought a portfolio of thirty houses and his idea was to renovate them, rent some and sell the others at a profit. The more money he made, the more he wanted.

He left before the children got up in the morning and most nights didn't get home until they were asleep. When their dad got home early enough to see them before bedtime, the excitement ran through the house. These were the moments Elizabeth cherished most. It was great having a lot of money, being able to do anything and go anywhere you wanted, but those evenings when Paul was at home, playing with the children, were by far the happiest of all.

"I promise," he would say, "once this big deal is through, I will take time off and we will go somewhere far away from the business. No phones honest!" But it never really happened like that. They had holidays to beautiful places. They visited sun-kissed beaches or went skiing, sometimes they went to a beautiful cottage deep in the forest beside a lake. But Paul always had his 'blackberry' with him, always took his laptop and spent so much time working, Elizabeth often thought it would have been better if he had stayed at the office. But the children loved it, even for short periods of time with their dad, they were thoroughly delighted. She could never take that away from them. Paul was a good man, just sometimes got his priorities wrong.

Paul knew what drove him. It was the fear of failing, the fear of turning out the way people expected him to.

They had gone to the cottage in the forest for the holidays. Elizabeth took the children into the forest, giving Paul a chance to catch up on some work. She picked flowers with Celia and watched as Aaron climbed trees. When she got back around lunchtime, she found him in his study, slumped over his desk. He was dead!! He was forty-eight years old, and his life was over!!!

Chapter 4
(Mick)

Mick lived with his mum, just the two of them. They lived in a nice enough area, though it wasn't posh, it was respectable. There were many different races in the neighbourhood. Mick and his mum were black, Mick's mum's family were from Antigua. Their next-door neighbours were Irish. There were a few English families on the street. There were also a few Indian families and some Cypriots and Greeks all living side by side. It was a good mix and Mick enjoyed their different cultures. He loved the Irish family next door as there was always music being played.

Mick had learned to play the trumpet when he was a little boy. He couldn't remember ever wanting to do anything else. He used to practise every day when he got home from school. While all the other children played football and other games, Mick would practise his trumpet. His Irish neighbours often asked him to come in and play for them, when they had parties. He was too shy though, but they used to listen when he practised and always told him how good he was.

He never took any exercise or played any energetic games, so as the years went by, Mick got fatter and fatter. The other kids in school used to laugh at him and called him porky. He hated the playground as he was constantly bullied. The worse he felt about himself and the way he looked, the more he ate. It was a vicious circle. Eventually, he couldn't walk up the stairs without being out of breath. This wasn't any good for the trumpet playing, not to mention his overall health. His mum made him go on a diet, and eventually he did lose weight, but it had taken its toll on his confidence.

He played the trumpet beautifully but wouldn't play in public because he was so self-conscious. His mum entered him into a talent contest without him knowing it. She sent a CD he had made for his own pleasure to the judges. They were so impressed they got in touch immediately and invited him to play for them.

His mum had to nearly drag him around to the hall. He was shaking so much he could hardly play the instrument. He closed his eyes and pretended he was at home in his bedroom. He started playing and it was as if he had been transported to a different plane.

He won hands down, everyone stood when he had finished, a standing ovation. Some women had tears in their eyes it had been so beautiful.

There was a talent scout in the audience that night and he rushed over to Mick at the end of the show.

"That's the best trumpet playing I've heard in years," he said. "Come into my office tomorrow and I'll make you a star."

Mick had just turned eighteen at the time and he knew he had a lucky break. The talent scout wanted him to go in for national competitions and appear solo at different venues, but he refused. He just couldn't do it. The talent scout was so frustrated with this young lad but no amount of coaxing would make him change his mind.

He eventually convinced him to record a few demos and send them to some recording companies. Once the recording companies heard the tapes, they were fighting each other to offer Mick a contract.

And so he started his career as a session player. Over the years, he played with a number of well-known bands, but always stayed in the background. He made it clear to them that he didn't want to be noticed. Though he had lost a lot of weight, he was still quite heavy and still very self-conscious.

He travelled all over the world playing at different venues. He enjoyed his life and everyone loved him. He was a genuinely nice guy. Nobody could understand why he never went solo, especially when they had jamming sessions, he stood out. When he played, everyone was mesmerised.

His life was simple, he never married. His music was everything to him. He made good money but no one could ever call him rich. That didn't bother Mick, he spent what he earned and more or less lived within his means.

When he wasn't playing, he liked tinkering with amplifiers and speakers. When any of his friends had problems with their equipment, they took it to Mick. He could take whatever it was apart, sort out the problem and put it back together like new. His friends loved him, not just because he was a good musician and could fix things, but he was a very likeable person. No one ever had a bad word to say against this lovely man.

Mick was still playing well into his forties, still going strong, but never out in front, always in the background.

He used to laugh and say, "Maybe one day I'll do a solo, but not yet."

In his heart he knew he never would, he was too afraid. Fear had taken root in his heart at a very young age and he couldn't seem to get past it.

Then one morning he didn't turn up for a practice session. This was totally out of character and one of his friends went to his apartment to check on him. There was no answer when he knocked, eventually, they called the police and when they got in, they found him slumped over the table. He was dead!!

Chapter 5
(The Voice)

"Harold," the Voice called.

Harold stood and moved forward in dread.

"What was your most precious gift?"

"My family," Harold replied.

"If you could change anything in your life, what would you change?"

"I'd give my sons more freedom in the running of the farm. I wouldn't insist it was all done my way."

"Why do you think you acted like that?" the Voice enquired.

"I was afraid, I was always afraid of failure, so I thought if I controlled everything, at least we wouldn't fail," Harold replied.

"Derek," called the Voice. "What about you? Have you any regrets?"

Derek moved in slow motion, his heart beating so fast he thought if he wasn't already dead, he may just have a heart attack.

"My biggest regret is not marrying Marianne. But just like Harold, I was afraid I wouldn't be good enough." He stuttered. "I thought, if we had children, I might be too busy for them and neglect them."

Mick was the next to be called.

"And you Mick?" the Voice asked. "What would you change?"

Mick was terrified to move, he stayed on his knees, head bent, afraid to look at anything but the floor.

"I would play and play and not be afraid to use my gift," he whispered.

Paul was kneeling and shaking. He hadn't been called out. Maybe the others were forgiven because they confessed. Maybe he would not be forgiven and be sent to hell?? *Oh please, please don't let that happen, please forgive me*, he prayed.

"I have heard your prayer," the Voice soothed. "I also heard the regrets you voiced before I spoke. "Why did you not spend the time with your family?"

"I too was afraid," Paul answered. "I wanted to be a success, I achieved that, but it wasn't enough. I was always told I'd amount to nothing, and those words rang in my mind every day, they pushed me harder and harder but I missed so much because of it."

The Voice spoke to all four men. "You are not dreaming, you have passed from your former life. You cannot go back. It's too late to change anything now. Your chances have gone."

"You, Harold, you were afraid you would lose the farm. You were afraid of change, so you wanted everything to stay the same. You had no faith in your sons, but more importantly, you had no faith in ME!!!

"Derek, you could have had such an amazing life, but you were afraid you'd fail, so you didn't even try.

"Mick, you were so focused on your fear that you forgot what your music could do for others.

"And you, Paul, you wasted so much time trying to prove to others how good you were. You were afraid that what they had said about you might be true. You were so blessed, but you let fear rob you of your blessings."

The four men shrunk, they actually felt so ashamed and so small in themselves. They still didn't know if they were on their way to hell. Each man bowed his head in sorrow and shame and waited.

Chapter 6
(The Great Outpouring)

The Voice broke through their shame and self-condemnation.

"I am a God of love. I understand what you did and didn't do. I also understand the reasoning behind it. You were all afraid. You let fear rob you of opportunities. You all missed so many of My Blessings because you didn't have faith in ME!!!"

"But I do not condemn, I am merciful. You are forgiven."

The love poured over each of them. The light shone even brighter (though they wouldn't have believed that was possible). A peace fell on each of them and flooded their souls. As they opened their eyes, they saw the indescribable beauty that was before them. This was where the 'rainbow effect' people had gone to.

They could hardly believe it. They were not going to hell. They were going to Heaven. This was pure rapture, each of them smiling and laughing and praising and thanking their God. It was wonderful.

Then the Voice spoke again.

"Too many of my people do not use or enjoy the wonderful gifts I give them. When my Son was on earth, He told the people that He had come that they may have life and have it more abundantly (John 10:10). What is wrong with people? Why do they run after things that fade and ignore the things that bring true happiness? Even the people who are dedicated to me are living 'half full' lives. They are always afraid to step out. Always worried about what others will think. I am frustrated with my creation. I have given them life that they may enjoy all things. Why do they chase after things in order to have life?"

The four men stood in silence. That's what each of them had done in their own way. They tried to do things their way, afraid to let others in. They had been afraid to step out in faith. Yes, they were definitely guilty. But the Voice had said they were forgiven? Were they? But even in the guilt and sadness of what they had missed, the peace and love flooded their beings. The joy burst through the sadness and melted the guilt. Though they knew they should be punished for wasting so many opportunities, the joy would not let them be afraid. What was this joy? If they had been on earth, their hearts would have plummeted to the depths of despair. But no, the joy inside each of them contradicted everything they 'should' be feeling. And so they waited for the Voice and in their hearts they were ready to accept anything that was offered.

The Voice spoke again, "I have a commission for you. I want you to go back to earth as a team, each one supporting the other. I want you to live and experience life on my terms. No one will recognise you. You will have the same gifts as before, but this time you will use them to help and encourage others. You will see when you go back that though it seems like only hours to you, two years have passed on earth. I will let you see your friends and families, but they will never know who you are. I want you to see how life has gone on without you."

The four men looked at each other astounded at the mercy they had been shown. This sounded so good, even though their hearts had longed to enter heaven. They knew that they had had a reprieve and they accepted it with joy and enthusiasm. Of course, they had no idea what the 'commission' entailed, but they weren't going to hell and that was all that mattered.

"Of course, we'll go!" they shouted in unison.

"We will listen and obey with all our hearts," said Paul. "Just show us the way."

Chapter 7

The four men closed their eyes, expecting to be rocketed through space. They were all holding their breaths. Nothing happened!!! Then a sudden sense of loss enveloped them. Each of them opened their eyes, they were back on earth. Actually, they were sitting in a car on the side of a country road.

They looked at each other in amazement. "We weren't dreaming, were we?" they said in unison. The road was just an ordinary country lane, fields on each side and trees scattered here and there.

"Where on earth are we?" asked Derek. "I don't recognise anything. How will we know where to go, how will we know which people we're to help?"

"Good question," said Paul. "But we promised we would follow and obey. I only hope we don't fail. Because if we do, what happens then?"

"He promised to guide us," said Harold. "I don't believe God will let us down."

Mick whispered (he was still in awe of what had happened), "We were told we would be given names and addresses of people who need help. I haven't got any instructions in my pockets. Has anyone else?"

They all checked, nothing, no slips of paper as they had imagined. No map reference that they could use and follow. This might turn out more difficult than they expected.

"What now?" Paul asked.

"Let's drive forward and see where the road leads," Harold said.

They drove for a few miles along the lovely country lane. Each lost in his own thoughts. Paul's words kept repeating in their thoughts. "What if we fail? What then?"

It was late spring and the sun was shining. All the buds were on the trees, a perfect day really. But for the four men who had experienced such beauty and love, their only sense was of loss.

Suddenly, Mick shouted, "Stop here. I don't know how I know, but I know this is where we've been sent."

Derek, who was driving, pulled over. They were outside a church with a small house attached.

"His name is Pastor John Humphries," Harold told them.

They all agreed. This was nearly as scary as when the 'rainbow people' had entered Paradise.

"Okay," said Paul, "what's the plan? Do we have a plan? Do we know what we should do or say?"

"I think we will know the words to use, just as we knew this was the place," said Harold.

"I wonder what he'll think when he sees four strange men walking up his drive towards his house," said Derek.

"Let's hope he doesn't have a shotgun and starts shooting at us," said Paul.

"Do you always look on the dark and negative side of things?" Derek asked laughing, though the laughter was more from nerves than actual amusement.

Paul didn't reply. "Actually," he thought, "that is exactly what I do. I never dreamt I'd be called the negative one of the group. I think I need to do something about that very soon." He smiled to himself, he was learning new things already, and they hadn't even started the commission.

Before they could knock on the door, it opened. A young man stepped out onto the porch.

"Good day gentlemen, how can I help you?" he asked.

Then they knew, they knew it in their hearts, this man was the one they had been sent to help. They could feel his troubled spirit. Although outwardly he was cheerful, they knew inside he was struggling with deep anguish and pain.

They could feel the pain as if it were their own.

"We've been sent to help you," said Mick.

His smile faltered a little. "I don't understand, in what way can you help me?"

"May we come in?" asked Derek gently. "We would like to have a chat if that's okay with you?"

John opened the door and led them into a spacious lounge. His face still showed surprise and a little concern.

"Would you like some cold drinks?" he asked. Suddenly, the verse 'many have entertained angels' came to his mind (Hebrews 13:2). He put it away quickly. *I'm being fanciful now, expecting God to send angels to help me. Maybe I'm being paranoid or something.* He smiled, but still, the thought had been put there. He believed totally in God. He knew God could solve all things, but was He that interested in John. That's what always got him.

He came back into the lounge with five glasses and a jug of juice. The men had seated themselves and looked to John as if they were praying.

"You've been praying and asking for help," Harold said. "We've been sent to help you."

"I don't understand how you can help me," John answered dubiously.

Mick continued "We know, outwardly you look happy and in control. Inside something is tearing you apart. What's causing this terrible anguish?"

"Oh!" were the only words that John could utter. He looked totally bewildered. "I'm sorry I don't know you from Adam. You come into my home and tell me that inside I'm falling apart. Well, no offence, but even if there was something tearing me apart, why would I break down and pour out my inmost secrets to four complete strangers? You are very welcome to finish your drinks, but then I'd like you to leave. Thank you."

He stood up and walked out of the lounge. They could hear him bustling around the kitchen.

"Well, that went well, don't you think?" asked Paul.

They all looked at each other at a loss for what to do next.

"Mmm, what do we do now?" asked Mick.

Derek took the lead, "I think we will have to go about this a different way."

Chapter 8

"Yes," agreed Harold. "I wouldn't let my sons know when I was worried or concerned. I know I wouldn't have opened up to strangers in a million years."

They finished their drinks. Paul decided to keep his mouth shut. The thoughts going through his mind were, well negative would be mild to say the least.

Derek, having been chosen as the leader, went to the kitchen and thanked John for his hospitality. He touched him on the shoulder, "I'm sorry if we've upset you. We are quite new to this and are more or less feeling our way around."

"You're quite new to what?" John asked.

"Well, to helping people in any way we can. It's like we've been given a job to do and we're just learning the ropes," replied Derek. "I think we more or less blundered into this without thinking too clearly as to what to say. So please accept our apologies."

John smiled sadly. "I can see that, coming to my home and telling me something inside was tearing me apart, well it's not exactly subtle, is it?"

"Sorry," Derek said again. "We'd like to stay around and help in any way we can, and I mean practically. But first, I think we could do with finding a bed and breakfast in the village. Do you know of any good ones?"

"There's a lovely B & B just five minutes up the road and I know they have rooms available. But I'm not sure you can help me and I don't want you to waste your time."

"We're not talking about reading your mind. We would genuinely like to help you in any way. Maybe there are chores we can perform that will help you out," Derek said.

"Okay," laughed John. "I can think of a number of chores that need doing. I never seem to have the time to do everything I need. If you get yourselves settled in the B & B and come back tomorrow morning, we can get you started on those chores. But I'm not promising they will be interesting."

"It's a deal," said Derek. He shook John's hand and went back to join the others in the lounge.

"Okay," he said to them. "I've told John that we will come back tomorrow morning and help with the chores around the church and grounds. He's told me about a B & B about five minutes up the road. Seemingly it has rooms available."

"Great," Harold said. "I can get stuck in with the gardens. They look as if they've been a bit neglected, also around the outside of the church could do with a bit of weeding. Right up my street." He laughed.

Paul and Mick looked at each other and shrugged. So be it. "Let's see what happens," said Mick.

They found the B & B quite easily. As they were parking the car, it dawned on them that they had no money and no clothes. How were they going to pay for their keep? And what would they do about a change of clothes?

Paul—determined not to be negative—was beginning to think he should have been called Thomas, doubting Thomas, put his hand in his inside pocket. He found a wallet and when he opened it, it was filled with bank notes. He was so shocked he didn't say anything. This was something he'd never experienced before. It was hard to believe. He had always relied on himself and always earned his money from hard work. He believed in God, but he'd been brought up knowing that it was hard graft that paid the bills and not presents from your Creator. And here he was having done absolutely nothing, sitting in a car with three other men looking at a wad of notes that had suddenly appeared. He couldn't keep the smile off his face.

The others didn't have any money so it was obvious that Paul would be the banker. He felt very humbled that he had been chosen to do anything in this adventure. He didn't expect to play any part except that of an observer. "Well, I think God had different ideas." He chuckled.

He paid the receptionist. "Any luggage?" she asked.

They were getting the hang of this now so Mick walked to the car and opened the boot. Inside there were four suitcases. He smiled to himself, "Wow, if someone had told me this could happen, I would have had them sectioned."

There were two rooms left at the B & B, two twin rooms. Without even a discussion, they knew that Paul and Mick would share one and Derek and Harold the other. It felt weird that they didn't have to speak to each other. They all knew what the other was thinking.

They left the B & B having showered and changed. They walked up through the village to a small restaurant on the outskirts. It was a real country restaurant with wooden beams across the ceiling and although it wasn't that cold, a fire was burning in the hearth, which made it very cosy indeed.

As they ate, they shared their life stories, achievements, regrets and the things that made them happiest in their past lives.

Then they tackled the problem at hand. What to do about John. How could they get him to open up? The first thing obviously was to gain his trust, but even then, would he open up to them? If they could only learn what it was that was troubling him, they could form a plan. It would be a start anyway.

Chapter 9

Next morning they were up bright and early. They had a good breakfast at the B & B. Paul asked the landlady to keep the rooms available for at least three to four days. She agreed and they set off towards John's house.

When they arrived, John was already up and about. He welcomed them in. He had made coffee and they sat around the wooden table in the kitchen, planning the day.

Harold volunteered to tackle the gardens and the grounds around the church. It was quite overgrown in places. When he saw it up close, it looked a lot more daunting than it had the day before. He wasn't sure if he could make much of a difference, but he was determined to have a go.

The four men went into the church with John. It was quite run down. John explained that he had taken over as Pastor recently. The church had very little money coming in to do any repairs. They looked around. It needed a coat of paint desperately. The pews needed sanding and re-varnishing. The floor, well that was another matter entirely. The carpet was threadbare. There was no hope of salvaging it. It would take them a while to sort this out, but the plan was in God's hands, so that's where they'd leave it.

"First things first," Derek said to John. "We need to order a skip. Then we can rip this carpet up and dump it."

Outside Harold told John that he would start on the grounds. John brought him drinks at regular intervals, though Harold thought it was more to keep an eye on him and check his progress. Harold realised he was not a young man so he understood John's concern. But then John had no idea where they had come from. It was hard work but he actually started to enjoy it.

Paul organised the skip and it arrived within the hour. They moved the pews to one side of the church. Then Derek, Paul and Mick started pulling the carpet from the floor around the altar first. It was hard work, much harder than they had envisaged. They worked on it all week but John insisted that they rest Saturday and Sunday. John never mentioned any service on Sunday, and the four men didn't want to push him. "We must give him space," said Derek, "he will open up when the Lord leads him."

The four men worked hard, it was a great feeling to be doing something to help. The work in the church was taking longer than they expected, but it was good. If they were honest with themselves, they would admit that they thought they'd come back to earth, sort the problem out and be back before the Lord within a few days. This was not how they imagined it would be.

Each night they went back to the B & B tired but satisfied. They had many conversations with John, but he still hadn't revealed anything to them. They prayed for a breakthrough.

John held the service on Sunday morning in the room at the back of the church. Only a few people attended church on Sundays so he didn't need the full church. But to his surprise, a few more than normal arrived. Then he saw the four men come into the church. He felt a bit intimidated but said a quick prayer and started the service. He didn't preach for very long. The thought going through his mind was 'short and sweet', that way they wouldn't get bored and might come again the following Sunday.

The four men were a bit disappointed at the shortness of the service. The worship was nice, but you couldn't say it raised the roof!!! Still it was early days and they needed to get to know John better and build up his confidence, maybe then they'd see a difference.

This went on for a couple of weeks, the men helping in the church and the grounds outside. It was hard work with just the five of them, well John spent most of his time making drinks and also seeing to his role as pastor in the town. Every Sunday John would hold a service, but the services were short and not very inspiring. The four men attended each week and prayed for a breakthrough with John.

The carpet was taking a lot longer to pull up than they had originally thought. In their hearts, they had thought this would be a doddle, and God would send angels to help them, but it looked as if it was going to be hard labour. Well, if that's what God had planned, then so be it.

Then one morning, some villagers were passing and saw the activity. They came and asked if they could help. The four men were delighted and said, "of course." Some went home to pick up tools, wheelbarrows, etc. It was like a minor miracle, well for John it was a major miracle. He never thought anyone really bothered about the church, apart from the few who were regular attendees.

Derek organised everyone, which was his forte. Before long he had a team of men helping to pull up the carpet. Others were moving pews to the back of the church as the carpet was being pulled up. It was quite a sight to see, especially as the villagers really got stuck in. A few of them went to see Harold and helped with the gardening.

The owner of the local garden centre was driving by in his van and stopped to see what all the activity was. When he saw how many people were helping with the grounds and gardens, he offered to supply shrubs and flowers to replace all the weeds.

Paul confessed that he really enjoyed sanding. One of the men had brought his toolbox, which included a sander. The men carried out some of the pews and Paul started on them. They weren't very bad but needed sanding down before they could be varnished. So he got on with that while people were still trying to pull up the carpet, which was proving to be very difficult.

Mick was helping remove the carpet when he heard one of the villagers speak to John.

"This is great," he said. "Why didn't we do this before? We'll have the church looking wonderful. It's just a pity about the sound system. They cost a lot of money but we'll try and tackle that once we get this lot sorted.

"What's wrong with the sound system?" Mick asked.

"It's old and hasn't worked properly for a long time. It's hit and miss with it, we never know whether it will get through the whole service or not. It's a shame really, but I know nothing about things like that and don't really know anyone who does."

"I do." Mick smiled. "Lead the way, I love a challenge."

John took him to where the sound system was. The villager was right, it was very old and not in proper working condition. But Mick, having witnessed the money and luggage suddenly appearing and people offering to help, had no doubt that this sound system would soon be working perfectly.

He asked some of the men to bring the PA system into the room behind the altar. That way he could work undisturbed and would be able to put the equipment to one side for the Sunday service. He was doing what he liked doing best—after playing that is—he loved fixing things.

Chapter 10

So Paul worked on the pews, Harold on the grounds, Mick on the sound system and Derek orchestrating the removal of the carpet and underlay. They worked all day. It had taken hours to remove a bit of the carpet with the help of the people. But it was rotten underneath and the underlay kept sticking to the floor. The floor underneath was black, at least that's all anyone could see.

A few women had brought buckets and mops. They started cleaning small patches of the floor. One of them shouted, "Look at this."

Derek went to her to see what was wrong. He expected, well he didn't know what he expected, rotten floorboards, tarred concrete, chipped tiles? He definitely did not expect to find what he did.

Underneath the dirt the floor was actually parquet flooring. *What on earth?* he thought. *Who would cover a beautiful floor like this with carpet?*

He looked at the woman, "This is fantastic! I expected it to be bare concrete, but this is beautiful. Thank you for finding it."

"Okay!" he shouted. "We need to sort teams to remove all the pews. We need to try and remove the rest of the carpet. Then we will start cleaning the floor in sections. And that doesn't just mean the women," he added.

They all laughed and started moving the rest of the pews. Some of the people worked on removing the carpet. As soon as there was enough space they started cleaning the floor, section by section—gently, so as not to damage the wood.

Some women came in with sandwiches and drinks.

"Time for a break!" Derek shouted and everyone agreed they deserved a well-earned break.

Paul also took a break. But he felt he needed to be alone for a few minutes, though sanding was enjoyable, he felt he needed time away from all the activities. As he was passing one of the pews, he noticed a Bible on the seat.

We must have missed this one, he thought.

They had placed the Bibles into cupboards at the back of the church.

He picked it up intending to put it with the rest, but something made him open it.

Strange, he thought. *I haven't prayed today, and we haven't prayed together. We've been so busy trying to find out how to help, we forgot to talk to the ONE who sent us.*

The Bible fell open at 'Mark 9:24 – 25' describing Jesus rebuking the demon from the young boy at the request of his father.

Paul always liked this story. The disciples had been helpless against the demon. But what Paul loved about this story was not just the wonderful miracle, though that was beautiful, it was what the father said to Jesus. "I believe, help me overcome my unbelief." Funny he should open the Bible at that particular story!

He sat reading the story and thinking about prayer. He didn't worry about unbelief anymore. He had seen the glory with his own eyes. He had heard the Voice with his own ears. He began to think back on his previous life. He was always busy, running around making deals, earning good money so his family could be comfortable. He had to confess that he had enjoyed the power. He liked being in control. Now, however, he was one of a team, just a cog in the wheel. Was this pride making him remember how he loved to be in control?

He began to pray like he'd never prayed before. "What is it You want me to do?" he asked.

"Trust Me," a voice said. This voice was like a whisper, was it in his head or his heart? He wasn't sure, but he knew he would do just that. He would put all his trust in God. He opened another page of the Bible. 'Eye has not seen, nor ear heard, nor has it entered into the heart of man, what things God has prepared for them that love Him' (1 Corinthians 2:9).

No sooner had he decided to trust God completely, he heard a quiet whisper again saying, "Be prepared, I will show you things you never thought possible."

Okay, this feels a bit scary, exciting, but definitely scary, he thought.

Someone called his name from inside the church. He walked through the doors of the church and couldn't believe his eyes.

It was a little like Bedlam. People were pulling up the carpet and underlay. Some were sweeping up the bits, and others were mopping, some even on their knees scrubbing gently. It was a hive of activity. But something caught his eye, something moving through the crowd unseen!!!

Chapter 11

It was flitting between people. It looked as if it was actually touching them, but nobody seemed to notice.

Is it some kind of animal? he thought. *I certainly haven't seen anything like it before, how weird?*

Then he saw another and another. He found it hard to describe them even to himself! They seemed to flit from person to person at an incredible speed. It took all his concentration to focus on even one of them. But as he looked they seemed to multiply. All of a sudden there were what seemed like hundreds of them. He thought he was hallucinating, just then Derek walked towards him.

"Sorry to drag you away from your sanding, Paul, but we really need your help. The men were doing okay, but I think they all want to be in charge. There is a lot of bickering going on and it's slowing everything down, and it was working like a dream. Everyone was helping and now all of a sudden they're all arguing! I don't know what's going on?"

Paul looked across the church. This was where he'd seen the creatures flitting from one person to another.

"I'll go and speak to them, don't worry, I'll sort it out," Paul said.

He walked across to where the men were, and he could hear the little snide comments that were being made to each other. He was shocked, especially as these people had actually volunteered to help, why on earth were they squabbling?

Once he was closer, he could see the creatures more clearly. They were small and not very pretty, well ugly was a better description. Then one of the creatures jumped on a man's shoulder. Paul couldn't believe his eyes, he let out a gasp. All the men looked at him.

"What's the matter, Paul?" they asked in unison. "You look like you've seen a ghost."

Paul started to say something, but no words would come out of his mouth. He couldn't take his eye off the creature on the man's shoulder. The creature stared at him. It sent a cold shiver down his back.

Can no one else see this? he thought. "What on earth are you?" he asked.

The creature started towards him. It moved so fast it nearly took him by surprise, but he was so disgusted at the appearance of it that when it tried to cling to him, he flung his arm out and sent it skittering across the room. All the other creatures stopped what they were doing and stared at Paul.

"He can see us," they screeched.

It was a horrible noise, Paul looked around the room, expecting everyone to have heard it. But the men were still looking at him waiting for an answer to their question.

"Sorry, I thought I saw something, but it was nothing really," he told them.

Everyone, including his friends, carried on with their chores. The men who had been bickering seemed to have got over it and worked together as before.

Paul watched the creatures. The one he had flung across the room limped back to the group. It scuttled away from Paul, terrified he would come after it. This had never happened before, and it hurt. "How could a human see us? No one has ever been able to see us, but this one was different. We need to be on our guard."

Paul looked around the room. They were everywhere. They were quite small, about the size of a lady's hand. They had big ears and mouths but tiny eyes and their heads looked as if they had been shrunk. Their overall appearance was peculiar. They were not brown, or black or grey, but a mixture of the three. As he stood watching them, and they him, he spotted a beautiful one. It looked female. She was tall and flowed through the crowd leaving a myriad of colours behind her. No one else seemed to see her.

The small ones, well they looked nasty. It was easy to spot them, but this one looked translucent. Paul could only wonder at what he was seeing. He had taken his eyes off the men who had been sniping, his eyes following the lovely creature. All of a sudden he could hear the bickering again.

He walked towards the men. There were dozens of the creatures climbing all over the men. They were on their heads, on their shoulders even inside some of their jackets. They made him feel nauseous.

What are they? he wondered. *What do they want?*

"Gentlemen, gentlemen," he admonished, "there is no need to get so uptight, we're a team and we need to work as a team."

Out of the corner of his eye, he saw one of the creatures whisper in one of the men's ears.

"I suppose you can do it better than the rest of us, can you?" the man practically shouted.

"Not at all," Paul replied. "You are all doing such a great job. I would never have believed so much could be accomplished so quickly when people work together. But what is the problem? Why are you arguing?"

He could see the creatures visibly shrink as the men looked at each other in embarrassment.

"I have no idea," said the man who had shouted. "Sorry, I don't know what came over me."

"I don't know why we started arguing," another man said. "It seemed to come out of the blue. Sorry."

Paul could hardly believe his eyes—the creatures were actually slinking away. They looked so tiny now, though he still didn't know what they were or what was going on. He was looking forward to telling the others about this little experience.

He stayed with the group of men, and before long they were all laughing and working together as before. He kept his eyes open, but couldn't see the creature anywhere. Little did he know what was to come!!

Chapter 12

What a great day, so much accomplished. The four called everyone together and thanked them for their hard work.

"If you are willing and have the time," Derek said, "there is still a lot to be done. Anyone who can and would like to, would you please be here around 10 am tomorrow and let's get this church back to its former glory. I know some of you have to work tomorrow but anyone who can, please come, we would be most grateful."

Paul couldn't wait to tell the others what had happened to him, but this wasn't something he could relate on their way back to the B & B. He would wait until they were at their evening meal to relay his story.

On the way back Paul looked at the people they passed. They were ordinary people going about the daily lives. There wasn't one person who hadn't at least one of the creatures on him or her. In some cases there were hundreds of these horrible 'things' clinging and crawling all over them.

The others were so delighted at how the day had gone they didn't notice how quiet Paul was. Their chatter was contagious, however, and soon Paul joined in the conversation, deciding to forget about it until the evening meal.

They went to their rooms and showered and changed. When they came downstairs the aroma from the kitchen was wonderful.

"Let's see if we can eat here." Up to now they had been eating in the restaurant in the town. "It smells delicious and I'm very hungry," Harold said.

They agreed and found a table in the dining room. As soon as they were seated, the landlady came with the menu. There wasn't a great selection, but it was good homely food and that's what they needed.

"We couldn't help wondering what you are cooking at the moment," Harold asked.

"It's a special recipe of my mother's," she answered. "It's meatballs in an Italian sauce."

"Sounds wonderful," Harold said.

The rest agreed and ordered their drinks.

As soon as she had left the table, Paul began his story.

"I prayed today," he said. "Do you realise we didn't pray today? We've been so busy helping, we actually haven't prayed. I mean I know we pray individually, well I do, but we haven't prayed together since we arrived."

The others looked shocked. He was right, after all that had happened to them, you'd think the first thing they would do every day would be pray.

"You're right," Mick said. "How easy it is to forget. We must all urge each other and I think we need to have a time of prayer together every day."

"Agreed," said Harold, "and there's no time like the present."

They bowed their heads and prayed, quietly but knowing God was listening, they understood they didn't have to say loud prayers.

Paul continued his story. "After I prayed, I read some scriptures. Then I heard the Voice. It was so clear although it was a whisper, I knew it was Him. He told me I was going to see things I never thought possible."

He then went on to describe the creatures and how they clung and crawled over the group of men who were bickering.

"Once I told the men how grateful we were and what a great job they were doing, I saw the creatures physically shrink and slink away. It was weird to say the least."

"Are there any on us?" asked Mick anxiously.

"That's the strange thing," Paul said, "I can't see any near or around us, but as we were coming back from the church, I could see thousands of them on and around the people. Some had hundreds others a few and some only had one or two."

"What can we do?" asked Harold. "Will you tell us if you see any near us, or coming close to us?"

"Of course," said Paul. "But I believe it is something you will see for yourselves. I don't think that I would be the only one from among us that would be shown these things. Four of us were sent back and I believe we were sent to work as a team."

He felt like a light had been switched on in his head. *Wow*, he thought, *I never thought I'd enjoy being part of a team. I was so used to doing everything myself and in my own strength. Now I know, not only have I God to rely on, but I have three other men with me who I know won't let me down.*

It felt like a weight had been lifted off his shoulders. Then he saw something move away from him. It was under the table so he had to bend down to see what it was. It looked like a sack of potatoes, brownish and slimy, but heavy. He knew immediately what it was. IT was the 'heavy load' you carry around when you try to do everything yourself and don't let others share the responsibility. He knew it in his heart.

"I don't think I'll ever get used to this," he whispered.

The others looked at him, confused. It was hard to understand what he was talking about. But the recent experiences had taught them to believe the impossible.

Then the door to the dining room opened and John walked in. They called him over and pulled out a chair for him.

"No," he said "I won't sit. I don't want to intrude on your evening. I've just come to say how thankful I am for all your hard work in the past two weeks. I wanted you to know that though some of the people from today need to go to their own jobs tomorrow, more people have volunteered to help in their place. If I didn't know better, I would say it's a miracle."

A huge creature appeared as if from John's chest. It looked grey-white and faceless, but consumed his whole body.

Paul nearly fell off his chair. It was the scariest thing he had ever seen. Though it was faceless, Paul felt eyes (that he couldn't see) bore into him. He couldn't take his eyes away. Then the creature reached towards Paul. It wasn't an arm, it was more like a mist but felt tangible. Then he heard the words—"We know you," it said. "We know you can see us. We're coming for you. Be careful and keep watching, we're never far away. Nobody can help you, you're on your own and there are so many of us. Look around you, you have no chance."

The mist clung to Paul's arm, he tried to brush it away but his hand just went through it. His heart was pounding in his chest. His throat was dry and he couldn't speak. He could feel his limbs becoming paralysed. It seemed the more frightened Paul became, the larger the creature became. He knew it was faceless, but he could actually see it smirk. Then he heard, though not as words, but as thoughts in his head.

"I've won," it said. "He is weak, he won't fight, he is not a threat to us."

Paul had spent most of his life trying to prove himself to others. He had neglected his family, those who loved him the most, he knew that now. He also felt the inadequacy creep over him again.

He knew that in this new life he'd been given, money or success didn't matter. He knew he didn't have to prove anything to anyone. But he also felt inferior to the other three. Was this the way he was going to feel for eternity? Inside his being a voice louder than any he had ever heard shouted "NO!!!! Enough is enough," and then a whisper—"It is finished."

"I know," he said, "but what can I do?"

Chapter 13

He must have had his head down trying to keep his eyes off the horrible creature because when he looked up, it looked smaller. Was this his imagination? It also looked angrier, it wasn't smirking anymore.

What is happening? he thought.

He looked around the table and back to John. Nobody seemed to notice anything. They seemed oblivious to what was going on around them. Then he heard the awful voice again.

"You can't win," it sounded very angry. "You're weak. You will never overcome us, there are too many of us. Look around you, just look at how many of us there are in this one room. We know you can see us, but we can see you and we know your weaknesses. Give up, you will not win!"

Paul looked around, it was like a veil had been lifted from his eyes. The dining room was full, but the people were blind to the thousands and thousands of creatures that kept flooding into the room. Some were small, like the ones at the church. Others were larger, but there were others who seemed to completely consume the whole restaurant. There were so many, he could hardly see the people, all he could see were the creatures.

The awful voice again, "You can't win so why don't you and your friends just pack up and leave. This is our town. Leave before something horrible happens. It may not happen to you, but what about John? Then you would have all failed before you even began. Better to give up before you cause some horrible incident."

Although the creature threatened, it didn't sound menacing, in fact, it sounded desperate.

Paul felt an overwhelming urge to pray. "Lord, please help me, I don't know what to do, please, show me!"

Then the 'still small Voice' whispered, "Open your eyes. See beyond what you're being told to see."

He loved the sound of this Voice. It brought a peace that he had never felt in his life. It sounded like waterfalls but also sounded like a loving father speaking to a small child, teaching him, guiding him.

He opened his eyes, what an amazing site he encountered. Yes, the creatures, or as now he could see were demons, were still there, around them everywhere there were angels!! Could they really be angels? Was it possible?

He started smiling. He didn't notice the funny looks he was getting from the others around the table. This was the best feeling ever. He wasn't alone, they weren't alone. The human race was not alone on this planet.

He looked at the creature again. It was shrinking. It was still trying to be menacing, but Paul was no longer intimidated.

"Bring it on!" was all he said.

The creature shrunk to the size of an insect. Paul was mesmerised, but before he could feel proud of his conquest, a touch on his shoulder made him turn around.

Behind him stood the tallest, strongest and fiercest looking warrior he could ever imagine.

The warrior winked and said, "I've got your back!" He smiled and said, "Well done, you've got a lot of courage, but more importantly, you have the ability and the desire to hear. You won't always see me, but just remember, I'm always here, as I said, I've got your back."

Then he was gone. Paul looked around he couldn't see any of the creatures. They seemed to have disappeared but he knew they were still around. He knew that to see them he had to let his physical senses go and trust God. Only then could he see with his spiritual eyes.

He turned his attention back to the table. John was now sitting with them and though they were chatting, they were all preoccupied by Paul's antics.

"Sorry," he said. "It's a long story, I will fill you in later." He turned to John. "How are things, John?"

"Fine, thank you, I've just come to say thank you for all you've done at the church. It has made such a difference already. I never thought I'd see so many people willing to help."

"Well, we're not finished yet," said Derek.

"Why were you so frightened when you came to our table, John?" Paul asked.

The other three men were embarrassed at Paul's question. It was a bit prying, and how did Paul know John was frightened??

John's face dropped. "What makes you think I was frightened?" he asked.

"It's a bit complicated," Paul said. "But believe me I know when people are afraid. What I don't know is what could have been so frightening about coming to thank us?"

"I don't know," John mumbled, closing his eyes. "It's stupid, I know, but it's just the way I am sorry."

He got up to leave, head down as if in defeat.

Paul put his hand on his arm. "Please stay, we need to talk," he urged.

John sat down, he looked crushed and exhausted.

"We've been sent to help you specifically," Derek told him.

The others nodded in agreement.

"We told you that when we first arrived at your house," Harold added.

"Yes, I know," John replied. "I didn't know any of you and although you said you wanted to help, well you were strangers, and I've never been in a situation like that before. I've never been approached by strangers offering to help me, just out of the blue."

"Okay," said Mick. "We were a bit forward I suppose, but nothing like this has ever happened to us either so we apologise for the intrusion. But I think now you must know that we are here to help you. Would you like to tell us your story? We know you are troubled and sometimes it's easier to share a problem with strangers than with people you are close to."

John smiled. It was a kind of sad smile as if he had finally thrown in the towel. He looked as if it was time to let go and let someone help him for a change.

Chapter 14

"Okay," he said. "I'm afraid. I can't tell you what I'm afraid of, well to be honest, I'm afraid of everything. It's not something to be proud of, a grown man scared of his own shadow, and in most cases for no reason at all. This feeling of dread just comes over me. It happens every Sunday I take a service. It happened when I walked through the door and saw the four of you sitting here. I came to thank you for your help, and I know there was no reasonable explanation for the fear and dread that came over me. But I wanted to run and it took all my willpower to walk over to you. My whole body seems to fall apart, and though I may (to most people, obviously not you, Paul) seem quite confident, I am constantly trembling inside."

"When did it start?" asked Derek.

"I was a pastor for a church in a large town, not too far from here actually. It started small but they were a great crowd and we worked together and prayed together. The church grew and within a couple of years we outgrew the building. Everything was going beautifully. I love kids. We had a Sunday school which was fantastic. We catered for children from birth to adulthood. We ran clubs throughout the week. It was extremely successful, and maybe I was getting proud."

"What happened?" asked Harold.

"We had a few kids in the clubs during the week. They didn't come to church but that's what it's all about, isn't it? Getting the un-churched kids to realise church is not all about rules and regulations."

He continued. "Some of these boys liked to disrupt the teaching every now and then. Then one night, one of them in particular, I believe he was one of the ring leaders, kept heckling the leader. He was obviously showing off, but it was spoiling it for all the others. We were very patient. We spoke to him and asked him to keep it down. He just laughed and shouted louder. Well, I'm sorry but there comes a time when enough is enough.

"He kept it up, shouting and being extremely rude. So I told him if he didn't quiet down, he would have to leave. But that just made him worse. He started throwing things around and generally getting out of control. I could see some of the other children were getting upset. Of course, I was getting more and more annoyed. I had warned him, but he'd lost it and nothing was going to stop him.

"I grabbed him by the arm and ushered him out of the hall. I probably dragged him out if I'm honest. I told him to call his parents and get them to pick him up immediately. I stood over him while he did it. I couldn't believe the difference in his tone when he spoke to his father, it was unbelievable. He was courteous and I think timid on the phone. When he came off the phone, he gave me a look and said:

"'We'll see who can push people around now!!'

"I have to say, I just thought, oh shut up you little upstart. When the father arrived, in a Rolls Royce I might add, he walked through the doors as if he owned the world.

"'What the hell's going on here?' he shouted. 'Are you okay, son?' he asked the boy.

"The boy just nodded and looked up at me accusingly. I started to say something, to explain what had happened and why I had insisted he be called, but he completely ignored me. He spoke to his son again.

"'What's going on, what happened?' he asked.

"'I don't know, Dad,' he answered. 'I was having a bit of fun, that's what it's supposed to be about at this club. Some friends and I were having a laugh, when this man grabbed me by the arm and dragged me out of the hall. He was shouting at me and made me look really stupid in front of all my friends. He's never liked me. Whatever I do or don't do, it's not good enough. I'm sorry, Dad, I didn't want to drag you out, but he made me call you. I was afraid because he threatened me.'

"I couldn't believe what I was hearing, what a liar, but what a very convincing liar. I was so angry. I actually called him a dirty little liar. Then his father pounced at me and threatened me. He told me if I ever spoke to his son like that again, he would make sure that I'd be thrown out of the church and never work in the county again.

"Well, I ignored him, I mean just because he obviously had money, doesn't mean he had any power in our church. He didn't attend church so what influence could he have? I told them to leave the premises, and unless his son was going to behave in a proper manner, he was not welcome back at the club. He stormed out, pushing his son in front of him. I thought that was the last I'd hear of it. I thought wrong."

The landlady came and asked if they would like more drinks. They ordered beers all around, including John.

"Carry on," said Mick. "What happened next?"

"A few days later I was called into the office of our trustees. The trustees consisted of four men and two women. The head deacon, Tony Kerr was quite influential with the other trustees. He was also a well-known businessman. He was the spokesman for the group. He explained that they had had a complaint from a very important businessman concerning the assault on his son at our club."

"'To be honest,' he continued, 'I was totally confused.'

"'What assault, when did this happen?' I asked.

"They told me what night it was, and even though I remembered the incident with the boy, I couldn't relate it to an assault charge. When could that have happened, I'd been there the whole night.

"They said that this businessman was considering bringing charges against the pastor of the church, which of course was me, for an assault on a young boy!

"It was so stupid, I actually laughed. What assault I asked again. I escorted the lad from the meeting because he was being disruptive and no matter how many times we asked him to behave, he became louder and more abusive. I removed him from the room as other children were becoming upset.

"They told me that they had to investigate the incident and until then I was suspended. I knew it was nothing really, though I was extremely hurt that they didn't take my word for it. But I had to see it from their side. They were concerned about the reputation of the church. So I was suspended for four weeks and moped around the house, not knowing what to do."

Chapter 15

He took a sip of his pint and continued. "The day of the hearing came. They called me in and explained that though the other leaders agreed I hadn't used force to eject the boy, they couldn't honestly say what happened outside the meeting. Seemingly, the boy had declared that I had pushed him and man handled him while we were waiting for his father to arrive.

"He had bruises on his arms. He also told them I had cuffed him around the head, which of course was a complete lie. They told me they had no option but to ask me to leave the parish. They explained that though the evidence was weak, and it was my word against the boy's, his father was very influential and could cause the church a lot of problems."

He hung his head, just thinking of it made him sick. But he continued with his story, "The result was, 'goodbye, John, thanks for all you've done for our church.' They gave me a good reference but couldn't take the risk of going against this man.

"It felt like my whole world had collapsed. What would I do now? How could I ever run a church again? I felt helpless and hopeless. I think that's when the fear started. It hasn't really left since."

"When did you come to this church?" Derek asked.

"About six months ago. I'd been without a church for a year and as you can imagine, I was struggling financially as well as mentally. I tried temping at different jobs, but I knew in my heart what I was called to be. Then one of my previous parishioners contacted me. She knew I had moved to this area and told me that the previous pastor had died and they were looking for a new one."

"I didn't want to apply, I was so nervous, but I also knew that if I didn't go for this, I would never get back to being a pastor. The fear was overwhelming. Even applying for the job was paralysing. The interview was dreadful. I stumbled over the simplest of questions. But I got the job, and I know it's because this is where God wants me to be."

"Saying that," he continued, "I haven't done anything really. Every time I try something or have some ideas for improving the church, the fear overtakes me and I back off. So here I am. I've always enjoyed preaching, but I have to say that lately it's lacked something, mediocre at best. To be honest, I think the only reason the people come to church is that they always came to that church on Sundays. It's habit more than anything. They certainly don't get any teaching from me. I feel such a failure, but that's where I'm at the moment. Well, for someone who wouldn't let anyone know about his failures or inner feelings, I've certainly bared my soul to you all."

Paul saw it again, the creature coming straight from John's chest.

John stammered, "S-s-sorry for g-going on, but you did ask."

Paul looked at John's hands, they were shaking. It nearly broke his heart to hear this lovely man's story and see what one incident could do to a person's life.

Paul prayed, "What can I do, Lord, show me how I can help this man."

The creature looked at Paul and said, "NO, he's mine, he's beyond help. I own him, he will never be free. I will pursue him for the rest of his life, he can't fight me, know this—I have won!!!"

Derek spoke after a pause, "We told you when we met that we were sent to help you. We weren't sent to help the church, though we are quite enjoying seeing it being transformed. We were sent to help you, and maybe in some way help the people of the town. If you will let us, we will. I promise we will not leave until we know you are okay."

John smiled and looked relieved. Paul noticed the creature shrink a bit.

Paul whispered to his warrior. "What can I do, how can I make him see the battle that's going on in this place?"

"All will be made clear to you, just listen to him for now and encourage him as much as you can."

They ordered coffee and encouraged John to stay a little longer. They asked him about his passions and interests.

His first passion was for God, naturally. He said that since he was a little boy, he had always wanted to be a preacher. He loved reading the scriptures and psalms, even when he was quite young. He went off the rails a bit when he was a teenager experimenting with some things he wasn't proud of, but he always felt the pull back to God and Godly things, it was too hard to resist. He finally realised that the only time he felt completely whole was when he was in church and in a relationship with God.

He explained that during the year he was without a church to pastor, he had visited many different churches and listened to many preachers. He learnt a lot during that year, he also learnt a lot about himself.

It was such a pleasant night. They listened to John and encouraged him. They spoke about all that had been accomplished at the church so far. They were so at ease with this man, he was so easy to listen to. They were all looking forward to hearing him preach when he had his confidence back, but one thing at a time.

John asked, "Were you able to do anything with the sound system, Mick?"

Mick laughed, "It's a bit old to say the least so it might take me a while to get it up and running. But it will be sorted, I promise."

They went through all the outstanding items that still needed to be rectified at the church. By the time they were finished, it was eleven thirty.

"We need to head off to bed," Derek said. "We have another big day tomorrow."

They said goodnight to John. Paul wanted to tell them about all that he had seen and heard, but they were all very tired, now was not the time. He would wait until tomorrow.

It was a lovely little B & B. The landlady was very friendly and fussed over them. The rooms were very comfortable and they had slept very well since they arrived.

The last thought that went through Harold's mind before he dropped off was, *I didn't think I'd be tired or need sleep on this venture.*

The peace that came over him was beautiful, a soft voice whispered, "Well done, rest now."

Then he felt his eyes droop and he drifted off to a dreamless, restful sleep.

Chapter 16

Paul, on the other hand, did not have such a restful night. In his dreams the demons fought for the souls of people. The angels battled with them constantly. Paul felt dragged into the battle and the creature that Paul now recognised as 'fear' loomed above him.

"I told you to give up!" it screamed at him. "This town is mine. I rule here and you are not welcome. Leave or something dreadful could happen. You have no idea who you are dealing with."

Paul could feel himself fold. He was bowed down under the pressure of this enormous demon. All the courage that he had felt when he saw the angels seemed to have been sucked out of him. He felt like he was drowning, not in water, but in fear. He had never felt anything like this before. He was paralysed and had no strength to fight, he was going under.

The fear was toxic. It touched every fibre of his being. His heart pounded, he couldn't lift his head. He could feel the sweat pour out of every pore in his body. He trembled all over. He couldn't do this, the demon was right, he wasn't strong enough. He was blinded by the fear so he was unable to see anything but the demons.

How can I get past this? was all he could think.

Then the warrior spoke. Paul heard the strong voice.

"Wake up, Paul, wake up."

Paul dragged himself out of the despair that he had fallen into. He opened his eyes, his heart was pounding and his body was soaked in sweat. The warrior stood at the end of his bed.

"Come with me," he said.

Paul pulled himself out of the bed. He threw on his jeans and t-shirt and followed the warrior out of the bedroom. But he couldn't stop his heart from hammering within his chest. The fear felt real and though he was with his warrior, he couldn't stop shaking.

Then they were floating. Out through the B & B and over the town. Paul couldn't grasp which of the two scenarios was the dream and the reality. Was it the terrifying experience he had just encountered, or this amazing feeling of flying with his warrior at his side? He knew that he wasn't on this adventure for nothing, though at this precise moment he felt like the boy in the film *The Snowman*. And because of this feeling, he was able to relax after only a few minutes.

The warrior took him to a hill above the town. It was a beautiful night with clear skies. Paul was hypnotised by the vast number of stars he could see. It was so beautiful. There was a warm breeze and he could hear the trees swishing. A peace came over him and poured into his soul, it was so lovely, he would have been happy just to stay there and never leave.

"My name is Adrian," the warrior told Paul. "I am your guardian angel, you don't know me, but I've been looking after you since you were born. I have been at your side through all the good and the bad times. It is my job to protect you and guide you. But now, you and I have a lot of work to do."

Paul was shocked. He had never even considered that he had a guardian angel throughout his life. He felt ashamed, he had someone watching his back all these years and he hadn't known and hadn't acknowledged it.

"I'm sorry," Paul said. "I never knew."

"Most people don't," said Adrian. "Don't feel ashamed, it was my assignment and I enjoyed it."

Then as if he was hit by a boulder, Paul blurted, "What happened to my family after my death? Are they okay?"

"It's one of the reasons I took you here," Adrian answered.

They turned towards the hill, their backs to the town now. Adrian moved his hand and a space opened up in the hill.

"Come with me," he gestured to Paul.

They walked through the space and went into a long tunnel. There was a light at the end of it and Paul was excited and worried at the same time as to what they would see when they got to the end. He wanted to see his wife and children so much it hurt. At the same time, he was worried that Elizabeth had met someone else and maybe the children had forgotten him. Which was understandable as he, looking back on his life, saw just how little time he had given to his precious children.

Adrian spoke into his thoughts. *Two years have passed since your death, your children will look older, so don't be surprised. I will show you both the physical and spiritual element so you can see the whole picture.*

Then they were at Paul's old house. Elizabeth was in the garden pottering as she used to call it. A lump came into Paul's throat. He could feel the tears sting his eyes. She was so beautiful. "Did he tell her that when he was with her?" he wondered.

The love he felt in his heart nearly broke it. *Oh, why didn't I spend more time with her? What a waste.* Sadness came over him and it took all his willpower not to cry.

Then he saw his two children, Aaron and Celia. They looked so big now. They were playing chase and running around the garden. Their laughter was the most beautiful sound he thought he had ever heard. Again his heart broke. *How could I have been too busy for my family?* Now the tears streamed down his face, he didn't think he would ever stop crying or would ever get over the guilt of what he had wasted in his life.

Adrian touched his arm. "Try not to feel guilty. Hindsight is 20-20 vision. Look with your spiritual eyes. What can you see?"

Paul looked, "Oh wow!!!" were the only words that escaped his lips.

The amount of lights, like sparkling stars surrounded the children. When he looked closer, he could see they were little angels circling around them. They kept touching the children. They touched their heads, their eyes, their mouths even their noses. He saw them holding the children's hands, leading them and dancing around them. Every time the angels touched the children, they laughed. It was spectacular. Again he didn't want to leave.

Adrian guided his vision to Elizabeth—behind her stood an enormous warrior. He was even bigger than Adrian.

Paul was taken aback at the size of this angel.

"He's huge," he said. Looking at Adrian perplexed. "Why such a huge angel?" he asked.

"She's been through a hard time since you died," Adrian told him. "The demons came on her heavily. They surrounded her and tormented her day and night. We knew we had a fierce battle to fight. That is why Thomas (Elizabeth's guardian angel) is so big, when we fight a battle and win, we grow. Thomas protected Elizabeth from the demons. They were fear, depression, worry, loneliness, guilt, insecurity, anger, bitterness and disappointment and many more. You humans accept these 'feelings' and think they are a natural part of life, but they aren't—they are demons. They do their utmost to break people and keep them in slavery. They wanted to drag her down. They tried to make her feel so low that she couldn't protect her children."

Paul felt his strength evaporate. He was going down into the pit again. The same one Adrian had pulled him out of.

Adrian touched his arm. "Elizabeth is a very strong woman. We, guardian angels, fight the demons and keep those in our care safe. But only the person can actually break the demon. Look at Elizabeth can you see any demons close to her?"

Paul looked and there was such a bright light around her, it looked like nothing could touch her. "The light," he said, "what is it, it's so bright?"

"It's her faith," Adrian answered. "After you died and she was being attacked, Thomas whispered in her ear and led her to your local church. You both used to go there every so often. Thomas knew she needed a place of refuge. She needed peace and hope that can only be found in God. That is why he led her to this church. Within a few months, she gave her life to Christ. Her faith is so strong it shines from her as you can see. But not only can you see this, everyone who comes in contact with her sees her shine.

"I brought you here to encourage you. You needed to know your family was safe, secure and happy. Now you do, so you will not be worried and you will be able to focus without distractions. You have a hard battle ahead of you. You must fill yourself with the peace that comes from above so you will be ready."

They moved into the house. Paul wanted to touch Elizabeth and the children, just to let them know he was around, but he knew he couldn't. They wouldn't feel his touch and if they did, it could open old wounds and he wouldn't do that to his family.

He sighed and followed Adrian. They came into the lounge. The first thing that struck him was a picture of Elizabeth and him on their wedding day. It was over the fireplace and looked as if it took place of honour in the house. All around the room were photographs of Elizabeth and him at various stages of the children's lives. Then on one of the walls was a picture of the four of them, it made him smile when he remembered the day it was taken.

"They haven't forgotten you. They still love and miss you, but one day, Elizabeth will have to move on. She will meet someone else, you need to understand this and accept it," Adrian told him.

"I understand," said Paul, but he didn't want to think of that right now. He was happy he was still a part of their lives.

Adrian broke into his thoughts. "We need to go, we have a lot of work to do and I need to show you so much more than you can yet imagine."

Paul reluctantly agreed. "Just one more look at them. I just want to see the smile on her face and hear the children laugh one more time."

They moved back into the garden, the three of them were spreading a blanket on the grass. They were going to have a picnic. It was a lovely picture and one Paul knew he would never forget.

He turned to Adrian, "Thank you for this. I'm ready to go with you now."

Chapter 17

They were back in the tunnel and heading for the hill above the town. When they arrived at the top of the hill, Adrian asked Paul to use his spiritual eyes to see what was going on in the town.

When he did, it was mayhem. The battles were raging all over the town.

"Is this what it's always going to be like?" He asked Adrian.

"Yes, until people are aware of what's going on in the spiritual realms," he said, "that's where you and your friends come in. We need you to show the people, starting with John, what's going on around them. Once he understands the concept of the war we are involved in, he can teach others about it, and in turn they can teach others and so on."

"Okay," Paul said. "That will be great for this town, but what about the rest of the world. How will they get the message to the people in other countries?"

"Let's take one step at a time," Adrian said. "You four men are going to be very busy for the next few months, and then…" He left it open and Paul did not miss the implications that were left unsaid.

Adrian led Paul back to his room. Paul fell into bed, one part of him elated having seen his family happy and coping and still laughing. The other part struggled with the loss of them. Then there was the battle. "Why on earth would anyone think that he could cope with, never mind help sort out this mess?" he wondered.

He was nearly afraid to sleep. He could still remember the despair he had felt earlier and he didn't want to revisit it. But as soon as his head touched the pillow, he was asleep. No dreams, no nightmares, just rest.

The morning came quickly. It seemed to Paul as if he had just got into bed, but funnily enough he felt totally rested.

I wonder what the others will make of what I have to tell them, he thought. *Will they even believe me?*

The four met for breakfast. Their spirits were high. They were getting somewhere with John. Last night he had actually opened up and told them his story. Now, what to do next?

Paul sat watching and listening to the other three plan their day. *Yes,* he thought, *I would definitely call them my friends. I don't suppose you go through what we've been through and remain strangers.*

He wanted to tell them all that had happened to him in the previous forty-eight hours. He could hardly contain himself but didn't want to interrupt their conversation. He was mulling these things over in his head and praying that what he said would somehow make sense to these men, when he looked up, they were staring at him.

"What?" he asked "What's wrong? Why are you all staring at me? Do I have egg on my face or something?"

Derek spoke first. "You look so different this morning. It's hard to put a finger on it, but you look stronger. It's like you've grown muscles overnight?"

"You also look more confident," added Harold.

"You look a lot less stressed," said Mick.

Paul just smiled.

"Okay, what happened?" Derek asked. "Something has changed within you since yesterday."

Paul began to explain, first about the demon of fear he had seen come from John's chest. Then he explained how he was shown the battle in the spiritual realm raging over the town. He told them about Adrian and what he looked like.

"Adrian," said Mick, "you even know his name? That is amazing. I wonder what mine is called."

"I think you will be told, Mick, but it's unbelievable what's going on around us," he said.

The others sat riveted when he told them how fear had tried to defeat him, how it taunted him and told him he was too weak. Then he told them how Adrian had led him and showed him his family.

"That must have been heart-rending," Harold whispered. Thinking how wonderful but very sad to see his family.

"Actually," Paul said, "It was so lovely to see them. Adrian explained that though they struggled in the early days, Elizabeth brought them through."

He described the aura around Elizabeth, and how she is kept safe from attacks because her faith is so strong.

Paul had such a feeling of peace when he spoke of his family. It was something he had never experienced before.

They chatted and asked Paul all kinds of questions. Paul explained as best he could, especially about fear saying the town belonged to him.

"What happens now?" asked Derek. "Has Adrian (it felt weird calling an angel by his name) given you any instructions on what we are to do?"

"First off," said Paul, "we need to let people know what's going on around them. We need to start with John."

"Easier said than done," Mick replied. "It's hard for us to take in, and we've heard the Voice. How will we explain to people who haven't had our experience?"

"I know," Paul answered. "But Adrian explained that if we tell John what's going on in the 'spiritual realms', and he sees where we're coming from, I think it will go from there. After all he is their pastor, and I believe he will be better at making people understand than we are. Then we'll see what happens."

"I don't know if I want to see one of these creatures, or demons or whatever you call them," Harold told them.

The other two agreed, though they couldn't help notice the difference in Paul.

"Make no mistake," said Paul, "They are demons, I was wrong calling them creatures. Creatures are visible to the human eye, these are not. We need to know what we are warring against. It's going to be tough, and believe me, last night I was ready to throw in the towel. But we've also got to remember that we're not alone. There is an army of warriors, and the angels are warriors, don't forget that. So it's not in our own strength that we will be fighting, we are on the side of the Lord!!!"

I want to share in this, thought Mick, though he didn't say it out loud. But he couldn't contain his curiosity. He also could see the difference in Paul, who up to now had been the pessimist. He bombarded Paul with questions.

"What exactly do they look like?" he asked. "Is fear the main one? What about the little demons you saw first, what are they? And the battle, can you actually see angels fighting demons? What does that look like?"

"From what I can see, so far, fear is the main one," said Paul. "It seems to dominate the others and when it is attacking someone like John it definitely has an effect on the others. You can see them grow and become more powerful, it's very frightening when you see it first, it's extremely frightening. I think what's more scary is that no humans see it, they are totally oblivious to what's going on."

"The smaller ones," continued Paul, "didn't scare me at all when I saw them first. They reminded me of the film *Gremlins*. Not pretty though, but not really frightening. They seem to go around in numbers so they can attack in groups. Now that I can see the warrior angels, I know the 'Gremlins' have no power at all. Well, they seem to whisper in the ears of humans, making them unhappy with their lot. But I didn't notice them being able to do anything else.

"There was one other demon, or spirit I saw. I can't be sure because it was there one minute and gone the next. It was beautiful, all different colours and very alluring. But I know it wasn't a good spirit, there was something about the way it slipped out of sight every time I tried to get a good look at it. I have no idea what it is, but I'm going to find out."

Chapter 18

It was hard to drag themselves away from the breakfast table, they were so enthralled at what Paul was telling them, but eventually Derek spoke.

"I think we'd better get started. They'll think we're not coming. But I think we need to pray before we go anywhere."

They bowed their heads, and each of them asked in their own way for help for their work. Then they got ready for the day ahead. When they arrived at the church, there was a crowd waiting. Even more people had come to help. They were waiting for instructions, or at least directions in what to do. Derek got everyone together, and before they started, he asked Paul to pray for their work.

"Lord," Paul prayed, "we know this is Your work we are doing. We ask You to bless each and every one of us. Keep us from evil, and keep us from harm today. Let everything we do, be pleasing in Your eyes. Amen."

Derek then organised everyone, giving each special chores. A few men came to Paul and asked if they could help with the sanding. They had brought their own sanders and Paul was delighted. They all got down to business and soon the whole place was buzzing.

Mick came over to Paul. "What can you see?" he asked excitedly.

Paul laughed. "You want to see them too, don't you?

"I suppose I do," he said. "It sounds so scary, but there's something in me that's not going to rest until I do. I can't explain it, but I know I need to see what's going on around us."

"Okay," said Paul. "I think you're ready so ask God to give you His Spirit so that your eyes will be opened."

"Great," Mick agreed. He was just about to pray the prayer, but then doubt came into his mind. *Was he really ready? Did he really want to see what was going on?*

Paul looked around at the people working, everything seemed quiet and peaceful. He turned to speak to Mick and saw a hoard of the little demons pressing into him. They seemed to be choking him, some were whispering in his ears. Then he saw fear and another spirit. *Mmm, what could that be?* he wondered. Fear wasn't as big as it had been in John, but it certainly was there.

"Mick," he whispered, "those little demons I told you about, are all over you, and I can see fear, though nothing like what it was in John. Also, there's another demon, not quite as big as fear, but it's big enough. What are you thinking?"

"I started wondering if I really was ready to see what was going on. Doubt came into my mind before I could pray."

"Ahh, doubt, we'll have to watch out for that. Never mind the prayer yet, just tell those demons to get lost in Jesus' name."

All of a sudden, Paul could see them shrink. They were squirming and screaming in what looked like agony. Then they were gone and so was fear and doubt.

"Are you okay?" he asked Mick.

"Yes, thank you," Mick replied, "I am now."

Paul looked around, everything was peaceful again. *All's clear today*, he thought.

Everyone did their chores with enthusiasm. There was an air of cooperation throughout the building. It really was a joy to be part of it. People were smiling and laughing together. If a person was struggling with something, someone would automatically come over and help. Paul was a little baffled. He had expected a battle and had come prepared for war. But everyone was in complete harmony. He wondered what the others thought. And wondered if they thought he had made it all up.

Harold did wonder what all the fuss had been about with Paul. He had been a bit reticent in coming this morning as he expected (from what Paul had said) "All hell to be let loose". But here they were in a lovely atmosphere of peace and harmony. He knew Paul wasn't lying, but this was the exact opposite of what they had all expected.

Derek felt a bit like Harold, but something in him made him feel on edge. He was waiting for something to happen. He kept himself on guard, praying constantly. What Paul had described was not something to be trifled with and it would be so easy to let your guard down in this kind of atmosphere. He was determined to keep his eyes and ears open.

Mick continued to work on the sound system. He was disappointed he hadn't prayed the prayer yet. In fact, from the way things were going, it looked like the battle was over and he had missed it. It was awful to feel disappointed that everything was going well, but he couldn't help it. He felt a failure, again. Then he remembered Paul's words. So he rebuked the demons that told him he was a failure and the demon of disappointment. He was determined to remain strong, so he prayed, not the prayer to see the demons, but to be filled with the Holy Spirit. He knew when the time came for his eyes to be open. God would make sure he was ready. So he felt calm and confident.

About an hour had passed when Paul and the other three became aware that John had not arrived. They had been so engrossed in their own jobs they had thought he was just running late, but an hour, that didn't seem right.

Paul went to Derek. "I'm going over to John's house to see if he's okay."

"Okay," Derek said, "We'll hold the fort here, everything seems to be quiet and peaceful at the moment. I hope John's all right."

Paul nodded and walked towards John's house. He knew he had Adrian at his back, but even so, the nearer he got to John's place, the faster his heart raced. By the time he reached the door, it was hammering in his chest. He rang the bell and waited. Nothing happened, no one answered.

Weird, he thought. *I expected John to be the first at the church this morning, maybe he's gone to get provisions for the people.*

He was about to ring the doorbell again when the door opened slightly. He stood just inside and called John's name. What he heard sent shivers down his spine.

The noise was deafening. It was shrieking, like something terrifying. It seemed to be controlling everything around it. Then he heard the sound of glass being smashed. He could see pottery being thrown and crashing against the walls. But the worst sound was the laughing, no, laughing was a lovely sound, this was more like cackling. It went right through him, the hairs on his arms and the back of his neck stood up. Paul understood that fear had had some kind of victory here, there was no doubt the house seemed to be drenched in it.

Adrian was behind him. "I believe you need to enter the house," he said.

"After you," Paul said, thinking there was no way he was going in there first.

"No, that's not the way it works," said Adrian. "Remember I have your 'back'. This is as much a test for you as it is for John."

49

"Thanks a lot," said Paul. In his mind, he felt paralysed, and he thought his heart would beat right out of his chest, but his feet seemed to be moving forward by themselves.

Chapter 19

What he saw when he entered the house made him want to run. Flies and insects swarmed the room. He took a deep breath and stepped inside. He couldn't believe his eyes. There were things flying in all directions. Paul could see the little demons. There were thousands and thousands of them. They were throwing the pots and pans at the walls. They opened cupboards and flung the glasses onto the floor. They opened drawers and threw knives and forks all over the room, it was mayhem. Some of them had a hold on the curtains, and they swung them outward so they were horizontal. It was a terrifying sight. They were laughing and dancing around John and around the room.

John couldn't see any of the demons, all he could see were things flying around his kitchen and lounge. He couldn't lift his head. Fear had engulfed him. He couldn't get free; he was imprisoned in his terror.

Paul saw from the corner of his eye, a figure huddled on the floor, he realised it was John. Above and behind him was what Paul recognised now as fear. Today he looked bigger by about ten foot and stronger. He also looked more evil than Paul had noticed before.

Poor John, he thought. "What can I do to help him?" he asked Adrian. *Funny,* he thought, *when fear attacked me, I felt like a little boy with no power, completely overwhelmed.* But this was different. John was a good man, a man of God, who loved God, in fact, was His child, fear had no right to terrorise him.

He wanted to distract fear and release John from his nightmare.

"Talk to John," said Adrian. "Let him know you are here."

"John!" Paul shouted over the din. "Look at me, I'm here, come over to me."

Paul could see the tears streaming down John's face. His heart went out to him. He watched as John tried to get on his feet, just to see fear push him back down, then it laughed that horrible laugh.

Paul was about to ask Adrian what he could do, when he saw an awful blackness, a darkness that permeated the room, it seemed to consume everything it touched. It was drifting towards John. Paul heard the screams of the little demons as they were enveloped by the darkness, they seemed terrified of it. He almost felt sorry for them as it smothered them.

It was getting closer to John. Paul began to panic. "Where's his angel?" he shouted at Adrian. "Surely, he must be doing something to help him?"

"Look through the spiritual eyes you were given," Adrian ordered. "Fear is trying to hide John's angel from your sight."

Paul watched transfixed. He could see John's angel, he was huge and he was fighting a fearsome battle. He was slaying the demons as they came towards, but it seemed the more he slew, the more they came at him.

"This is stupid." Paul was getting angry now. "I thought we were stronger because we have God on our side. What's going on?"

Adrian touched his shoulder and said, "Remember what Jesus said? 'You must believe with all your heart.' Nobody seems to have that kind of faith these days. There doesn't seem to be a lot of 'mountain moving' faith anywhere on earth anymore. (Matt 17:20) Jesus also said, 'When the Son of Man returns, will he find Faith on earth?'" (Luke 18:8)

"I'm going in," Paul said. "I can't just stand here watching the darkness smother John."

"Wait," Adrian held him back. "We have reinforcements coming. This will be the time when the demons are revealed to your friends. They will then know what they are fighting against."

"What about John?" Paul shouted. He had to shout to hear himself above the noise. "I know it's evil, but I've never seen or felt anything as bad in my life."

"I will explain later," Adrian told him. "Right now we need to call our brothers to help us stop this mayhem. Just call your friends in your mind now, make it an urgent call for them to come fast."

Paul did as he was told, though he felt a bit silly calling the others in his mind, but that's what he was told to do. He knew he was out of his league here and needed all the help he could get. But it was hard to believe that they would hear his thoughts, yet they had to, he couldn't leave John. The darkness seemed to be getting closer and closer. Anyway, it wasn't about him, whether he felt foolish or not, it was about John and helping him.

Back at the church, the others were working alongside the parishioners. They were oblivious to what was going on at John's house. All of a sudden, all three made their excuses to the people they were working with. They hurried from the church and ran in the direction of John's.

When they arrived and saw the door open and heard the screams, they hesitated. They looked at each other shocked.

"What's going on?" said Harold.

"It doesn't matter," Mick replied. "We need to get inside." It sounded so brave and in control that the other two just followed. But Mick didn't feel brave or in control, in fact, it felt as if fear had grabbed his heart and was squeezing it out of his body. But he didn't stop, he stepped over the threshold. He prayed, "Lord, if You will, then let me see what we're fighting, but only if You want me to."

As he walked into the hall, his spiritual eyes were opened. He was being led by the Spirit and could finally see. Yes, fear was squeezing his heart. He almost fell over, but felt a touch on his shoulder and turned to see what it was. He saw the most magnificent being standing behind him. Nothing in his imagination could have dreamed up someone so powerful. He looked to be at least ten to eleven feet tall. He was radiating power. Light was streaming from him and Mick could feel the strength from that being pour into his own heart. He looked down, fear had shrunk and was so feeble it couldn't touch him, never mind squeeze his heart from his chest.

"I am Andrew," the being said. "I am you guardian angel, I am here to protect you and fight alongside you. We have work to do. Prepare yourself, the scene in there is shocking, but remember I am with you."

Mick walked through the door into complete bedlam. He had never seen so many flies, wasps, bluebottles and other flying insects he couldn't identify. Then there were other things, all sorts of creatures, he was speechless. Paul had described them well, but nothing could have prepared him for this.

Chapter 20

Paul, he thought, *where is Paul?* He couldn't see him. "Oh no, please don't let anything have happened to him please!!!"

He couldn't see him anywhere. In the midst of all the confusion, turmoil and horror that was going on, he could see a bright shining light. As it moved through the room, the creatures, or demons as he knew them to be, shrunk and looked no bigger than the flying insects in the room. Some of them fell to the ground, extinguished by this light force, others tried to escape, but the light moved and as it moved, the demons became less and less.

What on earth is it? Mick thought. Then the light force turned and looked at Mick, it was Paul! Light was shining from him. It seemed to be coming through his pores. Immediately, Mick remembered the verse—'Let your light shine for all to see' (Matt 5:16). He'd thought about that verse numerous times but never quite understood what it meant until now. Paul looked positively glorious!!!

Andrew touched Mick on his shoulder. "Move closer to Paul."

Mick moved quickly to stand next to Paul, *Maybe some of the light will shine through me,* he thought.

Paul smiled at Mick. He didn't seem to be aware of how much light was emanating from his body, actually his spirit. "Well, in for a penny, in for a pound," he said.

Mick could only nod, he was a bit overwhelmed by the light that was coming off Paul. Funny, he was not afraid. He felt no fear of the demons or the flying creatures. For the first time in his life, he felt courageous. He wanted to be here, he wanted to fight. He was on the side of good and he knew in his heart that they would win. "What do we do?" he asked Paul.

"Pray, and demand that fear leaves," Paul told him. "When it sees we are not afraid of it, it loses its power, so just standing against it, is diminishing its power over us and John."

Mick watched as fear began to shrink. He turned to see Harold and Derek at his side, they were both full of light. Their light was not as bright as Paul's, but light was shining from them and they were smiling, and it was beautiful. He looked down on his own body, and yes, light was pouring through him as well. He felt stronger knowing the light was not of him, he knew it was the light of Jesus shining through him. He also knew Jesus had already defeated Satan, the battle was the Lord's, but the victory would be theirs. They couldn't lose!!!

The four of them moved towards John. They made a shield between John and the darkness. As they walked, they prayed. "In Jesus' name, we demand that you leave John alone." They kept repeating the prayer and kept walking towards John.

Mick looked over his shoulder. Their angels were standing shoulder to shoulder, facing the darkness, swords drawn. He could hardly see, their light was so bright. They marched on the darkness as the four men marched towards the demon of fear. The darkness tried to hide, but there was nowhere to go that the light could not penetrate.

Forward they moved, like an army advancing against the enemy. Well, actually that's what they were. Fear was getting smaller and smaller. Adrian spoke into Paul's spirit, *Don't show any mercy. Keep advancing until it has disappeared altogether.*

Paul heard and nodded. Mick heard the order too. They needed this. This was payback for all the time they had let fear dominate their earthly lives!!

They kept moving forward. Earlier fear had had John in a vice. It so completely overpowered him, all that could be seen of him was a bundle of fear lying on the floor.

John looked up and saw the men coming towards him. Strength seemed to flow through his spirit. Fear had to let go of his heart. It couldn't hold on any longer. It tried to whisper something into his ear.

John suddenly shouted, "Enough. Get away from me. I'm tired of living like this. Go and don't come back, I order you, in the name of Jesus!!!"

The four stopped so suddenly they nearly fell over each other. Fear was gone, it had disappeared, nowhere to be seen. Then all the other creatures that had been tormenting John fled. The curtains fell back to the proper position. The furniture stopped moving and then a Light filled the room.

This Light shone, it engulfed the room. It poured into every part of the house, seeping into the walls, flowing through the doors and over the windows. It was like no other light. It was like a thousand sunrises in one. All other light, as in the light from the angels and the four men, paled into insignificance before it.

The Light spread through the room. It touched each of the four men. It felt like they had been cleansed inside and out. They were purified and strengthened by it too. But they couldn't stand in its presence, it was too powerful, it was the Light of Jesus, and they knew it.

All men and angels fell on their knees before Him.

A voice, like many waterfalls spoke. "Well done, faithful and strong warriors. Today the battle has been won. The father has sent me to tell you, He is well pleased with you."

Then the light faded and there was a peace that none of them had ever felt before. It was almost palpable. They stayed on their knees and prayed, but not like they had done before. Words poured from their spirits, words in a language they did not understand. The angels did though, and they sang such wonderful songs, praising and thanking God. Worshipping Him, bowing before Him and their love for God filled each of the four men's hearts. It felt like Heaven and Earth were worshipping together, it was awesome and holy.

When the singing and praising faded, though it never stopped, the four men could still hear angels singing praises. Paul looked around the room, everything was back in its place. There were no signs that anything had happened in that house. He would not have believed it if he had not seen it himself. As he looked, he thought the room seemed more beautiful than he remembered. He could feel the peace and knew that the presence of Jesus had permeated the house and left total peace.

Paul asked Adrian where the darkness had gone. He had seen fear shrivel up and the other creatures flee, but as he had had his back to the darkness, he hadn't seen what actually happened.

"When humans pray in the name of Jesus," Adrian said, "the darkness has to hide. It cannot stand that name, it will be somewhere shivering and trembling, it is terrified of Jesus. Jesus defeated it at the cross. So always remember, when you pray, use the name of Jesus and power will be given to you from above. The darkness can never re-enter this house. Once the Divine Presence has manifested in a place, the darkness can never come near that place again."

Chapter 21

None of the men wanted to move, they could still feel the Presence of the Lord and each just wanted to bathe in it. They sat, eyes closed, each in their own praise and worship and deep wonder at the majesty of Almighty God!! None of them wanted to leave the peace or the beauty that had penetrated into their very souls.

Adrian touched Paul's shoulder, "It's time to go."

Paul opened his eyes and looked around. Each of the men's angels touched their shoulders. As one they all stood together.

"What are we to do now?" Derek asked. "Our help seems so redundant after what we've just experienced."

Adrian spoke, "Today we won a battle, but the war is still ongoing. Satan does not want to give up this town. He has been in control of it for so long and he will not surrender easily. That is why John was attacked so violently. The plan was to terrorise him so that he would leave and never return. But Satan didn't take John's courage, through his fear, and his tenacity into account. God heard John's prayers and pleas, that's why he sent you four men to help him."

Adrian continued, "You need to get him to tell you his whole story. There is something keeping him in bondage. He has hidden it so far down in his being he pretends that it has gone. But it keeps coming back to haunt him and keep him prisoner. Speak to him again, after today, he may open up and tell you, but pray at all times for him and for yourselves. You are fighting a very determined opponent."

He told us his story at the restaurant, Paul thought. *But there must be more to it than he shared. Well, all we can do is ask.*

Paul suggested that they go out on the patio and relax for a while. John busied himself getting drinks and taking them out to his new friends who were standing in a circle discussing their amazing experience.

When he brought the drinks out, they all sat together. Paul was the first to speak.

"I think there is more to your story than you told us John," he said quietly. "I've been told to ask you to share whatever it is that you have kept a secret for so long. Until you share it, it will always have power over you. You will be in bondage and Satan will have control over some part of your life. Tell us your story, I promise the pain will diminish, but if you hold on to it, you are giving it power."

"I was expecting this to happen, especially after the events of today. I have never told anyone, it has eaten away at me for years. It will be quite therapeutic to actually talk about it. But please bear with me, it's been buried for so long, and I have spent years pretending nothing ever happened," John told them.

The four men sat waiting for him to tell his story. It was clear that he was struggling and all kinds of thoughts were going through their minds of what this awful secret might be.

Then Harold spoke, "Let's all pray before you tell us. Let us pray that we will be patient and attentive listeners and compassionate to what you have to say. We will pray for courage for you to share this very heavy burden with us. You no longer have to carry it alone."

So they prayed, each praying and asking the Father to guide them. They were praying in different languages now, just as they had done when they were in the presence of the Lord Jesus. That wonderful peace descended upon them again. Their praising and worshipping lasted for over an hour. They were so overwhelmed by the Spirit they didn't notice time at all. Then it came to a natural end. It was time for John to share his burden.

Chapter 22

He started slowly and chose his words carefully. "When I was a young boy," he whispered. "I had a teacher in school. He was very charismatic and very good with the kids. All of us idolised him. He was funny and caring. He had a few 'special lads' he gave extra attention to, helping them with their homework and taking them on trips etc. We all wanted to be part of this small and elite group.

"I should start by saying that my father left my mother when I was about two years old. She never remarried and there was just the two of us. Obviously, we didn't have much money and couldn't afford trips or holidays. Though my mum worked hard, she didn't want to work all hours and never see me, so she curtailed her working hours to be at home for me when I got home from school. Up to the age of nine or so, that was great. She was always there for me it didn't matter about holidays or trips. We had fun together and had a good life. Then when I started in this teacher's class and heard the other kids boasting about the special trips he took them on, I started wanting to be part of that group."

"Looking back," he continued. "I see that the 'special kids' were not as carefree as we had imagined. After a few months in his class, doing all I could, to gain his attention, he invited me on one of his trips. We were going away for a weekend and staying in a house in the middle of the forest. You can imagine how excited I was, I couldn't wait. My mum wasn't happy, even in those days parents had to be careful who they let their children go away with. But I begged her. She insisted on meeting him before we went on the trip.

"I was so embarrassed. I explained to him and actually apologised for my mum. I still feel ashamed of myself for that. Anyway, she met him and, as I knew she would, was quite taken with him. He had the kind of personality that would charm the birds off the trees. She gave her permission and we went off for the weekend. We had a wonderful time. He was terrific and great fun to be with. I found out on the weekend that all the boys in his group came from families whose dads had either left or died. None of the group had any contact with their dads. This made him even more special in my eyes.

"We came home after a brilliant weekend and I suppose I was boasting to others now that I was part of the elite group. It was great. I was so happy. We went away a number of times that year. Always to remote places that I would never have seen with my mum, it all seemed so exotic. That year was probably the happiest year of my life."

He carried on with the story, but they had to strain to hear him as his voice was faltering. "The following year everything fell apart. We were away on one of the weekend trips. We had gone to a beautiful lodge in a forest, again in the middle of nowhere. All day Saturday we trekked through the forest. We played games in the early evening and then all of us helped prepare the evening meal.

"There were eight boys in all including me. Two of the boys were a bit older. I believed they were there to help the teacher. Every so often, through the previous year, one or two of the boys would drop out, but the place would be quickly filled by another boy desperate to be a part of the group.

"That Saturday night after lights went out, he came into the dormitory. It wasn't really a dormitory, it was a big room with about ten beds in it. We all slept in the same room, but obviously, the teacher had his own room. He came to my bed and whispered that he needed to see me alone. I, of course, thought that I was singled out for something special and jumped out of bed to follow him.

"When we got to his room, the TV was on and he suggested we watch a film before we got down to business. I had no idea what he meant, but I was more than happy to be with him watching a movie. I sat on the sofa with him, he had made popcorn. I remember thinking—this is what it would be like with a dad. The film started innocent enough, but after about ten or fifteen minutes, it seemed to change. It became a bit rude in places.

"Then we were watching young men walking around naked and touching each other. I was becoming very uncomfortable, but I didn't know what to do. He put his hand on my knee. I was terrified, my chest was so tight. I didn't think I could breathe. His hand travelled up my leg, I jumped off the sofa, sending the popcorn all over the room. I tried to reach the door, but my legs felt like jelly. I didn't know how to get away, where were we? All I knew was we were in the middle of a forest, with nothing but trees all around. Still, I was determined to get out of the room, I stumbled to the door, 'I need to go back to bed,' I told him. I was so shocked at what had just happened, it felt like I was dreaming or having a nightmare. I kept thinking, I'm going to wake up in a minute, back in my bed, and Mr Roles will be the nice teacher again.

"He jumped in my path and grabbed me. 'Where do you think you're going?' he snarled. 'What did you think I invited you here for? I've given you a full year of fun and enjoyment. Most of the boys only get a few months, but I thought you were worth the wait. And don't forget, you were the one who did all he could to get into my group. Now you don't want to pay the price? Tough, you don't have a choice. I decide what happens in my group.'

"I tried to wriggle out of his grasp, but he was very strong. I kicked him in the shin and made a run to the door. He grabbed me from behind and threw me on the floor. He kicked me in the ribs as I was lying there stunned. He picked me up as if I was a baby. I hadn't grasped how big he was until then. He towered above me. I had no hope of getting out of that room, never mind getting out of the lodge. He just carried me over to the bed and threw me on it. He started taking off his clothes and I kicked out at him. Then he punched me in the face, I lost consciousness. I must have been out for just a few minutes, I don't really know, but when I came to my senses, he was raping me.

"'Oh, this was worth the wait,' he sniggered. 'I haven't had this much fun in months.'

"Well, you can imagine the pain was excruciating, but the humiliation and degradation was much worse than the pain. I tried to think of something else, all I could see was my mum, and how she would feel if she knew what happened. When he had finished with me, he threw my pyjamas at me and smacked me again, saying, 'get out of my sight, you disgust me.'

"I crept from the room into the dorm. I didn't want anyone to see me. I was so embarrassed and ashamed of myself. I was in so much pain from the rape, but also from the beating he had given me. Blood was pouring from my mouth and I thought I was going to lose all my teeth. My ribs were bruised and I found it very hard to breathe. I climbed into my bed and started to pull the covers over my head when an older boy came and sat on the bed. I was paralysed with fear. It seemed to shoot through me. I couldn't speak, I was at his mercy if he wanted to do the same to me, I knew I couldn't defend myself. I lay trembling, expecting the worst, but praying for a miracle."

Chapter 23

"I didn't speak, I couldn't speak, the fear I felt that night totally overwhelmed me. He spoke to me in a soft and kind voice. Just hearing his voice started the tears rolling down my cheeks."

"'Here is some ointment,' he said, 'for the wounds, and take these painkillers. They will also help you sleep. We keep a supply with us whenever we are with him.'

"I just nodded and he gave me water to take the pills with. I spread the ointment in all the places he had abused and beaten me. I had never taken painkillers before, but then, I had never been in a situation like this before either. I didn't expect them to work so fast, I was asleep in minutes, and didn't wake until the next morning. I knew the pills had knocked me out, but in reality, I didn't want to ever wake up again.

"Up to then, everything in my life had been safe. Now it was all gone, innocence, trust, security, even love and friendship seemed false. I never felt more alone as I did that morning. He had destroyed my life. I was never the same again.

"We washed and dressed and went to the kitchen to prepare breakfast. Some of the boys gave me a funny look as I had cuts and bruises on my face, but no one said anything. Mr Roles was already there, smiling benevolently at us. 'I decided it was such a lovely morning I would get up early and make you all breakfast,' he said cheerfully. He looked over at me and winked. I had to rush to the bathroom, I threw up, but I was afraid to stay there as I thought he might come looking for me and catch me on my own again. I knew if I was in a crowd, he couldn't hurt me.

"We went hiking that morning," John continued. "He was his usual friendly, funny self and most of the other kids lapped it up. I noticed two older boys held back and weren't as caught up with him as the rest. One of these was the boy who had helped me the previous night. I asked if I could talk to him. I needed to know what happened. I knew what happened physically, but I needed to know if I had done something to make him do those things to me.

"'Don't let him see you talking with me, or we will both be in trouble,' the boy said. 'Meet me after school tomorrow and we will talk then.'

"The rest of the day was a blur. I hardly ate and I had retreated into my own solitary world. I just about got through the day because I knew we were going home that evening and he couldn't touch me.

"When we finally arrived at the school, he grabbed me by the arm.

"'Nothing happened this weekend. Do you hear me?' He whispered in my ear. 'You tell your mum that you got into a fight with one of the lads. Say anything about last night and your life won't be worth living. Oh, and don't forget your lovely mother, you wouldn't want the same thing, or something even worse to happen to her, would you?'

"I felt my knees buckle under me. He dragged me up, digging his nails into my armpit. The pain was awful. I had to bite my lip to stop me from screaming. My mum came over just at that moment. She looked at me and I could see the worry on her face, I tried to smile, but my split lip hurt too much.

"'Are you okay, John?' she asked. 'What on earth happened to you, you look awful.'

"He put his hand on her arm. I swear if I had had a knife, I would have stabbed him in the heart. I have never hated anyone so much before or since. I think the hatred is still inside me. But I was a kid, and he was the adult and as he said, I had no power. So I just bowed my head and listened to the lies he told my unsuspecting mother.

"'He had a bit of a disagreement with one of the older boys,' he told her. 'It got out of hand. I am so sorry, it is my fault. I was busy with some of the other lads and by the time I broke them up, John, well, you can see he was no match for the older boy. Isn't that right?' he sneered.

"My mum seemed to think it was a genuine smile. Before Saturday night, I would have too. She was preoccupied with the state I was in to really look at him. She thanked him. Then she put her arms around me and gave me a hug. I nearly broke down then and told her the whole story, but I knew he was watching. We went home and she put soothing ointment on my wounds, at least on the ones she could see. She had my favourite meal ready for me, meat pie and cheesecake for after. But I could hardly eat anything.

"She kept watching me, I knew she was worried, she kept hugging me and stroking my hair. Believe me, it took all my resolve not to tell her. But I knew I couldn't, not only because of his threats, but also because she had gone to see him and had given her permission for me to go. I knew my mum would never forgive herself if she knew, I just couldn't do that to her. I convinced her to let me stay off school for a few days until some of the bruising had healed. She could see I was hurting and kept asking who this brute was that had done so much damage to her son, if she only knew.

"So I nursed my wounds for a few days, she had been granted leave of absence from her job to look after me. She spoke to the principal of the school and explained that I was under the weather and could not attend school for at least a week. I begged her not to mention the incident and she agreed. She actually said it wouldn't be fair to the lovely teacher who had gone to all the trouble of taking young boys to places they may never get to see. The irony was not lost on me, even at that young age.

"As I was not actually sick, I asked my mum if I could go to the local shop. She agreed, though she didn't look too happy. I told her I needed the fresh air and she relented. I was able to meet the older boy as arranged. We met in a park near the school. When I arrived, he wasn't alone. The other boy who had lagged back on the hiking trip was with him. They were thirteen and fourteen years old. They tried to be quite macho about everything, but I knew deep down they were as traumatised as I was."

Chapter 24

"'How's it going?' The older boy asked. His name was Larry.

"'Okay,' I muttered, and hung my head.

"The other boy called Tom spoke to me for the first time.

"'You can't tell anyone about what happened at the weekend. It has to be our secret,' he almost whispered. I could feel his fear, he was terrified.

"'I know,' I replied. 'He told me he would make my life hell if I said anything. He also threatened my mum, saying much worse things would happen to her, if I mentioned what happened.'

"'He told us the same, and we believe him. He is evil and he doesn't care who he hurts or who he destroys.'

"'Why do you keep going on the trips?' I asked.

"'Well, he doesn't bother with us that way anymore—we're too old for him. He only likes the younger ones. He forces us to go on the trips so we can look after the boys, when he is finished with them. We've looked after a lot of boys in the past few years, like we looked after you. We are caught in his trap. If we don't go, he threatened to get one of his friends, one who prefers boys our age, to have his fun with us. If we say anything to anyone, they'll want to know why we've not told anyone before. And let's be honest, who would believe us against one of the most charismatic teachers in the school?' Tom answered.

"'You must have put up a fierce fight. I've never known any of the boys to be beaten up so badly before,' Larry said. 'He must have lost his temper with you, what did you do. I take it you didn't surrender easily?'

"I couldn't stop the tears now, they streamed down my face. 'He said he had waited for me for twelve months, and he reckoned I was worth the wait.'

"I told them exactly what happened and how I tried to get away but he had been much stronger than me. How I'd kicked him and that he had punched me in the face. I didn't know how many times he hit me, but that I eventually blacked out.

"I asked them again why they kept going with him, though he wasn't hurting them, they knew he was hurting someone else.

"'It doesn't work like that,' Larry replied. 'He doesn't do it every time. Sometimes we will go for months without an incident and you know yourself they are good times.'

"'Besides,' added Tom, 'if we didn't go, who would look after the other boys that he hurts. They would be left in agony all night without knowing someone was there for them. He gets us the pills and the ointment. I don't know who from, but I think they are sleeping pills, but he insists we tell the boys they are painkillers.'

"I knew they were right," John told the four men. "Looking back, I think it was what got me through the day on Sunday. I was very grateful that they had been there. And I thanked them for helping me. They told me that he had threatened them, telling them that he would decide when they were no longer required. If they dared defy him or deviate from his plan in any way, his initial threats to them and their families would happen. They told me they felt like his slaves, and although they no longer had to put up with the sexual abuse, every time he hurt one of the boys, it opened old wounds for them. I think I felt sorrier for them than I did for myself. They had no way out. Tom explained that not only was the threat hanging over them, but he had a younger brother. Mr Roles had said that as long as Tom cooperated, he would leave his brother alone. He was desperate to keep him safe but his mum and brother thought he was just being mean, not asking that the brother be taken on the trips. He was in a real state, but what could he do."

"And that", said John, "is the whole story. I saw both boys quite often after that, but when I did, they looked so downtrodden. Their eyes were dead. I felt like I should be helping them, but they kept me company and they were the only people (apart from Roles) who knew my story. I kept myself away from Roles and he kept his distance too. I knew my mum wondered why I never went on the trips again, but I made her think it was because of the fight so she didn't pursue it.

"I have lived with it for so long now—it's a part of who I am. It eats into me, the pain, the degradation the injustice of it all. I often experience flashes of memory of that night. That's when the fear is the worst, it courses through me. It feels like something toxic running through my veins. When I was in the previous parish, I tried to block it out totally. I bought books on how to manage pain and disappointment. I bought all the self-help books I could find. For a time they worked, they offer exercises for the mind, how to banish bad memories, etc. They give advice on how to deal with disappointment. I thought I had overcome it, but when the incident with the boy happened, I fell apart."

"It's no wonder you fell apart," said Harold. "I don't know what I would have done if I found out someone had done something like that to one of my boys." He put his hand on John's shoulder, "You don't have to do this on your own anymore. We're here for you and we will help you anyway we can, whatever way you want us to."

"It's mostly the guilt," John said, tears streaming down his face. "How could I just walk away knowing what happened to me was going to happen to other young vulnerable boys? Why didn't I do something? Instead, I ran away and tried to forget it, or at least block it from my memory as much as I could."

"You were young and vulnerable yourself," Paul said. He was boiling up inside at the thought of someone hurting his son. "What do you want to do now?"

They all expected John to fold and retreat into himself as he had done before. But he surprised them. He sat up straight in his chair and looked at each of them individually. "You have been sent to help me? Haven't you?" he asked.

"Yes," they answered in unison.

"Well, will you help me find Roles? I'd also like to find Larry and Tom," he asked.

His heart was beating hard in his chest, *What if they said no? What then?* He decided there and then, no matter what, he was going to find Roles and face him, man to man. But it would be so much better if he had friends stand with him.

The four men were beginning to think and speak alike. All of them said yes at the same time. "We would be delighted to help." They looked at each other and laughed.

"Well, one thing is for sure," said Mick, "we seem to be on the same wavelength, and then some."

"Okay," Derek said, "first things first. Let's get on the internet, what was the name of your school, John?"

"St James' school," he replied. "I have looked it up and he is no longer there. I have no idea where he went, but I think if we contact the school, they will be able to direct us."

"While you are doing that," said Paul, "I think one of us at least should go to the church to see how they are getting on. I don't want them to think we've abandoned them."

"I agree," said Mick. "I'll go with you, I want to sort out the sound system anyway, I'm not giving up until it's working properly."

The two men left the group and headed towards the church. When they entered, they could see the small demons flying around from person to person. They were whispering in the ears of the people, telling them that their pastor had gone off with his new friends and left them all to do the hard work.

Paul looked at Mick, "They're here again. They really are little pesky things, aren't they?"

Mick laughed and together they prayed, it was a short prayer, but they knew that it was heard. The little demons fled, they looked terrified. Everyone seemed to relax as they were left alone. Paul explained to the helpers that something had come up with John, and Harold and Derek were helping him. But they were there to finish off the job they started.

Everyone got down to work, they worked hard, the women started to mop the parquet flooring with great care. They could only do a small area at a time, the black underlay had stuck hard to the floor and it was taking longer than they had imagined. Paul helped the men with the sanding and the pews were beginning to look as good as new. Mick went into the back room to continue his work on the sound system. The creatures seemed to be staying clear of the church for the time being.

Chapter 25

Meanwhile at John's house, the three men were deciding on the plan of action. "I think I should ring the school," said John. "It's where it all started, and at least they will have a record of me there."

"Good idea," Harold said. "Let's pray for direction. We don't want to do this in our own strength. We need a power that is stronger than ours in this situation."

The three men knelt and prayed bowing their heads, Harold prayed, "Lead us Lord in the way we should go. You alone know all things and the heart of man. Let us be successful for Your glory and let us not try to do this in our own strength."

It felt like Heaven opened and a peace came upon each of them. Paul and Mick felt the peace too, even though they weren't in the house. They felt a confidence in their spirits and a new boldness. They knew in their hearts that their prayers had been answered, even before they started on their journey.

John rang the school and after giving his name was put through to the headmaster. His name was Mr Barlow. John was nervous, he didn't think he would be able to get the words out, but to his surprise, the words just flowed from him. He remembered the scripture, "Do not worry about what you will say, for the Holy Spirit will give you the right words at the time," (Matt 10:19).

"I'm enquiring about the whereabouts of some people from your school. The teacher was called Peter Roles. The two students were Larry Grady and Tom Sykes. The students would be in their thirties. Peter Roles would be in his fifties now."

"Can I ask why you want to know about these people?" Mr Barlow asked.

"It's of a personal nature," John replied. "I knew them when I attended St James' school as a boy and I need to look them up again."

Mr Barlow seemed to be on the defensive. "I can't give that information to you over the phone. Can you come to the school to see me?" he asked. "Can you bring proof of ID?"

John made an appointment for the following day and asked if Mr Barlow would object if he brought friends with him. Mr Barlow was quite happy with the arrangement and said he looked forward to meeting John. They decided to call it a day, and it had been quite a day. John looked exhausted but also peaceful, which was the first time any of them had seen peace in his eyes.

"Would you like to join us for dinner this evening?" Derek asked.

John smiled, "No, thank you, there is someone I need to see. I have neglected her, and I need to make it up to her. But thank you for everything today. Shall we meet for breakfast?"

"Perfect," said Derek. He looked at Harold and raised his eyebrows. He hadn't expected to hear John had a lady friend. Paul and Mick came back to the house, they were quite happy with the way things had gone at the church, it looked better than when they arrived.

Derek explained to the two of them that they had made an appointment to see the headmaster of John's old school. They were leaving just after breakfast the following morning.

Paul said he would go to the church first thing and explain to the people that they would be away for the day. He didn't feel worried that there would be a problem. He knew it was under control—the control of someone far stronger than him.

The next morning Paul came back from the church smiling. The people were happy to be left working in the church. Everyone helping each other, it was good to see.

John and the four men agreed that it should be Derek who visited the school with John. There was something commanding about Derek, people seemed to sit up and listen when he spoke.

It was about an hour's drive to the school. They arrived with about twenty minutes to spare.

"Can we pray before we meet Mr Barlow?" asked Derek. They prayed as they had done the previous day. They prayed for direction and guidance and to do it in His strength.

"Prayer is such a great thing, isn't it?" said John. "Even though I'm a pastor, I don't think I ever understood how empowered you can feel over a situation when you've brought it before the Lord!!"

They all agreed, what seemed like insurmountable problems seem to shrink into insignificance once they prayed.

"It's a bit scary," said John smiling. "It's probably the first time in my life that I've really known that God is interested in EVERYTHING we do and is watching over us constantly. It's still hard to take in."

They left the others in the car and entered the school. They were shown into Mr Barlow's office. It was organised, everything was in its place. He sat behind a large oak desk. He stood and shook their hands, introducing himself. He was a lot younger than they had expected, probably in his early to mid-40s. It seemed weird calling him Mr Barlow.

"My name is Tim," he said. "I'm so used to all the kids calling me Mr., it's become the norm. But I'd prefer if you called me Tim, please."

"You wanted to know about Peter Roles?" he asked seriously.

"Yes," John said. "He was a teacher here when I was in junior school here."

"I'm sorry if I sound like I'm prying, but can you tell me the nature of your business with him?"

"It's a very delicate matter," John started, "one that I've only recently been able to discuss with anyone. But I will give you the whole story."

So John retold the story of how he'd thought Mr Roles was the best teacher ever, and that he so wanted to go on the trips with him, also how happy he had been that first year. Then he told him what happened on the worst night of his life. He explained that if it hadn't been for Larry and Tom, he would have eventually committed suicide.

"I need to find him and expose him for what he is and what he did. Not just to me, but how many others were there? I also want to find Larry and Tom and thank them for what they did. They saved my life and my sanity. I also want to see if they will stand with me against this man and get justice once and for all."

Chapter 26

Tim Barlow looked stunned. "Dear God!!" he exclaimed. "It was before my time, though I did hear stories, but they were only rumours. The tale was that one boy accused Mr Roles of molesting him. To be honest, it was quite a few years ago, and I don't think people took kids seriously. I believe the school held an internal investigation. They interviewed a number of boys around the same age as this particular one. The census of opinion was that this lad was exaggerating. Most of the kids loved Mr Roles.

"Some said they didn't know anything as if they were saying 'no comment'. So the principal decided that the best course of action would be to request Roles' resignation. He didn't want to ruin him, but he didn't want to take any chances with a lawsuit against the school, if the family were able to find other victims and prove the child was telling the truth. He thought it best to sweep everything under the carpet and avoid any scandal.

"It's not how it would be handled now, we keep a close eye on all our teachers, and everyone has to have a CRB check before we will employ them. We also have outside agencies that come to the school to talk to the boys. If they have a problem, they are there to help."

John was horrified, but at the same time, it lulled some of his guilt. He probably wouldn't have been believed either. Then he thought—the same thing had happened to him at his last parish. He was asked to leave to avoid a scandal, but the difference was, he had done nothing wrong, whereas Roles had raped numerous boys. If both cases had been investigated properly, John would still be at his old parish, and Roles would be behind bars.

"Do you know where he went after leaving this school?" he asked Tim.

"I checked the files after our conversation," he handed John a piece of paper with the name of the school on it. "I can't say whether he is still there or not, but it's a good place to start."

"I can't believe he just got another teaching job so easy," John told him.

"Yes, I know what you mean, but as I said earlier, they were different times. People didn't have to have the checks that they do now. And I believe the principal gave him a reference, so he wouldn't have had a problem getting another job."

"What about Tom and Larry?" asked Derek. They had become so embroiled with Peter Roles, he was afraid they would forget about these other men. He wanted to make sure these men were okay. He also knew that without their testimony, John's story wouldn't be enough to put Roles away. They needed corroboration from others to finally nail this paedophile once and for all.

"I have their details here," Tim said. "One of their sons attends this school, so it wasn't difficult. I suggest you call them and arrange to meet with them. I'm not sure they'll want to bring it all up again, but you can only try. These are their phone numbers, I think if you speak to Tom, it's his son that is at our school. He will get in touch with Larry. Tom usually finishes work around 5 pm."

They thanked him for all his help, and as he had asked, promised to update him on any development. They both had a very good feeling about Tim. He was a genuine person and seemed truly concerned about what had happened previously.

When they left the school, Derek turned to John and said, "I didn't see any demons, or for that matter any angels around Tim. I think because I've seen them before, I expect to see them everywhere."

John understood what he meant, though he had never actually seen any supernatural beings, from the descriptions the four men had given him, he knew exactly what Derek was talking about. But then he felt the fear creep over him.

What if they don't want to remember? he asked himself. *What if they have left it all behind and don't want to be reminded of it again? What if I'm on my own and have to do this alone?*

He turned to Derek as they were walking towards the car.

"What if!?" he blurted out.

Derek took one look at John and could see the fear forming in him, it wasn't as large as it had been when they first met him, but Derek knew that John would need to fight this thing for a long time to come. He needed to keep fighting, only then would it leave him alone.

"You know what's happening, John?" he said. "You're letting fear take hold of you again. Only you can stop this. You have to do what you did at your house. Tell it to get lost in Jesus' name. You know there is power in the Name, but I understand that it is your battle, and you will have to fight it until you've finally overcome it and it leaves you alone. Remember, you are not alone anymore. You have your guardian angel in the fight with you, you cannot be defeated. And you also have the four of us watching out for you."

"You're right," John said. "I keep thinking, I'm on my own and I've no one to turn to. But that's not true. I need to train my mind and my spirit not to react to every possible negative experience."

They met with the others and decided that they would have lunch and head back home. They would ring Tom after five from John's house. Derek kept an eye on John, he knew that it was nerve racking for him, waiting until five or after to call Tom. He kept praying in the Spirit for him, he asked the others to do likewise. He didn't need to speak out loud, they knew in their spirits what was going on.

John constantly commanded fear to leave him alone, and it worked though it was very persistent. In the end, John felt a peace that he could not explain. He knew, no matter what, he would see Peter Roles face to face. Even if he had to do it without Tom and Larry, he could not let this situation go on.

They had a lovely lunch and chatted like old friends. Then they drove to John's. Paul headed over to the church to see how things were doing there. Everything was going according to plan, so he came back a happy man, no sign of the demons tormenting the people.

They waited with John and prayed. At five fifteen, John rang the number Tim had given him for Tom. A man answered and John asked if he could speak with Tom Sykes, the man replied that he was speaking to him.

"Who am I speaking to?" Tom asked.

"My name is John," he said. He was a bit apprehensive, but was determined to at least find out whether Tom and Larry would help him or not.

"You once helped me during a weekend away with Peter Roles," John continued.

There was silence at the other end of the phone.

"Hello, are you still there?" John said.

"Yes, I'm still here, and yes, I remember you, John. What can I do for you?"

He sounded distant and a bit angry to John's ears. John could feel the fear creep into his veins. He quickly rebuked it in Jesus' name before it took hold.

"I would very much like to meet up with you and Larry, if at all possible," he said into the phone.

"Why?" asked Tom angrily, "Why after all these years do you want to drag up the past?"

"Well, it's a long story," John answered. "I'm still trying to get my head around it myself, if I'm honest. But it's not something I can speak about over the phone. I need to see you to explain what's happened to me recently. Also, I would really like to thank you for looking after me when I was in such a mess. I really believe that you saved my life, I think if it hadn't been for you and Larry, and your kindness in the months that followed, I would have killed myself. I was so low, and your friendship in those months helped me more than you will ever know."

"Okay," Tom said. "I will phone Larry, we still keep in touch. When you've gone through what we went through, for those years, you need that support."

They arranged to meet around 7 that evening. Again the four decided that it should be Derek who went with John. The other three would remain behind. They didn't want to intimidate Tom and Larry by all four coming with John.

"You go," Harold told Derek. "We'll hold the fort. If you need help, just think it and we'll know what to do."

John and Derek found the small restaurant Tom had told them about. They had a beer each while they waited for the men to arrive.

Derek looked around the room. He was still amazed that he could see demons and angels fighting. He couldn't remember exactly when he had started to see this. *Must have been at John's yesterday morning!* he thought.

It just seemed normal to him now. As he looked around, he saw a few children in the restaurant. He could see their angels standing guard over them. They were surrounded with light. It was so bright it was beautiful. He also saw a few adults surrounded with the same light. Derek was smiling, though he knew the battle was going on, he also knew who would win. There were others who had demons prodding them and whispering in their ears.

When they saw Derek looking at them, they seemed to shrink as if they were trying to hide from him. Then, of course, there was fear presiding over them all. It looked huge and in control. Fear turned in Derek's direction as if challenging him. Derek smiled, in fact, a chuckle started to bubble up through his spirit and he started laughing at fear.

Fear looked so angry. It tried to come towards Derek, but then started to shrivel. The more it tried to get to Derek, the smaller it got. "You may have won this round," it shrieked at Derek, "but I'm still in control and I always will be!!"

Derek heard another voice, a very commanding voice saying, "You know your days are numbered. Even now, you are losing your power. More and more people will hear about you and you will diminish. Once people see what you are and they have the power in them to fight you, you will be defeated."

Chapter 27

All of a sudden, plates, knives, forks and spoons flew off one of the tables. It was where fear was hovering. Everybody in the restaurant jumped. They all looked around to see what had caused it. The two men sitting at that particular table sat paralysed. The waiter ran to the table and picked everything up and gave the men a dirty look as if they had deliberately thrown things on the floor. One of the men apologised, "I don't know what happened," he said. "I'm so sorry, let me help."

The waiter said it was okay. He seemed to accept the explanation. He'd probably seen worse.

John watched the men. They had come in after him and Derek, they hadn't looked at anyone, just sat whispering to each other.

"I think it's them," he said to Derek. "Unless I'm very much mistaken, it's Tom and Larry. They haven't changed very much since I met them all those years ago. They look just as scared as they did then. I feel awful asking for their help."

"Time for prayer," Derek said. Every time they were unsure of how to continue, they prayed. Once they prayed, the way was made clear to them. So they bowed their heads in silent prayer. Nobody really looked at them. The majority of diners were too wrapped up in their own worlds to notice anything. Except the two men who sat whispering.

Their eyes were drawn to Derek and John's table. Tom recognised John first.

"I know it's him," he told Larry. "He hasn't changed much in all these years. Older and taller, of course, but he still has that same look about him."

"Yes," agreed Larry. "I know what you mean about the look. There was always something about him, even when he was young. A kind of goodness in him that was evident. I know it's him. What do you want to do? Will we join him and his friend? "

"Yes, lets," said Tom. They both started walking towards the table.

Meantime, Derek and John were deep in prayer. Derek prayed "Lord, this is a very awkward situation for us. I know that if You are in charge, it will go smoothly. We want to leave the outcome to You, not what we want, but what You want. Help us get over our feelings of inadequacy so that we may accomplish all that You want us to."

As soon as he had he finished and John joined in the 'Amen', John felt a tap on the shoulder. He turned to see who it was. It was Tom.

"Do you mind if we join you?" he asked nervously.

John beamed and said, "Of course not, please take a seat."

They shook hands and John introduced them to Derek, he told them that Derek was a close friend and support to him at this time. The two men sat down at the table. None of them had eaten, and they asked the waiter to bring some menus. They decided to order their meals before they got down to business. As they were concentrating on what to eat, Derek was prompted to look with his spiritual eyes. He'd never heard the prompt before, but it didn't shock him as Paul had explained it all so clearly. It just seemed natural that all four men would see it eventually. He knew Mick could see into the supernatural. He hoped Harold could too—then they would be as one. Everything else they said and did seemed to come from one voice.

He looked around, and surprise, surprise there looming above Tom and Larry was fear. It looked huge, a lot bigger than before and a lot more menacing than Derek had ever seen it. It smirked at Derek, it looked so powerful. It took all his willpower not to be intimidated by it.

He understood that the two men didn't know that fear was, in fact, a demon, so they couldn't fight it. Then he noticed something else which seemed to hover over the two men. It was a grey mist and it was thick like a fog, he couldn't see through it. He felt a shiver go down his spine. Fear looked over in his direction and grinned horrendously.

Derek's angel touched his shoulder. "I am Mark," he said. "Don't be afraid, you are not alone in this. Look over there," he pointed over to a corner in the restaurant.

Derek could see a picture—some would call it a vision. He saw his three friends, they were kneeling in prayer. It was such an amazing site, it brought tears to his eyes. The four men had become so close in these past few days. He had never been this close to anyone in all his life.

Mark spoke again and when he did, fear physically flinched. "When someone prays in faith as your friends are doing, a huge army is released to fight beside you, so don't feel intimidated."

Derek felt better immediately and he felt stronger, both spiritually and physically. He was growing, just as Paul had, and he could feel it.

The four men ordered their meal and John, Tom and Larry began sharing what had gone on in their lives and what each of them was doing presently.

Tom spoke first, "As you know, after the weekend we met you, we continued to go on the trips. You know it wasn't our decision, but we didn't feel we had any option or any way out of it. We actually carried on for about twelve more months, and a lot of the time nothing happened and everyone had a great weekend. But there was always the fear in us of what might happen. It's hard to explain, but it's like waiting for the worst to happen, then when it doesn't, it is such a relief. But when it does, it's crushing.

"We were getting too old to go on the trips and other kids started arguing that they should be taken. It was getting around the school and people were taking notice of these weekends away.

"One teacher approached me, his name was Mr Kenny," said Larry. "He was one of the good guys. He asked why we kept going on these weekends with Peter. I tried to look cool and said we helped with the younger ones and helped Mr Roles to organise the activities, etc."

"'Why,' he asked, 'if you both go on all the trips, does Tom's younger brother not go with you? You could look after him. James is his name, isn't it?'"

Larry told how he was speechless, he could have lied and said James wasn't interested, or Tom's mum wouldn't let him, but if Mr Kenny checked, he would find out the lie. So he told Mr Kenny that he and Tom didn't want James along with them. They were able keep the other boys in check, but if James came, he'd be following Tom around the whole time, and then maybe the others would start doing the same thing. He said it was better for him and Tom that James didn't come.

"He looked at me suspiciously and nodded," Larry continued. "I knew he didn't believe me for one minute. I got away from him as soon as I could. I knew if I stayed talking to him, I'd tell him everything. He was that kind of man, someone you knew you could trust, but I was too terrified to let that happen. I think that was the beginning of the end for Peter Roles at St James."

Chapter 28

"Over the next few months," Tom took up the story, "a few of the other teachers started showing interest in the weekends away. At first, Roles carried on as normal, and as you know, we could go months without anything happening. But I think he noticed the other teachers taking an interest, and he became aware his days were numbered. We went a few months without any problems, nobody was hurt and everyone had a great time. But it had been quite a while since there was an incident, so we were getting ready, we knew it would happen soon."

"Then on one of the trips, he started acting like a man possessed. He took one of the boys to his room. We waited with dread in our hearts. When the boy came out, he was in a terrible state. He wasn't beaten up like you were, but he was so distraught and kept blaming himself. Larry and I had to take him to one side and quietly have a word with him. We explained that sometimes this happens and we gave him the pills and the ointment to help him. We told him that he couldn't tell anyone about it because we would all get in big trouble with Roles.

"I can still see the look on his face, when we told him. I have never felt so condemned in all my life," said Larry.

"The young boy shouted at me," he continued. "He accused us of collaborating with Roles, he was screaming at us, asking us how could we allow this to happen to him, how did we keep going on the trips when these things were happening to other boys. The tears were streaming down his face. He kept looking at us, saying we knew it was going to happen to him but did nothing to stop it."

Both men hung their heads in shame. Derek watched fascinated at what was going on around them. Fear had actually shrivelled a bit and just as Derek was about to feel triumphant about this, the thick grey mist covered the men's bodies and fear looked at him with that awful grin again.

Mark touched Derek's shoulder, telling him not to become discouraged. "Remember who is really in charge here. Don't rely on what you see, look up, always look up," he told him.

Tom carried on with the story. "Larry and I felt so guilty, we couldn't sleep. After the young boy had taken the pills, he fell into a deep sleep, but we lay awake feeling like killers. Then we heard Roles come out of his room again. This had never happened before. He looked like a mad man. He went towards one of the younger boys, one that had been with us on a lot of weekends. He was small and had blond curly hair. He was so innocent. We had hoped that he'd be the one who got away because Roles had never bothered with him.

"To be honest, he had never taken an interest in this lad at all. We thought he would be the one who got the best of the weekends without paying the price. So when we saw Roles taking this young boy, we jumped out of bed and ran over to him. We pulled the boy away from him and pushed Roles over.

"When Roles got to his feet, he was furious," Tom continued. "He started screaming at us to stay out of his way, or we would be really sorry. But we couldn't let it happen again. After the way that other kid had looked at us, we knew we would never let it happen again. We grabbed him and pushed him towards his room. All the boys were awake now with the raucous, except the one who had taken the pills. They were staring at us as if we were mad."

Larry picked up the story, "We shut the door behind us so they couldn't see what was going on. I've never been so scared in my life. But we were determined not to let him touch that lad."

"It came to blows between us and him," said Tom. "He did what he was good at. He picked on me and started punching me. Larry was trying to get him off me, but he was very strong, but we were very determined. He started screaming that he would get to James, no matter what it took. He would destroy my family and my mother would be blamed for being such a bad mother, then we'd both be taken into care.

"He thought it would make me cringe in fear like it had before. But instead it made me even angrier. All I could see was James being put through the same pain and degradation I had been because of this man's disgusting perversion.

"Then I thought, who does he think he is? Destroying so many young lives and threatening my mother. I started hitting him. Both Larry and I had been going to boxing lessons for a few months. We must have known this day would come. We weren't very good, but I think the shock of us standing up to him and hitting him back, even after his threats, gave us the upper hand.

"We both jumped on him," said Larry. "We pushed him to the floor and sat on his chest. We shoved sleeping pills down his throat and stayed there until he started nodding off. He was still swearing at us as he was falling asleep."

"When we woke the next morning, he was as quiet as a mouse. We all had breakfast as if nothing happened, except we knew and so did the boy who had been raped. We saw to the boy and took care of him all day, though he looked at us as if we were the betrayers. He hadn't seen what we did to Roles, but I don't blame him. In some ways, we were the betrayers. The problem was that we never knew what was going to happen on one of the weekends. If we didn't go along, it could be so much worse, but it didn't help our guilt really."

"Something I have to ask," said John. "All the months when I had gone and nothing had happened to me, were there other boys abused during those weekends?"

"Sometimes," answered Larry. "He could go for months without touching a young boy and everyone would have a great time. I think you might remember some of the lads that stopped going all of a sudden."

"Yes," said John. "I was thinking about if after the weekend it happened to me. When I looked back, even before I started going, every so often, one of the boys would decide he didn't want to go anymore. I remember thinking they must be mad, but when I look back now, I can see how subdued these boys were after they dropped out. What I don't understand is why none of the other teachers noticed anything."

"Well, if you think about it," said Larry, "one, they were not aware of anything suspicious going on. And two, most of the boys sang Roles' praise and wanted to be around him. He was very charismatic, he fooled a lot of people all the time."

"Including my mum and I," said John. "Sorry, carry on with your story, what happened next?"

"Well," said Tom, "things were never the same after that. He kept threatening me that I would rue the day I stood up to him. He promised he would get James if it killed him and he would make my life hell."

"You see that was his way," added Larry. "He would target Tom and leave me alone. He hoped that if anything happened again, it would be Tom's word against his.

He actually thought I would go my own merry way and forget all that had happened. He said I didn't have to go on the weekends anymore. I was relieved from that duty. He told me he had changed since Tom and I jumped him. He had seen his actions as others would and realised that people would not understand that he was just showing these boys how much he loved them. My skin crawls even now when I think of what he said to me that day. I was only fifteen, but I had more sense than to believe any of that garbage."

"He told me," said Tom, "that I would have to go on the weekends alone for as long as he said. Otherwise, he would invite James. At first, we both went along. That was more to show him that we were real friends and that he couldn't and wouldn't split us up. Instead of us being there to help the young lads after the abuse, we started to protect them.

"Every time he tried to corner one of them, we would come behind and ask him to help with some chore or other. He couldn't say no because he was the 'lovely' teacher that everyone loved, and the boys would wonder why he was being nasty. Every night, we dropped sleeping pills into his drink. We were always half afraid we would give him an overdose, but we managed to keep him away from the boys for a lot of months."

"Then he organised a weekend without us knowing," Larry continued. "He took just a few young boys away. Normally, we would know about the weekends, not just from him, but from the excitement of the boys. This time, he told the boys that it was going to be a 'special' weekend with his favourites, and he didn't want us tagging along. He instructed them not to say anything to us. Looking back, we understood that he knew what we had been up to. So the only way to stop us hindering him was not to let us know about it.

"The first we knew of it was Monday morning. Mr Kenny asked us if anything unusual had happened on the weekend away as two of the boys failed to show up for school that morning. We were dumbfounded, all the years he had forced us to go with him, to look after the boys and warn them not to say anything. Then this, we thought maybe he was cracking up."

Chapter 29

"We told Mr Kenny that we hadn't known about the weekend and hadn't been invited," Tom said. "He looked quite surprised but didn't say anything. He just nodded and walked away. We were waiting for the fireworks to start all day, but nothing happened. Then we heard he had visited the two boys who had not turned up for school. Still nothing happened, in fact, nothing happened for a few weeks. Roles looked very guarded. It was like he knew he was being watched.

"Then we heard he had arranged another weekend without telling us. We couldn't believe it, he knew he was being watched, but it didn't seem to matter, we think he must have been getting desperate. We only knew because we heard two young boys talking about it. They were so excited, I don't think they knew how loud they were speaking."

Larry continued with the story. "We decided to let Mr Kenny know about it. He told us to leave it with him and we did. He called us into his classroom after school that day. He had found out all the arrangements for the coming weekend. He asked us to accompany him in his car so that we could surprise Roles. He didn't ask us anything about what happened during these weekends, and we didn't volunteer any information.

"We went along with him that weekend. You should have seen the look on Roles' face when we arrived Friday evening. I thought he was going to have a heart attack." They both laughed for the first time since they had sat down. "Everything went smoothly, as you can imagine," he continued. "From then on, Mr Kenny started taking his wife along on the trips. Roles' hands were tied on these weekends, he couldn't object to Mr and Mrs Kenny joining him. Everyone, including the Principal, thought it was a great idea. This way, they said they could take more boys as the burden wouldn't be all on Roles. He was not pleased, but what could he do?"

Tom took over. "So, Roles was growing more and more frustrated. After a few months of being watched all the time, he just cracked. He told one of the young boys that he wanted to see him after lessons. The boy went to the staff room to see him. The story goes that the boy hadn't been in with him for more than a few minutes when he grabbed him. The boy screamed and pushed him away. Roles lost his grip on the boy and he ran from the room. In fact, he ran straight into Mr Kenny's arms. He was sobbing. He blurted out what had happened.

"Mr Kenny tore into the staff room after Roles, shouting at him. Roles was completely calm and said it had been a misunderstanding, and the boy was hysterical. Mr Kenny couldn't get him to say anything else. Roles looked down his nose at him and told him not to be so ridiculous. He more or less said that Kenny was just jealous of him because the boys loved him, and that was that. He actually told Mr Kenny to mind his own business. But Mr Kenny wasn't having any of it. He wanted to call the police in, but the principal declined. He decided to hold an internal investigation into the incident.

"They interviewed a number of boys, we weren't among them. The principal did the interviewing. He wouldn't even allow Mr Kenny to be present. None of the boys would say anything bad about Mr Roles. Any who had been abused were too frightened to say anything, and those who had got away without the abuse, thought Roles, was wonderful.

"The principal spoke to Mr Kenny afterwards. Mr Kenny wasn't happy and wanted to bring charges against Roles. But the principal was more worried about the publicity and the reputation of the school. You could see how frustrated with the situation Mr Kenny was. The principal came to an agreement with Roles. He asked him to leave quietly as Mr Kenny was insisting there be an investigation.

"Can you imagine that happening now?" Larry added. "There would be an outcry and the whole school would be under scrutiny. Roles left immediately and that was the last we ever saw of him. He disappeared into the sunset, as they say."

"Well," said John. "He went west all right. He moved to Manchester. That's one of the things I wanted to speak to you about. I want to confront him and I want to bring charges against him. I've lived with this for too many years and it's eating away at me. I have to do something, or I know I'll regret it for the rest of my life."

Derek couldn't believe his eyes. Fear had come from nowhere. One minute there weren't any demons around and then all of a sudden they pounced. Fear was huge. It grabbed both men's hearts and squeezed. Derek could actually see what it was doing in these men's bodies. Then other demons came from all directions. They were like sharks in water, moving, hunting. It took all of Derek's willpower not to move away. He wasn't shocked when the men couldn't speak. He could see why.

He looked over at John. Fear was seeping over towards him, creeping, closer and closer. Derek had to do something, but what?

"John!" he shouted, (louder than he meant to) "Guard your heart, pray NOW!!!"

John knew exactly what to do. He started praying in the spirit. He prayed against fear, and Derek saw it retreat. The two other men just sat looking at them. They looked stunned at Derek's outburst.

Derek spoke again, this time more gently. "I think you should know that this situation is not just in the natural, it is also in the supernatural."

They looked at each other confused and somewhat reluctant to stay sitting with these two men.

"Okay," Derek said. "Let me try to explain, though it won't be easy. My three friends and I were sent here to help John. God has a plan for John's life and this fear and guilt is crippling him. It's stopping him from becoming all that God wants him to be. We've been sent to show him how destructive fear, guilt and self-loathing can be."

Derek cleared his throat. He looked across at fear, it was smirking again, it started to come towards him, but he remembered Mark was standing behind him and he also knew fear trembled before Mark. So he smiled at it and told him (through his thoughts) to go.

"Fear is a demon," he continued. "But one that can be defeated. It controls the majority of other demons, which include, doubt, worry, guilt, self-pity, self-loathing, anger, rage, jealousy, envy, coveting. All of these and more! Its main purpose is to terrify people, so they can't become what they were created to be. It puts thoughts of worthlessness in their heads. It sniggers at them if they try to do something it doesn't want them to do. It paralyses, it tells people that they can't amount to anything. So many things could have been accomplished by so many different people, if they hadn't let fear take away their choices."

"I've heard it described as F.E.A.R.," he continued. "'False evidence appearing real!' When you stand up to it, it backs down, but it keeps trying to drag people down. It doesn't give up easily. My friends and I can see these demons. I can see what fear is doing to you now. It is literally squeezing your hearts. There are also minor demons whispering in your ears that I am some kind of crazy man. They're telling you to get up and leave and carry on with your lives as you have done for the past number of years. You see, I can hear them too."

"Before you give into them," he continued, "answer me one question. Has everything been good in your lives since your school days? Have you ever thought that you would like to see justice done against Roles? Do you think of the other boys he hurt, and the ones he is hurting now? It's all because of fear, Roles instilled it into your hearts, and fear has had so much power over your lives. Do you want to be set free? Do you want to know that you have done the right thing and be able to stand tall?"

Both men hung their heads, ashamed.

"I don't want you to be ashamed. You were only boys. I'm not here to judge anyone. On the contrary, I want to see at least three lives changed for the better forever. I won't pretend it will be easy, in fact, I can tell you that there is a great battle to be fought, but we have a Great God helping us. If we put our trust in Him, we can't lose."

"Remember the scripture says, 'our struggle is not against flesh and blood, but against the rulers, against the authorities, against the powers of this dark world and against the spiritual forces of evil in the heavenly realms'" (Eph. 6:12).

Chapter 30

Larry was the first to respond. "It's been a real struggle," he said. "I have a good life now. I'm married and have two children. I have a great job that I enjoy and everything, more or less, has been going smoothly. But every so often I have a dream of Roles. It's like I'm a young teenager again, living in fear. I've tried to suppress these emotions as much as possible, but the day after the dream, I'm in a mess and my whole day is ruined. I can't get him out of my mind. Then the guilt starts, how could I let him do those horrible things to young boys. It takes all my willpower just to get through the day. It's been a regular occurrence in my life since I met Roles."

Tom added, "I'm the same. I have a lovely life with my wife and son and daughter. My fear is that the last young boy we helped will turn up in my life and bring charges against us for aiding and abetting Roles. The fear of losing it all, my wife, my kids, my job, it is terrifying. Sometimes I can't get out of bed with the fear of what could happen. Everyone knowing what we did."

"That's exactly what happens," said Derek. "It is subtle. You think it's you and your thoughts doing all this. You start believing you are weak, you're like a jellyfish with no backbone etc. then down and down you go until it has complete control. But I think it gets its kicks from letting you carry on with your life as if nothing ever happened. Then it pounces. All of a sudden, you're terrified, incapacitated and you feel there's nothing or no one who can help you. You've never told anyone what happened to you, have you?"

"No," they both said together. Tom continued, "Who could we tell, it feels like we were a party to it, how can we tell even a counsellor that? It's okay for you two," he told John and Derek. "You have God on your side. We, on the other hand, are mere mortals."

"I'm trying to cope with the past, hoping nobody recognises me from my childhood, it's crippling me. My wife, when I get down like this, worries. She convinced me to start going to church with her. I knew it was the right time, I really felt the need to go. I can't think that I'd be much use to God, and I don't really understand why He'd be bothered with someone like me, but I've been learning His Word. And waiting to see what happens and now it has!"

Larry said, "My wife has been at me for the last few months to go with her to church. She takes my son and daughter. I haven't plucked up the courage yet. I keep seeing bolts of lightning striking me if I walk through the doors. Though for some unknown reason, I've been reading the Bible these last few weeks. Isn't it strange that both of us have changed and moved towards God, even in a small way, and then you both arrive?"

John and Derek looked at each other and smiled. "God works in mysterious ways," John said.

"Can Larry and I have some time to think this through?" asked Tom.

"It's a very big step and one that will definitely change our lives. We also need to share this with our wives. We've never told them what happened, it will be hard, please be patient with us," added Larry.

"What happens if we are prosecuted for aiding and abetting?" Tom asked again. Derek could see fear grip him. The grey mist was getting thicker around the two men. He didn't know exactly what it was, it was puzzling him.

Mark whispered in his ear. "It's dread," he said. "What they feared most in their lives, having their past laid out before the whole world, may just come to pass. The mist is the dread that works so closely with fear and helps paralyse."

What can I do? asked Derek in his mind.

Pray for them, Mark answered. *When you and John meet up with the other three, you all need to spend time together praying for strength for these two good men.*

Derek watched as fear moved closer to John. It seemed like it had suckers, it reached towards John. The suckers, when they touched him, seemed to suck out all his energy and strength.

"That's a great idea," Derek told the men, much to John's confusion. John gave the men his mobile number so they could contact him when they decided what they were going to do. His face looked so troubled Derek's heart went out to him.

They all said their goodbyes and shook hands vigorously. As they did, hope stirred in John's heart. He had immediately thought, once they said they needed to think about it, that he would never see or hear from them again. But something in the way they shook hands told him it would be okay. Anyway, he had the four men with him and he wasn't alone any longer. He didn't want to think about how he'd feel when they left. They'd become very close friends whose companionship he really enjoyed. He wasn't going to think about them leaving yet, right now, he knew they had to pray.

Derek and John drove back in silence. Each one lost in their own thoughts. Derek was concerned about John. It must be hard hoping yet not knowing whether Tom and Larry would stand with him. Something deeper had happened to Derek, he knew in his heart his three friends had his back. He also knew he could depend on the One who is always faithful. Nothing could take that away from him.

They arrived back at the B & B in just over an hour. Paul, Harold and Mick were waiting for them in the bar. John could see by their faces they were desperate to hear what had happened.

They sat together at a table in the corner of the bar so they could have some privacy. There weren't many people around at this time. Unfortunately, as they could see demons everywhere, it was a bit distracting. Mick especially felt this, he was constantly mesmerised by what was actually going on in the supernatural. All the years he had been a Christian and he had had no idea of the battles being fought around him.

John and Derek gave a precise account of the day's activities and encounters. You couldn't expect people to pray for exactly the right thing, if they didn't know the whole story. Once they had relayed the events of the day, John asked the men to pray with him. They agreed and John led them in prayer.

They had never heard him pray like this before. It was so powerful and so humble. It felt like water was flowing over each of them, giving them, yet again, an amazing peace. Mick, of course, had to open his eyes. This was probably one of the most powerful prayers, apart from the incident at John's house that he had ever witnessed. He knew he would see something spectacular. He wasn't disappointed.

Chapter 31

He looked towards John whose eyes were closed as were the others'. John looked on fire, there was a bright light around him. It was blazing. He looked above John's head, the ceiling, upper floors and roof had disappeared. The view was straight up through the clouds and the brightness shining down on them was blinding, and yet he could look at it without discomfort to his eyes.

Angels, and angels and angels in their multitudes, hosts of angels, were everywhere. It seemed to him that they formed a ladder or stairway to the 'Throne Room'. The colours were breathtaking. The sound of singing was unimaginable, the beauty of the angels' choirs, praising and worshipping was so extraordinary, he started to weep, he couldn't control himself, he had no idea there was such beauty, and he was allowed to be part of it. He tried to see through the light, but the tears made his sight blurry, though he didn't think he would be able to see through the light anyway, it was so, it was all encompassing. He sat and wept openly. Then through the light, something like a bolt of lightning touched his heart. He would never be able to put it into words, but he knew that he had just been touched by God!!!

The tears poured down his face, he kept repeating and repeating, "God touched me! Me, who spent my life afraid of my own shadow?" He couldn't move, he never wanted to move again. The peace, the strength, the power he felt within his spirit was so awesome, and then some.

Paul opened his eyes next. He too saw the 'stairway to heaven' and the brilliant light above. He quickly bowed his head in worship. *How does the Divine Creator find time to commune with someone like me?* It never ceased to astound him. *What an amazing God we serve, and I am serving Him,* he thought.

Unlike Mick, Paul could not stop smiling, he really wanted to chuckle out loud and jump up and praise God, but John was still praying and it might seem quite rude. So he held back, but he could not stop the chuckle from coming up from within his spirit. He actually laughed out loud.

Derek, Harold and John looked at him in surprise and confusion, especially as they looked at Mick, with tears flowing down his face, though he looked so at peace, more peaceful than any of them had ever seen him. Paul's face was radiant and the smile was so beautiful. Paul had never been that demonstrative, and none of them had heard him laughing like this, or smiling like he was. "What's going on?" Harold asked.

"Sorry," Paul said. "God is so awesome, look up, look up!"

All three looked up. Harold looked as if he would have a heart attack. His eyes were wide in surprise and adoration. Derek let out a shout, something else none of them had ever heard. But John's face was the best. It was as if all the light of the sun was shining through it. His smile was so bright and then the light started to pour through the rest of his body. He fell on the floor in worship. He was still smiling, but tears were streaming from his eyes.

The other four men followed, it was like the day they had been in John's house. Nobody could sit or stand in the presence of such beauty. Five grown men knelt together in a bar. Then one by one they bowed down to the ground in an act of worship.

The other customers just stared. Ordinarily, this would have caused a commotion and people would have ridiculed the men for such an outward act of devotion. Some would have even complained that it was not acceptable in a bar. But a quiet came over the whole room. It was as if the rest of the people understood that these men were experiencing the supernatural.

Harold alone said nothing, and though he was not ever the first to offer advice or comment, he always joined the conversation. The five men prayed with their faces to the ground, some out loud, others within their hearts. When it had come to a natural end, they all retook their seats.

Harold quickly went to the bar and ordered another round of drinks. The landlady was speechless, she just nodded. Derek watched Harold closely. They shared a room and had become quite close. Now Derek was worrying how this might be affecting his friend. Then he stopped himself. He was letting worry get a handle in his life, just like before. It starts small, but before you know it, you're worrying about everything. He had been worrying about John on the way home, and now he was worrying about Harold.

As soon as he stopped himself, a tiny demon leapt from behind him. It flew to the ever-present fear as if to apologise for failing. Fear swiped it away and the creature went scurrying out of the bar. Fear was angry, Derek could see that, it was also diminishing, but it clung on to people as if its life depended on it. *It probably does,* thought Derek. If only he had known how easy it was to banish fear and worry when he was alive. How much happier he would have been. Then he had to stop himself again, now 'self-pity' was having a go. He watched as another tiny demon scurried away.

Harold came back with the drinks. He was still very quiet.

"Are you okay?" Derek whispered.

Harold nodded. "Later," was all he could say.

The five of them sat and chatted. The four told John the whole story of their lives, where they had lived, who they had loved, and what they were like in their previous lives.

John was fascinated. He had thought of them as warriors, and rightly so, but they hadn't always been this way. As he listened to each of their stories, all of them seeming to understand exactly what and where they had gone wrong, somehow, it made him feel stronger and more confident than he had ever been.

"There is something else I need to tell you," he said, catching them all by surprise.

Harold nodded for him to proceed before anyone could comment. They sat still in anticipation of what he was about to share with them. They half-expected him to tell them of another atrocity that had happened in his life and their faces were grim in expectation.

Chapter 32

John started laughing. "Stop looking so worried," he told them. "This is something nice, well I think it could be."

That put a different slant on things, they were all eager to hear something nice was happening in John's life.

"Well," said Mick. "Don't keep us in suspense, come on, out with it," he laughed.

"There is a woman whom I'm very fond of," John told them. "Her name is Jennifer."

Harold's eyes misted over for a second, he was remembering his own darling Jenny. "That's my daughter's name," he told John. "We called her Jenny."

"She's not your daughter, is she?" John asked nervously.

"No," said Harold, "my Jenny is married to David and the last I knew she was pregnant with her first child. If she's anything like her mum, she'll either already have a few more around her, or be planning on it." He smiled at the thought. "Anyway, tell us about Jennifer."

"We've been seeing each other for nearly a year now," John told them. "She is the most wonderful person I've ever met, (present company excluded)," he laughed. "We met at a party and I know it sounds corny, but as soon as I saw her, I knew she was the one for me. She is beautiful, with long dark hair and big brown eyes, her family is Italian. She has such a great sense of humour, and I love hearing her laugh, but when she smiles, I just melt.

"I've told her about the incident at my previous church, but I've not confided in her about what happened to me as a child. Every time I try to tell her, I get all tongue-tied and can't get the words out. I've been praying for the courage to tell her, and then you guys came along. I never realised that God really listens to our prayers, I know that sounds dreadful coming from a man of God, but now I know first-hand that He does and He answers them." He laughed embarrassed.

"I want her to know everything about me," he continued. "Until I finish this and deal with it, I'll have no peace. I'm going to phone her and arrange to meet her later, if we can. I will tell her everything, including what happened this evening. She is a true believer and I know she loves the Lord. So I'm asking you again, would you pray for me, pray I would get the right words to explain everything to her, including why I haven't told her before. I want to marry this woman, but I can't go forward with my life until I sort out my past."

All four men agreed to pray for him that evening. John got up and left the table. The three men, Paul, Mick and Derek turned to look at Harold.

"What's wrong?" asked Mick.

Though Harold and Derek had become quite close, there was a certain bond between Mick and Harold. It was as if they knew each other's thoughts. The same bond was between Derek and Paul, they were definitely the leaders in the group, and though Mick and Harold mattered just as much as Paul and Derek, they were inclined to let the other two take the lead.

Harold closed his eyes and tears spilled down his cheeks.

"I'm sorry," he said. "It's hard for someone as simple as me to grasp the enormity of what goes on in the supernatural. I'm not one for changing as my boys would gladly testify. So this has been hard for me to grasp."

"You have seen the angels and demons though, haven't you?" asked Derek.

"Yes, I have," Harold answered. "To be perfectly honest, I thought that big one, fear, was going to wipe me out when I saw it first. It actually came towards me and it seemed to soak into my body, it grasped my heart in its hand, if that's what you would call them. I nearly fell down in a dead faint. I told God He'd picked the wrong person for this mission. I was too scared to listen to my boys' ideas when I was alive. I'm not much better now."

"But then something extraordinary happened," he continued. "I felt a strong hand on my shoulder and a scripture came into my head. 'You will hear a voice behind you, telling you which way to go, whether to the left or to the right' (Isaiah 30:21). After that, I experienced great peace, I can't really describe it. I still don't feel very courageous, but I know who the voice belonged to and I'm determined to obey. But you see, I was being obedient I didn't expect anything in return. I was always taught to obey and not question, and just put up with whatever happens. Then when I looked up and saw the angels, I could hardly take it in. Who would ever believe that God Almighty would give someone like me a vision like that?"

"There is something else that I'm overwhelmed at," he said.

"What?" they all asked together.

"I heard a voice," he whispered, as if saying it out loud would diminish it. "I heard God speak to me, not a scripture in my mind or a voice in my heart, but a voice that was loud and clear."

Mick, who had felt like a bolt of lightning go through him during the vision, whispered, "What did the voice say?"

Harold choked back the tears as he answered them. "The voice said, 'I am pleased with you, you are a good and faithful servant. Tell this to your brothers, I have chosen each and every one of you, and I am very pleased with my choice. Listen to your guardian angels, they are My messengers, they will direct you and lead you, so don't be afraid, you are all over comers.'"

They all sat stunned, God was pleased with them. Each of them had been going through a battle of his own. Each thought they were not worthy, or not up to the task. Each was afraid that they would let the others down and cause the mission to fail. When they all voiced how they had felt, every one of them had been struggling with inadequacy at the task at hand. It made them smile.

"Here we are fighting with John against fear and all the time, doubt and low self-esteem are trying to get a foothold," said Paul.

"I can understand Harold and I having doubt," said Mick, "(No offence Harold), but you and Derek have always looked in control. How could we not see the demons on each other?"

Chapter 33

"We hid them too well," said Derek. "You ever notice, in our past lives, some people always seemed to hold it together and some couples always looked as if they were the perfect match. Then you'd hear they split up or that 'held together' person had a breakdown, or went completely off the rails. Well, I believe that's what these demons—doubt, low self-esteem and worry—are. They hide and scratch away until they're embedded into your very soul."

"If I'm honest," said Paul, "it's also pride. Don't let anyone see you're struggling. Don't show your emotions in case they might be misinterpreted. Its pride, but I must admit, I haven't seen anything that you would call pride, in the demon world. Have any of you?"

"Good question," Derek commented. "I remember the first time I could see the demons. The ones we call gremlins, they were so small, I remember laughing to myself at the size of them. I thought, these will be a doddle to annihilate. That was before I encountered fear. But I remember a fleeting figure move by me. It was actually quite beautiful, all different colours that seemed to glimmer. Then it disappeared, it wasn't something that I thought of as 'good', even though it was beautiful, there was something about it that looked a bit menacing. I haven't seen it since."

"I saw that figure," Paul exclaimed. "It was really beautiful, and like you, I only caught a glimpse of it and it was gone. I too felt something menacing about it, I can't put my finger on it, but there was just something about it I didn't like."

"What were you thinking when you saw the creature?" asked Harold.

"I don't think I was thinking anything," Paul replied. "I was looking at the 'gremlins' and trying to figure out what they were. The creature I saw just floated past, touching some of the older men. They were the ones who started bickering. Could that have been pride? It wasn't very big, bigger than the 'gremlins' but a lot smaller than fear."

"The one I saw," said Derek, "was the size of a lady, not quite as big as fear, but human size definitely, and much larger than the 'gremlins'. I'm wondering why it would be getting stronger and bigger."

"Let's be on the look out and see what happens," said Mick. "I'm struggling with the fact that I can see the demons and angels as it is. Nobody else is aware of them, though we weren't aware of them before either. If only people could see what's going on around them, they would definitely behave differently."

"Before we do anything else, let's pray for John," Derek said. As always, they bowed their heads. They started with thanksgiving and worship. Then they asked for courage and boldness for John as he told Jennifer his whole story.

When they had finished praying, they agreed that they should turn in. It had been a long day and they were tired, they also knew they would have an early start the next day.

Mick laughed, "Funny, I never thought we would be tired when we took on this mission, I thought we'd be like supermen and not need sleep. I thought we'd be filled with unending energy. But I have to say, I'm shattered and I haven't been through what you have, Derek, you must be exhausted."

Derek nodded, he was too tired to talk anymore, just the thought of putting his head down, was wonderful. They went to their rooms, Harold and Derek to theirs, and Paul and Mick to theirs.

"Before we go to sleep," Harold asked, "do you mind if we pray?"

Though Derek was exhausted, he was quite happy to pray. "I would be delighted to pray," he told Harold. "I love praying. I must say that though I was a believer in my past life, prayer was just something I did. Now I feel that every time we pray, we are coming into the presence of the Lord. Communicating with the Almighty!!! Knowing when we take the time to stop everything for Him, He is glad and listens to us and answers our questions and requests. I've never known such confidence in prayer before."

They both knelt side by side in the room. Neither of them uttered a word, both silently acknowledging the Lord and His greatness within their own spirits. It was a very special time, they didn't have to speak out loud, their spirits were communicating with the Lord and also each other. A very special time!

They stayed like that for quite a while. The peace in the room was tangible. Who could possibly imagine that the Love of God would pour down on them from Heaven? But that's what happened, they couldn't move, they knelt and received the outpouring of love from above. When the Spirit was finished pouring this love into their hearts and spirits, their angels touched them on their shoulders.

When Derek turned to say goodnight, it was as if he was looking at a different person. Derek's jaw literally dropped. Harold was kneeling beside him, but the rainbow colours that had surrounded the people in the waiting area were running through him. He was positively glimmering and shimmering and it was beautiful. Derek had never seen a more exquisite human being ever. The light shining from Harold was as bright as the sun, Derek just looked in awe.

Harold looked across at Derek. He couldn't believe his eyes. Just like Derek had seen in Harold, he could see in Derek. The colours were so vivid and so bright, normally they would hurt the eyes, but Harold didn't want to even blink in case this beautiful vision of Derek would disappear.

They stared at one another, tears streamed down their cheeks. They both closed their eyes and bowed in thanksgiving. When they opened them again, the shades had faded and both returned to normal, but yet, not quite normal, there was a glow flowing from their bodies that hadn't been there before.

They both retired to bed, hardly speaking. There wasn't anything you could say after such an encounter. As soon as their eyes closed, they were asleep. They slept in a deep and restful sleep throughout the night.

Chapter 34

Meanwhile in the other room, Paul and Mick were in deep conversation. "I can't say I've ever felt so excited in all my days," Mick said. "This thing that is happening with us is beautiful. We don't have to worry, or sort things out, or stand up to anyone, or even go out on a limb. Everything is being taken care of and all we have to do is be obedient and seek guidance."

"I know what you mean," Paul replied. "All my life, I made things happen. I would go out on that limb, always worrying what would happen next. I was the one who sorted everything out and stood up to the bullies. I don't think I ever consulted God, or asked Him what He wanted from me. I presumed, He put us on this earth and it was up to us to make the most of it."

"Now I'm looking around me," he continued, "and seeing things I never thought possible. I'm able to let others lead the way without feeling a failure. I can't tell you how liberating it is to actually work as a team. Pity I never experienced it in my past life." He laughed at the thought.

"I know what you mean," Mick said. "I was probably the exact opposite to you. I worked with a fantastic team. They all helped each other, all I had to do was play. Now looking back, I see that I was quite good at it."

"Mmm, what's that colourful creature I see hanging around you?" Paul laughed.

Mick almost jumped, but realised Paul was just ribbing him. He started laughing. "That's what I was always afraid of in the past," he told Paul. "Instead of just getting on and playing the best I could, I would hide away and only play if I was with family or very close friends. I used to think people would believe I was conceited. You know, the stupid thing about it is? They actually thought I believed I was too good. It's so stupid, when I look back, I could kick myself for not going out on that limb, just once."

"Anyway," he continued, "that's history and we've been given a job to do—one that I'm relishing. Okay, I'm not in the forefront of things, but that suits me. The fact that we are a team is what matters, and none of us is better than the other. We can relax and let God show us what He wants us to do."

"I agree," Paul said. "I feel so relaxed I don't have all the fears and worries that I used to have. It's just a matter of taking each day as it comes and seeing what new thing God has in store for us."

"I agree," said Mick. "I think it's time we turned in. God alone knows what tomorrow will bring. But whatever it is, we need to rest."

They too slept soundly and all four felt rested and refreshed when they awoke the next day.

They met for breakfast at eight thirty am. The landlady liked fussing over the men. They had such hearty appetites and never left a scrap on their plates. It was a real compliment to her cooking and gave her that extra bit of enjoyment in what she did. She was preparing the breakfast for them and humming to herself. It was an old hymn she had learned at Sunday school.

"What on earth brought that into my mind?" She said to herself. There was something about those four men, something she couldn't put into words, but since they had arrived, there was a peace throughout the building and a peace within her that she hadn't felt in years.

She always worried about her B & B. Would people like her cooking? Would they sleep well? Was it clean enough? Were there enough towels etc.? The list seemed to go on and on. She always felt on edge and she worried about each and every guest.

Then these men arrived, what was it about them? They made her feel—good, whole, content and happy about herself and what she was doing. It was as if they confirmed that she was in the right place at the right time in her life. She loved running the B & B and since they had arrived, she realised how much she enjoyed doing it. She wasn't worrying about silly things as she usually did. She was still humming the hymn when her husband came into the kitchen.

"You sound very happy," he said. "I haven't seen you this relaxed since we opened the place. Is there something I should know?"

She turned to face him and saw him smiling at her. She loved him so much. He was the kindest, gentlest man she'd ever known. The B & B was her idea. She was the one who wanted to start it. He went along with her and called it her precious dream. When they had bought the place, it was very run down. It needed a lot of work and they used up all their savings—including the money they got from selling their previous house—getting it up to their standard. Her husband, Robert, had done a lot of the work himself and anything he couldn't handle, his friends helped with. They had lived in this area all their lives. They had been childhood sweethearts. This was the dream, living the dream, though sometimes it seemed more like a nightmare.

They'd had tourists from the city stay for a week, in the early months after they opened. They complained about everything, from the bedrooms being too small, to the windows not overlooking the gardens. You name it, they had complained about it. As they hadn't opened that long ago, it knocked her confidence, and since then, she had been trying hard, sometimes too hard, to make everyone happy.

"So tell me, my lovely Alice," said Robert smiling, "what's making you so happy? You haven't found another man, have you?" he said laughing. Then more seriously, "Those men that are staying with us, you're not going to run off with one of them, are you?"

Alice couldn't help laughing. "Aha, do I detect a touch of jealousy?" she giggled, she slipped her arms around his waist.

"Well, a man can't be too careful when he's married to as beautiful a woman as I am. I have to be on my toes, and not let any other man slip into the picture." He bent down and kissed her lightly on the lips. "Come on out with it, you look radiant, practically glowing," he smiled.

"I don't know what it is exactly," she answered. "Since those men arrived, I've felt happy and my confidence in this B & B has come back. I can honestly say that for the first time since those awful city guests came, I am enjoying every minute of my life!"

"Well, that's all that matters to me," Robert said, pulling her close and whispering in her ear. "As long as you're happy, my world is a better place."

They both kissed, and then Alice smelt the bacon burning. "Oh my word, now look what you made me do, it's all your fault, distracting me with your flattery and fine talk." She laughed and pulled away from him to see to the bacon.

How wonderful it is to see her so happy! he thought. They'd been together eighteen years now, since they were both sixteen. He had known as soon as he met her at the school disco that they would spend the rest of their lives together. It wasn't a bad life at all. Now she had her B & B, she could keep herself busy. She needed that. They'd been trying for a baby since they were in their twenties. The doctors said there was nothing wrong with either of them, but Alice had never conceived. They were both thirty-four now, so time was running out, that's why he had ploughed all their money into this place. He would have bought her the moon if he could. Just seeing her like this, so happy, it did his heart good and he couldn't help but smile.

"What are you smiling at?" Alice asked as she caught that cheeky grin of his. "What's so funny, me burning the bacon, because that was your fault, not mine. I'm a great cook, if I'm not interrupted." She laughed.

"Nothing darling," he answered, "just counting my blessings. By the way, what's that tune you were humming earlier? It's been going through my head for the past few days. Don't know where it came from, but I can't stop humming it."

"I'm the same," she smiled. "I think it's that hymn, 'Love divine, all love excelling'. I don't know where I heard it, but, like you, it keeps going round and round in my head. How very weird that we should be thinking of the same hymn at the same time. But my dear husband, I have breakfasts to prepare, I can't spend all day chatting to you, don't you have a job to go to?"

Robert worked with his friend. They had a small business doing repairs on houses and overall DIY. Robert was a qualified electrician and his friend Dave was a plumber. Both could put their hand to anything, so they were usually kept very busy.

"Okay, okay, I'm going," he laughed and kissed her again. "Take care of our guests, but no running off with any of them, promise me?"

"Go on, you need to go to work and let me get on with my day." She laughed as she pushed him out the door.

Just as she was about to close it, he pushed back in and took her in his arms. "I love you so much and I thank God for you every day," he whispered.

"I love you too, and I promise not to run off with any other man. Nobody could ever compare with you, you've made me a very happy woman, now get to work." She laughed. He kissed her again and finally left.

By the time she came into the dining room, it was eight forty-five, she was fifteen minutes late.

Chapter 35

"I'm so sorry for the delay," she said to the four men who were sitting, chatting and praying.

"Don't be silly," Harold said. "A few minutes is not going to make much difference. Anyway, we don't have to leave until ten so we have plenty of time."

As he said the words, he reached out and took her hand. She was a bit surprised, but it felt right and though normally this sort of gesture from a guest would make her feel uncomfortable, this didn't.

He looked different today. It was hard to put it into words, but he looked like he had a light shining from him. She felt such a peace being near them that she didn't want to move away. There was something about the way they spoke and acted, she felt drawn to them in her spirit. This had never happened to her before.

As Harold held her hand, he said, "I believe congratulations are in order."

She was completely flummoxed now. "I don't know what you mean, why would you want to congratulate me?"

"The baby," Harold told her. "You're pregnant, a few months I would say."

She tried to take her hand away, but he held on to it. "Wh… what?" she stammered. "I'm not pregnant, I couldn't be."

"Why?" asked Harold.

The others were staring at him. *What's he doing?* Each thought. *This isn't like Harold. The poor lady looks so embarrassed. Does he know she's pregnant because he'd had four children of his own?*

"It just didn't happen for Robert and me. We've been trying for years and I just can't get pregnant," she said, her eyes welling up with tears.

He held her hand tightly, "Speak to your doctor, but I'm telling you, you are pregnant."

She was clearly shocked and agreed to speak to her doctor. It was possibly more to release her hand from Harold's grasp than anything else. She continued to serve breakfast, though her hands were visibly shaking. She brought them freshly ground coffee, except for Paul, he loved his tea.

When she had gone back to the kitchen, the others turned to Harold. "What was that about?" asked Mick.

"Well," said Harold, "you know we have our guardian angels?"

"Yes," they replied in unison.

"Mine, his name is Daniel, told me to tell Alice that she was pregnant. And as we agreed, no matter what, we will be obedient. I did what I was told." He smiled.

"Brilliant," said Mick, "we are getting the hang of this, aren't we?"

They all laughed and agreed. This was good, caring for others. The four felt genuinely happy for Alice. What a privilege to be a part of this. They finished their breakfast and went into the large sitting room to wait for John. He arrived about half an hour later. No one asked if he had told Jennifer his whole story, they knew he would tell them when he was ready.

"Is there any news from Tom and Larry?" Paul asked.

"Nothing yet," said John. "I'm not worried though. I understand how they are feeling, it's a big decision. The lives they have lived will never be the same again."

Paul just sat and stared at John as if it was the first time he'd seen him.

"What's wrong?" John said, feeling slightly uncomfortable. "Why are you staring at me like that?"

Paul laughed and said, "It's just that it's the first time I've seen you without those pesky demons attached to you. I was looking for them in case they were hiding, but they're nowhere to be seen."

"You mean I'm free of them?" John asked incredulously. "Wow, fantastic, I felt free but it's so nice for someone else to confirm it."

They all shook his hand and congratulated him, patting him on the back and encouraging him. He was laughing and he looked so different from the first time they had met him, it truly was a miracle.

Alice came in when she heard all the commotion. "Is everything okay?" she asked smiling. "Can I get you gentlemen some coffee or tea?"

"That would be great, thanks, Alice," said Paul. "But tea for me please, and coffee for the rest, thank you."

"Are you okay?" Harold asked her. They had all seen her angel fighting off fear and something else. Something they didn't recognise. It wasn't as big as fear but it kept reaching out and trying to get into her head. Her angel was strong and was constantly warding off the two demons.

"I'm just a bit scared," said Alice. "I've called the doctor but the surgery isn't open yet. I keep panicking in case what you said is not true. I'm trying not to build my hopes up. I know you are different from other men. I knew it as soon as you arrived. I believe you are men of God, so I believe what you told me. But doubts keep coming into my mind. I have to keep pushing them out. So there is a battle going on around me, please forgive me if I'm all over the place, but it's quite scary for me."

"Have you spoken to your husband yet?" asked Harold.

"No, not yet, I've been too scared to build his hopes up, just in case."

"Well, my advice is to take that step of faith, and call him and tell him," Harold told her. "You'll be surprised how the doubts will stop coming when you have faith."

"Thank you so much," she said, her voice shaking. Tears were welling up in her eyes as she gave Harold a hug. Then she practically ran from the room.

All five men sat in a circle and Derek led them in prayer.

"Father," he began, "You know all things. You know before they happen and You know the hearts of man. We ask that You would give Tom and Larry courage and strength in the decision they are about to make. Whatever the outcome, Lord, we ask for Your will in this situation to be done. Amen."

"Amen," they echoed.

"What should we do while we are waiting?" asked Mick.

"Well, there's still plenty to be done at the church," John replied. "We could go over and see how far the people have got to."

They all agreed and walked across to the church. John was right, and though it was amazing what had been accomplished in the couple of days by the villagers, there was still a lot of work to be done. They rolled up their sleeves and got stuck in immediately. Mick picked up the pieces of the amplifier and started putting it back together again. It looked as if he might need some replacement parts. He asked one of the men where he might buy them.

Having been given directions to the local electrical shop, he explained to the others where he was going and why.

He walked up the street from the church. He thought how blessed he was with this second chance. He saw things so differently now. The sky was bluer, the grass greener, the fragrance and beauty of the flowers were so much more intense than he could remember. All the things he had taken for granted before now seemed to have come to life and it was as if he was in the centre of its creation. It was all so vivid, even the air he was breathing seemed fresher. He savoured it all and took enjoyment in each thing he saw, smelt and heard, like the blackbird singing. It felt like the whole of creation was worshipping the Lord. He was wrapped up in praise and worship as he walked, it was a perfect day.

Chapter 36

He came across houses along the road, just before the village square. Some of the houses had a golden aura around them, not always the ones he would have expected. Some of them were dishevelled and in some ways, looked uncared for, but the golden light made them look beautiful. Others that were actually beautiful houses, spotless and well looked after, had a grey aura around them, which took away from the beauty.

It goes to show that God views things differently to man, he thought.

He began to watch the people now. There were demons around all of them. Some had their angels fighting for them and the battles looked fierce. Others, he noticed, were completely overpowered by demons, when he looked closely, he could see these angels tied and gagged.

"What is that about?" He asked his angel.

"They are the unbelievers," the angel answered him. "Their angels can't help them because of their unbelief. They imagine they have to do it all themselves, they don't believe in God, or His helpers."

"That is so sad," Mick said. "They look so bogged down in their troubles." He noticed a woman walking towards him. It looked like she had millions of worms wriggling inside her. They looked like they were squeezing her heart and her lungs. Her angel was strapped up, unable to help her.

"What on earth are they?" Mick asked.

"It's worry," said the angel. "It grips their insides and wraps itself around the heart. You remember the feeling you had when you were worried about something? Your heart felt tight, and sometimes you could hardly breathe? Well, now you can see exactly why."

"I thought all those symptoms were in my mind," Mick said.

"Now you know."

All this, of course, was going on in Mick's mind. He could see people looking at him. Then he caught himself grinning at what Andrew had just said.

"Mmm," he thought, "how funny, if I was walking with my head down, or walking along crying, everyone would turn away. But because I'm smiling, everyone is looking at me as if I'm mad."

He reached the shop and they had what he needed. He put his hand in his pocket and there was enough money to pay for all the equipment and some left over. He left the shop but couldn't get the woman he had seen out of his mind. She looked tormented. "We've been sent to help people. I can't just ignore her. Okay, Lord, please give me the right words to help this lady."

He rushed down the street and caught up with her. She was hardly moving, she had so much on her shoulders. He walked alongside her and bid her good morning. When she looked at him, he could see the worry in her eyes. She just nodded and said nothing.

"Excuse me," he said. "I know you may think this is none of my business, but you look very worried and upset. Is there anything I can do to help?"

She looked at him, confused. "Yes, if you have £100 so I can buy food for my children, and maybe some clothes." She laughed cynically.

He put his hand in his pocket and pulled out exactly £100. "Is that enough?" he asked.

Her hands shook. "What do you want me to do for that?" she whispered. A look of terror came into her eyes.

"Just chat to me while we walk along, if you don't mind," he said. "What has been going on to make you so worried?"

"I lost my husband twelve months ago," she told him. "We had no insurance. We couldn't afford it, but it never occurred to us that he would die, he was only forty. Now I have three children, and only a widow's pension coming in. I've gone to the social, but they make me feel like a beggar, it's so humiliating. I never thought I would be in this situation."

"Can I pray with you?" Mick asked.

"Eh, I don't believe," she stammered.

"That's okay, just because you don't believe doesn't mean God doesn't exist," he told her. "I have enough belief for both of us, so if you will let me, I will pray as we walk. All I ask is you keep an open mind."

She just nodded again but didn't utter a word.

Mick bowed his head and prayed silently at first, then out loud. "Father, You know this lady, You know what she's been through. Bless her Father and help her unbelief. Show her Your love for her and how You care for all You have created. Thank You Lord."

He looked over at the woman, she seemed shocked. "Are you okay?" he asked.

"I've never heard anyone pray that simple before. I thought you had to have 'special' knowledge in order to pray. But you pray as if you are on first name terms with God Almighty."

"Well," he laughed, "I wouldn't go that far, but I promise that He is real and you have a guardian angel, who will take all this worry from you, if you let him. Just trust God, He sent me to you, didn't He?

"I suppose He did," she said. "Nobody else even noticed I was worried, I suppose they are all caught up in their own worlds."

"Are your children boys or girls?" Mick asked.

"I have two girls and a boy! My son is the youngest, he has just started school. The two girls are eight and ten."

"What did you do for a living before you were a mum?" he asked.

"I worked with sound equipment, fixing things like speakers, etc. I also worked in the office, but unfortunately, the company moved to another part of the country."

Mick couldn't help himself, he started laughing. She looked shocked. "What did I say?" she asked, offended.

"You worked with sound equipment," Mick said. "We are working in the church down the road. I have just been to buy some equipment to try to fix the sound system. It's very old, but I think it can be fixed. How would you like to earn some more money, come and help me fix the system? What do you say?"

She looked so surprised. "Okay" is all she said. So Mick and she walked towards the church. He learned her name was Melanie, but she liked to be called Mel. They walked and chatted and he told her about the Lord. He could see her guardian angel becoming untied. He told her about fear and worry and what they did to the body. He told her that she could fight them, if she had faith, nothing could stop her.

"Tell me more about this God of yours," she said to Mick. So he explained how his Lord loved everyone and wanted only the best for them. But if they had no belief, even God couldn't do anything. He must wait for you to come to Him, he told her.

They arrived at the church as everyone was sitting down to eat. They pulled chairs for Mick and Mel. Mick introduced her to his friends. He told them her story, John was intrigued. "You worked in an office and worked with sound equipment?" he asked.

"Yes," was all she said.

"Are you by any chance looking for work?" John asked her.

"Yes." Again one word, it was as if she couldn't manage any more.

"When can you start?" he asked her.

She looked at him and then at Mick. "Is this real?" she asked Mick.

"I think so. John here is a pastor, I don't think they're allowed to lie." He laughed.

"I can start now," she said.

"But first," Mick told John. "She's going to help me put the sound system back together."

"Fair enough," John said. "But after it's sorted, I have so much paperwork to do, I haven't got around to it in months."

Mel looked as if all her birthdays had come together. "Thank you," she said to Mick. "This 'Faith' that you speak of, it works, doesn't it? I think I will take a deeper look at this. I will pray and ask for the gift of faith, thank you again."

Alice had brought sandwiches and drinks for everyone and sat with them as they ate. She and Mel chatted and Alice told Mel about her faith. Everyone around the table was chatting and laughing. Mick watched and enjoyed. The food was delicious, this was part of their new lives, it was as if every sense in their bodies was alive, everything tasted, looked, sounded and smelt amazing. Mick just couldn't get enough of this new sensation.

Chapter 37

Later, when they had finished for the day, they went back to the B & B. Each of them showered and changed for the evening meal. They met in the dining room and Alice and Robert came in immediately, holding hands and smiling. Harold beamed at Alice.

"How are you tonight?" he asked.

"I am so happy," she said. We've been to the doctor and did a pregnancy test, it came back positive. The doctor says I'm fit and healthy and everything should be okay."

"I know it will," he said. "You will be fine, and I have a feeling there will be more children on the way for you both."

"Whoa," said Robert. "One thing at a time, I'm just trying to get used to being an expectant father." He laughed.

"It's nothing to do with me," Harold told him. "I'm just the messenger, but it's great to be able to deliver such a lovely message."

"How did you know?" Robert asked him.

"My angel told me," Harold said casually.

"Oh!" was all Robert could utter, "Well, thank you so much for telling Alice and for encouraging her to call me. This is one of the happiest days of my life." He turned away quickly and walked towards the kitchen. The others smiled as they saw him wipe his eyes. This was indeed a good day.

"Are we seeing John tonight?" Mick asked.

"I'm not sure," Derek said. "I spoke to him earlier and I think he's seeing Jennifer tonight."

"Has he told her his story?" asked Mick. "I was out all morning, so I don't know if he said anything to any of you?"

"Yes," Derek told him. "He finally plucked up the courage and told her everything, including the fact that he wants to confront this man and have him locked away."

"And?" asked Mick.

"He says she cried and hugged him. She told him she would support him no matter what he decided to do. She even offered to accompany him to confront Roles." Derek smiled. "She must be some woman."

"Yes," agreed Harold. "I'd like to meet this lady she sounds like a good woman to have by your side."

Derek's phone rang, it was John, asking if they had eaten. "We're just about to order," Derek told him.

"Will you wait for me, I'm bringing Jennifer. She's really looking forward to meeting all of you."

"Wonderful," Derek said. "We'll get Alice to bring another table over. What time do you expect to be here?"

"Give me twenty minutes," John said.

Twenty minutes later, John walked through the doors holding hands with a very pretty lady.

"He didn't exaggerate when he said she was beautiful," commented Paul. They all agreed.

Introductions were made all around. Then they ordered their food, and Alice did not let them down, everything was delicious. They sat chatting, and Jennifer told them all about her childhood and her trips to Italy when she was young. It felt so comfortable to be around her, it was as if they had known her for years. When Derek finally looked at his watch, it was eleven o'clock.

John tried to pay for dinner, but all four men made him put his money away. This is our treat, they agreed. As they were saying their goodbyes, John's phone rang. He looked at caller ID and his face paled.

"Hello," he said into the phone. "How are you, Tom?"

The others held their breaths and each prayed in their spirits.

"Yes, of course," John said. "What time tomorrow? Okay, see you then."

He closed his phone and looked towards the men. He had become so close to them in the past few days. They were standing with their eyes closed. He knew they were praying for him.

"Tom would like to meet with all of us tomorrow morning at eleven. Is that okay with you all?" He said.

"Of course," said Derek. "What about Larry, is he coming too?"

"I don't know, Tom didn't mention him."

"Well, let's wait and see what tomorrow brings," Paul said. They all headed towards their rooms. As they were going up the stairs, they looked at each other and knew they had to pray. They decided to use Mick and Paul's room.

They knelt together and prayed, each praying in his heart at first then Derek prayed out loud.

"Lord, only You know what's going on in these men's hearts, grant them courage and strength to face the demons that have tormented them through their lives. Only in Your strength can any of us be over comers."

Harold continued, "We are Your instruments, Lord. Show each of us what You would have us do. Thank You that You care for all of Your creation. Thank You for guiding us today with Alice. You are an amazing God. Thank You for answering her prayers. Thank You for giving Mick the courage to approach Mel. Lord, draw her to You. Bless her and give her a strong faith. Amen."

The Light poured down on each man and peace filled the room.

Chapter 38

The next morning was glorious. Mick looked out the window and smiled, how could he have missed all this beauty before? It was like he had spent his time going around with his eyes closed. After their prayer time, the previous night they were all feeling very positive. Derek and Harold were first down to breakfast, followed shortly by Paul and Mick. Paul was laughing as he sat down.

"What's funny?" asked Harold.

"It's Mick," Paul said. "I couldn't get him away from the window this morning. He is completely enthralled by everything he sees."

"I know how you feel," said Harold to Mick. I am in constant wonder at everything, it's all so beautiful."

"I feel a song coming on," Mick smiled.

"Noo-oo," said Derek, "it's too early."

They all laughed and chatted, it seemed that every time they thought they knew everything about each other, some other little fact would be mentioned and they were off again. Nobody would have known, had they watched the men, that they had an important, possibly life changing, meeting to attend in just under two hours. They were so relaxed and carefree.

Alice came in and took their orders for breakfast. She'd already brought the coffees and tea. They ordered a full breakfast, and when they had finished, their plates were practically clean. They asked Alice if they could use the small sitting room to pray. She hurried away to open the windows and let some air in, also to check that it was clean, but it always was.

They each knelt to pray. Derek began, "Teach us which way to go, Father. Send Your Spirit on us so that everything that we speak of today will be guided by You. Let nothing of ourselves come into this meeting. Let it be Your will and not ours."

"Thank you, Father," continued Paul, "For all You have done and shown us in this short time. Stay close to us and guide us as we do Your work here on earth."

Mick and Harold joined in, thanking God for His provision and beauty.

When they had finished praying, it was nine forty-five. "It's time to move!" Derek told them.

They left the B & B and walked across to John's house. John was just coming through the door.

"Where are we meeting Tom?" asked Paul.

"We'll meet at the café where Derek and I met him last time. It will take us about an hour to get there depending on traffic."

"Are we all going?" Harold asked, confused. Usually, it was only John and Derek.

"Please," John asked. "I want Tom to see that we are not on our own. I also want him to know that if he decides not to go through with it, I am not on my own. I don't want him to feel guilty. He won't, when he knows I have friends with me. Is that okay with you all? My car is a people carrier, so should fit us all in comfortably."

"Great," said Harold, "let's go."

They drove to the café, the traffic was light, it only took forty-five minutes to get there. It didn't look like a bad café, but Mick said, "I hope we don't have to eat here, the breakfast we had this morning was very filling."

The other three men agreed laughing. John said, "I think I'll eat if I can, unlike you lot, I've had nothing since last night."

"Must be love," said Paul.

"What a lovely young woman you have there, John," Derek told him.

"Jennifer," answered John, "I know, when this is over, I'm going to ask her to marry me."

"Why wait?" asked Harold. "This could go on for a long time, and you don't want to let someone as beautiful as that get away."

"I know," said John. "I'm always putting things off, it's a bad habit of mine. I'm always saying, when this happens, I'll do this etc. etc. Just like with my paperwork back at the house. Poor Mel, she doesn't know what she's letting herself in for. But you're right, I'll ask Jennifer the next time I see her. I wanted to go to a posh restaurant and propose down on one knee. Though she's not really bothered about posh restaurants, she's too down to earth for that. I can't very well take her to Alice's because you are always there, and she would expect to eat with you."

"Mmm, you have a point there," said Harold. "Let's see how it goes today then we can think of some way around it."

"Actually," Paul interrupted. "Why don't you make arrangements with Jennifer, say for tomorrow night. We'll talk to Alice and she can put a table in the small sitting room for you both. Knowing Alice, she will make it very romantic. Then later if you both want to join us, we'll be next door."

"Ha-ha, great idea," said Derek, "What about it, John?"

"Am I being railroaded into a proposal by you four?" asked John, laughing. We haven't even looked at engagement rings, how can I propose without offering her a ring?"

"Is that another excuse?" asked Harold, smiling.

They slapped John on the back and they all began ribbing him about his indecisiveness.

That was the scene Tom walked into. Five men laughing and joking and looking totally at ease. He himself was a bag of nerves, his stomach felt as if it was in a vice. His heart felt like all the blood was being squeezed from it and he couldn't catch his breath properly.

Mick looked towards the door and saw him. He knew instantly it was Tom. He could see worry squeezing his organs and fear loomed over him. His angel, Mick noticed, was fighting with all his strength, but didn't look like he was a match for worry and fear. It seemed to Mick that this angel was fighting a losing battle.

"No," Andrew whispered in his ear. "Tom is here, isn't he? Fear and worry did everything in their power to stop him coming this morning, but Tom's angel was too strong for them. So though they are doing all they can to terrorise him, the angel is winning."

"I never thought of it like that," Mick said.

The others noticed Tom standing in the doorway. John stood up immediately and went to him. They shook hands and as they did, the four men noticed fear shrink a little. The nearer John and Tom came to their table, the smaller fear got. As they approached, Paul turned to Mick and asked puzzled.

"What on earth is that crawling around his heart and lungs? It looks like millions of worms wrapping and strangling the life out of him."

"It's worry," said Mick. "My angel Andrew showed it to me yesterday when I went into the village. I had passed Mel and saw these things squirming all over her, as you say, trying to squeeze the life from her. Andrew said it was worry and that's why you feel so weak when they attack."

"Wow, they are ugly," Paul said as he stood to meet Tom.

Harold watched as each of their angels stood with Tom's fighting fear and worry. He had overheard Mick explaining to Paul. He remembered he had lived most of his past life with this demon, sucking the energy out of him.

"If I'd only known what I know now," he said to himself.

"That is why you are here," Daniel, his angel, said into his heart. "You need to show people the things they feel, fear, anxiety, worry, dread, are demons sent by Satan to destroy humans. Once people are aware of what they are and understand that they are not just feelings, they can learn to fight them."

Harold nodded his head, he still didn't feel quite up to the task, but if God said He was happy with His choice, then Harold knew God would give him the strength to carry out whatever work He had for him.

Chapter 39

Tom shook everyone's hand and took a seat at the table.

"What would you like to drink?" Paul asked.

"A coffee would be great please," Tom said.

After the waiter had taken the order, the men got down to business.

"I didn't expect to meet this many people," Tom told them. "Were you all victims of Peter Roles too?"

"No, no," said Harold. "We are John's friends, we want to support him and you and do what we can to help. That is, if you want to proceed with all this."

Tom remembered Derek telling him about the other three men. His face was bright red with embarrassment. He had thought they were more victims. He didn't know if he was pleased or disappointed that they weren't.

"Have you spoken to Larry?" John asked. "I take it he's not coming today."

"I'm not sure," Tom told him. "We spoke before I rang you last night. He was very undecided and said if he was here, then well and good, but he wasn't promising anything."

"What's been happening with you since we last met?" Derek asked.

"Well, after our meeting, I decided to tell my wife everything. We have a good marriage and she's a great wife, but I didn't think she could take knowing all the ins and outs about my past life, so I never told her."

"What happened when you told her?" asked John.

"She was really angry with me," Tom told them. "To be honest, she was so angry I thought she was going to hit me or throw something at me. I felt devastated. I must say, I nearly cursed you, John, for bringing it all up again. I thought our marriage was over for sure, and in a way it is."

They all gasped, and John said, "I am so sorry, Tom, I never meant for this to happen."

"No, no, don't worry," Tom told him. "When I said she was very angry and she was believe me. But she was angry that I never told her. She said she couldn't understand how I could keep all that pain and hurt inside and not tell her or let her help. I don't think I ever understood how strong my woman is. When she had got over being angry at me, for not telling her, we sat holding each other and I cried for a very long time. I don't think I've ever cried so much in all my life, but it was such a relief to have it out in the open at last. So when I say our marriage has ended in a way, I mean it's a new start and all the secrets and pain I experienced I can now share with her."

"Have you decided what you want to do about confronting Roles and bringing charges against him?" asked John. "There is no pressure, if you don't want any part of it, there's no hard feelings. That's one of the reasons I brought my friends along, to assure you that I'm not on my own in this. So you are free to make whatever decision you choose."

The four men looked at John, he had changed so much. He was so strong and positive. They noticed his angel, he seemed to have grown about two feet and he looked so much like the warrior he was. John didn't notice them looking at him, he was concentrating on Tom, making sure he was comfortable with whatever decision he made.

"I have already made up my mind," Tom told him. "I am with you, whatever happens. I can't let this man get away with this evil anymore. Too many young lives have been wrecked because of him. I want him stopped."

"Praise God," John said, they all answered "Amen."

Just then the door opened and Larry walked in. The fear was looming over him. There was a grey mist all around him. Derek knew it was dread. Then Derek looked closer, he could see through the mist. There was a horrible creature stuck to Larry's chest. It was grey and slimy and looked heavy as it clung to him. It seemed as if it was trying to pull Larry down. Derek could imagine just how it could pull someone under. He didn't know which was worse, fear or dread.

John jumped up when he saw Larry and went over to shake his hand. Larry looked shocked to see so many men around the table.

"What's going on? Who are all these men?" he asked John warily.

"They are my friends. They are the ones Derek and I told you about. I didn't want to put you or Tom under any pressure, so I wanted you to know that I'm not alone in this, come and meet them," John answered.

As they walked towards the table, the four could see fear shrink again, just like it had with Tom. Dread still clung to Larry, as if it would never let him go free. Derek prayed in his spirit for release for him.

Larry shook the men's hands and he and Tom hugged.

"First," said Paul, "what are you drinking?"

"Black coffee please," Larry told him.

Paul signalled the waiter, who took the order and was quickly back with a black coffee.

Larry sipped it looking around the table, waiting for the bombardment of questions to come at him. He had taken about three or four sips and looked at Tom. Tom looked so calm and in control. If he thought about it, he didn't feel quite as terrified as he had when he walked through the door. *How is that possible?* he asked himself.

Paul was ordering another pot of tea, the others were sipping their drinks, everything was so normal, it was scary. Was he the only one who was on tenterhooks? He waited until Paul had his tea and decided to go for it.

"I want to go with you, John," he said. Once it was out of his mouth, the relief he felt was overpowering. It felt like a big dark cloud had been lifted from him. And of course that's exactly what happened.

Derek and the others were smiling as they watched dread fall away. It tried to cling on but it couldn't get a hold any longer. Larry's angel stood guard so it couldn't get near him again.

"Thank you," said John. "Tom (as you probably know) will be coming too. It's time to stop this man once and for all."

Tom leaned across to Larry and asked, "Did you tell Barbara?"

"Yes," Larry said and shook his head. "She was fuming that I hadn't told her before now. But when she realised how guilty I felt, she understood. We had a long chat. It was quite a night, she cried and I cried and we just held each other. To be honest, I don't think we've ever been so close. She wanted to be here today, I think she might be meeting Maria and the two of them might just surprise us. How did it go with Maria last night?"

"The same as you," Tom told him. "She was so angry, but when I explained how I'd felt all these years, she calmed down. We both cried as well, it feels as if something has been released."

"I know what you mean," said Larry. "I felt better after telling Barbara, but when I came here today, I was terrified and dreaded meeting everyone. Then I sat down and it was as if everything lifted. It felt like a low dark cloud lifted from me. I can't explain it, but I feel so much better."

"I was the same," said Tom, "and like you, was dreading meeting up with these men, but as soon as I sat at the table, it lifted. Can't explain it, but I'm glad it happened, I've lived with that low black cloud long enough, it feels as if I've lost a couple of stone."

They both laughed because each understood what the other had gone through.

Five minutes later, the door opened and two women stood looking around the café. They spotted Tom and Larry, but they too were quite shocked to see five other men seated with their husbands. They approached cautiously and tapped their husbands on the shoulders.

Tom and Larry introduced Maria and Barbara. All the men stood when the women arrived at the table, the waiter brought extra chairs and took their drink orders. Both men were pleased and proud their wives had taken the trouble to come to the meeting to show their solidarity.

Derek looked around the table, no demons, none at their table anyway, but fear wasn't far away and it was staring across the room at Derek. He ignored it, it wasn't worth worrying about.

Chapter 40

"Do you mind if we start the meeting with prayer?" John asked around the table.

Everyone agreed and bowed their heads.

"Lord, show us the way. Guide us and teach us Your ways. Grant us courage and strength for the battle ahead. And give us Your wisdom in all we do. Amen."

"Amen," they answered.

"Okay," said John, "where do we start? We know he moved to Manchester after he left our school. He seemingly started in some inner city school there. But we have to have a plan to find out where he is now. I can't see him being in the same school, I don't think he lasts more than a few years in each school. He's not as young as he was and kids are becoming more switched on to people like him. We will have to contact the school in Manchester, and take it from there."

"What school did he move to?" asked Barbara. "How did you find out?"

"We spoke to the school that John, Tom and Larry attended," Derek said. "The principal gave us the information after John explained what had happened with Roles. The school he moved to was called St. John's. It's somewhere in Manchester, but I don't know exactly where it is."

"Don't worry," said Barbara, "I can check that out on the internet. If he's moved on, I will try and get them to tell me where he went. This could take a while, if he's been changing schools every few years, we're in for a long search. Larry will ring you as soon as I've found out anything."

"Great," said John. "Once we find him, what then? If we go into the school all guns blazing, he might just disappear again. We have to go carefully. Remember how charismatic he is, he will have fooled a lot of people, and people are proud, they won't admit they were tricked by him."

"Once we find out where he is, we can go to the nearest police station. We need to be sure we have the right man. Then we can report him to the police."

"Sounds like a plan," said Derek. "Let's eat, is anyone hungry?"

The waiter brought the menus and after they had ordered, they sat around the table and chatted. When they had finished lunch, Derek insisted on paying for everyone. The ladies decided that they wanted to make a start on finding this monster so they left the café first. The men sat and chatted for another half hour running different scenarios past each other.

John made the first move to leave. "We had better be on our way," he said, "to avoid rush hour traffic."

"He has a big date tonight," Mick told them laughing.

"It's tomorrow night," John said blushing.

The four men left the café, but John stayed behind to thank Tom and Larry. "It's a big step you've taken," he said. "I know it wasn't easy, but I just want to say thank you from the bottom of my heart. I'm so glad to have met you both again, and glad you are with me on this."

Tom and Larry shook his hand and in turn thanked him. He had changed their lives. Their marriages were closer and they felt a freedom that they had never felt before, they were very grateful.

When John had gone, Tom suggested he and Larry go to their local for a pint. The two left the café different men than they had entered.

Meanwhile, the other five men discussed their next move as they were driving back. What if Barbara and Maria can't find him through the internet? What would be the best way to catch up with him, what would be the quickest way?

"We were given the information from the original school," John said. "I suppose if it's not available on the internet, then we do it the old fashioned way. Go to the school he moved to first and try to pick up his trail."

The others could see the determination in John's face. He had started this and he was not going to stop until he finished it.

Later that evening Larry rang John. "Not good news," he said. "Let me put Barbara on to you, she can explain it better than me."

Barbara came on the phone. "We pulled up the school whose name you gave us, but they did not list the teachers individually," she told him. "We got the name of the headmaster, a Mr Bryant, but he wouldn't give me any information over the phone. So we don't know if he's still there or has moved on. You seemed to have been more successful with your old school. Have you any ideas what to do next?"

"I thought this might happen," John said. "I will ring Mr Barlow at our old school. I'll ask him to speak to Mr Bryant, headmaster to headmaster. That will probably add more weight. I'll also ask if he can make an appointment for us to meet with Mr Bryant. Sometimes it's better face to face. Do you have the number for the school?"

She gave him the number and he thanked her for all her help and support at the café. "As soon as I know anything, I will contact you."

"Thank you," said Barbara. "I mean thank you for starting all of this. I have been with Larry for a long time and have always known there was something bothering him. He would never speak of it and would get very angry if I kept prying. Over the years, I can't count the times he woke me up shouting, 'no, stop it'. Then he would wake in a sweat. He said they were just normal nightmares, but I knew it stemmed from something in his past. To be honest, I thought at one time that his mum had been cruel to him when he was a boy. He denied it, of course, but I always harboured a feeling of resentment against her. Yet I knew when I saw them together that whatever it was, he had forgiven her. I, on the other hand, could not."

"I feel so ashamed," she continued. "His poor mum. Don't get me wrong, I was always nice to her, but somehow I just couldn't let myself get too close. Now I want to go and apologise for all the hard feelings I had against her. I feel so guilty now that I know the truth."

"Don't let guilt take over your life, Barbara," said John. "It will drag you down. Believe me, I know all about guilt. Wait until we catch Roles. When it's out in the open, you can explain to your mother-in-law how you felt. But Larry will need to be the one to tell her. He will also be free of any guilt he felt. That man has spoilt so many relationships, but God will have the victory."

"Thank you, John," Barbara said. "You are a very good man. I am glad I met you."

"Thank you," said John quite humbly. "I will keep you all updated. Do you want me to contact only you or does Larry want me to speak to him?"

"No," she told him. "Please speak to me or Maria. The men work full time and it's not always convenient to have that kind of conversation over the phone where people might overhear. We have discussed this with Tom and Larry and they are happy with us being the go-betweens. I hope that's okay with you, and you are comfortable with it?"

"Of course," said John. "I am delighted that you and Maria are involved, especially for Tom and Larry, it must be such a weight off their minds."

She agreed and gave him Maria's mobile number. "I work mornings until twelve noon. Maria works afternoons. We do a job share, just so you know when we are contactable."

"Great, thanks Barbara," he said, "have a good evening and I will be in touch. God bless."

"And God bless you, John," she replied.

Chapter 41

John rang Jennifer and filled her in with the day's events. "Have you eaten yet?" he asked.

"Actually, I was just preparing a lasagne," she replied. "There's plenty to share, why don't you come over and bring a bottle of red wine with you. Give me about an hour, and everything will be ready when you get here."

"Mmm sounds great," he said. "See you later." He jumped into the shower. Then he put on his black jeans and black shirt. When he looked at himself in the mirror, he changed his mind. "I look too much like a vicar," he said to himself. He found a grey shirt. That felt more like it.

He decided to go across to the B & B before he went to Jennifer's, to see the lads. They had become so close, Derek and Harold were like the father he never knew, and Mick and Paul were like older brothers. He wondered how he'd feel when they finally had to leave. Thinking of this brought him to a decision.

Harold was right, he thought. *Why am I procrastinating over asking Jennifer to marry me? I know she's the one for me so what's stopping me?*

He suddenly realised that because of what happened when he was a child, and again in the previous parish, he didn't have much confidence. He was afraid Jennifer would say no.

He walked across to the B & B. The four men were in the middle of their evening meal. He remembered the first time he had walked over to them at that table. The terror he had felt, unrealistic fear had pierced his heart. Now, as he looked at them, they felt like family, this was the closest he had ever felt to other men.

Mick spotted him first. "Hi, John," he shouted across the dining room.

The others looked and immediately pulled up a chair for him.

Paul noticed the bottle of red wine in his hand. "I don't think Alice would be too pleased with you bringing your own wine into her establishment." He laughed.

"I'm on my way to see Jennifer, she's cooking lasagne."

Harold raised his eyebrows. "Do you want us to talk to Alice about the small living room?" he asked.

"Yes, please," John smiled. "You are right I don't know what I was waiting for. One thing, if she says yes, will you be able to stay for the wedding?"

Derek laughed. "That all depends on how long you intend to keep us waiting for the wedding. I don't think the Lord will be happy with us hanging around here for a couple of years."

"I know," said John. "I must admit, now that I've made the decision to ask Jennifer to marry me, I want it to happen sooner rather than later. I already have a house so we won't need to save for that. But you know women? She will want her family there and probably half of Italy too. I understand if you have to move on before then, but I will try and organise it as soon as possible."

"First things first," said Paul. "Ask her tomorrow night and we'll take it from there."

"Okay," said John and smiled at the way his life had changed since these men had arrived.

"Any news?" Mick asked.

"Barbara rang earlier," he told them. "She couldn't find the information we needed from the internet, only the headmaster's name, it's Mr Bryant. She said he was less than helpful. I thought I'd speak to Mr Barlow at my old school and ask him to speak to Mr Bryant on our behalf."

"That sounds like a very good idea," Derek said. "He was quite helpful when we met him and you and he seemed to hit it off, so I'm sure he'll do it for you."

"I'll contact him in the morning," John said. "In the meantime, I have a lovely lady cooking me lasagne, so I'd better not keep her waiting."

They waved goodnight to him and Paul called Alice over to the table.

"John is planning a special night tomorrow night for him and his lady friend," he told her. "I said I would ask you to set up the small sitting room with a table for two, making it look romantic. Is that possible?"

"Of course," said Alice. "It will be a pleasure. I'll make sure we have romantic music and lighting sorted. What do you think they'd like to eat, ours is a set menu, it's not like a normal restaurant?"

"Alice," said Paul, "you are a great cook. Whatever you have on the menu will be great, but not lasagne, she's cooking that for him tonight."

"Good job you told me," she laughed. "I'll check my cookbook and come up with something a bit different. I'll get Robert to sort out the living room tomorrow. Will you need it for prayer?"

"We'll need it just in the morning after breakfast," he told her. "It will probably be for about an hour or an hour and a half. Will that be okay with you?"

"Oh yes," she said. "I love it when you pray in my house. I know you have brought blessings beyond measure to my home. Thank you."

Chapter 42

John arrived at Jennifer's house with a few minutes to spare. He took this time to pray. "Father," he said, "I know this lady is the one I want to spend the rest of my life with. If this is from You, will You please bless our relationship and let it flourish as only You can. Amen."

He knocked at the door and when she answered it, she took his breath away. She looked even more beautiful than he had ever seen her. There was something about her tonight, it was like there was an aura around her and everything about her shone. He couldn't speak, and before he even thought of it, he took her in his arms and kissed her. It was a long, lingering kiss full of tenderness and love.

When they finally broke away, they were both breathless. She led him into the dining room by the hand.

"You behave yourself, remember you're a pastor." She laughed.

John held up his hands in surrender, "I promise I'll be good." He laughed.

They sat down together and held hands to say grace. Then she served up the food.

"What have you decided to do about finding this monster?" she asked him, she couldn't bring herself to mention his name.

He explained that he was going to speak to Mr Barlow and ask him to speak to Mr Bryant.

"Sounds like a good idea," she nodded. "And even if he doesn't want to ask about 'him', at least he may be able to make you an appointment with this Mr Bryant."

"Yes, that's true," said John. I know Roles went on to the school in Manchester, but it was a long time ago, I can't see him still being there after all these years. Someone would have found out about him, or at least become suspicious as Mr Kenny did in my old school."

"I agree," she said. "To be honest, I think he'll have left a long time ago. I think someone like him would have to keep moving. There are different associations going into schools now. They make themselves available if a child needs to talk about anything that's bothering them. They also make them aware of what is right and what is wrong behaviour. Someone somewhere is going to blow the whistle on him."

"Yes, you're right," John sighed. "It nearly happened with that young lad at my school, the one the lads told us about. I wonder whatever happened to him."

"Tomorrow," he continued, "I will contact Tim Barlow, and get the ball rolling. If Mr Bryant agrees to see me, or gives Tim the information we need, at least we're on the right track. Even if it means going from one school to another until we find him, then so be it. I am not giving up until I do."

Jennifer smiled. She could see the change in him, since the four men arrived. She had loved him before, but looking at him now, he seemed so much stronger and more self-assured. Her heart swelled, and she stretched across the table and squeezed his hand.

"I love you," she said smiling.

"I love you too," John told her. He had to stop himself from asking her to marry him there and then. The lads were asking Alice to set up the small dining room for him tomorrow night and he didn't want to spoil it. They talked well into the early hours of the morning before John looked at his watch.

"I'd better go," he said. "I'll never get up in the morning."

Jennifer smiled. She didn't want him to leave. She hated saying goodbye. *Oh, how I wish we didn't have to say good night and go to our separate homes each night,* she thought. *But he hasn't mentioned marriage, and with all this going on, I don't expect him to. I will just have to be patient and wait until it's finished. Then maybe he will ask me to marry him. If not, I will ask him. I know in my heart, this is my husband.*

With sighs and resignations, they held each other and said good night.

"Oh," said John, "can I take you out to dinner tomorrow night? Alice is doing some special meal tomorrow and the lads suggested we eat there. She's a great cook, what do you say?"

"Yes, of course," she said. "That would be lovely. What time will I meet you?"

"I'll pick you up at eight o'clock, if that's okay with you?" he told her.

"Yes, great, see you then." She gave him a quick peck on the cheek before he left. As the door closed, a little pang of jealousy hit her from out of the blue. "What on earth is that about?" she asked herself. "Feeling jealous of Alice, that's ridiculous, she's happily married to Robert. I know John doesn't fancy her, so why should I feel jealous?"

Then it dawned on her. Since the four men arrived, John had spent so much time with them she had felt a bit left out. Now here they were arranging to have dinner with them again. It wasn't a very strong feeling, but it was a bit irritating. The she remembered what John had told her about the demons. How they came in all shapes and sizes. She knew she was being attacked because they had had such a lovely night. Jealousy was so subtle, so dangerous, it seemed to just creep into her mind, out of nowhere.

"No!" she said out loud. "I love John and he loves me. These men have only helped him. I refuse to feel resentment or jealousy against any of them, so get lost."

At once, her spirit lifted and she started laughing. *Just as well no one can see me,* she thought, *they'd think I'd gone insane.* She didn't see the creature slink away, completely flattened by her refusal to let it have control.

Chapter 43

The next morning John rang Tim Barlow. He explained what had happened with Barbara and how Mr Bryant, the head teacher in Manchester, hadn't been very forthcoming. Tim agreed to speak to Bryant on John's behalf and make an appointment for him. John thanked him and hung up. All he could do now was wait!

In the meantime, he had work to do at the church. He walked over towards it and as he looked, he could see a light coming from it.

Someone must have turned all the lights on, he thought. *I can't understand why, it's a lovely day and it's a well-lit church on the dullest of days. That light though, it seems to be coming from everywhere.*

As he got nearer, he could see that the light was not from electric bulbs. It was too bright. It looked like an aura surrounding the church. The light was pouring into the church, not out of it. It seemed to seep through the masonry. He was nearly afraid to go closer in case the light would diminish.

But this wasn't the time for nerves. He walked through the doors and the sight took his breath away. Around the altar, on their knees, were the four men. They were surrounded by at least twenty-five of his parishioners. The tears stung his eyes. His whole body trembled. The people were engulfed in light. It poured in through the windows and the brickwork, but it also poured out through the men. At first, he couldn't move, he just wanted to stand and behold this wonderful sight. Then he knew in his heart, he had to be a part of it. He walked slowly down the aisle and joined them in prayer.

Mick was leading. The peace that flowed through them and over them was beautiful. It reminded John of Philippians 4 vs 7: 'And the peace of God, which transcends all understanding, will guard your hearts and minds in Christ Jesus.'

When the prayers had concluded, nobody moved. No one wanted to move. Then one of the parishioners spoke.

"It's like we've been touched by angels," he said. "As if heaven had come to earth for a time."

They all nodded in agreement. John noticed he wasn't the only one with tears running down his face. He looked around the group and everyone was crying. Some, it seemed with joy, others looked as if something or someone, (John knew who!) had broken through their hard exteriors and touched their hearts. They remained kneeling for another ten to fifteen minutes, no one wanting to come away from the peace. Nobody spoke, each communicating with God in their own spirits.

Then they all looked up, it was as if each of them were told at the same time that it was time to start work. John thought it would be hard to be motivated to do physical work after that, he didn't want to lose this peace. He was wrong, the peace stayed with each of them, and far from feeling a lack of motivation, he was charged with energy, as were the rest of the people. They were soon at their chores with more energy than they had ever had.

Later he thought, *Normally, I would be a bit vexed at someone else leading the people in prayer. How insecure was I?* He smiled to himself, he felt so different these days. He had regained his confidence and with it a freedom from needing to be 'the pastor'.

One woman walked quietly over to Mick and touched him on the elbow.

"Thank you for leading us in prayer this morning," she said. "I have never encountered anything quite like it. This peace that I have is physical. Can we do this every morning before we start work? I feel so energised, I think I could run a marathon." She laughed.

"Of course," said Mick. "It's the only way to start the day."

One of the men came over to John. He was quite wealthy, but he wasn't a regular at church and John didn't know him very well.

"I'm Craig," he said. "I think what you are doing here is just short of a miracle."

"I think, from what has happened so far, with all the help I've received, plus finding the parquet flooring under the old carpet, would constitute as a definite miracle." John laughed.

"You're right. I wouldn't have believed it, if I hadn't seen it with my own eyes," Craig told him.

"You are not a regular here?" John asked. "What made you come and help? Some of my regulars have not had the time, or the inclination to help out. I was wondering what brought you here."

"I can't say for sure," answered Craig. "All I know is, I had a very strong urge to come here this morning. Normally, I would pop into the office and check a few emails etc. But to be honest, they don't need me there, the place runs itself and my staff are excellent. It's just something to do I suppose."

"And this morning?" asked John.

"Well, like I said, it was an overwhelming urge to visit the church. I have seen all the activity over the last few days, maybe it was curiosity, but I think it was something more than that.

"When I arrived and those men started praying, it wiped me out. I have a very prosperous business and a great staff to run it, but something has been missing in my life. I can't put my finger on it. It feels like there is a hole in my spirit and I need to fill it, but nothing seems to do the trick. Then I came here this morning, and now I know what I need. I know we have just finished praying, but could you pray with me for guidance, I want to believe, I think I do believe. But what if it's too late for me, I've been 'in the world' for so long. Using every bit of my energy to make money, now I find it's not enough. I need this faith, this belonging. Do you think God will forgive me and let me come to know Him?" Craig sighed.

"Do you know the parable of the prodigal son?" John asked. "Or the story of the shepherd, who left ninety-nine sheep to find one lost one? Well, Jesus tells us there is more joy in heaven over one sinner who repents than ninety-nine righteous people (Luke 15:7). So the answer is yes, God has been waiting with open arms for you to come to Him. Do you believe Jesus is the Son of God?"

"Yes, I do, of course," Craig replied.

"Well, the Bible says, if you confess with your mouth that Jesus is Lord and believe in your heart that God raised Him from the dead, you will be saved (Rom. 10:9) You do not have to be afraid, God is Love. Pray and ask Jesus into your life, it sounds as if He's knocking on your door, do you want to open it?"

"Yes, oh yes," Craig whispered.

"Then it's a done deal," John said, smiling.

Craig knelt where they were and asked Jesus into his life, he never thought he would publicly kneel and pray, but here he was and it felt wonderful. John knelt with him and together they worshipped and prayed, and Craig gave his life to Jesus.

When they had finished, Craig said, "I think you need your walls painted. What else do you need?"

John explained how they were tackling one thing at a time. The first thing was to remove the black underlay from the parquet flooring. Paul and some other men had nearly finished sanding the pews, they need varnishing afterwards.

Craig asked, "Would you be offended if I paid for the paint and the varnish? I want to share my good fortune with you, will you let me help?"

John laughed. "Of course, that would be great. God has done so many miracles already I was just waiting to see where the paint and varnish would come from. He hasn't let me down."

"I also employ some painters," Craig said. "I don't want to step on anyone's toes, but if you let me know when they can start, I will send them to you. Here's my number, if you think of anything else you need, just let me know. What colour were you thinking of for the walls?"

"White," said John. "I think it will look clean and bright. Could we have either sheen or silk please? Not matte, it's too hard to get marks from the walls, and I expect this church to be overflowing very soon, so I need to keep things simple."

"Great," said Craig, "consider it done. In the meantime, I need to give these people a hand with the cleaning, etc." He smiled and walked over to the others. John could not help but smile and say a prayer of thanks. This was much better than he had ever imagined.

Chapter 44

They worked all day in and around the church. Mick worked alongside Mel, she was great, and what a difference in her from that first day he met her. She looked radiant and very peaceful. She was also a very hard worker—it took him all his time to keep up with her. Inside the church the team worked hard on the floor. The carpet had been down so long, the under felt was well and truly stuck to the parquet flooring and it was a painstakingly slow job. But each person cleaned their patch very carefully so as not to damage the flooring underneath. John looked around, he watched as people from all different backgrounds were working side by side. They were laughing and chatting with each other, John had never seen some of them passing the time of day with each other.

He kept his mobile switched on, hoping to hear from Mr Bryant, or Tim. It was Friday and he also needed to work on his sermon for Sunday. So much had happened this past week, he hadn't even thought about his sermon for Sunday.

Around twelve thirty, he got a call from Mr Bryant.

"I've been speaking to Mr Barlow," he told John. "I believe you want to know the whereabouts of Peter Roles?"

"That's right," John said. "Any information you can give me would be greatly appreciated."

"I don't want to discuss it over the phone," he told John. "Can you meet me?"

"Just tell me where and when," John said.

"I know tomorrow is Saturday, but would it be possible for you to come here to Manchester?" Mr Bryant asked John. "It could take you about three hours depending on traffic. You are better leaving around ten am. Manchester United are playing at home and most of their fans come from down south, so traffic could be dreadful. "Sorry," he laughed, "I'm a Manchester City supporter, and we don't get along."

John smiled, he wasn't a big football fan, but he knew about the rivalry between the two Manchester clubs. "Okay," he said. "We'll leave early and call you when we're nearly there. What junction should we come off at?"

"Junction 19 on the M6," Mr Bryant told John. Then he gave him exact directions to their destination. They were meeting at a hotel called The Four Seasons, just off the motorway. He told John that the hotel catered for business meetings etc. so it was ideal.

John thanked him and told him how much he appreciated his help.

Mr Bryant said he was looking forward to meeting John the next day. They said goodbye and John immediately rang Barbara to give her the good news. "Tell Tom and Larry that I have a meeting with Mr Bryant tomorrow," he said. "It looks like things are starting to move."

"We'll all be praying for you," Barbara told him.

He went to find the four men to inform them of the meeting the following day.

"What do you want us to do?" Paul asked.

"I would really like you all to come, if that's okay with you?" he told them. "I know it might feel heavy-handed but good things happen when we are all together. I

113

don't know what to expect from Mr Bryant. He sounds like a good man, but you can never tell and I would appreciate you all being with me. I've told Barbara about the meeting and she and the others will be praying."

They all agreed, there was an air of excitement in the church. They all felt like a breakthrough was coming at last.

They worked most of the day stopping when Alice brought the sandwiches and drinks. Harold asked her how she always knew just how many sandwiches and drinks to bring over. She admitted that she would come over in the morning and check how many people were working so she would know how many to make. Everyone thanked her and the food was devoured. They finished up around four thirty. It had been slow going, but they could see the difference from when they had started.

"Okay," John told the people. "Time to pack up, have a great weekend, and if you can come again on Monday, that would be wonderful."

He looked around the church, there was still a lot of work to be done. The floor was a mess and probably a trip hazard. *I suppose I could come back tomorrow and try and fix it up for Sunday,* he thought.

Alice had come to collect the plates etc. She always left it as late as possible so as not to disturb the work. She heard John telling the people that work would resume on Monday.

"Will nobody be working tomorrow?" she asked.

"No," he replied. "The lads and I are off to Manchester for a meeting and I think everyone has worked very hard this week, they need a couple of days to rest."

"What about Sunday?" she asked. "How will you get the church ready for the Sunday service? It doesn't look very safe for old people especially, and you would have to sort out the pews, you can't do all that on your own, it's impossible, especially if you are going to Manchester in the day."

"I know," he said. "I was thinking that I would come here after I got back from Manchester and try and sort everything out. I know the lads will help, but it is a mammoth task."

Then he looked at her and smiled. "I don't suppose we could use your house for Sunday service?" he asked.

"Of course," she laughed, "what a wonderful idea, how many chairs will we need? Have you got song books? What about the sound system?"

John shushed her, laughing. "I will bring the song books over to you later. We should need around thirty chairs, sofas, stools whatever you have. Don't worry about the sound system, it's a smaller area than this church, so people will hear what's going on, anyway, remember this is not only our responsibility. God will orchestrate everything we just have to trust Him."

"Oh, I trust Him completely," she said, touching her tummy. "You'd better let everyone know where we will be worshipping on Sunday. We don't want people turning up to find the church closed."

"Good thinking," he said. "I'll put a notice on the door of the church, I'll also let everyone here know and ask them to spread the word." Then he turned to the people, who were packing up and told them what was happening, asking them to let their friends and neighbours know. They agreed and finally he was able to close up and go home. Obviously, though there were other things going on in his head, his main thought was this evening. He would propose to Jennifer. He knew in his heart that she would say yes, but a little voice kept whispering—"You don't really know, what will you do if she says no? What then?"

It started again as he walked towards his house, he could feel a small tightness around his heart. "Get out of my head," he shouted. "I'm not falling for your lies anymore."

The tightness left him, he suddenly felt free and full of energy. It seemed every time he rebuked that little voice, or the fear that was constantly trying to undermine him, he felt stronger, more energised and freer than at any other time in his life.

"I'm going to ask Jennifer to marry me, and she's going to say yes. That's all there is to it," he told himself, and the demons that were hanging around listening. And there were quite a few! It was a shame he couldn't see how they shrivelled from his words, they practically disappeared.

In the meantime, the four men decided to visit a local pub for a beer. They ordered their pints of bitter. It was a real ale pub and they were looking forward to tasting the local brew.

"Thirsty work," Derek said as he sipped his beer. "Is it my imagination, or does everything taste a hundred times better than before?" he asked.

"It's not your imagination," Mick told him. "Not only does everything taste better, everything sounds better, looks more beautiful. It's wonderful."

"I've heard more birds singing," said Harold, "than I ever knew existed. I can actually hear the different sounds each bird makes. Working on the farm, I was used to different birds, but sometimes when you get used to something, you don't always appreciate it, the way you should." His voice trailed off.

Paul put his hand on Harold's shoulder. "I couldn't agree more," he said.

Chapter 45

"You got the chance to see your family," Harold replied. "Do you think I'll be allowed to see mine?"

"You need to speak to Daniel, your angel," Paul told him. "I don't see why you wouldn't be allowed, if you ask."

"I keep thinking maybe it's because they are not doing too well and it would be more upsetting for me to see them, I don't know," Harold said. "It's the only thing that makes me sad."

They all understood how he felt, and each said a prayer that his wish would be granted.

Derek thought about his previous life and though it made him sad that he hadn't made any commitments, he was also glad. He didn't have that tug on his heart.

They sat and chatted for over an hour about past, present and future. They had become so close there was nothing they didn't know about each other.

"It's a big night for John tonight," Harold said. "I can't wait to see the joy on his face when she says yes."

"I think we should make a move," Derek laughed. "We'll want to look a bit respectable when they come and tell us the great news."

They strolled back to the B & B. Mick looked over at the church, "What's that light?" he asked the others.

They all looked, there was a bright haze around the church, but it looked as if it was seeping out from inside. They walked towards it and now it was very clear that the light was emanating from within.

"It's beautiful," Mick said.

They tried the door and it opened. "I was sure John locked this when he left," Harold said a little confused.

They walked inside, the light shone all around the church. It seemed to touch and soak everything with the brightness. They couldn't get past the vestibule, they couldn't walk. They each remembered the 'Old Testament' story. When the priests brought the Ark back to the temple, the Glory of the Lord filled the temple and the priests could not continue their service, for the Glorious Presence of the Lord filled the temple (1 Kings 8:11).

That's exactly what it felt like, they knew, 'The Presence of the Lord' filled the church, and all they could do was fall down in adoration.

They knelt there, none of them knew for how long, an hour? Ten minutes? Time seemed to have stopped. Then gradually the light faded and finally disappeared. They were devastated, but then the peace fell on each of them as if to remind them that He was still near.

The Light had terrified and excited them, it was beautiful beyond description. Then they heard a voice behind them, calling their names.

"Derek, Harold, Paul, Mick—listen to this message."

They turned as one and saw a warrior, so big, so strong looking—he was bigger than any of their angels. Again, they fell on their knees.

"No, do not bow to me, I am just a messenger, from the One who is worthy of all Glory," the warrior told them. "Stand and heed my words."

They stood, each of them glad he was not alone. They drew closer together as if on their own they would fall down again.

"The Light you have seen," the warrior explained, "is from my Master, the Lord God Almighty. The Alpha and Omega. The Light of the world has shone in this place for you to see. This Light quenches darkness, remember this. This Light is all around you. It is in your hearts and spirits and coursing through your bodies. It is giving you strength and building you up for what is to come."

"My name is Michael," the warrior told them. "I've been sent to warn you, you will come against a darkness that you've never encountered before. The darkness you saw at John's house had all but been defeated. This is something so evil, it will try to overcome you, but you have the power to defeat it. You must be on your guard at all times. It will try to weaken you. You must put on the full armour of the Lord. Read it in Ephesians 6, and make sure you put it on every day. Tell John to do the same. The battle is about to begin, and you are God's representatives."

They were speechless. *What was to come?* Harold thought, feeling that sense of inadequacy run through his mind, but as soon as it entered his head, it was gone. He knew in his heart at that precise moment that he was up for the task. He was not alone, they were not alone. This was not a battle of flesh and blood, this was spiritual warfare, and he was on the winning side.

"Exactly!" said the warrior and woke Harold from his reverie.

"Are you Michael the Archangel?" Harold asked sheepishly.

"Yes, that is who I am," Michael replied.

"What do we need to do to prepare?" asked Paul.

"Pray, and as I told you, put on the armour. Soak yourselves in the 'Word of God' and remember the promise. You are mighty warriors, and God is with you. The battle is the Lord's, but the victory will be yours," he told them. "Now you have a time of rest. Tonight relax, celebrate with John and Jennifer. Tomorrow, as you travel to Manchester, keep praying and reading the Word. Nothing is going to start yet, that is in the weeks to come. Now is the time for rest and preparation."

Then he was gone.

"Wow," said Mick. "Talk about being in the thick of it. I wonder if it's okay to be a bit scared."

"I don't think you'd be normal if you weren't a little scared," Derek replied. "Just don't let fear in."

"It can't get in," Harold told them. "It tried with me when Michael was speaking to us."

"What did Michael mean when he said 'exactly', what was that about?" asked Paul.

"Well, like I was saying," Harold explained, "the inadequacy thing came into my head when he was telling us that we had to be prepared for what was to come. But, I can't explain it, it just couldn't take hold. I knew then, in my inner being, that everything was going to be all right. I finally grasped the fact that we are never on our own. I understood that this is a spiritual fight, and we are on the winning side. That's when Michael said 'exactly'."

"Amen to that," they all shouted. Then they left the church, still feeling the peace. They walked back to the B & B with smiles on their faces.

Alice happened to look out the window as they were passing. "There's a light around those four men," she said to Robert. "I've never seen anything quite like it."

"I can't see the light around them, but I know what you mean," said Robert. "There is something different about them, it feels supernatural."

"I'm glad they're on our side," said Alice. "I think they may be very powerful men of God."

If only she knew!!!

Chapter 46

John's nerves were jangling. *Funny*, he thought, *I'm nervous, but I'm not afraid.*

He wore a pale blue polo shirt and a pair of black jeans. He didn't want to be too dressed up, but at the same time, he wanted Jennifer to know he had made some effort. He looked at himself in the mirror and was pleasantly surprised. He no longer looked haunted. The dark rings around his eyes seemed to have vanished. The lines around his mouth that made him look like a sad clown, (in his eyes) had definitely diminished. He felt stronger and in control, and it showed. "Well, here goes," he said to himself. "This is probably one of the most important nights of my life so far."

He picked up his keys, checked his wallet to make sure he had enough money and he was out the door whistling a lovely hymn that had been going through his head all day.

When he arrived at Jennifer's house, he still had five minutes to spare, he used the time to pray. He asked the Lord to bless the night, just saying that prayer lifted his spirit even higher and he felt his confidence rise.

Jennifer was putting the last touches to her makeup when she heard John come through the gate. She felt quite nervous about going to dinner with the four men. They were very courteous and friendly, but there was something different and powerful about them, and it scared her a little. Though she couldn't put her finger on it, she felt a bit in awe of them. She checked herself in the mirror. She was wearing a black camisole top with black flowing trousers. Over the camisole she wore a cream lace cardigan. It was a present from her parents from one of their holidays in Italy. She thought she looked okay, she hoped John would too. She said a silent prayer and asked God to bless the night. She was looking forward to the night, but in her heart of hearts, she would have preferred to spend it just with John.

She opened the door, he stood there smiling. He looked so handsome in his blue polo shirt. It showed off his tan. His eyes lit up when he saw her. "You look beautiful," he told her. "I am a very lucky man."

They both laughed and then kissed. John pulled away. "Let's get to the restaurant," he said, "or we'll be late."

Jennifer tried to hide her disappointment. She smiled and grabbed her bag and they were out the door. It was a lovely clear night and the stars seemed to be shining in abundance for the two of them alone. They chatted as they walked and Jennifer could feel John's nervousness but decided to keep it to herself.

When they arrived at the B & B, Alice greeted them. Instead of directing them to the large dining room, she ushered them into a small room to the left of the hall. The room was dimly lit with one table in the middle of the floor. Only two chairs were placed at the table. Jennifer looked at John confused.

"I thought we were joining the four men?" she asked.

"Well, maybe we'll have a drink with them later. I hope you don't mind, I wanted you to myself tonight," he told her smiling.

"I don't mind at all," Jennifer said, "this is very romantic."

John pulled the chair out for her, ever the gentleman. They both sat looking at the little room. Alice had gone to so much trouble. There were fresh flowers on the bureau, fresh flowers on the table, and as well as the dim lights, Alice had put on a CD of love songs.

They both smiled at her as she arrived with the menus. "I hope it's okay, but we have just a set menu tonight. You can have a choice of starters and desserts, but the main course is beef in red wine," she told them.

"Sounds great," said John. "And thank you Alice for this."

She smiled pleased that they appreciated the little effort she had put into getting the room ready. They ordered their starters and she left them to it.

"You are very fidgety," Jennifer said. She was thrilled that he had just wanted to be with her tonight.

He took her hand across the table. "I've wanted to ask you this for a very long time," he said, "but I thought I'd get things sorted first, but I can't wait any longer. Will you marry me, Jennifer?" he asked, looking deeply into her eyes.

At first, she didn't answer, she couldn't speak. She had dreamed of this moment for so long. When she finally caught her breath, she smiled and said, "Yes, of course, I'll marry you."

John stood up and pulled her to him and kissed her with a tenderness that took her breath away. The door opened just as they were pulling away from each other, and Alice came in with the starters.

"She said yes," John told Alice.

"Oh, that's wonderful," Alice said and hugged them both. "I hope you will be able to eat your food with all this excitement."

"Ha-ha, try and stop us," said Jennifer. "It looks wonderful."

Alice showed them a buzzer on the wall. "This is a very special night for you both. I don't want to keep barging in and interrupting you, so when you are ready for your main meal, please just press the buzzer. It will sound in the kitchen and I'll know I'm not disturbing you."

"Thank you, Alice," said John, "That was very thoughtful, you needn't have gone to all that bother, but we appreciate it very much." He smiled.

Alice laughed as she left the room. "It was no bother at all," she said, "Robert enjoyed fixing it up. Enjoy your starters."

John and Jennifer chatted as they ate.

"You know I'm going to Manchester tomorrow with the men?" John said. "Can you get a day off work in the week? I want to take you out and buy you an engagement ring. I didn't want to choose one for you. I want you to choose it, seeing as you will be the one wearing it. I don't know your ring size either. All the romantic novels and films where the man produces a ring when he proposes to the girl, how does he know the girl will like it? Or if it will fit her?"

Jennifer burst out laughing. It was one of the things John loved about her. She wasn't afraid to laugh like some women he had known, who would just titter in case it spoilt their image. Not Jennifer though, she was always up for a laugh and saw the funny side of everything. "What's so funny?" he asked her.

Jennifer wiped the tears of laughter from her eyes, hoping her mascara hadn't run as she answered. "I never knew you watched romantic films, and when did you start reading 'Mills and Boon'?"

"You know what I mean," John said. "I've just heard women talking about romantic novels, and I'll have you know, I've seen a few romantic films in my time."

"You are full of surprises," she laughed. "Maybe you will take me when the next very romantic film comes out? But I have to say, I agree with you. I don't know what ring size I am, so how would you? Anyway, I think it will be more romantic if we buy it together. I'm not sure about taking a day off work though, we're very busy at the moment, how about waiting and we can go together next Saturday?"

John agreed, and they discussed dates for the wedding. But both agreed to see what the outcome of the meeting in Manchester would be, after that they could set a date.

Jennifer was so happy. All her doubts and that bit of jealousy trying to warp her mind, she was glad she hadn't given into it. Now, here she was with the man she loved and they were making wedding plans. They hadn't set the date yet, but they were discussing where and how and who to invite.

John was wondering how many of Jennifer's family would come over from Italy for the wedding. *There could be hundreds,* he thought, but decided if there were, they would manage. They were a pair and they had the Lord in their lives, so there really wasn't anything to worry about.

They finally rang the buzzer for the main course. Alice brought it through and they both ate. It was delicious, the beef was so tender it melted in the mouth, and the vegetables were done to perfection.

Alice actually apologised that the presentation was not up to the standard of many of the high-class restaurants. Hers was a simple meal without the fancy artwork that went with food these days.

Both John and Jennifer told her it was perfect. They were quite happy without the art.

Alice was proud as punch. She felt elated as she walked back to the kitchen.

Chapter 47

"Liked your cooking, I see," said Robert, as she brought the empty plates through. "I don't know why you were wound up about it today. I haven't seen one plate with food on it come back into this kitchen. You are an amazing cook, enjoy your gift." He bent down and kissed her.

She smiled at him and said, "Thank you, you always encourage me. I am well and truly blessed."

"You certainly are," he said and kissed her again. She pushed him away laughing. "I have guests to attend to." But she turned and kissed him again.

When John and Jennifer had finished their food, John paid the bill. John asked if Jennifer would mind if they had a drink with the lads.

"Of course not!" she said smiling.

"I want to tell them the good news," he said. "That's if Alice hasn't told them already."

They walked into the little bar next to the dining room. The four men were around a table and looked as if they were praying. As they approached, Mick looked up and smiled.

"Mind if we join you?" John whispered.

Mick pulled out two chairs, and the three joined the others in prayer.

Derek was leading tonight. They were asking God for guidance for the meeting the next day. "Lord," he said, "we need Your Holy Spirit with us and in us tomorrow. Give us discernment and open doors that you would have us go through in Jesus' name. And arm us Lord, with Your armour for the battle that is about to come."

They all said Amen.

Harold had a glint in his eyes as he asked John and Jennifer if they would like a drink. John smiled and asked if they would like to hear their good news first.

Harold sat back down, "Drinks can wait," he said with a smile.

"Jennifer said yes!" John told them. They all cheered and Harold waved to Alice to bring the bottle of champagne she had chilling.

"I thought Alice would have told you," John said as Alice came with the glasses.

"No, she never said a word," Paul said smiling at Alice. "You knew?"

"Yes," she said. "John and Jennifer told me when I brought their starters. But it was not my place to tell anyone. I knew they would want to tell you themselves."

She placed the glasses on the table, Jennifer asked if she could bring two more and asked her and Robert to join them in their celebration.

Alice went pink and thanked Jennifer, she got Robert from the kitchen and they opened the champagne.

Jennifer was the first to make a toast, "to my wonderful future husband and to the lovely people he has introduced me to. God bless you all."

John, not being outdone, said, "And to my beautiful bride to be and my new found friends. Thank you all for everything." Then he leaned over and kissed Jennifer and all the others cheered.

The rest of the night was spent in pleasant conversation. Jennifer noticed that no matter what the topic was, the conversation always came back to Jesus. She felt she was in the company of angels, and she was right. The angels looked across at each other and smiled. The battle was about to begin, but tonight, they could enjoy their charges and share in their celebration.

John walked Jennifer home at the end of the night. When they arrived at her door, he said, "I don't want a long engagement, Jennifer. I hate saying goodnight to you and going home alone."

"I know," she said. "I feel the same way. But let's get tomorrow out of the way first and see where that takes us."

He smiled, she was right, of course, but just at this moment, all he wanted to do was close the door behind them and never leave her side again.

She pushed him gently out the door and whispered in his ear, "It won't be long now, so just be patient, you have a big day tomorrow and you need your rest."

He kissed her again saying "I'll call you tomorrow. Keep praying for a breakthrough for us."

"I will, of course," she said. "Ring me as soon as you have news. I love you."

"I love you too," said John, then finally backed away and Jennifer closed the door. He praised and thanked God all the way home. The night had been perfect, better than he had expected. God certainly answered his prayers to bless the night—that was for sure. It was wonderful how he and Jennifer thought alike and wanted the same things from life. "She truly is my soul mate." He smiled to himself.

The four men went to their rooms—Harold and Derek to theirs, Mick and Paul to theirs. Both pairs knelt to pray before they slept. They too thanked God for a wonderful night and for Jennifer saying yes to John. He looked so much stronger every time they saw him.

They all turned in and were soon asleep.

Chapter 48

Harold fell into a deep sleep and dreamt of his family. In his dream, he had split the land between himself and the boys. James had sold his portion, Joe was trying out different crops and they were doing really well. Jason was using his share to carry out research on certain crops. It was this research that had enabled Joe to grow his crops so abundantly. Harold had his little bit of land, where he eked out a living and struggled to make ends meet.

He felt the touch of a hand on his shoulder. He was awake immediately and was glad to be. Above him hovered Daniel, his angel.

"It is time to visit your family, come with me." Daniel stretched out his hand, Harold took it. He felt his body rising up through the room, up through the roof and as he looked down, he could see the town below him. He was scared, not about flying—that was wonderful. He remembered all those dreams he had had as a young man, of him flying through the sky. This felt just like those dreams. They had been so real, sometimes he would wake the next morning and believe he had actually been flying, and sometimes he believed he could fly. But gravity kept a firm hold on him. Then he would laugh to himself at the silliness of it.

Daniel whispered in his ear, "they were not dreams, they were the times when you let yourself go, and worries and anxieties left you and then you soared with the Lord."

Harold was speechless, how could he not have known. But he couldn't think of that now. Now, he was on his way to see his family. What had become of them? Had Trish met someone else? How would he feel if he saw her with another man? What about the boys? Had they let the farm go? Maybe they had drifted away from farming, after seeing what a mess their dad had made of it. What about Jenny, was she happy with David? What had she called her child, was it a boy or a girl. All these thoughts ran through his mind taking the pleasure of the flight from him.

"Relax," Daniel told him. "Have patience and all will be revealed."

Daniel took Harold over the tops of the houses, he guided him through clouds and when they came out on top of the clouds, Harold saw, not thousands, not even millions, but billions of stars and planets. The beauty was immense, and he simply looked and it took his breath away.

Then Daniel touched a hill and it moved. Harold remembered Paul telling him about the hill. They headed down a tunnel towards a light shining at the end. When they finally arrived at the end of the tunnel, the light was so bright Harold had to shield his eyes. When he opened his eyes next, he was above the farm.

"You are being granted a very special gift," Daniel said. "You will be allowed to speak to your family, but not as yourself, you will speak to them as someone who knew Harold a long time ago. That way they will be able to show you how everything is working."

They gradually descended and Harold found himself on the porch to his old house. As he trundled up the steps, the door opened and Trish walked out to meet him. It took all his willpower not to rush to her and take her in his arms.

"Hello," she smiled, "can I help you?"

"Hi," said Harold, "my name is Gerard," using his given middle name. "I was a friend of Harold's."

"Oh," she said, "I don't recognise the name, but I have to say there is something very familiar about you. Will you come in?"

He walked through the door and caught a glimpse of his reflection in the hall mirror. He looked completely different. His hair was a dull blond and he looked a lot thinner. His eyes were brown and a completely different shape than his usual. Yet somewhere in there he could still see Harold. He wondered if that is what Trish meant. He looked down to make sure he was wearing clothes, he hadn't had time to dress when Daniel had taken him. Yes, he was ok—jeans, boots and a cotton shirt, he would pass.

He walked through the next door, the one into the dining room. His whole family was there. He had to make a conscious effort not to cry. Trish introduced him to them all and as always, they were very hospitable. It was Sunday here, and they asked him to join them for lunch. It was good to see his boys and their families, but where was Jenny's child.

"Please God, don't let anything have happened to that baby!" he prayed.

As if to answer his prayers, a squawk came from one of the bedrooms.

"I'd better go and get him," said Jenny, "before he brings the house down."

She came back with a beautiful, dark haired little boy of two maybe three. "This is Harold," she said brightly. "Called after Dad, but we call him Harry."

Harold's breath caught in his throat. He couldn't speak for a few seconds. When he found his voice, he said, "He is a beautiful child." That was all that he could say. He was completely overwhelmed.

"Yes," Jenny said, "I think he looks like Dad as well."

"And acts like him too," laughed Trish.

"You mean he likes doing things his own way?" Harold asked, testing the water.

They all laughed in agreement, but then they looked quite sad.

"We miss him very much," said James.

"I wish we could tell him how much," Jason added.

"Yes," agreed Joe, "and show him the farm, so he'd know we didn't change it that much."

This was getting more and more difficult for Harold. He wanted to hug them all, he was so glad they were still close. *That would be because of Trish,* he told himself.

"How did you know Dad?" asked Jennifer.

"We knew each other on and off all our lives," Harold told them. "We used to be very close, but we kind of drifted apart. I heard about his passing and wanted to meet his lovely family," he finished lamely.

Everyone smiled. "It's good to meet someone who knew Dad," Jason said.

It had to be the Holy Spirit blinding them to who Harold really was. He was looking at them with such love, surely they would notice, but no, they just chatted as if it was the most natural thing in the world for a long lost friend of their dad's to turn up out of the blue.

Then he looked across at Trish, she was staring at him.

"Oh no," he spoke to Daniel, "I'm so sorry, I think I've blown my cover."

A small whisper came into his ear. "Don't worry, she just has a feeling and you remind her of you. Just relax and enjoy the time with them," he was told.

Easy for you to say, he said in his mind. When he looked into Trish's eyes and saw how beautiful she still was, it took all his strength not to blurt how exactly who he was.

After a delicious lunch, the boys asked if he'd like to see the farm. He told them he'd love to. David walked out with them, having been ushered out by the wives so they could get on with tidying up.

"We used to argue with Dad," said James, "about how to run the farm, and how we could make it more profitable. He always worked so hard and never really got time to enjoy himself with other things. We wanted to try and lighten the burden and bring in more revenue so he could have more leisure time with mum. But it wasn't to be."

"Did you all follow your separate paths?" he asked them.

"Well," James said, "after Dad died, we got together and looked at our options. We could sell part of the land and have one-storey offices on it. I spoke to some developers and got some prices. But in the end, I couldn't do it."

"We decided," added Joe, "that if Dad loved the farm so much, we had to honour his memory and continue to work it as a farm."

Harold couldn't believe what he was hearing. They decided to continue working the farm? Incredible!!

"We don't do it all Dad's way," Jason said. "We have modernised it a bit. We are growing different crops throughout the farm."

"Using Jason's expertise in soil conditions, we have been able to grow a great variety of crops and we also sell at the farmer's market, which brings us together with other farmers and we swap ideas," James told him, looking proudly at his brothers.

"We've been able to help other farmers produce better quality crops and they pay us for our expertise. We sell our techniques and that side of the business is growing quite rapidly," added Joe.

Harold was at a loss for words. His boys had made him so proud. He thought he might feel guilty about not letting them do things their way, when he was alive, but he knew it had worked out exactly as God planned.

"Your dad would have been very proud of you all." He looked to heaven and said, "in fact, he is very proud of you."

"Thank you," they said rather sheepishly.

Harold felt a touch on his shoulder, and Daniel whispered it was time to leave.

They walked back to the house and Harold thanked them all and gave Trish a kiss on the cheek, she squeezed his hand. It was as if she knew it was him.

He walked out the door a very happy man, so proud of his family. He had kept the tears at bay, thank God. Then he looked back and Harry ran out the door and ran to him. He put his arms out and Harold picked him up. "Bye, bye, Granddad," Harry said and kissed him on the cheek. Then the tears came flowing down as he put the boy back on the steps, he turned and walked quickly away.

Suddenly, he was at the edge of the tunnel with Daniel. A peace came over him and he was so thankful that he'd been allowed to visit with his family. He smiled as the tears continued to flow. His boys had carried on his work. All this time he had felt he had failed his family. But he knew now that he hadn't. He knew they had loved him and he them. "Thank You, Lord, for this wonderful time," he prayed.

Daniel spoke to him, "The others will be joining us shortly. Paul has already been shown, but Adrian will bring him along again. We have been instructed to show you the battle going on over this town."

That jolted Harold out of his reverie. "I'm ready," he said, and knew in his heart that whatever happened, he was ready, and he would do whatever he was asked.

They stood on the hill overlooking the town, waiting for the others to join them.

Chapter 49

In the meantime, Adrian, Andrew and Mark had woken their charges.

The six figures soared from the roof of the B & B. Paul knew what they were going to see and in his spirit knew that this was the beginning of the battle that was to come. Mick and Derek, on the other hand, were enjoying the flying experience and the sense of lightness.

They met with Harold and Daniel. Adrian spoke, "Open your spiritual eyes and see the battle over this town."

As they did, they could hardly believe their eyes. It resembled a scene of a battlefield from the 'first world war!' There were thousands of demons fighting thousands of angels. When a demon struck an angel, you could see the light fading. When the angel struck the demon, a thick black substance poured out of it, it looked disgusting.

The demons were screaming, it was a dreadful sound. It pierced their ears. It took all of Derek's willpower not to cover his ears against the screeches. It looked like the angels were winning, but only just. All the while, the humans were going on with their lives oblivious to the battle.

"It looks bad, but it's not as bad as it was when I saw it a little while ago. What happened?" Paul asked Adrian.

He explained, "With your help, John has been set free. He is no longer dominated by fear. Because of that, he has touched others, who in turn have been set free." He turned to Mick, "The same way you touched Mel and she was released from her worries." Now she tells others about the Lord and what He did for her. Her children pray and that delights the Lord. Each person who has been set free has in turn told others and set them free."

"John's church," he continued, "will lead the people of this town to victory. The Holy Spirit is, as we speak, encouraging him and giving him the words to speak to the people on Sunday."

Paul thought of all the people who had helped in the church. Then there was Alice and Robert, Jennifer, of course, and the man Craig who had come to help and then gave his life to Jesus. And he had offered to pay for materials needed for the restoration of the church. "If they in turn influence others, it will be like a pebble in a pond, the ripple effect."

"Exactly," said Adrian, reading his thoughts.

"God's light came into the world, but people loved the darkness more than the light because their actions were evil," (John 3:19) Mark said sadly. "Pray for the people of this town, Satan doesn't want to give it up. That's why the battle is so fierce. Satan is losing his grip on the people and he is not happy."

"And that's just the way we like it," said Andrew. The four angels literally beamed, the light shining from them was beautiful.

Harold, Mick and Derek had been very quiet whilst watching the battle from the hilltop.

"The four of you are mighty prayer warriors," said Daniel. "Remember Michael told you that the 'light' was coursing through your bodies, souls and spirits? You must keep that message in your minds and in your hearts at all times. The coming weeks or maybe months will challenge you all, more than you can ever imagine. But, you are ready, don't be afraid."

The scene in front of them faded.

"It's time to rest now," said Adrian. "Tomorrow you are all travelling to Manchester. Pray without ceasing. Remember that even your conversations are prayers and heard by God."

Then they were soaring over the town again and descending into the B & B and into their beds.

I won't be able to move tomorrow, Harold said to himself. *I've been up all night and I'm not used to this.*

Daniel spoke to him, "First, you must rid yourself of all negatives words or thoughts. And remember always, when the Lord gives you rest, you will rest indeed."

And so he did. He woke the next morning with the energy of a twenty-year-old.

When they were ready, he and Derek walked, well practically skipped down the stairs smiling and humming praises to God.

Mick and Paul were already at the breakfast table.

"What kept you?" Mick asked laughing.

Paul nudged him and said, "It must be an age thing." They both laughed.

"Hey," said Harold, "less about the age thing, I feel about twenty, how about you, Derek?"

"Yes, that would be about right," he laughed. "I feel I could do forty or fifty press ups at the drop of a hat."

"Let's not get carried away," Harold told him, "just in case we need to conserve our energy."

"Oh, okay," said Derek, pretending to be disappointed. And everyone laughed.

They ordered full breakfasts for each of them, which had become the norm. While Alice prepared it, they bowed their heads in prayer.

"Father," Mick began, "we come before You on this beautiful day to give You thanks for all Your great blessings. Thank you for this lovely house we are staying in and for the wonderful people who own it. We ask special blessing on Alice and Robert and their unborn child. We thank You for John and his mighty spirit and for releasing him from fear. Thank You for Jennifer and her beautiful spirit. Thank You also for Tom and Larry, for their courage in agreeing to stand with John at this time. Also, for their wives, Barbara and Maria, who are standing beside their husbands at this important time. Thank You for letting us be part of this battle, lead us we pray. Thank You for our guardian angels whom You sent to guide and direct us. Let Your Holy Spirit fall on each one of us today, that we will know Your holy and perfect will for us. Grant us the grace to obey and follow Your leading. Amen."

"Amen," the others concurred.

"Bless our food and thank You for it," Derek added.

Again they said, "Amen."

With the last amen, John walked through the doors of the dining room towards the four men, he looked radiant.

"Good morning," he beamed.

"Good morning to you," the men replied.

"You look in good spirits today," smiled Harold.

"Who wouldn't be?" John answered. "Jennifer said yes and we are not going to wait long for the wedding. Both of us feel we've waited long enough."

Just then Alice brought the breakfasts for the four men. Seeing John sitting at the table, she asked if he was hungry.

"Famished," he replied smiling, "but I don't want to put you to any trouble."

Alice laughed, "Just one minute, Sir," she said and turned to go back into the kitchen. Just then Robert brought out the extra plate with a full breakfast on it.

"We had a feeling you might need nourishment for the journey," Robert said. "Alice prepared your breakfast with the others."

"Ahh, Alice," said John, "you know me so well."

After they finished eating, they prayed again. They thanked God for the nourishment of their breakfasts. Then they prayed for strength and wisdom for the fight ahead. They stood together and each picked up their Bible.

When did we start carrying Bibles? thought Derek. *I don't remember always having a Bible with me, but I can't remember not having it with me.* It was another of those little mysteries that seemed to happen to them constantly.

They piled into John's car and started off for Manchester. As one of them spoke to John, usually Derek as he was in the front passenger seat, the others prayed and were given scriptures. This continued along the M6 towards junction 19. When they came off the motorway, they found the directions Mr Bryant had given them, extremely easy to follow. Within ten minutes they were parking the car in the car park of the hotel.

Chapter 50

They walked into the lobby and through to the lounge which was used for meetings. There were little cubicles and small and large round tables. They saw him sitting at one of the tables. No one could say how they knew it was him, but they did. They walked towards him and he stood and extended his hand to John, who was the first to reach the table.

"John, I presume," he said, "nice to meet you."

John shook his hand and said, "likewise, and thank you for meeting with us." Then he introduced him to the rest of the men.

They took their seats in the cubicle, which was larger than it first appeared. Mr Bryant, or Kevin, as he asked them to call him, was a man in his late fifties or early sixties. He was slim and fit looking and there was a kindness in his eyes that was noticeable immediately.

They ordered coffees and, of course, tea for Paul. Then they got straight down to business.

"What can you tell me about Peter Roles?" asked John.

"Well, after he left St James, that was your old school, wasn't it? Kevin said.

John nodded.

"He came to work at ours, you must remember, we are going back twenty years or more," Kevin continued. "At first, he was just a good teacher, good with the lads and everyone really liked him. He started taking boys away for weekends, the ones who had no dads and belonged to the poorer families. It was quite impressive, to be honest. I was working as a teacher then, I taught maths.

"I can remember thinking, what a great person he must be to give up his weekends to look after these boys and take them to places they wouldn't normally see. He didn't take a lot of boys, just about six or seven, and for the first few times, everything was great. Don't get me wrong, he didn't do it every weekend, but about once a month, he would take them in his Zafira. Meet them at the school on Friday evening and drop them off on Sunday afternoon. As I said, at first the kids were full of it and talked of nothing else."

"Then," he continued, "After three maybe four months, one of the boys, who in honesty, had been a quiet boy anyway, didn't want to go on the trips anymore. I can remember the weekend it happened. It was the long weekend in May. They went on Friday and weren't due back until Monday. This particular boy didn't come to school on Tuesday. His mum rang to say he was ill."

John's heart was racing and he could feel the dread and guilt seeping in. His hands began to shake and his mouth went dry.

Mark whispered in Derek's ear, "Pray for John now, touch his arm and tell him to put the full armour of God on. It's starting. The demons are trying to get a foothold again."

Derek prayed in the spirit, praying in tongues. He didn't know what he would have prayed for in the natural, but he knew this had to be a supernatural prayer and led by the Holy Spirit. He prayed against the demons of dread and guilt, without even knowing it. Then he touched John's shoulder and it was like a light coursed through John's body, and the demons fled. When Derek opened his spiritual eyes, he could see the demons lurking in the crevices all around the hotel, but guilt and dread had collapsed to the floor, they looked like flies.

"We were talking in the staff room," Kevin said, "and I was taking the 'mick', eh no offence," he said to Mick, who just smiled. "As I said, I was taking the mick out of Peter Roles. I congratulated him on his patience and giving up his weekends for the boys, but I laughed and said, 'what did you do to poor little Mikey? He didn't turn up for school today.' I was only joking, and only meant that maybe he had tired the lad out with climbing and trekking, etc. But Roles jumped up, red in the face, but checked himself and laughed. He told me that some of the boys just couldn't hack it."

"I have to tell you," Kevin told them, "I am a believer, and something shifted in my spirit. I know that may sound weird to all of you, but it's what I felt."

"On the contrary," said Paul, "we know exactly what you mean. I think God has been working on this for a long time. Don't you, John?"

John just nodded,

Kevin continued with his story, "I knew something was amiss, but when I spoke to young Mikey, he looked terrified. He swore nothing had happened on the weekend away so my hands were tied, but I decided to keep my eyes on Roles from then on. I thought of befriending him, but I couldn't, there was something a bit off about him. He made my skin crawl, but still I couldn't do anything about it.

"Young Mikey never went on another weekend away, but there were so many others waiting in line that his place was filled before the next weekend away. The next few months went without incident, but I was keeping tabs and checking with the boys that the weekends were good and they were all enjoying themselves. They all agreed they had a great time. Then, just as Roles was arranging the next weekend away, a new teacher came to the school, in a supply role. His name was Mr Kenny. Roles came into the staff room on the Wednesday morning. When he saw Mr Kenny's face, all the blood drained from his."

He continued with his story, "One of the other teachers laughed and said, 'what's wrong, Peter, you look like you've seen a ghost.' Honestly, I've never seen anyone pale so quickly in my life. Mr Kenny stood up and greeted Roles with a big smile. 'Nice to see you again,' he told Roles. 'I believe you are still doing your good deeds, taking some of the boys on weekends away? I'm delighted to say that my wife and I would love to help out again as we did in our previous school.' Roles blanched and just muttered 'thank you'.

"It was peculiar watching them. Mr Kenny seemed to be taking great delight in Roles' squirming. The atmosphere in the staff room was quite tense and nobody seemed to know why. Everyone was fidgeting and, well I can't explain, but it was like there was a battle of wills (or something else), going on. Everyone felt very uncomfortable. Mr Kenny seemed to be the only one enjoying himself. The teachers rushed to their classes before the bell went, they were so eager to get out of that atmosphere."

"Of course, I stayed within earshot of the room, well if I'm truthful, I eavesdropped. I could hear the conversation as clear as anything. They weren't arguing or raising their voices and I really wanted to know what Kenny's part in all this was. I was already suspicious of Roles, but God forbid if there were two of them. To be honest, I'd made up my mind that I was going along on the next weekend with Roles. The fear was," he looked sadly at the others, "that if anything happened, I could be thought part of it. I was in a quandary as to what to do. Then I heard Mr Kenny speak. He told Roles that no matter where he went, he would follow him. He said that he may miss one of the weekends, but he would find him and protect the boys from him, if it took everything he had to do it."

"I heard Roles snigger, it was probably one of the most horrible sounds I have ever heard. I'm not exaggerating, it was pure evil and it sent shivers down my spine. All he said was, 'We'll see if you can stop me.' Then he walked out of the room. I went cold all over. I didn't know what to do. I waited until Roles had walked down the corridor and was out of sight. I went back to the staff room to speak to Mr Kenny. There was such a difference in the atmosphere now that Roles had left. It was lighter, in both aspects. 'Light' as opposed to 'dark' and 'light' as opposed to 'heavy' if that makes sense?"

He carried on with his story, "Mr Kenny was standing by the window. He seemed to be praying. There was a light all around him. I thought at first it was the sun shining through the window, but it was a cloudy day and there was no sunshine, it was very unusual."

The four men looked at each other, knowingly. *Angels,* popped into John's mind. In the last few days, he had seen so much of the supernatural that the thought of angels walking among them was just natural.

"I spoke to Mr Kenny," Kevin told them. "I asked him what was going on and what was the history between him and Roles? He wasn't very forthcoming, in fact, he was quite enigmatic in his answer. His exact words were: 'For evil to flourish, all it needs is for good men to do nothing. I am here because good men are doing nothing about Roles.'"

"He walked from the room as the bell went, leaving me speechless."

"Did the weekend go ahead?" asked Derek.

"Yes, actually it did," said Kevin, "but without Roles. Mr and Mrs Kenny and I took the boys away for the weekend. I suppose I was a bit put out, I have to say. Man City were at home, and I never miss their home matches, but I believed this was more important. To be honest, I enjoyed the weekend so much I actually forgot to find out the scores until we got back. To see the faces of those young boys when we arrived at the campsite, will stay with me for the rest of my life. We had great fun. In fact, Mrs Bryant and another couple and I take boys away for weekends once a month. So, although Roles was doing it for all the wrong reasons, it has turned out to be a blessing now, and we really enjoy it and make sure the kids enjoy themselves, and no one is ever left out, there is enough adults to look after as many as want to come. Though, I have to admit, I try to organise the weekends when Man City are not at home." He laughed.

They all laughed with him, they liked this man. There was something about him that was spiritual and yet earthly, yes, he was a good man.

"What happened to Roles after that?" asked Mick.

"He resigned from the school and moved on, so did Mr Kenny, I might add. It was like his life's work was to keep an eye on Roles," Kevin replied. "But those words, Mr Kenny spoke to me about good men doing nothing, never left me. It's one of the reasons I took it on myself to arrange weekends away. But something else stirred in me, I needed to keep an eye on where Roles went and what he was up to."

"The headmaster received a request for a reference for Roles. At that time he was talking about retiring and was keen for me to take on the job of headmaster. We became quite close friends. He told me where Roles had applied for a teaching position. It was in another deprived area in east Manchester. I didn't know what to do.

There was no evidence against him. According to our records, he'd been a good teacher and very well-liked by the boys he taught, except for poor Mikey. I couldn't recall another complaint, or incident for that matter. Even Mikey hadn't made a complaint. The really sad thing was, he was too afraid to come away with us on weekends after what had happened to him. My wife was determined to get him to come, to show him that there are nice people in the world, who would take care of him. She wanted him to enjoy these trips without any worries. So she went to see him and his mum. She explained that she would be there the whole time, looking after him. His mum didn't know what was going on, but she urged him to go, and eventually, he started coming and enjoying it again. In fact, he's one of our helpers now, and believe me, he won't let anyone hurt any of the young boys, he is very protective. He's a teacher himself now and is great with the young boys."

"Anyway, I digress," he apologised. "I have a brother, Jim, he is a superintendent in the police now, but then he was a sergeant. I told him my suspicions about Roles. I explained that the headmaster had been asked to supply a reference for him, but I wasn't too sure. I asked him to make enquiries and see if there had been any complaints about Roles in any of his previous schools. Jim said he would check into it for me.

"Jim came back to me after a few days and said they hadn't had one complaint against Peter Roles. But he also said the Roles seemed to flit from one school to another on a regular basis. I decided then that I would keep an eye on him. So every so often, I would ring the school anonymously and ask to speak to him. When they went to get him, I would put the receiver down. Sometimes they would say he had left and gone on to another school."

"Why didn't he just work as a supply teacher?" Paul asked. "That way it wouldn't have been so obvious him going from school to school."

"Well, for one," Kevin told him, "he might not get a long enough contract to build a rapport with the boys. And two, he might be sent back to the same school more than once. You have to remember, he only seemed to leave if it looked like others were catching on to him, like Mr Kenny. If he had to go back to a previous school, there could have been a nasty shock waiting for him."

"What else did your brother find out?" Harold asked.

"Ah well, now comes the interesting part," Kevin smiled. "My brother has friends who investigate child abuse. Mostly these are within families, but they liaise with 'child porn' detectives who can have information of a paedophile ring in certain areas. Jim told one of the leading officers about Roles and asked him to check into it for him. The officer requested a photograph of Roles. That was easy to acquire, there was one on his application to our school. I got it from the headmaster and sent it across to him. They come down very hard if they think there is any kind of child abuse taking place. So they checked his previous school, and Tim gave them the name of the previous one to that, and so on and so on. I was able to supply them with names of schools he had moved on to after ours. Do you know that since the beginning of his career, he has taught in over sixty schools?"

"It's ludicrous that nobody checked why he jumped from school to school. The detectives had their work cut out for them, I can tell you. They spoke to as many headmasters as they could. Some of the previous schools were dead ends as their records didn't go back that far. There were some who kept records of past staff and how long they had worked at the school. Of these schools, there were a few who actually remembered him. They said he was very good with the boys and took them away for weekends every month or so. But then he just left suddenly. Every case they looked into, it was the same answer. The same information came from the schools that he moved to after ours. I've been trying to keep a watch on him for nearly twenty years."

"The police got the bit between their teeth," he continued. "They found which school he was working at and sent in an undercover police officer to the school. When Roles arranged a weekend away, the officer volunteered to accompany him to help him. His report said that nothing untoward had happened on the trip, but Roles seemed very irritated. He said he noticed a lot of boys seemed to be bewildered as their 'lovely' teacher was in a seriously bad mood for the whole weekend. But what could he do, nothing had happened on the trip and apart from the boys being confused because Roles wasn't his normal pleasant self, there was no evidence of foul play. Shortly after that weekend, Roles resigned. We believe he felt the net closing in on him."

"Do you know where he is now?" asked John. This conversation was bringing up memories that he did not want to think about. Memories of the 'good' weekends away with Roles, of the fun they used to have and the friendships he had forged with other boys. Bile came into his mouth and he felt sick, it was like something was taunting him saying, "You enjoyed those weekends, didn't you?" It was as if something was jeering him, it made him feel even guiltier than before. He lowered his head, trying to fight the jeering, but he felt too weak.

Chapter 51

Paul was the first to see it, the little maggoty demon that sat on John's shoulder, whispering into his ear.

"John," he shouted, "stop it now." He wasn't asking John to stop doing something to himself, he was telling him to stop the demon in his stride. Stop the demon whispering in his ear.

Everyone around the table jumped when Paul shouted. The three, Derek, Harold and Mick, saw what Paul was talking about. Kevin just looked at them as if they were mad.

John closed his eyes and rebuked the demon, in Jesus' name. To the four men's surprise, the demon shrivelled to nothing and fell off his shoulder like a piece of fluff. They smiled at each other. They hadn't heard John utter a word because he knew he didn't have to shout at the demons to defeat them. Once the name of Jesus is spoken to them, they can't hang around, they have no power. They have to let go, or as in this case, shrivel up and fall away. The problem was, most people, including John, let the demons antagonise them, instead of rebuking them as soon as they hear that horrible voice.

John opened his eyes and smiled. Kevin was looking at him questioningly.

"Eh, what just happened?" he asked.

John answered, "When you were describing the weekends away that went without any incident, I was reminded that I used to enjoy those weekends too. I started to feel guilty. I was enjoying myself, oblivious to other boys being abused."

"B-b-but," stuttered Kevin, looking shocked. "Are you saying you were abused by Roles?"

"Yes," said John and his head went down. Paul nudged him. It was obvious Paul wasn't going to let John sink back into that guilt that had imprisoned him for so many years. John looked up, not exactly smiling, but not cowering either. "Yes," he said again. "I was one of those boys. I've lived with the guilt for years and it's only since I've met these men, that I've decided I need to face my demons."

"Couldn't have put it better myself," Harold quipped.

What John had said was a common enough phrase, 'facing your demons' but the five men knew just how true that was.

"So that is why you asked to meet me?" Kevin said. "I was unsure at first, but as soon as I met you all, well I can't explain it, but I knew I had to tell you everything."

"I'm sorry I interrupted," said Paul.

"No, no, don't worry. I am just curious how you knew John was feeling guilty?" Kevin asked.

The men laughed, "It is a long story, one you might find a trifle hard to understand," Mick told him. "But before we go into that, as John asked, do you know where Roles is now, or have you lost track of him?"

"Well," said Kevin, still looking shocked at John's revelation. "He moved to the Isle of Mann, we lost track of him for about eighteen months. We thought that he had gone to Ireland, maybe to one of the inner city schools in Dublin. Jim contacted the Irish police the Gardai, but they had no information about him, though they agreed to do a little investigating of their own. They came back to Jim, they'd heard nothing, and there had been no reported incidents, or worried parents. So we were back to square one. Then out of the blue, we had a call from Yorkshire. When we lost track of him, my brother sent Roles' photograph to many different areas in the UK. On the off chance that someone would hear or see something. He spoke to different police forces and told them that it was just a routine enquiry. Though Roles wasn't wanted for any particular crime, the police in Manchester would like to ask him a few questions regarding a certain incident. He asked, if they came into contact or knew his whereabouts, they would contact him immediately. That's how Yorkshire got in touch with him."

"It seemed Roles was getting a little careless in his actions, after he moved to Sheffield," Kevin continued. "Instead of taking boys away for many weekends without incident, something happened on the second trip. A young boy's mother went to the police. She said her son had been very outgoing, full of fun and mischief. When he came back from the second weekend with Roles, he was a different child. He didn't want to go to school. He curled up in his bed every evening when he came home from school. She'd heard him cry himself to sleep on more than one occasion. She went to speak to the headmaster of the school. He sent for the child, but the boy wouldn't say anything against Roles. The headmaster could do nothing. You can't accuse a teacher, one as charismatic as Roles of doing something bad, when nobody would corroborate the story. But the mother would not give up. She reported it to the police."

"If the principal or headmaster could do nothing," asked John, "what could the police do?"

"You have to remember," Kevin told him, "the police take any accusation like that very seriously. They knew from the information I supplied to Jim that there had to be something amiss. The fact that we had more than twenty years history of Roles going from school to school, really whet their appetites. The Yorkshire police spoke to the headmaster. They obtained a recent history of employment for Peter Roles. And yes, he had worked in Dublin. He probably thought that Ireland was a bit too small to get away with what he was doing. We think that's why he came back to the UK.

"One of the police officers in Sheffield remembered the Manchester police asking questions about Roles. He checked the records and sure enough, it was the same person. He contacted Jim and told him the mother's worries. When the police went to the school to speak to Roles, they found that he had already left. There was no record of his whereabouts. The headmaster said he just didn't turn up for school one morning. He explained that he had asked Roles why the police might be looking to question him. He never saw him after that. It was so frustrating, Jim nearly had him, but to be honest, they still had no evidence. There's no crime moving from one school to another. But Jim knew there was something wrong here. He was determined to get to the bottom of it.

"He contacted heads of police departments all over the country, this time instructing them, should they find where he is, they must notify the Manchester police immediately. The police who chase paedophiles got on the case. Jim arranged a meeting between police forces throughout Great Britain. He was a chief inspector by this time. They met in Birmingham. The biggest concern was that it seemed he had disappeared off the face of the earth. They alerted every police force in every big city. They worried that if he found a school somewhere in a poor area of London, because London was so big, they wouldn't find him. And although there was no proof, Jim

136

knew in his heart of hearts, that there was something bad in Peter Roles. Their main aim was to stop him hurting any more children, but how? They had no solid evidence against him.

"He explained that the police didn't have the manpower to go from school to school looking for him, or warning the schools against him. They couldn't do that, innocent until proven guilty. It was very frustrating.

"But now, having met you, we have some information. You are ready to give evidence against him, aren't you?" Kevin asked John.

"I certainly am," said John, "that is, if the police can find him."

It looked like stalemate.

The men left Kevin thanking him for all his help. "You have my number," John said. "If you hear anything, please call me."

"Of course," said Kevin, "you will be first to know."

The men left the hotel. "What do we do now?" John muttered. The others could see the disappointment in his face. They had travelled all the way to Manchester, prepared for the battle of their lives, and though they had a lot more information, they were still no closer to finding Roles.

"One thing to remember," Paul said to John. "Because the police now have a witness, you, against Roles, they have something to go on. Kevin will let his brother know as soon as he can, so we are further on than we were. Don't get disappointed, this has been going on for years, you can't expect to fix it in a day."

"Anyway," he continued, "let's get back and pray. We are not doing this in our own strength. We need all the spiritual help we can get."

They all agreed and set off back south. "The match must be over," said Mick. "The traffic is terrible."

They used the time in the traffic jam to pray for guidance. "Remember when we started out," said Harold, "we were afraid we'd fail in this mission. Anyone feel that that's a possibility?" he asked.

"No," the other three men shouted in unison.

"Exactly," said Harold. "We've come so far, nothing will stop us from completing this assignment."

They all agreed and it seemed to lift their spirits. They were on a God given assignment. How could they fail?

At last they reached home, tired but determined. "Can we go to the church to pray?" John asked them.

"Of course," the men said. They headed towards the church. The five men pulled up chairs and sat in a circle. Derek led them in prayer.

"Thank You Lord for today! Thank You for the new information we received. We know now that as soon as we find where Roles is, we will need to act quickly before he vanishes again. But for this Lord, we need Your guidance. Show us where he is at this time. Help us stop him before he hurts another boy. Lead us Lord, You alone can see where he is, open our eyes and our minds to see and hear You when You speak."

"Amen," they said in unison.

All five men sat with heads bowed waiting, listening for the Spirit to reveal Roles' whereabouts. They prayed and asked for guidance, each in his own way. They were eager to find him and have him brought to justice. They sat and waited and waited. They had sat for at least an hour, nothing happened. The Lord was silent, their angels were silent. What was going on?

Chapter 52

"What's going on?" Paul turned and asked Adrian.

"It's not time yet, remember, this is to happen in God's timing not yours!"

Paul explained what Adrian had told him to the others.

Then Daniel spoke to Harold, "This is a major battle that you are about to take part in. You need to arm yourselves with the full armour of God. Keep praying in the Spirit until the battle is won. There is more going on than you can see at the present time. Just pray and fast and keep praying until the Lord tells us to move."

Then Harold spoke to the others, they read Ephesians 6 and clothed themselves with the full armour of God. Then they prayed again, this time they prayed in the Spirit.

After half an hour praying and worshipping, the five sat in contented silence, waiting to hear if the Lord had any other instructions for them. John knew in his spirit that the prayer time had come to an end. He knew he had to prepare his sermon for the following morning.

"I need to take the hymn books to the B & B," he said to the men. "Then I need to work on my sermon."

The men were surprised, the last time they had heard John's sermon, it was weak, to say the least. Maybe he had realised and was spending time preparing, it hadn't seemed like he had prepared the last one.

"It's been a long day," Harold said. "I for one am hungry. The others agreed and offered to take the books for John. He went to his house to prepare his sermon.

The four men had a lovely meal and discussed the day's events. Then they prayed for John and for the sermon he would give the next morning and also for peace for him at this time. Then they retired to bed.

The next morning when they came down for breakfast, Alice and Robert had the dining room prepared for the service. The men were directed into the small sitting room. Alice was serving the other guests' breakfasts when the men walked through the door.

"Expecting a large crowd for church this morning, Alice?" Derek asked.

"I like to be prepared," she laughed, "I would rather have too many chairs than too few."

Once they finished breakfast and prayed, the service was due to begin. Each of the four felt a bit nervous for John. When they had heard him preach before, he'd had no fire, and his sermon was lame. But they knew something had happened to him in the previous weeks.

When they walked into the dining room, they were shocked to see so many people, and people were still coming through the door. They looked at each other confused. "What's happened to these people between that first Sunday and today?" Paul asked.

"Maybe it's the fact that they are getting involved with the refurbishment of the church," Derek replied.

They sat at the back of the room, there was a projector mounted, and a screen was placed on the wall opposite. They presumed it was for the hymns.

John walked into the room. He looked so different to the previous weeks. He looked in control and confident.

The worship was led by three young people, with three or four other young ones playing instruments. It was wonderful, what a difference. *When had John arranged all this,* they wondered. The songs were modern and easy to follow. The three people who led the worship had lovely voices and seemed to be filled with the Spirit. Jennifer was in the front row, offering her support to her man.

Then the worship finished and John stood up to speak. He welcomed everyone and nodded to Robert at the back of the room to start the slide show. Everyone sat watching, wondering what was going on.

The first few slides were of the church before the work had been started.

Next were slides of Harold on his knees alone in the garden, weeding. Harold blushed. He didn't remember seeing John with a camera. Then he brought up other slides of Derek, Mick and Paul as they tried to pull up the carpet. They in turn blushed and looked at each other, they didn't remember John with a camera either. When they saw themselves in the photos, they smiled. They looked exhausted and grubby from the dust of the carpet. Then the final slides were shown, they were of the townspeople helping in the church and on the grounds with Harold.

The four men looked at each other, those weeks when they worked and prayed that John would open up to them, he had been watching them. 'Since we are surrounded by such a huge cloud of witnesses...' (Hebrews 12:1-2) came into their minds simultaneously. Then John began speaking, his voice was vibrant, the strength and purpose in it had everyone's attention.

He spoke on Haggai, chapter 2 vs 3-4 and 7-9. He explained that God told Zerubbabel and Jeshua to be strong and to get to work. God asked the people if they remembered what the temple was like in its former glory and promised He would fill it again with His glory and the future glory of the temple will be greater than its past glory.

He told the people that maybe without even knowing it they were obeying God's command for the upkeep of His house. The people were delighted to be told they were part of something much bigger than themselves. That they might play a part in bringing God's glory back to the church, they were smiling and chuckling and sitting a lot taller in their seats. The people were enthralled, they couldn't get enough. It was a great sermon.

The four men looked around the room. There wasn't one demon to be seen. Obviously, the demons knew better than be in the presence of God's people as they gathered to worship the Almighty.

John finished speaking he asked the worship team to finish the service with 'How Great is our God'. It felt like Heaven touched Earth. The words 'And the Glory of the Lord filled the Temple' came to mind. Nobody moved, the peace filled the room and everyone just sat and bathed in it. Some people were kneeling, some were crying, others were sitting with their eyes closed, praying. God was being honoured in this place and no one wanted to leave.

Eventually, John gave a small cough to get everyone's attention. "Thank you all very much for coming." The place erupted and the whole congregation stood and applauded. John joined in the applause, looking towards Heaven, towards the One who had made all this possible.

The four men moved towards John, congratulating him on a fantastic service. They had to stand in line as so many people were shaking his hand. He looked overwhelmed at the reception he had received. Then, the four with John and Jennifer met for lunch.

There was such a positive atmosphere in the restaurant, they were laughing and smiling and chatting. They were relaxed and John looked strong and ready for battle.

Chapter 53

They were so ready to go to war that they were up and ready very early Monday morning. They met for breakfast and afterwards used the sitting room for prayer. Surely after yesterday's service, God would send them into the battle. They felt ready for anything.

But nothing happened, and the Lord stayed silent. So the men hauled themselves over to the church to continue with the manual work. They had been so touched by the atmosphere yesterday, they were ready for spiritual work, but as they promised to be obedient, they got on with the mundane.

A full week went by and still they didn't hear anything. It was very frustrating. They were up at the crack of dawn every morning. Paul paced up and down. Harold sat with his head in his hands, praying. Derek picked up the Bible and searched the scriptures. It was Friday morning. They had worked hard and prayed hard all week. They fasted as Harold had been instructed, but still there was silence from heaven. Mick went back up to his room and knelt to pray.

All at once a light shone down on him, it was so bright he couldn't lift his eyes to look at it. Then the Voice said, "It is time, get everyone together and move now."

He ran down the stairs and met the others. They obviously had been instructed to get ready too. They left the B & B and collected John from his house. They still had no idea where they were going, but Derek just let his angel lead the way as he drove the car.

John rang Tom and Larry, he told them that they were to move, but he had no idea where they were going. "Just get in your car, and drive," he said. "Let the Spirit guide you, that's all we're doing." Then he spoke from the back seat. "This is the way to my old parish," he said surprised.

Tom and Larry heard him and headed in that direction.

Paul looked at John and said, "Really? This is the way to my old house. My wife and children still live here. It looks like the same area anyway."

When they pulled up outside the church, John's face dropped. "It can't be here?" he said. "He should be at school, and what on earth would he be doing at my old parish?" He rang Tom and Larry and gave them directions, "we are going in," he said. "We'll see you inside."

Paul looked at him. He could see fear trying to grip him again. It looked as if it was growing. "John," he shouted, "Be on the alert, put on the armour, this is a big battle. We need to be ready. But remember, we are not alone, God is on our side, and fear is terrified of Him so keep praying in the Spirit."

John nodded and closed his eyes. He prayed in tongues, he knew nothing could penetrate the armour of God.

They walked up the steps to the church. It was open and as they walked through the doors, they saw two men sitting in one of the pews at the front of the church. They seemed to be in deep conversation. The conversation looked quite heated and the two didn't notice the others come through. John knelt in one of the pews and began to pray.

Now that the time for confrontation was at hand, he felt quite frightened. Then he shook himself and told fear to get lost, his confidence returned, but still he remained kneeling before God asking for His protection.

Paul, on seeing the demons that surrounded the two men, was nearly knocked out by their ugliness and depravity. It was something he hadn't witnessed before.

Adrian whispered, "Take your eyes off the demons. Fix your eyes on Jesus. They can't harm you, but you in particular need to be strong, especially for the next few hours."

Paul conceded and started praying, but he couldn't get into the spirit as he normally did. The thought that he might have to lead the fight in this situation actually made him feel very good. Then he looked over his shoulder and saw a very beautiful looking spirit. She was touching him and moving around him. He was quite pleased with himself, but when he felt more pleased, the spirit lost some of her beauty and clung to him rather than float around him. He was very confused and spoke to Adrian.

"What's going on?" he asked.

"It's pride," answered Adrian. "Remember you saw it when you were first allowed to use your spiritual eyes?"

"Yes," replied Paul, "I'm sorry. I got carried away, thinking I was going to lead the battle."

Adrian touched his shoulder and said as gently as he could, "No, Paul, the next few hours will be the hardest battle yet."

The two men were still oblivious to the others in the church. The four gathered together, said a silent prayer. "We've all got our armour on?" Mick asked.

They nodded, when they looked towards the men, they were surrounded by darkness. It was horrible and as Paul had noticed earlier, the demons inside the darkness were vile and depraved.

The men moved forward towards the front pew. All of a sudden, it was as if the darkness had seen them for the first time, it turned and screamed at them. All of a sudden—power much greater than they expected—shot from within the darkness. The four men were thrown back as if hit with a cannon ball. They literally flew through the air like rag dolls and hit the back wall of the church. The darkness loomed and the men felt like insects against this power. They lay dazed, they hadn't expected to feel so weak against this evil force. Harold stood first.

Daniel spoke to him, "Stand in the Power of God and keep praying in the spirit. Remember you're clothed in the armour, use it."

Harold turned and shouted to the others, "We have the armour of God, stand with me in the power of God."

The others stood as one, side by side, praying in the spirit, remembering they were covered with the armour. They looked at each other and then down at themselves. They were actually covered and looked like the old Roman soldiers. Helmets on each head, 'Helmets of Salvation', so they would see and hear and speak and think as the Lord led them.

Each had a strong belt firmly fastened around the waist, the Belt of Truth. Jesus said, 'I am the Way, the Truth and the Life' (John 14 vs 6). Satan was unable to penetrate them with his lies.

Breastplates covered each of their chests, Breastplates of Righteousness, Jesus was their righteousness.

Shoes of Peace, though they were more like boots, but the men knew that wherever they walked, they would bring Peace.

In each of their hands they held a shield, the Shield of Faith, which extinguishes the fiery arrows of the evil one.

And in the other hand they held swords, the Sword of the Spirit, which is the Word of God, which cuts through bone and marrow and soul and spirit.

John continued to kneel and pray. The door opened and Tom and Larry walked in. They joined him and knelt to pray with him. Jesus' words seemed to come into each mind, 'Where two or three are gathered in My Name, there also am I!' (Matt. 18:20)

Chapter 54

The four men looked at each other. They too had heard the words. They knew it was time. Their angels were standing with them. Harold looked over his shoulder, he had to blink twice. He thought he was seeing things. Now he understood what a 'Host' of angels looked like. It was a huge army, he couldn't see to the back of it, it seemed to go for miles and miles. He nodded to the others, to check it out. When they turned and saw the millions of angels ready to go into battle with them, their faces lit up.

"We go now," Harold said. They started walking towards the darkness. They pressed in against it. It was like walking against a hurricane. They had not expected this at the beginning, but now they were ready, they could feel the power from above emanating from them. Suddenly, they were not afraid, they walked forward, slowly but defiantly. The darkness rose, it was as if it was becoming stronger rather than weakening.

Adrian reminded them to keep praying in the spirit. The darkness was trying to squash them, they could feel the pressure, but they kept advancing. It was hard and they had to keep strong, but they were still marching towards it.

Then out of the darkness flew thousands of demons. They were ugly creatures, drooling, cackling and screaming at them. Their screams were designed to deafen the men to the voices of the angels, but the men's heads were covered with their helmets so the screams and vile words of the demons were totally blocked out.

Then the demons flew at them, trying to strike terror into their hearts, but the men held their shields high. The demons literally bounced off them. And still the men advanced. The darkness sent out another battalion of demons, these were sent to crawl into the men's chests, to grab their lungs and squeeze the breath from them. They flew at them. They were like shots being fired from a gun. The men swiped with their swords, the angels joined in and soon the demons were split down the middle and fell in agony.

The men moved closer to the darkness, it was roaring at them, threatening them, their families, everything they held dear. It started threatening John, Tom, Larry and their families. Still the men advanced. They glanced across at the three men in prayer. They were covered by their guardian angels. John, Tom and Larry were oblivious to the battle going on around them. Or were they? They were deep in prayer, and the more they prayed, the stronger the men got.

Darkness was sending everything it had now. Demons were flying around the heads of the men. Trying and failing to get close to them. The men kept swatting them with their swords. Soon it seemed darkness had nothing left, its demons were limping back to it. They were slashed and defeated. Some of them were crawling to get back inside the darkness to their own type of safety. And still the warriors advanced. Then the darkness withdrew. One minute it was raging and firing things and demons at them, then, it just disappeared. But the four men did not stop. They were heading towards the front pews where the two men were still in deep conversation. The four walked towards them, there were still a lot of demons covering these men, but they looked terrified.

One of the men looked to be in his late sixties or early seventies. The demons surrounding him were vile.

He turned when he heard them approach. "Can I help you gentlemen?" he asked in a soft voice.

John's head shot up, he knew that voice. He recognised it immediately. He stood up and said, "Hello, Tony," then walked towards his friends.

"My goodness, John, what on earth are you doing here?" he asked.

"I am a pastor; this is a church; I came to pray. Is that a problem with you, Tony?" John replied.

Tony went pale. He looked as if he'd been slapped in the face. John could see he was at a loss for words, which in John's experience was a first for Tony Kerr.

"Who is your friend?" John asked conversationally.

Up to this, the other man had not moved or turned around to see who his friend was speaking to.

"This is Peter," Tony replied, not guessing that John already knew who he was.

The other man stood and turned to look at John. He looked as if he had been caught in an illegal act or something. The guilt was written all over his face.

John recognised him immediately, though the years had not been kind to him. It looked as if every sin he had committed was etched on his face. John could hardly take his eyes off him. The cause of his years of fear and guilt just stood and stared right through him.

John's tongue seemed stuck to the roof of his mouth. All the years, practising what he would say to this man who nearly ruined his life seemed inadequate.

Tony interrupted his thoughts asking, "Do you have business here, John? It's just we are having a very important meeting and it's a bit inconvenient at the moment. Maybe you could call and make an appointment at a more convenient time, okay?"

Suddenly, John found his tongue. "No, it's not okay, Tony. I didn't come here to see you. I came to see your friend here, Peter Roles."

"Wh-what, how on earth do you know Peter?" Tony asked astonished.

"Do you want to tell him, or should I?" John spoke directly to Roles.

"I'm sorry, I'm at a loss, I have no idea who you are," Roles told him, looking warily from one man to the other.

Derek was watching, he took John by the arm to have a chat. "Is this the same man who assaulted you?" he asked John.

"Oh yes," John replied. "He's obviously aged a great deal. He was just a young man when he attacked me, but I will never forget his face, ever!!"

Derek asked, "Do you want us to intervene, or are you okay talking to him?"

"I'm okay, thank you," he said. "As long as I know you have my back and are praying for me. You know the scripture, 'I can do all things through Him who gives me strength' (Phil 4:13). I'm standing on that scripture."

Derek couldn't help but smile, the difference between this young man standing before him and the man they first met was nothing short of miraculous.

"We're right behind you, John, all the way."

John looked at the other three men and smiled a 'thank you'.

The three nodded, and John knew he had nothing to fear.

He turned to Peter Roles, "Do you remember teaching at a small school when you were a young man? Mostly poor parents, it was in a bit of a rundown area in Leicester? It was about twenty years ago, it was called St James. Do you remember it? Or have all the schools you have taught in blended together. How many have you worked in, around sixty? That's quite a lot of schools to get through."

Roles looked uncomfortable and pretended he didn't know what John was talking about.

"Oh you remember all right," John told him. "Those weekends away with young boys who had no dads? I do. Especially one particular weekend in the country, when you beat me unconscious and raped me, then threw me out of your room when you were finished with me. John is the name, but then how many other young boys have you done that to?"

"Now, now, now, what's this all about?" Tony asked. "Peter and I go way back. I've never heard anything so farfetched in all my life. Come on, John, you obviously have the wrong man, and you are getting carried away. You have a habit of that, don't you? This story of yours sounds very fanciful indeed, are you sure you haven't dreamt it all up to make up for accosting that young boy at the youth club?"

"Of course not, Tony, I'm not stupid. I know what happened to me and I know it was at the hands of this man." John shook his head. "How do you know him, by the way? I never saw you with him when I worked here, what's going on?"

"Hold on one minute," Tony blustered. "What gives you the right to storm in here shouting accusations? I think you need to leave and leave immediately."

John was taken aback, he knew Tony was a bit pompous and full of his own importance, but he'd never heard him speak to anyone like this before.

"Okay," he said. "I'm leaving, but I won't be going far. Neither will my friends."

John turned and nodded to the four men. He started walking towards Tom and Larry. He didn't know what to do, all he could do was trust in God. He felt too shocked to do anything else.

Chapter 55

Adrian touched Paul's shoulder. "Don't let him leave this place. Under no circumstances can you let him leave. Watch the faces of the two men, they are hiding something. As soon as we leave, they have something planned. Stop John before he leaves the church."

Paul stood up. He noticed how the demons turned to stare at him. He remembered John's words to Derek and kept repeating the scripture in his mind and heart. It would block anything the demons would try to plant, this was huge. It was a battle of wills as well as a spiritual battle. He walked over to John and put his hand on his arm. "You can't go, something is going on here and we need to get to the bottom of it. Adrian has warned me, we need to check this place out. Look at the faces of Tony and Roles. They are definitely up to no good."

"Okay," John said smiling. He didn't want to back down in front of Tony, but up to now, he didn't see what else he could do. Now he had his backup standing beside him.

All four men stood next to John, then Tom and Larry joined them, they all stood staring at Roles.

"What is this? What's going on here? You all look like you're looking for a showdown," Tony shouted. "Get out of here now before I call the police."

"Oh, that won't be necessary," Tom said. "They are on their way." He looked over at John and nodded, "Larry and I called them as a precaution, looked like we were right to do so!"

John smiled at him and thanked both men for their support and for their wisdom to call the police.

Tony raged, his face was puce, "What right do you have coming in here and causing a disturbance? What on earth did you call the police for?"

"Oh, I'm sorry," said Derek, "isn't that what you were about to do?"

The men started walking closer to the two at the front of the church. Paul noticed that the demons didn't look so bold now. In fact, some were positively shaking as the men and their angels approached.

All of a sudden, Peter Roles made a break for it. He ran to the back of the stage. He opened a door and pulled out a young boy who seemed oblivious to what was going on.

"Take one more step and I promise I'll hurt the boy!" he shouted.

Paul immediately recognised the boy, it was his son Aaron. Fear raced through the church and was about to clutch Paul's heart. The look of triumph on its face made Paul remember he was covered with the armour and he stood firm. It was like fear hit a brick wall, it went flying in the opposite direction.

"What are you doing, Peter?" shouted Tony. Then he turned to the men and said, "I know nothing about any of this. Yes, I was his friend, but I had no idea that anything like this was going on. I want no part in this. I'm leaving."

John stepped in his path and blocked him. "You are not going anywhere. I think you have a bit of explaining to do. You can wait with us for the police."

"Get out of my way," Tony screamed at him. "How dare you. Have you forgotten who I am?"

"No," John said mildly. "How could I forget the man who orchestrated my removal from this parish, and under such a cloud? You, I will never forget."

Then Roles shouted, "I'm not going down on my own. I'll take you and all the rest with me, Tony, I promise you that."

John looked at Tony shocked. He always knew there was something he didn't like about this man, but he never thought that he was a paedophile.

Tony shouted, "Shut up you stupid man, they can't prove anything. It's all in this man's head, all in his imagination. Just keep hold of the boy to keep him safe from these seven intruders into our church."

Then Tom and Larry walked forward. Larry spoke for the first time. "It's all in one man's imagination, really? Is it in ours too? We are here with John, Peter Roles knows us all right, we might be older, but he won't forget us, will you, Peter?"

Paul looked at Aaron, he looked so confused. He kept looking from one group of men to the other.

Derek stepped out of line and walked towards Roles. "Let the boy go," he said. "Are you thinking about a hostage situation? If so, get real, the police are on their way, it's time you paid for your sins. You've nowhere to run. The police have your description. Police all over the UK are on the lookout for you. What did you think? That nobody would ever talk about what you did to them when they were boys? Believe me, we've been following your tracks for a while now, but the police were onto you before us. You just kept slipping the net. Well, now the net is closing in and you're in the very centre so make it easy for everyone and give yourself up. The police will be here any minute."

"No, no, no," Roles screamed. "I am not going to prison. I am never going to prison, I'll make a deal with the police. I have plenty of evidence on a certain ring operating throughout the UK. They can have that for my freedom."

His face was a mask of pure evil. The demons danced around him in delight. Egging him on, pushing and prodding him to dance to their tune. There was one in particular who seemed to be whispering in his ear, telling him what to say, goading him. Roles was practically frothing at the mouth. He was delirious at the thought that though the others would be caught, he would go free. "I'll leave the UK," he told them. "I'll go somewhere nobody has ever heard of me, the police will have their hands full with all the evidence I have, the deal is in the bag."

Paul watched as Roles became more and more animated with his own proposal. He took his hand off the boy for a split second. In that second, Paul stared into the eyes of his son. "Now," he barely nodded, but it was enough. The boy shot away from Roles and ran straight into Paul's open arms. The tears began to flow down Paul's face as he held his son in his arms.

He took control of his emotions and asked Aaron, "Are you okay? Did he hurt you?" The panic was trying to get back in, but Paul resisted it. He was stronger than fear, stronger than panic and his son was safely in his embrace. Then a peace came over him. It was like a cloud, engulfing him and the boy. Later, he would recall it as 'perfect peace'.

Just then Roles made a run for it. He ran to the door he had brought Aaron through.

Chapter 56

"There's a way out of the church from that room," John shouted and ran after him.

He caught up with him as he was trying to unlock the door. Peter pushed John away from him. Then it was as if all the anger and frustration that had built up in him over the years exploded. He shot out with his right fist and caught Roles under his jaw. The punch sent Roles spinning across the room and laid him out cold.

By the time Derek got there, John was standing over Roles and saying, "It is over. Over for good, you will never hurt another child as long as you live. You disgust me!!!" He turned and saw Derek standing in the doorway grinning. Rubbing his knuckles, John chuckled and said, "Never knew flesh against flesh could be so painful."

"I think it's more like bone against bone, and you did very well," Derek smiled.

"What about Tony? Don't let him get away," John shouted.

"It's in the bag," Derek told him. "Harold and Mick are practically sitting on him, with Tom and Larry guarding the doors, just in case. He isn't going anywhere."

As they walked out of the room, they saw Mick and Harold holding down a very irate Tony Kerr, he was not a happy man.

But one man was very, very happy. Aaron looked up at Paul, "You remind me of my dad!" he said.

Paul bit back the words that he so longed to say to his son, that had been the deal, and though with all his heart and soul, he wanted to let this child know who he was, and how much he loved him, he would not disobey.

"Thank you, I hope your Dad knew how lucky he was to have a son like you."

"Oh yes, he did," Aaron said innocently. "My dad worked very hard because he wanted us to always have the best. But sometimes he would take time off and they were the best times. I really miss him."

"Well, just remember that he loved you and is looking after you and your mum and your sister Celia."

"How do you know I have a sister, and she's called Celia?" Aaron asked.

Paul touched the side of his nose with his finger, 'Special Branch', we know lots of things. Then he winked.

Aaron's mouth made a perfect O, "Okay," he said, "it will be our secret."

"NO," Paul nearly shouted, but checked himself just in time, "no secrets, nobody keeps secrets from their mums. If someone tells you to keep a secret, walk away. And always tell your mum anything that's troubling you. She will know what to do. Mums are like that, they're kind of 'Special Branch' too."

Aaron smiled and held on to Paul's hand. It was so hard for Paul not to break down and take on all the guilt for not enjoying his previous life. Then he remembered Adrian's warning, "This will be your hardest battle." He had thought it was when he saw Aaron with Roles' hand on him, but this was harder, not to let the guilt overwhelm him.

The police arrived within minutes of the skirmish. They stopped in their tracks as they saw Harold and Mick holding down a very irate, but still pompous, Tony Kerr.

Tom and Larry stood aside and let the police do their duty. "Okay, Sirs," said the lead policeman. "We can take it from here. But this isn't Peter Roles. We were told that he was on the premises, what's happened to him?"

"He's in here," John said, "he's a bit less irate than Mr Kerr!"

They came into the room and picked Roles up unceremoniously and practically dragged him out. They put Tony Kerr in handcuffs, read him his rights and two officers took him to another police car.

Harold stopped the leading police officer. "Peter Roles stated that he intended to make a deal with the police. It seems he has extensive evidence of a certain paedophile ring working throughout the UK. He intimated that Tony Kerr was part of it, but I think he could be one of the ring leaders."

The police officer introduced himself to the men. "My name is Detective Inspector Tate," he told them. "I don't suppose you know where this evidence might be hidden?" he asked.

"No, unfortunately he didn't mention its whereabouts," said Harold. "But it must be somewhere close by, the way he spoke, it was as if he could just go to a cupboard and produce it."

"We'll need to get a search warrant for this place and his home address and that of Tony Kerr's," the Inspector said.

"Mmm," said Mick, who had remained very quiet, "I doubt he would have kept it at his house, he has been moving from place to place for years. That would have been very inconvenient, I think he has hidden it somewhere very safe, but with easy access. And I don't think Tony Kerr would keep it at his either. When Roles was shouting about the evidence he had, I watched Kerr's face. It was puce, he was so angry, but he kept looking at the base of the stage. Once he saw me watching, he tried to look anywhere but there."

"I can't see any opening at the base here," said Tate. "Hold on a minute, the carpet looks as though it's coming away from the edges here." They bent down and pulled back the carpet to find a key stuck to the underside of it.

"Roles must have been in a hurry to have left the carpet like that," Harold said.

"I think he must have been disturbed," Tate said. "Maybe he was hiding it from Kerr? It is possible that Kerr didn't know Roles had this information."

"I think Roles was here trying to blackmail Tony Kerr," Tom said—who had remained in the background with Larry. "Kerr looked furious with Roles when we first joined John in prayer. They were whispering and Kerr was threatening Roles. I think Kerr noticed the carpet and knew what was under there."

"We didn't see any of this," Derek said to the other three. They had been busy fighting off the darkness. They looked across at John. He said he'd had his head down in prayer. He was praying for guidance. He had known Roles was here, but until he spoke, he hadn't recognised the man with him.

"Good thing you both came when you did," Derek said to Tom and Larry, "now we can see the full picture."

"So what happens now?" Asked John?

"Well," said Tate, "the key looks like a key to a safety deposit box, or something to that effect, finding what it opens is going to be the hard part."

"You won't let them make a deal with Roles?" John asked anxiously. "I couldn't bear it if any other young boy was hurt by him."

"That's up to the courts to decide," said Tate dejected. "If we can't find the evidence before he offers the deal, then I think they would rather have a ring of paedophiles off the street than keep one under lock and key. I'm sorry, but that's just the way it is."

John felt like someone had kicked him in the gut. Paul had to fight another battle, this time with rage. He was speechless. To think the man who had kidnapped his son and would have held him hostage, actually tried to hold him hostage, might go free? It was just too stupid!!!!

Chapter 57

Mick watched the others go through all the emotions, anger, disbelief, dejection, failure, rage, frustration, and he prayed silently for wisdom as he was not in the habit of putting himself forward. This was going to be a challenge to his courage, or lack thereof!

Mick's angel, Andrew, whispered in his ear. "With man this is impossible, but with God, nothing is impossible!" (Matt. 19:26)

Mick smiled and his face lit up. The others looked at him bewildered!! "Look," he said, "with God, nothing is impossible! Why are we all of a sudden working and thinking in the flesh, let's pray."

Officer Tate made his excuses and took Aaron by the hand to leave the church. Half way down the aisle, Aaron pulled away and ran back to Paul and hugged him.

"Remember you said I shouldn't have any secrets from my mum?"

"Yes," said Paul

"Can I share one with you about my teacher Mr Roles and that other man?" Aaron asked him.

"Of course," said Paul, his stomach dropping, hoping it was nothing bad that had happened to Aaron.

"I go to the children's club in the week at the clubhouse near the school."

John's ears pricked up, "I know the clubhouse you're talking about, what happened?"

"I was there one night," Aaron told them. "It was my first time there and I needed the loo. All the other kids were playing games and I was embarrassed to ask anyone where it was, so I decided to look for it myself. I tried a few doors and they were either locked or empty. Then I saw a light, the door was open, so I looked in.

Mr Roles and the other man were sitting, looking at a computer screen, it looked like they were looking at photos. There was no sound from the computer. There were papers and photos all over the desk. I didn't know what they were, but the men were comparing some of them to the ones on the screen. Then the older man must have heard me cause he shouted 'whose there'. So I started to creep away, but I heard him tell Mr Roles to get everything back into the box and to make sure he put it all in the safe. I ran down the corridor in case they caught me and shouted at me."

"Do you know which office it was?" Inspector Tate asked, "Do you remember?"

"Of course, I can," said Aaron indignantly. "I've got a great memory."

"Okay," Tate said, "we'll need a search warrant. We can't just saunter into the offices of the parish and tear everything apart."

"How long will that take?" asked Paul anxiously.

"Just depends on who the judge is and if they think we have just cause," Tate told them. "I'll make a phone call and, as your friend here advised, start praying."

The seven men looked at each other and smiled. Tate didn't know the half of it. They knelt in the front pew to pray, Aaron still holding Paul's hand. This was such a blessing to him and such a heartache, but his mind had to be on his God.

As they knelt, much to the bewilderment of the police officers in the church, who looked slightly embarrassed. They had expected the men to bow their heads and say a quick prayer discreetly. Very unusual to see seven grown men and one little boy kneel as one to pray.

"You just never know what you will come across from day to day on this job," Tate whispered to one of the officers. Still, if they got the search warrant and found evidence, it would be a real coup.

As the seven men prayed, Tate rang the courts. He was told judge Lacy was in chambers. He was put through to her immediately, once he had explained the urgency of the matter.

"Judge Lacy here," she answered the phone. Tate went through the whole scenario that had played out in the church. He explained that the boy, who had been abducted by Roles, had seen some kind of photos on a desk in the offices of the parish, and also believed there was a computer with something on it as well.

Once she had all the information, Judge Lacy was more than happy to issue a warrant. Inspector Tate could hardly keep the excitement out of his voice. Of all the judges that could have been in chambers, she was the fiercest against paedophiles.

Mmmm, he thought, *maybe this prayer thing works!*

He turned to the men who had finished praying, and said, "Okay, gentlemen, you can leave the rest to us. Just leave your details with the PC here so we can be in touch to take statements etc."

John stood up, "Please, Inspector Tate, this man nearly ruined my life and the lives of these two men here," he said pointing to Tom and Larry. These other men and I have been trailing him and finally caught him. No offence, but the whole police force in the UK was supposed to be on his trail, but he kept outwitting them. We really need to see this through. We will not interfere with the search, but we need to be there to the end of this."

"Well," said Tate, "it's against all regulations, but I see where you're coming from. Okay, but please do not hamper the search. You will not be allowed to enter the room. You may have to wait outside. We can't have any trace evidence of you in there. It could jeopardise the case."

"We understand," said Paul. "We can wait outside, but I'm not going to let this young man out of my sight until I hand him over to his mum, is that okay with you?"

Tate nodded, "No problem. The rest of you carry on to the building, you know where it is, I believe?" he said to John.

John nodded yes.

Tate turned to Paul, "You, Sir, can come with the lad in the police car. I'm not letting him out of my sight either."

Everyone was quite happy with those arrangements. They all trudged to their cars, Harold, Mick and John went in one. Derek said he would like to travel with Tom and Larry. They would follow in theirs.

Tate stopped at the court, and as requested, the search warrant for the premises was at the front desk. He jumped back in the car. He radioed the police station. "Hold everything," he told them. "We have a warrant for the search of the premises as requested. Get a team of forensic people over to the parish hall immediately."

He turned back to Aaron, "Would you like the sirens on?" he asked him.

"Yes, please," said a very excited Aaron.

Paul looked down at him, *All in all, this experience has been more of an adventure to him than anything else. Thank You Lord. How You can change things around is amazing.*

"Can I ask you a question?" he asked Aaron.

"Of course," said Aaron.

"Why were you in the back room of the church? Shouldn't you be in school?"

"Yes, but Mr Roles is our new teacher. He hasn't been here very long and he doesn't know his way around very well. So he asked my teacher if I could accompany him on his errand. He said it was quite important and the whole school would benefit from it. He told my teacher that he had rang my mum and asked her for her permission. My teacher tried to contact mum, but couldn't get through. He told Mr Roles that I could go, but we had to be back before lunch. I guess he'll be very cross by now."

Yes, thought Paul, more than cross, *he should be fired and if I have anything to do with it, he will. Imagine letting a child go off with a teacher, a new teacher at that, one you knew nothing about. That's totally irresponsible, unless???* But he wouldn't let himself think like that. He looked at Aaron, who was enjoying himself so much, flying along in the car with the sirens full on and a big smile on his face. He would never forget this moment.

Chapter 58

They arrived at the building. The others were already there. "Okay," said Tate, "let's do this." They walked into the building. The receptionist looked up from her screen, alarmed when she saw all the police and forensic people converge on the building.

"What on earth is going on? You can't just barge in here, these are parish offices. What do you want?" she asked exasperated.

"We have a warrant to search the premises," Tate told her. "Please hand over all keys to offices and cupboards throughout the building, thank you," he said as he handed her the warrant.

She looked completely taken aback, but she handed her full set of keys over to him, without another word. She picked up the phone to call somebody. "That won't be necessary," Tate told her. "Keep an eye on her, and don't let her speak to anyone," he said to one of the officers.

"What's this all about?" she asked.

"You will find out in due time. I advise you to sit comfortably until the search is concluded."

Aaron led the way to the office. Paul was so proud of him, he seemed so grown up all of a sudden. He pointed to the door of the office, it was locked. Tate went through the keys, *We'll be here all day at this rate,* he said to himself. Then the next key opened the door.

"Thank you, Aaron," he said, "Officer Ryan, can you stay with Aaron and the gentleman please?"

The forensic team entered the office with Tate and two other police officers. They searched through all the drawers and filing cabinets, nothing! Nothing seemed to be out of order. "Where on earth can it be? There's nowhere else I can see that they could have hidden it." He told the team.

Aaron tugged at Paul's hand. "Why are they looking in those drawers?" he asked. "They had a big box on the desk with them, that wouldn't fit in any of those drawers."

Tate looked frustrated. He was going around in circles, trying to think where they would keep something so sensitive. "There's nowhere else they could hide it." In his frustration he sent up a silent prayer.

Paul shouted to him, "Aaron says the box would have been too big to fit in any of the drawers or filing cabinets. Remember he heard Kerr telling Roles to put everything in the safe."

Of course, Tate said to himself, *but where?* He was walking between the desk and the wall, moving pictures to see if there was anything behind them, nothing. He sat down at the desk to gather his thoughts. "It's got to be here somewhere," he said to no one in particular. "Come on think!" He stamped his foot in frustration. What was that? It didn't sound like the rest of the floor. He bent down on his knees and lifted one of the carpet tiles and low and behold there is was. A safe! Nobody would ever know it was there.

"Okay," he smiled and turned to give Aaron 'a thumbs' up. "Well done," he told Aaron. *Only one problem,* he thought, *what is the combination? I suppose we could get someone in to drill it open, but that's going to take time and I don't want Roles making any arrangements with CPS. I need to think.*

He started going through the various account books and diaries that were on the desk. Nothing! He opened drawers and rifled through them. Time was running out, if he didn't find something soon, he would not only be letting John down, but the young lad Aaron as well. Plus he might be letting a known paedophile go free. He was trying not to panic. "Okay," he told himself, "do this rationally, forget everything that's going on around, just be methodical, it usually works."

So he took out all the papers, diaries, appointment books and painstakingly looked through everything, still he could see nothing. At the back of the drawer, there was a very small book. It looked like a child's notebook. He had nearly overlooked it. Opening it, there were dates and times and some names, it didn't make any sense. But he carried on diligently, going through each page and searching for anything that could be a combination. Then on the last but one page, he came across a random number. It was so small, he nearly missed it. If he had let himself be stressed, he would definitely have missed it. Even now, he couldn't make out the figures, they were too small. *This has got to be it,* he said to himself. *My eyes are not good enough, maybe a trip to the optician is in order.*

He took the book out to the hall where Aaron and Paul stood waiting. "Aaron," he asked, "do you think you can read this number for me please?" He showed Aaron the number, but didn't let him touch the notebook.

"Yes," said Aaron, obviously confused as to why inspector Tate couldn't read it himself. Then he read out the numbers in a flash.

The officer standing with Paul and Aaron wrote the number down and handed it to inspector Tate. Tate went straight to the safe and punched in the numbers. "Yes!!" The safe opened and just as Aaron had told him, inside there was a large box. The box was locked, but he took a letter opener from the desk and prized it open.

What he saw inside made him want to throw up. Not only were there photos of young boys, but there were also photos of men with young boys, including photos of Kerr. The photos seemed to go back a long time, maybe even into the seventies or eighties. It made him sick to his stomach to think that this evil had pervaded his watch. Under the photos was a laptop that would probably be password protected, but that didn't bother him. The evidence he had in his hand was enough to send Kerr down for a long time. Then he came across another book, this one was hidden under the laptop, it was a book of names and addresses, plus phone numbers. He doubted the addresses were kosher, but the phone numbers might turn out to be useful. Also, he found a number of memory sticks and at least six CDs. He had his work cut out for him.

"I think we've hit the mother lode!" He said. "Okay, let's get all this to the station and let's interview our two boys and see what they have to say for themselves."

As they were leaving the building, a car pulled up. It was Elizabeth, Aaron's mum. She ran over to him and threw her arms around him.

"Are you okay, honey?" she asked.

"Yes, Mum, it was great, I got a ride in a police car with the sirens on. It was brilliant," Aaron told her.

Tate came over and said, "He is a real credit to you. You have a fine young man there. He has been such a big help, we wouldn't have done it without him." He turned to Aaron, "Keep up all this good work and you will make a great policeman one day."

"Wow," said Aaron, "that would be so cool."

Tate introduced Paul to Elizabeth. "I've been keeping an eye on him, and like inspector Tate said, he is a credit to you. He is a very brave boy." He ruffled Aaron's hair and Elizabeth gave a gasp.

"Sorry," said Paul immediately. "I didn't mean to be over familiar."

"No, no," Elizabeth laughed, embarrassed. "It's something his dad used to do. He has never let anyone else do that since we lost him."

"I'm sorry," Paul whispered, trying to hold it together. He wanted so much to take Elizabeth in his arms, just once more. The feeling was overwhelming, *This battle just gets harder and harder,* he thought.

Then Elizabeth said, "Sorry, I've left my daughter in the car, just let me get her." She quickly let Celia out of the car and brought her across to Aaron and Paul. She was the image of her mum. Paul couldn't take his eyes off her. His two beautiful children had grown up so much in the past two years. Why had he taken it all for granted when he had had them so close to him?

Then another car pulled up and a tall, very good-looking man got out. Aaron took one look and ran to him. "Sam, Sam," he shouted, "I've been in a police car with the sirens on."

The man called Sam picked him up like he was a feather and spun him around. Aaron was laughing and screaming with delight. Celia ran to Sam. "Me next, me next." He picked her up and swung her around, she screamed and laughed just like Aaron. Paul's heart cracked then. He tried to turn away before he broke down completely, but Elizabeth put a hand on his arm to stop him.

"Aaron," she shouted, "come and say thank you to this nice gentleman for looking after you." She looked into Paul's eyes, "Do I know you from somewhere?" she asked.

"I don't think so," he said, gathering all his strength to sound cheerful.

"You look so familiar," she said, "must be my imagination."

Sam walked over to them, Elizabeth introduced him. "This is my friend Sam," she said. Paul could see the love in her eyes and see it was reciprocated by him. "Sorry, I've forgotten your name."

"It's Paul," he said quietly. He could see she was trying to register something in her mind, but just then, Aaron came running over and gave Paul a huge hug.

Elizabeth and Sam looked at each other in amazement, at the show of affection Aaron had shown for this stranger. Paul hugged him and said, "Take care of your family, big fella."

Aaron looked at him and said, "Okay, Dad," in a whisper.

Paul's knees nearly buckled. Then Celia ran to him and hugged him, "Thank you for looking after my big brother," she said.

This was nearly more than Paul could handle. Now he understood Adrian's warning. That this was going to be his hardest battle yet. Would he ever get over this, or would he ever want to?

They said their goodbyes and Sam put his arm around Elizabeth's shoulder and walked her to her car with the children.

The other men had been standing at a distance watching the proceeding. They walked across to him and stood by him. It was as if they were columns holding him up with their strength.

"Now I know what it must have been like to be a musketeer," Harold chirped up. "One for all and all for one!"

They all laughed and it broke some of the pain Paul was feeling.

Inspector Tate joined them. "We've got more than enough evidence against them and against some leading men as well. I can't believe they were so pompous, but from the photos, it looks like this has been going on for a lot of years, so I suppose, having gotten away with it this long, they thought they'd never be caught," he told them. "The night Aaron saw them they must have been reliving past glories. They won't have a leg to stand on, we've got them now. Thanks to young Aaron, we've got the names of the entire ring. It won't be hard to track them down."

Chapter 59

"What happens next?" asked Derek.

"Well, we need to get to the station fast. I want to interrogate them myself. It's against procedure, but if you want, you can watch through the two-way mirror," he said.

"Yes," John nearly shouted. "I've waited for so long for this, I want to see what they have to say for themselves."

They drove to the station, Roles and Kerr already had their solicitors present.

Roles looked so cocky, "I can give you the entire ring," he offered, "in exchange for my acquittal." He smirked at Tate.

"What makes you think Kerr hasn't already offered us the same deal?" Tate asked him.

"Ha-ha," said Roles, "because he will still be protesting his innocence. He actually thinks you believe he had nothing to do with it. When it was him who first groomed us!"

"What age were you then?" asked Tate.

"Ten years old, but he gave me sweets and other treats. He took me to football matches and sometimes we went to nice restaurants, places where my stupid, poor parents couldn't take me. I started to enjoy the lifestyle. He paid all my college fees, and he taught me the business. It all seemed to come naturally to me," he said smugly.

"So, if he treated you so well, why did you rape and beat boys into submission? Why, if he taught you the business, did you not follow his example? It seems to me that you enjoyed the violence, more than the sex?" Tate asked.

"Yeah, I did, so what?" Roles said. His solicitor tried to shush him, but he was on a roll. "I hated those poverty stricken schools, and the pathetic kids that went there, but I had to keep a low profile, and nobody bothers too much about what goes on at poor schools so I had no choice. It amused me in the beginning to be the charismatic teacher that all the kids loved. The excitement of the months deciding which one I would pick out of the group. Then when I was ready, well any of the boys were fair game, they trusted me, ha! Who would listen to one pathetic boy when all the rest thought I was wonderful. So the one I picked out didn't come on any of the trips again, so what? There were always boys eager to come on the trips with Mr Roles." He sniggered.

"But you used to bring two older boys along, didn't you?" asked Tate, "What was that about?"

"They were there to give the kid a sleeping tablet and patch him up so he didn't wake the other kids with his whining and crying. They were my insurance. I couldn't be bothered even looking at the kid, once I'd had my way with him." He practically snarled.

The seven men stood on the other side of the mirror. John felt sick at the callousness of Roles, it was like these boys were little more than rag dolls to him, to be used and then discarded. He looked around at Tom and Larry, they looked so ashamed. He could feel it emanate from them. They looked as if they would shrivel up.

He went over to them, "Are you both okay?" he asked.

Tom replied, "I don't know about Larry, but I feel so sick, he used us and we let him. Why didn't we stand up to him?" He turned to Larry who just nodded, his head bowed.

John touched both men's shoulders. "Firstly, you were young yourselves, what were you, twelve, thirteen, fourteen? How could you stand up to someone as devious as Roles? You were the good guys. You were the saviours of all the lads he hurt. Remember, if it wasn't for you, I wouldn't be here. I said before, I think I would have committed suicide. You both saved my life and probably the lives of many of those boys. You have nothing to be ashamed of. Don't let shame and guilt rob you anymore. Shame and guilt have taken enough from us, they're not getting any more."

Both men looked at each other and smiled sadly. "Thank you, John," they both said.

Derek came over, "Remember to put the armour on, if you feel like you're slipping at all, just cover yourself in the armour. Satan wants you to feel defeated, but you are warriors, as John says, you're the good guys."

They both stood that little bit taller and watched the proceeding without that feeling of dread around them. John, Tom and Larry stood together. They listened to Roles as he went on and on about his exploits. The way he spoke, the utter disregard for what he had done, left them speechless.

Derek returned to the other three, they could see a much more terrifying site. The demons were crawling all over Roles. Slithering all around him! They looked as if they were climbing into his ears and coming out of his mouth. It was not a pretty sight.

Roles was going on and on spilling his guts, believing that he would get full immunity when he told them where the evidence was.

Then Tate interrupted him, "I've got some bad news for you," he said. "We already have all the evidence in our possession. Everything you thought you had well hidden has been found. You haven't got a leg to stand on, good luck in trying to make a deal, you have no chance."

Neither he nor Roles' solicitor were prepared for the rage that overtook Roles. He jumped up screaming, his face contorted into a mask of pure evil. He lunged across the table at Tate, grabbing him by his lapels and trying to pull him towards him. The solicitor tried to stop him but he threw out his hand and sent the solicitor flying from his chair.

Three police officers ran into the room and eventually dragged him off the inspector. They had to handcuff him to the chair. Tate was clearly shocked, nothing like this had ever happened to him in his career. "Interview suspended," he said into the tape. He gave the date and time and rushed out of the room.

The police officers helped the solicitor off the floor and he followed close on the heels of Tate.

The four could see the darkness penetrate the room. They wanted to shout at the police officers to get out before it touched them. In the end, they didn't have to worry, all four, the three that had rushed in and the one standing on guard during the interview, came out of the room at such a speed, it was like a stampede.

They stood and watched as the darkness flooded every corner of the room. It looked the same as the one they had battled with at the church. They thought they had defeated it, but here it was again, large as life and looking more menacing than ever. Roles sat, he was slumped over the table. They couldn't see his face, was he smiling or crying, they couldn't make out. The darkness was like a thick black twister, flying around the room. Still Roles sat with his head bowed.

John, who could not see the darkness invade the room, asked the officers what was going on. "We don't know," one of them said. "But we're not hanging around in there to find out."

Tate, who had gone to tidy up after the incident, came down the corridor. "What are you doing outside the room?" he shouted. "Get back in there now. He's handcuffed to the chair now, he can't harm you. One of you, get back in there, that's an order."

The officers looked at each other, then at Tate. "Sorry," said one of them sheepishly, "we can't."

"What do you mean you can't?" he shouted. "You load of nancies." He opened the door and was nearly thrown back by the sheer wall of evil that filled the room. "What the hell was that?" He asked as he quickly shut the door.

Derek went to him. He rested his hand on his sleeve and said, "Some things are very hard to explain."

"Try me!" Tate said angrily.

"Well," Derek explained, "the rage that Roles has plunged into has brought, what only can be described as, a dark evil into being."

"How on earth do you know that?" he asked incredulously.

Derek cleared his throat and said, "We can see it!"

Tate's face went pale, what on earth was he dealing with here. Paedophile rings were one thing, but this, 'evil personified' even tactile? What was he to do with that?

"What can we do?" he asked Derek.

Derek turned to John, now it was John's turn to go pale.

"Do you know what you have to do?" Derek asked him.

"Yes," he answered in a whisper, "I need to go in there and forgive Roles. To be honest, I don't know if I can. All these years of anger and rage and fear and guilt, it feels too hard to let it go."

Larry came over to him. "If anyone can understand how you feel, it's Tom and I. And if you want us to go in there with you, we will. Though we both feel terrified of what's going on in that room, you have made us aware that we don't need to be in bondage to that terror anymore. So we are more than willing to go with you."

"Thank you," John said, "that means so much to me, but I know that I have to do this by myself, for myself. Thank you for showing me that it's possible."

"Now you know you are not on your own, you are never on your own," Derek told him. "We are all here praying for you, our angels will cover you. But you have to overcome the fear and the bitterness that has robbed you of so much, do you want to pray?"

"That's an understatement, if ever I heard one." John chuckled.

All the men circled John, and their angels circled them.

Derek prayed, "This Lord is in Your hands. Your word says we must forgive. Please grant John the grace and courage to forgive Peter Roles, and in turn, give Tom and Larry the grace to forgive him also in Your strength Jesus. We pray against the darkness in Peter Roles' soul, we command it to shrivel in the light of Your presence."

The four men watched as John got ready to face his nemesis. As they watched him straighten himself, they could see the light begin to shine from him. It was like it was pouring through every pore, they couldn't take their eyes off him. It grew brighter and brighter until they had to lower their eyes, they knew it was the Light of Jesus shining through. John, of course, couldn't see it, but he knew something was happening.

"Okay, ready?" Derek asked him.

"Yes," John said decisively. He knew in his heart something had shifted. All the years he had held on to the anger and bitterness, let it build up to a hatred that he didn't think he was capable of, he could see it now, it was like a cancer preventing him being the man God created him to be. *Well, no more,* he said to himself. *It finishes today.* Then he prayed for the full armour of God from Ephesians 6.

Tate didn't know where to look. This was nothing like he'd ever encountered in his whole career. Could he let a civilian just walk into this room, with a possible mad man? Though at least he's handcuffed to the chair, he mused. *That's something, well I hope it is.* This could go terribly wrong, but he didn't know what else he could do. Whatever was in that room—be it darkness or evil—it was too strong for him or any of his men to combat. Then he sent up another silent prayer.

Chapter 60

John walked to the door. Funny, all the years he had lived in fear of everything really. Here he was facing his biggest challenge yet, and he felt no fear at all.

Then a voice said in his ear, "Mmm, what if it doesn't make any difference? What if the darkness overpowers you, what then? Can you really be sure that God is on your side? After all, you did lash out and hit Roles, is that what the God you serve expects of you?"

John just smiled at the other men, he knew that voice, but it no longer had any control over him. "I think we have them on the run," he said. "That ugly voice that has whispered in my ear all these years is telling me not to go. Now I know I'm doing the right thing." He opened the door and walked through.

From Tate's point of view, literally, he saw John walk towards a very aggressive man who was handcuffed to a chair. It didn't look that scary. It would have looked totally harmless had he not experienced the force when he opened the door earlier. Again, he prayed, (this was becoming a habit), "Lord, if this is from You, and we get it sorted, my family and I will be going to church on Sunday, and every Sunday from now on. This situation is completely out of my remit."

As John closed the door, he could feel the total weight of the evil come over him. "You're not alone," he said to himself. "Not only have I my friends praying for me, the angels are surrounding me, but more importantly, I'm filled with the Spirit of God, and nothing can come against me and no harm can come to me."

Suddenly, the oppressive weight of evil lifted. John walked towards Roles, who sat with his head bent. "Do you remember me?" he asked him.

Roles sneered at him. He was actually drooling, "From when?" he asked. "From today when you punched me or from when you were a little, pathetic, whining kid, whom I had great pleasure in seeing to?" He sniggered.

"Both, I suppose," John answered calmly.

"Yeah, yeah, I remember you both times. I hope you're not waiting for an apology for what happened years ago. I'd say, don't hold your breath."

"No," said John, "don't need one thanks. I've come here to tell you I forgive you. I understand now that you didn't do all these things completely on your own. You see, you have all the anger and bitterness inside you. You've let it mould your life. Instead of reporting what Kerr did to you when you were a boy, because you didn't think anyone would believe you, you pretended it was what you wanted. I overheard you telling the Inspector that you were fine with it, but you never were, were you?"

Roles tried to jump at him but he was restrained by the handcuffs. "How the hell can you know what I was feeling when I was a kid. You weren't even born."

"We all have to make a choice in life!" John said. "It's those choices that determine how your life will turn out. You were a bully when you were a child. You knew, or thought you knew, that even if someone believed you, they would probably say you deserved what was coming to you. You couldn't believe that anyone would have sympathy for you, so you turned it around and pretended it was okay. Then you could ask Kerr for anything and he would give it. But you started hating yourself then, and the hatred has just built up over the years until it has finally consumed you."

Roles was snarling now, he looked like a caged animal.

John placed his hand on Roles' shoulder and said, "I forgive you in Jesus' name."

Outside the room, looking through the two-way mirror, the men could see the demons screaming and literally climbing the walls, the darkness seemed to have shrunk because a great light shone in the room and permeated everything. The stronger the light, the smaller the darkness became. It seemed to shrivel, until it had nearly disappeared. They kept praying and the light got brighter and brighter.

The eyes of the four men were on the spiritual battle. Tom and Larry could feel it, though their eyes couldn't see what was going on, they knew the atmosphere all around them was changing. They also felt their hearts change towards Roles. They hadn't expected it to happen so quickly, but all of a sudden, they could feel no hatred for the man handcuffed to the chair. They felt a peace pour over them. It felt like oil, pouring over their heads and into every cell of the bodies. They looked at each other in amazement, there were no words to describe this, but then they didn't need any words. They just smiled and continued to pray.

Tate, on the other hand, was looking solely on the physical side of the situation. He saw, (but couldn't quite believe) Roles go from an aggressive, sneering bully, to a little old man in front of his eyes. Roles wasn't that old, but he seemed to have shrunk inside himself. He was no longer snarling and shouting. He sat with his head down, a man defeated.

John saw the same image. "God is so amazing," he said to himself. "One, I never thought I could forgive this man, and two, I definitely never thought I could feel sorry for him, but my heart goes out to him. This is from God. I know I couldn't feel this, without His Spirit in me." He asked Roles if he could get him anything.

Roles seemed to be in a daze. "Erm, some water please, if that's okay?" he practically whispered.

John saw a broken man, someone who made the wrong choices through his life. Now all he had to look forward to was prison. Instead of feeling a great deal of satisfaction, all he felt was pity.

Paul went to get the water and took it into the room. Here was the man who intended to kidnap his son, and he didn't even want to think what Roles had planned after that. Paul thought he would hate him, but like John, all he saw was a broken man, who would never harm another child again, and for that he was very thankful.

They both walked out of the room and looked through the two-way mirror. Roles lifted his head and said something.

Tate asked if it was safe to enter the room and the men agreed it was.

Chapter 61

They all stood and watched as Roles spoke to Tate. Tate came out again and signalled for John to go back in.

This time, John walked through the door unafraid, knowing the battle with Roles was over and the good guys had won.

Roles looked at him with tears in his eyes and said, "I'm sorry, I'm sorry for what I did to you and I'm sorry for what I did to all the others. In the safe with the rest of the files, there is a book with names and addresses."

"Yes," said Tate, "we've seen it. It's the names of the members of the paedophile ring?"

"No," said Roles, his voice catching, "they're the names and addresses of the boys I abused all through the years. I used to pretend to myself that I kept them to gloat over, but I didn't. I think somewhere deep inside me, I knew that one day I'd be caught. So you can contact these boys, some will be men now, and they can go as witnesses against me. It also has names of boys that Kerr abused. He didn't know I knew of them, I haven't got all their names, but there is quite a few. Now it's finally over, I'm so tired, but I'm glad it's over."

John thanked him for his apology. Then John and Tate walked from the room.

Tom and Larry came to them, "We have to tell him we've forgiven him too," Larry said. "Not so much for him, as for ourselves. We need to finish this, and until we say it out loud, it could still have a hold over us. Is it okay with you if we enter the room with Roles?" they asked Tate.

"Eh, yes of course," he said. It didn't matter anymore, everything that had happened since he met these men went against all he had ever believed or understood. If it was against procedure, well so be it, he didn't feel that he was in charge anymore. *Someone or something far more powerful than me is in charge now.*

Tom and Larry walked through the door. Roles looked up, half expecting to be shouted at. He knew he deserved anything he got from these men, so if they were here to berate him for all he did to them, well it was nothing less than he deserved. But to his utter astonishment, they both put their hands on his shoulders and forgave him. He started to cry and couldn't control the sobs that shuddered through his body. Tom and Larry turned to leave. Both of them had tears of pity in their eyes for the man who had controlled them through their early teens. His past actions had also controlled them in their adult life. But they could only feel pity and forgiveness.

John was watching the proceedings through the two-way mirror again. "How can he have changed in such a short time?" he asked the four men.

"It was 'The Light'!" Derek said. "It permeated everything in that room, including Roles. Nothing can ever stay the same when touched by 'The Light'.

"What happens now?" John asked Tate. "What's happening with Kerr? Surely, he is more evil than Roles. What does he have to say for himself?"

"Let's go and ask the detective that interviewed him." They walked down to the next window and looked through the window at Kerr. He was completely subdued, not the pompous, overbearing man John had known previously.

John turned to the others, "Why is he so different to Roles?" he asked.

The others shook their heads in bewilderment. Then Adrian spoke to Paul. "Roles built himself up with hatred, he let it consume him. Hatred for himself first, then for Kerr and then he transferred all that vileness onto young innocent boys. It took over his life. Every time he hurt a boy, the hatred took another piece of him, until at last there was only evil, where once there had been a human heart. That is why, when the Light touched him, he was completely broken. The Light extinguished the evil from his heart. Now he has nothing, but God is merciful and if Roles will allow Him, God will transform him."

Paul explained this to John. "Okay, but what about Kerr?" John asked.

Adrian spoke again. "Kerr did what he did, he believed he was made like this and so does not hate himself. In fact, he believes he loved the boys he abused. In his mind they didn't suffer, they were happy because he rewarded them. You see, Roles was violent with the boys, and as he did to John, would throw them out, away from him. He said they disgusted him, but in reality, he disgusted himself. Not so with Kerr, he is still of the opinion that he did no harm and the boys were willing participants."

As Paul told John what Adrian had said, he thought, then asked, "Why is this room not filled with the darkness? Surely Kerr is much worse than Roles, I don't understand."

"The demons you saw climbing all over Roles were his tormentors. They weren't just evil from him. They were torturing him with what he had done. He has been held captive by this darkness for a long time. That is why there was such a battle at the church, and why the darkness thought he could control him here. He had no peace. All he ever felt was hatred and the darkness thrives on pure hatred. Kerr, on the other hand, did not hate the boys, nor does he hate himself. The darkness is inside him, dormant. It is waiting for the time when, once Kerr has been confronted by his victims and grasps what he put them through, then it will attack. You must remember that Satan is patient so he lets Kerr believe it is a quirk of nature."

Tate had been speaking to the detective who had interviewed Kerr. "What's the story?" he asked.

"Well," said the detective, "he was denying all knowledge of Roles and what he was up to, that was until we showed him some quite explicit photos of him with young boys. His bravado disappeared then, and he confessed to everything. He's saying the boys liked it and it's just a quirk of nature."

"He'll know just what a quirk of nature he is when he's in prison," Tate replied. "Has he given you any names of the others involved, it turns out, the book of names and addresses we found was a list of young lads abused by Roles and Kerr! It's not a list of the paedophile ring as we thought."

"Oh, he's singing like a canary. He's given us some quite big names. This will bring a lot of people in high places down. I think he actually believes that because he is cooperating with us and giving us names of some very important people, he'll get off scot free."

"Not if I've got anything to do with it," said Tate angrily. "Get on to the computer guys and speak to the paedophile division, update them with what we have so far. See can the computer guys pick up anything we might have missed."

The other detective turned to leave, Tate was happy with the outcome so far, but still frustrated that they hadn't found the actual list of members of the ring. He put his hand in his pocket and touched the key they had found at the church.

"Oh," he practically shouted, "what an idiot!"

The other detective turned, "What's wrong?"

"Because I found the safe and the list of names etc., I forgot all about this key. It's a key to a safety deposit box. I'll ring judge Lacy, we need another search warrant for whatever this key opens."

He turned to John, "Do you think you could get Roles to tell us what bank this key is for?" he asked.

"The way he is at the moment," John said, "I think he will tell us anything we want to know."

He walked into the room with Roles. Roles looked up at him. John saw a pathetic broken man. He spoke to him in a gentle voice. "The key to the safety deposit box we found, what bank is it from?"

Roles gave him the name of the bank immediately! Tate watched through the two-way mirror, once he had the information, he rang judge Lacy and requested another warrant. They had to hurry the banks would be closing soon. He wanted this sorted out before close of play.

Judge Lacy agreed and had the warrant written up there and then.

Tate took another officer and raced to pick it up from the court house, then sirens on full, they sped to the bank. They arrived twenty minutes before closing time. Tate was shown to the manager's office. He produced the warrant and the manager took him down to the safety deposit boxes in the basement of the bank.

When he opened the box, there were more sickening photos. It took all his willpower to control his anger against these men. At the bottom of the box, he found the list he was looking for. There were reams and reams of paper and rows of names, addresses and occupations. "YES!!" he shouted, to the consternation of the bank manager. He looked towards heaven and gave thanks.

Now back to the police station, this was definitely the list. He recognised some of the names on it.

He rushed into the station, "We've got it, and this is the right one this time," he told the other officers. "You won't believe some of the names on this list, there will be a lot of people, shall we say, 'surprised' when we do our dawn raid in the next few days. But this has been a good day. I, for one, think we could all do with a beer to celebrate. Saying that, if it wasn't for these men and their tenacity, we would have still been chasing shadows and not aware of exactly what was going on under our noses."

He walked down the corridor to the seven men. They were standing in a circle actually they looked as if they were praying again. "Ahem," he coughed, "sorry for interrupting."

"No, no," said Derek, "we were just giving thanks for everything that happened today."

"Amen to that," Tate replied. "Oh, while we are on the subject, could you direct me to a good church please? I really want to know more about this God of yours."

They laughed and turned to John. "I think this is your area of expertise," Harold said.

John chuckled, "I would be delighted to give you directions, over a pint of beer at your local? Drinks are on you, of course!"

Tate looked quite taken aback. "I didn't think religious men would frequent pubs," he said.

"Correct," said Harold, "but we're not 'religious' men; we are followers of Jesus and Jesus was quite at home with everyone eating and drinking."

"Well said," John slapped Harold on the back.

"Sounds like my type of man," Tate said.

"You have no idea!" John laughed. "Okay, where is this local of yours?"

"It's just down the road to the left of the station, we can walk together." He shouted to his colleagues to follow them to the pub. After the day they'd just had, they could all do with a pint. It didn't take long for the rest of them to pack up what they were doing, everyone was in good spirits.

They all enjoyed a few pints and some food which, not quite as good as Alice's, was still tasty enough. They'd forgotten to eat lunch and they were ravenous. John gave Tate directions to his church. After all, it wasn't that far from the station.

The seven men left the pub after the meal, leaving Tate and his men to enjoy another pint or two. It had been an exceptional day and there was a lot to discuss.

Tom and Larry took their leave promising to speak the following day.

The five drove back to the village, singing praise songs and worshipping God all the way. The angels sat on the roof of the car and joined in with the songs.

John couldn't wait to get back to his beautiful Jennifer and tell her all the amazing things God had done that day.

Chapter 62

John dropped the men at the B & B and drove straight to Jennifer's. She opened the door as soon as she saw his car drive up.

"You know," he said, "we talked of marriage before I went off on my adventure?"

"Yes?" she answered, a little doubt creeping into her thoughts, *What if he's changed his mind? What if something happened and he's met someone else?*

John saw the doubt cross her face. It was another thing he loved about her. He could read every emotion of hers in her face. She didn't have to say a word. His heart went out to her. He knew she was worried in case he changed his mind. "Do you want a very large wedding?" he asked, smiling at the relief he saw in her.

"No, not really," she answered. "I would like to keep things simple, why?"

"Well, how quickly can we arrange the wedding?" he said. "I just don't want to wait any longer. I was thinking we could have the reception at the B & B, they have a nice restaurant and there's the outside area for extra guests. I thought we'd have close friends and family in the day and have an open house to all villagers, etc., in the evening. What do you think?"

Her eyes sparkled and her cheeks took on a pink hue. "Actually, I've just been speaking to Alice, seeing if it was possible to hold it there," she said shyly. "I asked her if she would cook the main course for the day menu and get caterers for the evening. She is adamant that she can do both, though I'm going to get some of the young girls from the village to help. She's quite advanced in her pregnancy now and I don't want to overburden her. By the way, what date were you thinking of?"

"Mmmm, tomorrow!!!" John replied.

She smacked him then, "Don't be silly, it will have to be at least a few weeks from now." She laughed.

John dropped his head as if he was disappointed, "Okay, if you say so," he muttered.

Jennifer couldn't help but laugh, "Stop being silly, you know what arrangements have to go into this. And anyway, don't you want to get married in the church? I don't think it will be ready by tomorrow, do you?"

"Okay, point taken," he laughed. "I'll get on to Thomas to do the honours. I've known him for a long time and he keeps asking me when are we going to tie the knot? He'll be delighted that we've finally organised something. He will take the service. I know he'll be delighted."

"Well, you'll have to make sure he is available," Jennifer replied sensibly.

"I'll do that tonight, I need a suit, we need invitations, your dress, flowers, etc. etc., should be simple enough."

Simple according to man! she thought. There was so much to do, the dress first, she wanted it lovely, but not too expensive. Her sister she knew would wear a dress of her own choosing, which saved a lot of hassle. Then there would be the invitations, her and John would need to decide between them. The flowers would be the easiest part she knew just what she wanted.

"You'll have to let me know what date Thomas can do. Also, how long do you think the church will take to be finished, we could be talking months?" she teased.

The look of horror on John's face was priceless. "Noo-oo-oo," he said adamantly. "I can't wait that long, I'll talk to the men and see how quickly we can get everything arranged in the church. Maybe we could even sort it for next week?"

"Not a chance," she said smiling. "I have a lot of organising to do, and you have as well, so a few more weeks won't kill us."

"I suppose so," he laughed, "it was worth a try."

He could smell something cooking in the kitchen. "What are you cooking tonight?" he asked.

"I'm trying out the recipe of Alice's, meatballs in red wine sauce."

"Good job, I didn't eat too much at the bar earlier," he said.

"Oh, you think it's for you, do you?"

"Of course, my future wife, I have to sample your cooking, it's what I will be eating for the rest of my life." He kissed her and food was the last thing on his mind.

Over at the B & B, the four men were discussing the day's occurrence.

"Okay," said Mick, "what happens now? John seems to be in a good place, and it looks like we achieved what God wanted us to, where do we go from here?"

No one said anything. Each man was thinking his own thoughts on the subject. Did they do as they were asked? Did they do it right? Each angel was silent too. Mick said, "Let's turn in, it's been a long day." The rest agreed.

Three of the men went to their rooms, but Paul stayed in the lounge. "I would just like some time to pray," he explained.

It was so peaceful and comfortable here and he had a lot to think about. He didn't feel like sleeping, his mind was in a whirl after the day's events. Suddenly, a bright light shone down on him. Adrian came and joined him on the sofa.

"How are you doing?" he asked.

"To be honest," said Paul, "I don't know. It's been a very unusual day and that's saying something after the past few months. I don't know what I'm feeling. It's as if my emotions are on a roller coaster. I'm so glad I saw my family again. I'm filled with 'what ifs'. If I could go back in time, I'd change everything. I'd spend more time with them. I wouldn't be so obsessed with work and making money. I'd enjoy life, it's so fragile, so short. Why didn't I wake up and notice before it was too late."

Then he couldn't control his emotions anymore, he broke down and sobbed. His body shook and he couldn't lift his head. All the regrets of his previous life came pouring in. He couldn't contain the anguish anymore. It was too much to take, his heart cracked, he didn't think he could take the pain anymore. It was too much to ask one human being to endure, but he knew he didn't have a choice, which in its own way made it all the more painful.

Adrian covered him with his wings. He understood Paul's pain. It was why he'd given him the warning earlier in the day. "Please, Lord," he prayed, "give him peace. Today would have broken an ordinary human, this man is extraordinary."

Then God granted Adrian's request.

Peace poured over Paul, peace he had never experienced before. He knew there and then that he was in the right place with God, and actually, nothing else mattered.

He stayed as he was letting the peace pour over him, touching every part of his being, pouring into his soul, his heart, his mind and spirit. Then the verse came: 'And the peace of God which transcends all understanding shall guard your mind and heart in Jesus.' Phil. 4:7.

He lifted his head at last and looked at Adrian. He couldn't imagine life without this warrior at his side. "Thank you," he said. "I'm where I'm supposed to be. I got a second chance. I also got another chance to see my family. I take it this Sam is the new love in Elizabeth's life, is he?"

"That's not up to me," said Adrian. "That's up to God, but God didn't create humans to live alone. Would you want Elizabeth to be lonely for the rest of her life?"

"No, of course not!" he replied. "And I want my children to have a dad who will spend time with them and enjoy them. That's the truth, yes, my heart is broken, but only because I didn't appreciate what I had. But I don't want my family to be deprived of a loving husband and father. Though I don't understand, why did Aaron call me dad today?"

"Well," said Adrian, "you have to remember, you were Aaron's hero. He will never forget you and when you ruffled his hair, it was like a light switched on in his spirit and he knew you for a split second. It's the purity and innocence of children. They are so much more perceptive than any adult."

Paul smiled, a little part of him was very pleased that his son knew him and acknowledged him, that would stay with him forever.

"Okay," he said to Adrian, "I think I will turn in for the night."

When he walked into the bedroom Mick was sitting up in bed reading the Bible. "Sorry," Paul said, "were you waiting for me?"

"Not really," Mick replied. "Though I wanted to make sure you were okay. It was a very tough day for all of us today, but especially for you. Are you doing okay?"

"Yes, thanks, Mick," Paul smiled. "I've spoken to Adrian. And though in some ways my heart is broken seeing my family again, in other ways I'm happy they have found someone who loves them. So I've got peace, Adrian prayed, and wow, do I have peace, perfect peace."

Mick smiled, "That's all I was praying for. I can go to sleep now, in peace. Good night, Paul."

"Good night, Mick," Paul whispered.

Chapter 63

The next morning all four men were up bright and early. They were all eagerly awaiting news from inspector Tate. John came across to the B & B. He joined them for breakfast and then they made their way to the sitting room to pray for the days ahead.

Having finished praying, John asked, "How long do you think it will take to finish the church?"

"What a funny question to ask." Harold laughed. "After all we went through yesterday, I thought the state of the church would be the last thing on your mind."

John laughed. "Well, it's just, well, as soon as we finish the church, Jennifer and I want to get married. So although everything else may take months to sort out, if the church is ready, I can marry my lady."

They all laughed and agreed. "Let's get across and see how things are going," Harold suggested.

They crossed over and entered the church. It was amazing what had been accomplished in such a short time. The majority of the underlay had been removed, and though there were still patches to be cleaned, they were being seen to by some very efficient ladies. Craig and his men had started on the walls, it looked so bright. Some men were cleaning the windows, letting the sun shine through. It was always a bright church, but with the windows cleaned and the walls painted, it was beautiful. John was thrilled. Paul went to see the men who were sanding the pews. They only had a few more to go.

Mick went into the back room to see Mel. She was deep in concentration. There were pieces of the sound system all over the floor. Mick was a bit taken aback, it looked like she had taken the whole thing apart and was putting it back together again.

"How's it going?" he asked her.

She looked up startled, "Ah, Mick, you're back, well as you can see, I've still got a bit to go, but I'm getting there."

"It looks as if you've taken it all apart and are putting it back together again. Are you?"

"Mmm, yes," she said nervously. "It really was a mess. I thought if we start from the beginning, then we should be able to sort it out."

Mick laughed, he hadn't realised just how good Mel was. "Well, let's get cracking," he said and knelt down beside her so she could show him what she was doing.

The hours flew by, everyone working as hard as possible, word had got out that as soon as they finished the church, John would get married to Jennifer. It gave everyone a little more urgency. They worked side by side, rich and poor alike. John was humming a hymn and before he knew it, everyone had joined in. It was a good place to be. Alice came at lunch time with sandwiches and drinks. Everyone took a break. Mick noticed Craig had managed to sit near Mel. They were laughing and chatting like old friends. He remembered how desolate she had looked. How long ago was that? Not that long really, now she was happy. She had a job, could pay her way, and if he was not mistaken, there might even be a romance blossoming.

John went to see Jennifer after they had finished at the church. She heard his car and opened the door before he could knock. He took her in his arms and kissed her and thought how wonderful to come home to this every night. When they broke away, they sat holding hands, he explained, "Thomas said he can perform our wedding service two weeks on Saturday, or the following Saturday if that suits you better."

"Okay," said Jennifer. "Let's make it the following Saturday. We have a lot to sort out. I want to give my family some notice," she laughed. My mum will be very cross with me for not giving her at least six months' notice. She'll have to buy an outfit. My sister will be bridesmaid, but she wants to choose her own dress. Mum, my sister and I will need to go shopping for my wedding dress. You wouldn't want to get married to someone in rags, would you?"

"If it was you," John told her, "I wouldn't care, but I know that your wedding day is very special and I want you to enjoy every minute of it. I know you won't if I rush you too much. So okay, we're looking at three weeks on Saturday. I'll tell the gang at the church they can slow down a bit. Word has got out that as soon as the church is finished, you and I are getting married, so everyone's working double time. I think if they keep this up, it will be ready this Saturday and then they will be disappointed. And we don't want that!" He laughed.

"You haven't started cooking yet?" he asked her. "Do you fancy going to that posh restaurant in Marlow. I can pick you up at around eight?"

"That would be wonderful," replied Jennifer, "but what brought this on?"

"I would just like to spend the evening alone with you without interruptions."

"I'd love that, thank you. Now go home so I can get myself ready for this special night out."

He kissed her and turned towards his car, as he was walking down the drive, his phone rang. It was Tate.

Chapter 64

"Hello, Inspector Tate," he said.

"Hello, John, I hope I haven't caught you at a bad time?"

"No, not at all, I'm on my way home to get ready for my date tonight. Have you any news?" John asked.

"Yes," said Tate, "they have both been remanded in custody, pending a hearing tomorrow morning. Then the courts will set a date for their trials. There are a lot of big names on that list. They will take longer to arrest and prosecute, but Roles and Kerr will go down first. I wanted you to know how grateful we are for your courage and tenacity. We had no idea how big this was. We've spoken to Superintendent Bryant in Manchester. It looks like he'll have his hands full rounding up the members in his neck of the woods as will Birmingham police department. Scotland Yard are on the case too. In fact, every big city in the UK will be working this. It is the biggest coup we've ever had fighting against paedophiles, and it's all down to you and your friends."

"No, no," said John, "we are just instruments, the real orchestrator is God, when He's on our side, we can't lose. By the way, I wanted you to know I'm getting married in three weeks' time at the church I minister at. I would like to invite you and your fellow officers to the evening service, with your spouses, of course. The following two weeks I hope to be on honeymoon, so if the trial comes up then, I won't be available."

"Thank you," Tate said, "how nice of you to invite us. I'm sure the lads will be delighted to attend. I most certainly will be there. Mrs Tate will love it, another excuse to buy a new outfit." He laughed. "I'll let the courts know your arrangements, though to be honest, I think it will take longer to set the date for trial, probably a couple of months at least."

"That's great," said John, "I can get married and go on honeymoon without worrying about the trial. Have you spoken to Tom and Larry yet?"

"No, not yet, they are my next call. We've also been going through the list of victims. We will be contacting them in the new few days, may even be weeks, there are so many of them. You can see why it may take some time for the trial to come around. Tom and Larry have already agreed to give evidence. Do you know, Roles not only made a list of his victims, he also made a list of Kerr's victims. He named Kerr's victims separately, starting with himself. We've decided to follow up on Kerr's list first, if we get a few witnesses willing to give evidence against him, it will be a slam dunk on both cases. Your services may be required when we find these men and boys."

"How do you mean?" John asked.

"Well, you are a pastor, and I presume you have some experience in counselling? I think a lot of these people will need someone who they can relate to, someone who can relate to them, and I don't know anyone better equipped for the job," Tate said. "I'll let you get yourself ready for your date. If I don't see you before, I'll see you Sunday, with my family."

"Great," said John, "don't forget the service will be held at the B & B, we're still working on the church."

"No worries, we will definitely be there, after today, I don't think I'll ever miss church again."

They said their goodbyes and John hurried home to shower and change. He picked Jennifer up at eight as promised. They had a lovely evening in Marlow, planning their wedding day. John could hardly believe that, in three weeks, this beautiful woman would be his wife.

Chapter 65

The four men ate at the B & B, Mick told them about Mel and how she had taken the sound system apart and was now putting it back together. Then he told them how he had noticed Craig and her chatting. "I hope it will develop into a lovely romance, she deserves it. She is such a lovely person, it's so nice to see her happy."

"I think we should all do what you did," Paul said. "You noticed someone hurting and you helped her, you've been instrumental in changing her life for the better. We should watch out for people who are hurting, worrying, or plain ill and help them. Surely that's what God would want?"

"I agree," said Derek, "who knows how long God will want us to stay here. The church is nearly finished, that won't take long, especially the way everyone worked today after finding out John's plans. Let's make the most of it while we're here."

They retired to the sitting room to pray, they sat around in a circle. Harold led: "Lord, we cannot do anything on our own, show us what you would have us do, and give us the courage to obey. Our angels have shown us the battle over this town. Show us what to do and who to help in Jesus' name."

They sat and chatted, Paul said, "You made a difference in Alice's life, Harold, because you obeyed. Now look at her, she is truly blooming, she looks so happy and healthy. We need to take heed to what is going on around us, we may not have very long as Derek said, let's make the most of it."

The four decided that the next day after working in the church, they would take a wander around the town and let the Holy Spirit guide them.

They went to their rooms. As Paul was in the bathroom, Mick knelt to pray. "I'm not very confident, Lord, in what I'm supposed to do. Please help me!"

Andrew touched his shoulder. "Why do you doubt? What's happened to your faith? You saw Mel hurting and went immediately to help her. I, not even God told you to do that. That goodness is in your spirit. Don't let Satan try to take it from you. You are a good man, and you want to help others. That's all the Lord is asking of you. Don't worry, He will lead you, just rest now and leave it to Him who knows all things?"

Mick smiled and then felt dumb. *Why do I continue to doubt?* he thought. Then he remembered how many time Jesus said to His disciples, 'Why have you so little faith? Why did you doubt? Why did you not believe?' He felt a bit better then, after all, they had spent three years with Jesus and they still doubted. So there was hope for him. He was still smiling as Paul came out of the bathroom.

"What's happened?" he asked Mick. "Have I missed something?"

"No, no," said Mick, "it's just me, I'm still trying to get used to having this faith. I keep thinking I can't do it, I keep feeling that I'm not good enough. But in the end, it's not up to me, it's up to God, and He sent us here, so we just follow His lead."

"I know what you mean," said Paul. "Sometimes I think I'm way out of my league here, and, of course, I am. But like you say, it's not up to me, it's up to God, so we have to forget our own insecurities, but it's hard at times to forget ourselves and our own inadequacy, even though we know we are not alone. I've just thought we are struggling and we've seen the angels and heard the Voice, what must it be like for people who haven't? Can you imagine how muddled they must feel? Derek is right, we need to get out there and do as much as we can before we are moved on to somewhere else."

"Do you think we will be moved on somewhere else?" Mick asked. "I thought that once this assignment was over, then we would be taken into paradise."

"I really don't know, but when I saw the battle going on just for this little town, I thought, what about the rest of the world?" Paul said.

They both turned in for the night, they knew they had a full day ahead tomorrow.

The next morning, the four men had their usual breakfast and prayer session. As they were walking towards the church, they saw a young lad, probably in his late teens. He was sitting on the ground. It looked as if he was begging. They walked up to him to pray with him. When they approached, he looked terrified. The four could see all kinds of horrible creatures crawling all over him. They were in and out of his ears, his eyes, his mouth. Fear was towering over him, consuming him.

Harold bent down so he was at eye level with the lad. "Hi," he said. "My name is Harold. Can I help you?"

The lad started screaming at him, Harold nearly fell over, the lad was so aggressive, he shouted into Harold's face. "Get away from me, I know who you are. You are servants of the Living God, what business do you have with me?" The sound was dreadful. It wasn't a screech as such, but a screech inside a roar. Derek held Harold by the shoulders.

"Are you okay?" he asked.

"Yeah, fine thanks," Harold whispered, though clearly he was shaken.

Then Daniel touched Harold, "This lad is possessed," he said. "The demons have taken over his mind and his body. This is what they want to do with the youth of this town. There is a lot going on in this town and nearby towns that nobody knows about. Reach out to him and place your hand on his arm, and pray in Jesus' name."

Harold did as he was told, though clearly he was afraid he would be attacked. He reached out and took the lad's arm. The boy literally flinched and drew back from him in terror. Harold closed his eyes and concentrated on Jesus. When he opened them again, the boy was sitting staring at him. Fear looked as if he would tear Harold limb from limb. But Harold just smiled at it, which caused it to shrink considerably.

"What's your name?" Harold asked.

"Colin," whispered the young lad. "What do you want? I haven't got any money, please leave me alone."

Harold spoke gently to him. It seemed the demons were afraid to show themselves when the name of Jesus was mentioned. He could see nothing of them as he spoke to him. "We are just here to help you, if you want our help, that is?"

Then Colin started laughing, it was not a pleasant sound. "Why on earth would I need your help," he sniggered. "Go away old man, you can't help me. I'm beyond help." Then he started laughing hysterically.

Harold's heart went out to him. "Nobody is beyond help," he said. "Come with us and we'll get you something to eat, you look as if you haven't eaten in a while."

"Noo-oo-oo," the lad shouted. "Get away from me, I know what you want, you disgust me, leave me alone!!!"

People were walking past and when they heard the lad shouting, they hurried on, not wanting to get involved.

Paul shook his head. "What if we were doing something to this young lad? No one cares. They just cross the street and pretend they didn't see anything."

"And that is the biggest problem with this town," Adrian told him. "It's not just the amount of evil going on in it, it's the complacency among the people. They are afraid to get involved in case it might take up too much of their time or money, so they ignore it and go on with their own lives."

"Isn't that what we all did?" Mick asked.

Adrian smiled at him, "No, actually it's not. Though you were caught in your own insecurities, you still had a heart for others, but these people are afraid of everything. That's why fear has such a hold on this town."

"What can we do?" Derek asked.

"Take the boy into the church, he won't resist you. The demons are afraid of the name of Jesus and they are hiding. So take him with you and lay hands on him. Get John to join you, this is one of the many battles that he will have to face."

Harold and Derek took Colin by the arms and pulled him from the ground. Nobody looked in their direction. Each person passing put their head down and pretended they couldn't see anything unusual going on.

As they reached the doors of the church, Colin suddenly went rigid in their arms. He tried to pull away. "No, no, no, please, let me go!" He cried. "I can't go in there, please leave me alone, nobody can help me, it's too late for me. Please don't torment me anymore."

Mick shouted at the demons, "Be quiet!" he roared, much to the shock of the other three men, who had never heard him raise his voice.

The demons ducked, and Mick held the door of the church open as the men practically dragged Colin through.

Colin started to howl then, it was a pitiful sound. John came rushing to the back of the church to meet the men. "What's going on?" he asked, concerned.

"This young lad—his name is Colin—is possessed," Harold told him. "We have brought him here to pray over him, but we've never done anything like this before."

John looked at them incredulously, "Of course, you have," he told them, "What about the day in my house? What do you think that was?"

"Ahhh," said Paul, "but you weren't exactly possessed, were you?"

"What would you call it?" asked John, "I felt possessed, and you four men were used by God to free me. Why do you doubt yourselves now, especially after all we've been through?"

The four looked at each other ashamed. Here they were, they could see the angels and the demons and had heard the Voice, and they doubted. Here was John, who could see and hear nothing of these things, and he believed.

They sat the boy on a chair and circled him. They began to pray, as they prayed, some of the people working in the church came and stood with them, soon more joined them. Before long, everyone who had been working in the church was standing around the boy praying.

Harold looked up and saw a Light streaming down through the ceiling. That beautiful Light he loved so much. It poured into Colin, covered him from the top of his head to the bottom of his feet, and it kept shining and shining and nothing could quench it.

The men saw the demons scurry away. They were climbing over each other to get out of the way of the Light. As they hit the floor, they disintegrated. Fear hadn't even made it through the doors of the church.

All of a sudden, Colin collapsed. If Harold hadn't been holding his arm, he would have fallen from the chair. He looked as if he was dead. The men closed their eyes and prayed. When they opened them again, Colin was coming out of his stupor.

"Are you okay?" Harold asked.

Colin looked totally confused, "Where am I?" he asked.

"You are in the church," they told him. "Do you feel okay?"

"Em, yes, I think so," he said.

John introduced himself to Colin and shook his hand. "Have you had breakfast yet?" he asked him.

"I don't know when I ate last," Colin told him.

"Okay, let's get you some food and get you cleaned up a bit," John said and took him to his house. The rest of the people smiled at the difference in him and carried on with what they had been doing.

The men followed, knowing they had to hear Colin's story. As they were walking towards John's, Mick said, "Look at the difference between the people in the church and the ones outside. It's as if they are on different planets. As soon as we started to pray, everyone joined in, whereas when we were on the street, everyone hurried by, terrified they might have to get involved."

"There's a lesson here somewhere," Paul uttered. "Imagine if more and more of the townspeople started coming to church, think of what that would mean to the complacency that is killing the place?"

They all agreed. Now they knew what the main problem was, it didn't seem that insurmountable.

Chapter 66

They arrived at John's house. He was making a bacon sandwich for Colin. They sat with Colin and asked where he had come from. "I'm from Marlow," he said. John looked across at him. He and Jennifer had had such a good night there the previous evening. Now here was this young lad in a state, it made him feel sad that while he and Jennifer were having a lovely time, someone was hurting and he was oblivious to it.

Paul looked across at him. "John," he shouted. "Don't do the guilt thing."

John laughed, "I'm sorry, we had such a good night there last night, it breaks my heart to know there are people like Colin here who feel so lost."

"I know," said Paul, "but I really believe God would like you to have some happiness now. This is not the time for guilt. Actually, it's never time for guilt. So you had a good time? Well, thank God that He blessed you, now you can bless others."

John looked at him, "That's a great way to look at it, I will bless as many as I can and enjoy my life too."

They all sat around the kitchen table. "Tell us your story," John asked Colin. "You're from Marlow, where are your parents? Do you have a job? Sorry, I'm getting carried away. Tell us in your own time."

"My name is Colin Wentworth," he said. "My dad left when I was little, then my mum got ill and couldn't look after my sister and I. We were taken into care, they separated us. I haven't seen her since I was nine years old. I was shunted from one foster home to another." His face went crimson and he hung his head.

"What's the matter?" asked John quietly, "It is okay, you are among friends here."

"I was abused in some of those foster homes, also in the care home. I am so ashamed, I should have fought back, I should have done something, but I felt so powerless."

"How old were you when the abuse started?" John asked.

"It started when I was around ten years old. The first foster home was okay, the people were very nice, but I couldn't stop crying about my mum and I missed my sister. In the end, they couldn't handle it. They wanted a child who was happy to be with them. I don't blame them, they were nice and the house was lovely, but I missed my mum and just didn't want to smile and pretend everything was okay, because it wasn't.

When they sent me back to the care home, the people there were disgusted with me. They told me they had placed me in one of the best foster homes in the area and I was very ungrateful. So they weren't bothered who took me after that. They sent me to a horrible place, there were a lot of other foster kids there, and it was filthy. The man didn't work. He was always around, watching. After a few weeks, I knew what was going to happen. I could see the other kids looking at me, it had happened to them too and I was the new kid, so they knew what was coming. He called me into his room. I have never been so terrified. I thought of all the times the last people wanted me to smile, I would have given anything to smile for them once more, but I knew where my destiny lay now. Anyway, he did me, you know what I mean."

180

"Yes," said John, "I really do."

Colin looked at him as if he was a fool. *How could this 'put together' pastor know what it had felt like?*

"Anyway," he continued, "I ran away from that one, then social services caught up with me and put me in another one. The cycle continued, sometimes the people were lovely, but I couldn't relate to any of them. I was so afraid to trust anyone, so they would send me back and say I was unmanageable. In the end, I ran away. I was fifteen.

"I found a group of kids on the streets in London. We slept rough and begged for money. Then one of the kids introduced some tablets. They took the edge off, so we started taking them, then we went on other stuff, stronger stuff, the tablets weren't having much of an effect after a while. Sometimes, I did things to pay for the drugs. So you see," he looked into Harold's eyes, "I'm way past saving, I'm not worth anything, that's why I wanted you just to leave me be."

"Well," said Harold, "that's not the way we do things here." He smiled at Colin. "Nobody is beyond saving."

Paul looked across at John, "What do you want to do?" he asked. "Shall we leave Colin here with you and go back to the church?"

Colin jumped up, "You're not leaving me anywhere with someone I don't know. I'm out of here now."

John caught him by the arm, "Calm down, no one is going to hurt you here. We want to help."

"Yeah," replied Colin, "I know all about that kind of help, thanks, but no thanks. I'll get by on my own."

Paul blocked his way, "I think you should sit down and finish your sandwich and cup of tea. John here might just share something with you that could change your life. Will you at least give it a try?"

Colin looked doubtful and turned to Harold, "You stay with us, please?" He sounded so frightened. Harold had a lump in his throat, again thinking of his three sons.

"Of course, I'll stay," he said.

Colin sat back down at the table and continued eating his sandwich, he looked ravenous. Harold poured him another cup of tea. He could see that Colin was trying to concentrate on the food, afraid of what was coming next, but at least determined to get some sustenance before his ordeal.

John asked Harold to pray with him. They both prayed out loud, much to the consternation of Colin, who didn't know where to look. John asked the Lord for guidance and wisdom, then Harold asked for understanding for Colin and that God would grant him an open heart.

After they had finished praying, John told him his story. He didn't leave anything out. He explained how he had felt, and what it had done to him through the years. He told him how they had finally caught up with the monster that nearly ruined his life, only to find he was now just a pathetic old man.

Colin sat with his mouth literally open. He couldn't believe what he was hearing. *This man had been abused? It didn't seem possible, why wasn't he in the gutter like me?* he thought.

Harold had heard his thoughts and spoke to John, "I think you need to tell Colin the reason you are here today, and why."

John told him about Jesus. He told him that nobody was beyond saving. Jesus had died for all, including Colin, and if he could reach out and ask, Jesus would heal him.

Colin wasn't having any of it. "Sounds like a fairy tale to me," he said. "Thanks for the sandwich and the tea, but I think I'll be on my way."

John rose from the table, "Okay," he said. "But, how about you pay for the tea and sandwich before you go."

Harold looked at him shocked. What was he doing?

Colin, smirked, "Yeah, I thought there would be some catch. What do you want me to do?" he asked sarcastically.

"Well," said John, "we are doing up the church and we need as much help as we can get. How about giving us an hour or two of your time? That is unless you have other pressing engagements?"

"No," said Colin sullenly. "Lead the way." He shoved his hands in his pockets and walked out after John. Harold followed behind laughing to himself. John was very good at this.

They came into the church and Colin took a step back as if he was afraid he would be hit by a bolt of lightning. Harold was behind him, "Don't worry, you're safe here, I promise."

"Okay, what do you want me to do?" Colin asked John in a surly voice.

"We've been trying to get the final bits of underlay off the floor," John told him, "it's proving harder than we thought. We have to do a little at a time. It is stuck to the floor beneath." He took him across to show him a part of the floor that had been cleaned thoroughly. "This, believe it or not, is parquet flooring. Do you know what that is?"

"Eh, no," said Colin, totally uninterested.

"Well, John said, "it's very expensive flooring, we couldn't afford to replace it so we have to do a little at a time so as not to cause damage. See these women? They have been working on this for a while, but they are very patient and have done a fantastic job."

"Okay," said Colin, "where do you want me?"

"I think if you could help the women. One, you won't feel threatened, and two, they need someone to fill their buckets and freshen up the water for them. Can you do that?"

"Of course," moaned Colin and plodded across to the women who were working on the underlay.

He watched as they knelt and soaped and brushed the underlay from the floor. As he watched, he saw how much this washing was changing the floor. At first, it was totally black, then, little by little the parquet flooring became visible. Then there was no black left, just a beautiful floor underneath. He was fascinated.

John saw his face and walked across to him. "See how it works?"

"Yeah, it's amazing. It looks so different to what it was like before, it's like it's brand new."

"Yes," said John, "that's what Jesus does for you when you put your trust in Him. He makes all things new, the old is gone forever."

Colin looked at him and swallowed. He turned away quickly in case John might see the tears stinging his eyes. How had this happened? Why had he come to this town? All he could remember was feeling homesick and wanting to be near where he had lived with his mum. Now here he was in a church with people who believed in something or someone bigger than them, and being told that he could have a clean slate? Was it possible?

Chapter 67

They all continued working on the church. Some of Craig's men had started cleaning more walls preparing for the painting. They had come into the church as if they were coming to do a normal job, but there was something in the atmosphere that was different than anything they had encountered before.

When everyone stopped for a break, Craig's men sat together at a table. They watched as people shared their food, the laughter and the chatter was contagious. They sat watching, wondering what these people had that they didn't. John came across to them. "Hi, lads," he said, "I hope you are okay, have you got enough to eat?"

"Eh, yes, thank you," said the older of the men. "It's a very happy atmosphere here. We are enjoying sitting and watching the people."

"Yes," John replied, "they're a good lot. They have helped me so much in and around the church, we're hoping, when you have finished painting, for the church to be back to its former glory. But we couldn't have done it without these people, and of course, the Lord. He has blessed us so much. We can't begin to thank Him for all He has given us."

The other painters looked down at their plates, slightly embarrassed that John was speaking about God so openly. John could see the thoughts going through their minds. 'He's going to start giving us a sermon now, better not to look at him, then maybe he'll get the hint.'

John smiled and said, "Enjoy the lunch, but remember there is plenty more over here if you're hungry. And if you come tomorrow, don't worry about bringing your own, there is enough for everyone to share." With that, he stood and headed back to the four men.

The painters looked at each other, 'What was going on? He could have used that as an opening to give us a lecture on theology or religion. He could have told us that we were sinners and needed to get to church. What a funny pastor, that doesn't try and drag you into the church. Weird!!!'

John spoke to the four, "I could see they were terrified that I might start lecturing them. I hope I read it right, I'm always afraid that if I don't tell people about Jesus, I'm letting Him down, but at the same time, I don't want to force anyone to come and join us if they're not interested."

"I think you read it perfectly," said Harold, who had watched the scene with interest. "They are confused now. I think they'll want to know what kind of church leader doesn't force people to attend. Well done!"

"Thanks," said John blushing. It is such a good feeling when someone backs you up, and somehow it was even better coming from Harold. John thought of him as the father he never had, there was something so humble about Harold—John was filled with a kind of awe of him.

As they sat eating their lunch, John looked across and spotted Colin sitting at the edge of the table. Others at the table were chatting with each other. He looked as if he was in a world of his own. He didn't join in with the conversation around him and just nodded when anyone tried to include him. John was about to go over to him when Harold held his arm.

"Watch," he told him.

John was confused. This poor lad looked so lost, but he did what he was told and watched quietly. People were standing up and returning to their chores. Mel and Craig excused themselves from their table and approached Colin. When he saw them coming, he bowed his head. He looked like a trapped animal. John's heart went out to him. Mel touched Colin on the shoulder and he nearly jumped out of his skin. He really looked terrified. Then he looked up at her face, she had such a peaceful look, he was instantly drawn to her.

"Do you mind if we join you?" she asked.

"Eh, no, of course not," he replied, but his body language said something completely different. He shifted his eyes towards Craig, he was trying his best to look hard, but the look didn't quite reach his eyes.

They sat with him, Mel next to him and Craig opposite. "It's quite different than anything you've experienced before isn't it?" Mel asked, stretching her arm out to take in all the tables that had been full of people, sharing food and conversations and laughter.

"Yeah, just a bit," he muttered.

Mel would not be put off. She put her hand on his shoulder, "Let me tell you how I got here," she said. She proceeded to tell him her encounter with Mick in the street and how her life had changed dramatically after that meeting.

Craig then told him his story, though not as dramatic as Mel's, it was still quite difficult for Colin to take in.

Mel continued, "We're not trying to grab people in off the street, so we will have a bigger congregation. But we honestly want to help people who are hurting. And you look as if you are hurting inside, will you tell us your story?"

Colin bowed his head again. He thought to himself, *I've told it once already, so one more time won't kill me.* Then he relayed all that had happened to him from the time he went into care and all the bad decisions he had made since. Craig and Mel could see how much he was struggling telling them. His hands never stopped moving, and his legs were shaking. He looked as if he was about to jump up and run. He kept looking around him. He was so agitated, his whole body was in constant motion.

Craig had seen these signs before. They were withdrawal symptoms from the drugs. "What were you on?" he asked Colin.

"Heroin, coke, anything I could get my hands on really," Colin confessed.

"Would you like to be free of all this pain that's going through your body now?" Mel asked him.

"Yes," he whispered. He looked exhausted. "I can't stand these feelings, I feel like there are millions of insects crawling around inside my body. My skin feels itchy and sore at the same time. The only way I know how to stop it is to have another fix. I don't have the cash to buy anything so watch your purse and warn the others. I'll take anything to get rid of this constant feeling that something is crawling inside me."

"You'd take anything?" Craig asked. "I suppose you'd do anything as well, would you?"

Colin sneered, "Huh, should have known, I suppose you want me to do something for you?" He smashed his hand down on the table. "Is there anywhere that isn't infested with perverts like you? Just leave me alone, I don't need your type of help, thanks."

Poor Craig, he pulled back in shock at what Colin was implying. He only wanted to help this lad. He felt like an older brother to him, he couldn't believe that what he had said could be so misinterpreted.

"Oh my gosh. No, no, no, I'm so sorry, that's not what I meant at all. But look around you, we are just normal people. I only gave my life to Jesus a few weeks ago and so did Mel. We've found a peace that's hard to describe, I've never felt anything quite like it. We want you to experience this peace as well."

Mel agreed, "If you had seen me before I met Mick, you would not have believed I was the same person. I felt like my insides were being eaten up by maggots. I wasn't using anything, but I was so worried about money and how I was going to get through the next month and feed my kids that I couldn't think straight. He brought me here, the people were friendly. They helped me out financially and gave me a job.

"Then they told me about Jesus and how precious I was to Him. I couldn't quite believe it at first. I've never had anyone do anything for me before. I never heard of a God who loved me so much that He would give up His Son for me. It sounded unreal, but the more I spoke to people and the more I prayed, the easier it became to believe. Don't get me wrong, I still struggle with the fact that God gave His only Son. I have two daughters and one son. If God asked me to give up any of them, I don't think I could. Then I'm only human, I'm not God, so though I struggle with it, I believe it and it's changed my life."

"So you want me to become a Bible basher, do you?" Colin asked incredulously. "Cause you see, I've seen a few of them at the care home too…"

"Oh," Mel said, "that's awful, I know there is no way you can have a relationship with Jesus and continue to do what these monsters do. Some people use their roles in church as a cover for who they really are. That's why we need normal, ordinary people who are good and kind and want to help others. People without ulterior motives. The people in this church want to help the helpless and down trodden. We want to show the world that there are good people around, people who can be trusted and depended upon."

She stopped suddenly, her eyes bright with tears, but her face was radiant. She noticed the silence. As she looked around, she saw that everyone had stopped what they were doing and were listening to her.

She bowed her head in embarrassment, "I'm sorry for being on my soap box, but I'm very passionate about this subject."

Alice started applauding and everyone joined in, that made Mel even more embarrassed. John walked over to her and put his hand on her shoulder, "I couldn't have put it better myself," he said smiling.

Colin just sat staring at her. He'd never heard anyone speak so passionately about anything in his life. He was still desperate for a fix, but he couldn't move. Where would he go? The thoughts going through his mind were so confusing. Yes, he wanted and needed a fix, but he didn't want to rob from these people who had only shown him kindness and asked nothing in return. He didn't want to betray the trust that they had in him. It had never bothered him before, he took what he wanted and felt he deserved and to hell with the consequences, but this situation was quite different.

Chapter 68

Harold and the others could see the demons crawling all over Colin. They looked like they were scratching and stroking him all over his skin and the ones inside him were worse. They looked as if they were eating him alive from the inside out.

"We need to do something for that boy," Harold told the others. "We can't just sit here and watch him being attacked like this."

"We will help him, if he will let us," Derek said. "He's been through so much. You can see how hard it is for him to trust others, especially men."

Mick looked at Harold, "He trusted you, Harold. In fact, you're about the only one he seems to trust. When we were at John's house, he begged you to stay with him. Will you approach him?"

"Yes," said Harold rising. He walked towards the table where Colin sat with Mel and Craig. They stood up as Harold approached the table, but he motioned for them to stay. The three other men joined them at the table. They sat around Colin, he looked as if he was about to make a dash for it, he truly looked terrified. Harold put his hand on Colin's arm. Immediately, the demons started screeching and digging their claws into Colin's skin. They chanted the same thing they had the first time the men encountered them.

"Get away from us, you men of God. You can't have him, he's ours forever."

"NO, HE'S NOT!!!" Harold shouted. A few heads turned in his direction.

Colin was staring down at his arm where Harold was holding him. It was the only place on his whole body that wasn't screaming in pain. He looked into Harold's eyes, "What's going on?" he asked in a small, frightened voice.

Harold could have cried for this young lad. He wanted to take him in his arms and hug him as he would have done for one of his sons, but he restrained himself. He knew this was not the time.

"Will you take a few minutes to hear what I have to tell you, and will you trust what I say?" he asked Colin.

"I think so," Colin whispered in fear.

"First," said Harold, we'd like to pray."

Colin bowed his head, *Don't they do anything here without praying?* he asked himself.

Harold began, "Lord, we need Your help. We have no idea what to do, this is a completely new situation to us, so we are relying on You to show us the way. We need divine inspiration. Amen."

Everyone agreed and said Amen.

Harold told Colin the men's stories. How each of them, though they had lived good lives, never used the gifts they were given and died before they truly embraced the blessings they had been. He described the 'waiting area' and the 'rainbow people' to perfection. He shared how terrified they were when they thought they were hell bound. He explained how 'The Voice' of God reassured them and gave them this assignment. "We're not on our own on this planet," he said.

Colin tried to pull away, *Bloody aliens now,* he muttered to himself. *How am I going to get out of here?* He didn't know that the others could hear him.

Not only could they hear him, but the four men could see the demon whispering in his ear and knew exactly what was being said to him.

"No, I don't mean aliens." Harold told him.

Colin's head shot up, "Did I say that out loud?" he asked, shocked.

Harold only smiled. "Can I ask you a question? When you were young, before your mum died, did she speak to you about your guardian angel?"

Colin's eyes widened, "Yes," he said. "She told my sister and me that we had guardian angels watching over us. I don't know about my sister, but mine hasn't been much help to me in my life. I suppose he gave up on me and is looking after someone whose life is not such a mess."

Harold looked over Colin's shoulder at his angel, who was standing behind him with his head hung low. He was bruised and battered. One of his wings looked as if it was hanging off. Harold felt such a deep sympathy for this angel of God who was battling daily for the soul of this young man. Though he looked torn to shreds, he still stood guarding the boy and doing his best to shield him.

"No," Harold said, "he hasn't left you. He has never given up on you. If you could only see him and know the battles he has fought on your behalf, you would understand how amazing your warrior angel is."

Colin's angel looked up, Harold could see tears in his eyes, but he just nodded at Harold and whispered, "Thank you."

"So you see," Harold continued, "we see the angels, and we also see the demons. I can tell you now that every part of your body, except where I have my hand, is screaming in pain. It feels like you're being torn apart, as if you're being eaten from the inside out. Your skin feels as if it has been stung by a million nettles all over your body, except this arm."

Colin looked him in the eye, tears started flowing down his cheeks and he just nodded. He couldn't speak. The lump in his throat was blocking his voice box.

"Do you want to be free of this?" He asked Colin.

Colin choked out a yes.

"God can take all this away. You can be cleansed and healed of your addiction. The demons will have to flee, but first you must believe."

Immediately the demons started their screeching and chanting. "He's ours, he's ours, he's ours!!!"

Harold commanded them to shut up. It was like they had been whacked. They continued to claw at Colin, but they were mute. Then the four men saw fear loom over him. It all but engulfed him. His angel was helpless because of Colin's unbelief. Fear whispered something into his ear and his head shot up. He looked past all those sitting around him towards the gate into the church's grounds.

He couldn't believe his eyes. It was the nicest sight and yet the most awful sight he had seen. There, standing at the gate with his usual sly grin, was his dealer. Colin wondered how on earth he had known where to find him, but he didn't care. If he could just get a fix, maybe he could take in all Harold was telling him. He jumped up, pulling away from Harold's grip. The pain immediately shot to that part of his body, but he didn't care. Now was not the time to be thinking of these things, he could see the solution to his problems and it was just a few feet away. He moved away from the group and headed towards his dealer.

As one, each person seated around the table bent their heads in prayer. "Please protect him," Harold prayed. It came straight from his heart. "There, but for Your grace

Lord, goes one of my boys. Help him, strengthen his angel, send Your army Lord, we are desperate."

Colin nearly ran to his dealer. As he got up close, he could see the coldness in his eyes. His smirk said, "I'm in control, you're a pathetic loser. Your life belongs to me, I have power over you and you can't escape it."

"What have you got?" Colin asked him in desperation.

The dealer just sneered, "I've got anything you need. You want your usual?"

"Yes," Colin almost shouted. "I've no cash on me at the moment, but I can get some if you'll just give me the fix now, I will pay you later."

The dealer looked towards the people praying around the table. "I see you've made some nice new friends, they'll be easy picking for someone like you. Nice churchy people, you can bleed them dry, then get me their addresses, you can have the next fix free as well as this one. Is it a deal?"

"Yeah, yeah," Colin hurried him. "Just give me the gear and I'll meet you later with your money and their addresses."

"Where will you shoot up?" the dealer asked him. "You can't very well walk into the church and do it in front of everyone. I've got my car around the corner. I can get you to an alley where you can shoot up in private. Then when you're sorted, you can come back all innocent and fleece these losers." He looked towards the people around the table with their heads bent in prayer. He started sniggering, "What the hell are they supposed to be doing? They are so dumb, they have no idea that they are about to be fleeced by St. Colin. They won't know what hit them."

Colin looked at him properly, for the first time since he had met him. That cold stare, the sneer, all of a sudden he could see through him. The stare and sneer were a cover up for fear. He could feel it emanate from him. He was afraid, of what? He turned to look in the direction the dealer was looking. He realised that he was afraid of the people bowed in prayer. He was terrified of the church. No wonder he wanted Colin to go around the corner and into his car. He couldn't wait to get away from the church. The dealer hopped from one foot to the other, obviously agitated.

"Come on, come on," he growled. "I don't have time to hang around places like these. Do you want to score, or not? If you do, you'd better get a move on, I haven't got all day."

Then, as if a wave had washed over him, Colin felt a peace flow through him. He had never experienced anything like it before and it stunned him. No fix had ever had this effect on him. He couldn't move, he didn't want to move. "Just let me stay like this forever and I'll be happy," he prayed.

The dealer pushed him and brought him down to earth. He knew he had to make a decision, and quick. *Do I take the fix and carry on as before? Or do I give the new life a go?* he asked himself. The crawling and scratching were starting to come back. Should he go with the dealer? But how long would the fix last? How long before he would need another one? If he took the fix, the dealer would want him to rob these people blind. The only people who had taken the time to listen and understand what he was going through. Is this the way he wanted to live his life? He looked towards the people praying, Harold lifted his head and looked straight at him.

What was it that Harold had said? Yes, he remembered, 'You can be free of this, God will set you free, but you must believe.' Then he remembered Mel's story and how she had felt previously. When he looked at her now, she looked so peaceful. "Can I have that?" he asked God.

He heard the voice in his heart say "Yes!"

He looked into the dealer's eyes, "Thanks, but no thanks," he told him.

The dealer nearly fell over in shock. "What????" he screamed at Colin. "Are you stupid? Do you think all these churchy people will give a damn about you once they've heard all you've done? Get real!!! This is your last chance. You won't get a second chance with me. I promise you, you'll be sorry. I'll make sure all these 'nice' people hear about all the things you did. I wonder how they'll feel when things start disappearing. Hah, they'll turn on you so quick you won't know what hit you. I will let them know who is to blame for it."

His face was crimson with rage. Colin could see blotches come out all over his neck and face. He started scratching and pulling his t-shirt away from his neck to relieve the burning itch. A thin film of sweat appeared over his lip. His eyes were bulging so much that Colin was afraid he was having a seizure. "Keep the damn drugs," he shouted, "you'll need them later, when your stupid righteous self comes back down to earth. I'll be back to collect my dues, one way or another. Then he turned and almost fled, he couldn't get away quick enough. Colin was left still holding the drugs, what was he to do now?

While Harold had been praying, he had been watching Colin and the dealer. He could see Colin's angel. He looked beaten and battered, still with one of his wings hanging off. His head was bent low in defeat. Harold's heart nearly broke just watching him. As he watched the scene play out, he nearly fell off his chair. He looked around the table, and everyone was deep in prayer for Colin. All their angels were praying and worshipping God, it was beautiful to see.

At first, it looked like Colin's angel would be defeated. The darkness around the dealer was just like it had been around Peter Roles. It kept reaching out to touch Colin, but his angel kept fighting it off. Then because of the prayers, he saw the sky open and hosts upon hosts of angel warriors came marching to stand with the angel. They surrounded them. Two huge warriors stood each side of him and held him up. The darkness began to shrink. Above Colin, a great light shone. It completely enveloped him. Harold could barely make out his form because the light was so bright. And it stayed and engulfed him, permeating every pore and protecting him. The darkness fled and with it the dealer, the light was too strong. Harold watched as the strength poured back into Colin's angel, he stood with the warriors, now as strong as they were, ready for battle again.

Harold could still see the light shining over and all around Colin. He knew this light was the light of Jesus, there was no other light like it. He couldn't stop smiling, yes, the demons were doing their best to hang on to Colin, but even they had to know they were defeated.

Chapter 69

The itching and stinging was back again. It was worse than ever now. He looked down at his shaking hands desperate for a fix. He could just slink off down the road and shoot up and get rid of this horrible feeling. Then he thought for how long this time?

He looked up towards the church, the people who he had only just met were still bowed in prayer. He knew it was for him. He played back the tirade his dealer had spewed at him. Even with the stinging and itching and the crawling feeling all over him, he had to smile. The dealer had called him St Colin and righteous, two names he had never been called in all his life.

Can I do this? he asked himself.

"With My help—yes!"

It was that voice again, the one he heard in his heart. He looked back towards the church. He was scared, but not terrified. *Well,* he said to himself, *there is no point standing here doing nothing. It's time I tried something different with my life.*

He opened the gate and started towards the group still bowed in prayer. Only Harold was watching, and he was smiling. It was like he knew something had changed in Colin. He still felt the physical effects of withdrawal, but he kept his eyes on the group. These people had only known him for such a short period, and here they were praying for him. They had befriended him, not knowing anything about him. They welcomed him into their group. The thought astonished him. He wanted to be like them. It was like they saw people differently. He reached the table, but he couldn't speak.

Harold stood up and put his arms around Colin. He hugged him and patted his back, saying "Well done."

Colin felt the lump in his throat again, *Will I ever stop crying?* he asked himself.

Harold pulled away and offered him a seat. "You are a very brave boy," he told him. "We are very proud of you and the way you handled yourself with that—" he was going to say 'lowlife', but the saying 'there but for the grace of God' came into his head so he just said, "—young man."

"I'm not too sure I handled it so well," Colin told them. "He's promised to come back and rob you all and blame it on me. I'm so sorry I've brought trouble to you. Maybe you should have left me where I was," he finished lamely.

Derek was the first to respond—"This is why we're here. This is what we were sent to do. You've no need to feel guilty, we'll be waiting for him and so will the police. Now we need to concentrate on you. How do you feel?"

Colin looked down at his hands, they still held the drugs and were shaking badly. "Physically, I feel terrible. I feel worse than I did when I first walked to the gate. It feels like the symptoms have magnified themselves and are pulling at every part of my body. But inside I feel peaceful, like I know this won't go on forever. Does that sound weird?"

"No," all four men said together. They could see the demons hanging on to Colin, trying to scratch and pierce him. They were doing their best to convince him he was not healed. They stood around Colin and prayed. Mick ordered the demons to leave Colin's body, in the name of Jesus. The four had to put their hands to their ears the screeching was so fierce. But they couldn't hang on. The light was shining through Colin now, he was healed. He only had to believe.

"Have you made a decision?" Derek asked him.

"Yes," he said boldly. "I want what Mel, Craig, John and the others have. I want that peace, I want to see people as you do and not always think the worst of them. I'm not sure if God would be interested in me though, but I really want to give it a try. What should I do?"

The four knew that this was John's territory and turned to him. He touched Colin on the arm and led him into the church. This time he went in without fear. They walked to the back of the church and through into the small room behind the altar. As they sat facing each other, John asked Colin if he wanted to make a commitment to God.

"I really do, I want to believe all of this, but I can't get my head around the fact that God would be interested in someone as screwed up as me," Colin told him.

Then John picked up the Bible and read the parable of the prodigal son. Then he read another parable about the shepherd leaving the ninety-nine sheep in search of one. He told him—as he had told Craig—that Jesus said, 'There is more joy in heaven over one sinner repenting than many righteous.' What can you lose?" he asked him. "When you put your trust in Him, you become a new creation. The old is gone, you are given a new start. John showed him the prayer that people usually prayed at this point. Colin read it and nodded, but asked if he could just say what was in his heart to God. John was amazed at this young man. "Of course," he said. "That is what praying is, just letting God know what's on your heart. You don't have to pray it out loud, God can hear you. You don't have to be embarrassed."

Colin looked John in the eye. "I never thought I would be able to do anything like this," he said, "but I want to say it out loud, I want you to be a witness of my promise to God today."

John was truly humbled. "Thank you," he whispered.

Colin bent his head and prayed, "Lord, You know me, You know all I've been through, and all I've done to others. I am so sorry for all the hurt I've caused in other people's lives. I want to change. I want to belong in You. So today, I surrender everything into Your hands. Whatever You have in store for me, I will embrace it, but You know I need Your help every day for the rest of my life."

He lifted his head and smiled. He looked back down at his hands, they were not shaking. He had no stinging or itching over his skin. The turbulence inside him had subsided and the peace that he had felt at the gate now engulfed him. "What happens next?" he asked eagerly.

"Well, I'm organising a course very soon," John told him. "It's called the Alpha course. It's designed to teach about Jesus. Who He is, what He did for us, how He alone paid for all our sins, and how we can come to the Father through Him. It will show you how He treats everyone the same and all are welcome at His table."

"Can you put my name down for that please?" Colin asked.

John smiled, "Of course. Usually the course is held once a week and goes for about ten or eleven weeks. Mel and Craig have asked if we can condense it by meeting a few times a week. You may have heard, I am getting married in a few weeks so we would like to have completed the course before I leave for my honeymoon. We are actually starting it tomorrow night. How does that sound to you?"

"Great, it sounds perfect, thank you."

"Then when we have finished the course, we will have the baptisms. The majority of people who complete the Alpha course want to be baptised. We are hoping that you will feel the same."

"Baptism?" Colin asked shocked. "I was baptised when I was a baby, why do I need to be baptised again?"

John laughed, "I know, it sounds weird, but let me ask you a few questions. Do you remember being baptised? Did you make that decision for Christ yourself?"

"Well no," Colin said. "But my mum was very religious woman and she believed in God so I know I was baptised."

"Okay," said John, "I understand your confusion, most people feel the same. The difference between this baptism and the one performed on you when you were a baby is this. This baptism represents burial and resurrection. When you go down into the water, and it is full immersion, it represents your old life dying and being buried. Then when you come back up from the water, it represents your resurrection into your new life. The old is dead and the new has come to life. Do you understand?"

"Yes, I do," said Colin. "I like the sound of that, the old life dead and buried, that would be wonderful."

He had been so caught up in the prayer and the thought of a brand new start, he'd forgotten about the drugs which he had slipped into his pocket before he started praying. Now he took them out and showed them to John. "What should I do with these?" he asked.

"It's entirely up to you," John said. "You can flush them down the toilet, or keep them and hand them over to the police. They will have some questions for you, especially about your dealer. They would probably find him and arrest him. It may mean you have to go as a witness against him in court."

Colin looked so scared. "I just want to start fresh, I don't want the police asking me about the dealer and digging up my past. I promise you I haven't got a record, and though I may have hurt people's feelings, I've never been aggressive. I don't want to cause any more trouble for you or the people at this church, and I know if my dealer gets wind of me talking to the police, he will cause trouble."

"Okay," said John, "let's flush them, but going forward, you may have to give an account of yourself. If, as I believe, you've been sent here for a reason—we could have quite a battle on our hands. Just always remember, the battle belongs to the Lord, and the victory is ours. Can you commit that to memory?"

"Yes, definitely," Colin replied.

"Do you think you would like to help kids before they get drawn into that life?"

"Oh yes, that would be so good, but do you think I'd be any good at it?"

"I do," said John, "but God needs to heal you completely first, physically, emotionally and spiritually. So we'll take it slow and wait on His timing. It's no good rushing into things without first consulting Him."

Colin and John walked out of the church. Colin looked like a new person, actually that's exactly what he was, a new creation!!! Everyone stood and shook his hand, Mel and Alice hugged him. This was his new family. It was very hard for Colin to take it all in, but he felt that he could start a new life here and he couldn't stop smiling.

The day was getting on so John called a halt to the work. "Let's have an early finish today," he said, "it's been quite eventful and I think we need to preserve our energy. The church is looking great, it will be perfect for the wedding, but I for one have a lot of chores waiting. Have a good evening everyone. See you all bright and early tomorrow morning."

He turned to Colin, and saw that it had just dawned on him that he had nowhere to sleep. He was looking totally lost. "You are welcome to stay at my house tonight, if you'd like?" he said.

"Oh, okay," Colin answered in a small voice.

Chapter 70

Alice interjected, "Sorry, John," she said blushing, "but Colin needs a good, wholesome meal and someone to look after him until he gets back on his feet. So he'll come back to the B & B with me, if that's okay with you? Are you okay with that, Colin?"

"Yes, thank you," he whispered. He was completely overwhelmed. He felt safe and loved for the first time since his mum had died.

Craig tapped him on the shoulder, "I'm looking for apprentices, would you like to try your hand at painting and plastering?"

"Wow, yes please," Colin grinned. "I think I could do that, thank you for giving me an opportunity."

"No problem," Craig said, "I think you will do a great job."

So all was agreed and each went to their relative homes. Mick noticed, just before they left, that Craig pulled Mel aside and whispered in her ear, then gave her a small kiss before he left. He couldn't stop smiling. *I don't think it will be long before we have another wedding in this church,* he thought.

The four men accompanied Colin and Alice to the B & B. Alice took Colin to his room. "This is yours for as long as you want it," she said. She handed him the key, "You can lock it and you will always be safe here. But we need to do something about your clothes, they're a bit of a mess. I think you are the same height as Robert. He has a couple of pairs of jeans and a few t-shirts that he has outgrown. I'm not the only one who has developed a big belly in the last few months." She laughed. "I will bring them along to you and some fresh towels etc. You have a nice shower and I will leave it all outside you door. Evening meal is a 7 pm, I'll see you downstairs for that."

"Thank you," Colin uttered. He thought he was going to cry again, Alice patted him on the arm, "you're family now," she told him.

The four men went to their rooms. Harold asked Derek if he could shower first. Derek was more than happy to oblige. As Harold was gathering his things for his shower, Derek took out an A4 notepad and started writing or doodling in it. Harold had noticed it before, but had never asked about it. When he came out of the shower, feeling clean and refreshed, Derek was still sitting at the desk doodling.

Harold couldn't contain his curiosity anymore. He looked over Derek's shoulder to see what he was doing. He couldn't believe what he was seeing. "Derek," he practically shouted, causing Derek to jump. "I never knew you could draw, you are amazing. These sketches are excellent."

Derek flushed with pleasure, "Yes, I've always enjoyed drawing and painting," he said. "I just never had the nerve to let anyone see them. Since we've been here, I can't stop drawing. I keep seeing things that take my breath away and I just have to get it on paper. Today, I wanted to capture the 'before' and 'after' of Colin."

"Well, you certainly did that. Colin's poor angel, he looked bedraggled when we first saw him. When we prayed and Colin stood up to the dealer, I could see the change in the angel. Then when he and John came out of the church, it was like he had been reborn too. You've captured it perfectly. Can I have a look at the rest?"

Harold turned the pages back and started from the first page. It was John. Derek had drawn him as he looked when they first met him. He also captured fear looming over him. The sketches were incredible. He turned page after page, Derek had caught each person perfectly.

"I think you need to show these sketches to Mick and Paul," Harold told him. "Then let's show John, Mel and Colin. Look at Alice before she knew she was pregnant. She was consumed with disappointment and worry, and the heaviness that surrounded her, you captured it so well. Then look at her as she is now, the light shining from her. You truly are an exceptional artist. I take it this is another of your talents you've been hiding under a bushel!"

Derek laughed embarrassed, "Yes, I guess it is. I really enjoy drawing, but I've never really known whether I was good or bad at it, so I didn't do anything with my drawings. Except put them in a drawer in the house where nobody could see them."

"I see one of the lesser demons looming," Harold said. "We've been concentrating on the really big and dangerous ones. We've missed these little pests and let them move in. We need to pray."

They both knelt where they were and prayed. Derek rebuked the demon of self-doubt, while Harold thanked God for getting him to notice the sketches. They both finished praising and worshipping and Derek went to shower and shave. Harold looked through the book again, it was fantastic. The fact that Derek could put on paper what was going on in the supernatural would be such a blessing to the people affected. When they were ready to go for dinner, Harold picked up the book—just in case Derek might 'forget' it!!

They met Paul and Mick in the bar and Harold showed them the sketch book. Paul was incredulous, "Talk about hiding your light under a bushel," he laughed. "These are tremendous, wait until John sees these, he will be able to see with his own eyes how much he has changed, inwardly and outwardly."

Colin crept into the bar where the men were sitting around talking and laughing with each other. They looked so comfortable together. He wished he could have friends that he could feel like that with. He walked towards their table, even now, he still didn't know if they would welcome him or not. Guilt was hanging on to him, dragging his newfound confidence down.

Harold was the first to notice him. Again, his heart went out to him, he could see the guilt clinging to him and the loneliness that surrounded the boy was tangible. He held out his arms to him. Colin was embarrassed, but he didn't want to leave the other man hanging, so he walked into the embrace. Harold hugged him and said, "You remind me of my youngest son, Joe."

"Thank you," Colin whispered. He never really had a father figure until now, but since meeting Harold, he had felt a certain connection to him. "Your son must have been very proud to have a dad like you."

Harold smiled, tears welling up in his eyes. "I'm not sure proud is the word, but I have three sons and a daughter. I know they loved me dearly, even though I was as stubborn as a mule sometimes. I know I was loved and you can't have a better gift than that, so I'm a very happy man."

"You certainly feel like a father, I would have loved to have you as my dad," Colin said quietly.

Harold blushed, "Well, while I'm here, I'm here for you. But I have to tell you, you still have a lot of those demons hanging around you. I see guilt is the most dominant one at the moment. You need to deal with that, if you don't, it will hold you back and you will not grow into the man God has ordained you to be!"

"Me??" Colin stuttered, "God has a plan for my life? Are you sure?"

The other three men turned towards Colin. Their faces sombre now, he felt a bit intimidated. Paul spoke, "Yes, God has a plan for your life. In fact, God has a plan and purpose for everyone's life. Unfortunately, we humans get caught up in the cares and worries of the world that we miss the blessings. Don't make the same mistakes we did, especially me."

Mick put his hand on Paul's shoulder. He knew what was going through his mind. "We've all made mistakes," he said. "That's why we're here, and thank God we got a second chance. Let's move to a bigger table over there. What would you like to drink, Colin?"

"Orange juice, please."

Alice came with their order. "Harold is really a father figure, even to me," she whispered to Colin. It was loud enough for the other men to hear.

The three men smiled, but Harold went bright red, though he couldn't help smiling himself. He knew in his heart what God wanted him to do. Help the lonely, especially the young and vulnerable. Well, he could do that, as long as God sent the young to him, he would look after them.

Mick turned to Derek, "Did you bring your pencil with you?" he asked.

"As a matter of fact, I did," Derek told him. He took out the pencil and began to draw Colin. Before he started, he showed Colin what he'd been like when they first met. How he had been covered with demons, small and large. They were pulling him in different directions. Now he wanted to sketch him with just a few demons clinging to him. But as he sketched, he noticed Colin stare at him with fear in his eyes. Derek saw fear loom behind Colin and envelope him. It was so sudden that the others hadn't seen it happen.

Derek quickly sketched it so Colin could see exactly what was happening in the spirit world. Then he looked behind to see what Colin was so terrified of. Two men had entered the bar. They were standing, waiting for Robert to pour their pints. One of them looked extremely rich and powerful. The other looked like his lackey.

"What's wrong?" Derek asked Colin. "What frightened you just now? You look terrified."

The others finally took notice and Harold put his arm around Colin's shoulder. But instead of him relaxing into the embrace as he had before, he pulled away and moved stiffly to the other end of the table. Harold was shocked and not a little hurt at Colin's reaction. Derek looked at Harold and said, "One or both of those men at the bar has terrified Colin."

Alice came to the table to check everything was okay. Harold asked if she'd mind them using the small sitting room for a while.

"Of course not," she told them, "feel free."

Harold and Paul guided Colin into the small sitting room. Derek gestured to Mick to stay where he was for the moment. "I'm going to move around to the other side of the table so I'm sitting opposite you," he whispered. "We'll pretend I'm sketching you, I want to sketch those two men at the bar, there's something about them that scared Colin."

So Mick moved around and Derek started sketching. When he looked with his spiritual eyes, his hand froze over the page.

"What's wrong?" Mick asked shocked.

196

"I thought I'd seen depravity and evil in Roles and Kerr, but it's nothing like I'm seeing now. He got himself under control and started sketching as fast as he could. First, he sketched each man without the ugliness around them. Then he began to sketch the demons. It took pages of his sketchbook to capture all the demonic creatures crawling and hovering over the pair. By far, the most possessed with evil was the rich and powerful looking one.

Derek had to use all his willpower not to stop and stare. He had never seen so many demons in one place. One or two of these demons tried to latch on to Alice as she cleaned tables, but they bounced straight off the light around her. Derek quickly prayed for Robert, he wasn't sure if he had made a commitment to the Lord so he prayed for protection for him. Then lo and behold, the demons bounced off him too. Derek finished his sketches and he and Mick moved to the sitting room.

Chapter 71

As they walked through the door, they saw Colin sitting with his head bent. Harold and Paul were praying over him. Derek could see the mighty battle going on over their heads. It was hard to tell who was winning. The battle was ferocious. Colin's angel was out in front slaying everything that came at him. His wings covered Colin, protecting him from the onslaught. It was a bloody affair, Mick and Derek rushed over and joined in prayer.

Alice came into the room, she could tell by the posture of the men that something beyond her comprehension was going on. She rang John immediately asking that he come quickly, something very strange was happening. He in turn rang Craig and Mel. Craig said he'd be there in minutes. Mel had the children to look after, but agreed she would be in prayer until she heard back from him.

John arrived and Alice ushered him into the sitting room. A few minutes later, Craig arrived. Alice spoke to Robert, "Will you be okay here on your own? I feel I need to join the others in prayer." She had a funny feeling about the two men at the end of the bar. She couldn't put her finger on it but somewhere deep within her, a feeling of unease crept over her. She pretended to give Robert a hug and whispered in his ear, "Be careful of those two men, there is evil around them."

Robert told her he would be okay. Normally, he would have laughed at her for her vivid imagination. These last few months, however, had changed his attitude to the supernatural completely.

"I've put the armour of God on me. I didn't like the atmosphere that those men brought in. I'll keep praying. Alice, I need to ask you something."

She looked at him expectantly. "When this is over, and maybe even before that, I'd like to ask John to baptise us. Are you okay with that?"

Her face lit up, "Of course. I felt the Lord telling me to wait for you to make the decision. It's been a bit frustrating, but it's worth the wait. I'll come back as soon as we've won the battle."

She joined the others and as Derek raised his head, he could see the angels had the upper hand. The demons were being slain, fear was retreating. Guilt was shrivelling. They kept praying in tongues. Alice and Craig, heads bent, kept praying in their hearts. Harold had his hand on Colin's shoulder the whole time. He finally felt the lad relax. It was like all the tension poured out of him, he practically slumped onto the table. He looked exhausted. He lifted his head eventually and looked around. Six men and Alice surrounded him, praying for him. He could feel the strength return to his body. He still didn't want to see those men at the bar, but as long as he was away from them, he could cope.

As the prayers ceased and each of the four men watched the demons flee, Harold squeezed Colin's shoulder. "Do you want to tell us what happened?"

Colin didn't think he could speak, the memory of what those men had done, especially the older one, was too terrifying, even after all these years. But then something broke inside him, it was as if he had buried something deep inside him and locked it with a big padlock. All of a sudden, the padlock snapped. He knew he could finally speak of the dreadful things that he had seen during his time in care.

He looked at Harold, he really was like a dad to him. He started to explain, "Between foster homes, I had stays in care facilities. It wasn't pleasant, and the abuse was rife. It was mostly physical and mental abuse by the male care assistants. We were to tow the line or face the consequences. Most of us towed the line as much as possible, but we knew they were waiting for an excuse to hurt us. So if any of us stepped out of line at any time, we were for it. Then one night, that man, the one at the bar, came into the dorm. He handed one of the staff a wad of notes and told him to disappear. In the bed beside me was a young boy, he was only six or seven, he was shy and timid. We older ones knew what it meant when someone like that man came to the home.

"He walked over to the young boy's bed and pulled the blankets off him. 'You need to come with me,' he told him. The boy looked terrified. The man looked at each one of us and said, 'Go to sleep and forget what you've seen, unless you want to be next.'

"Then he took the boy into another room, we could hear the boy crying and then screaming. The more he screamed, the more that monster laughed. He came out after about half an hour, the boy was nearly unconscious. 'I'm taking him with me, but don't worry, I'll come back for a few more lucky boys. It depends on how long it takes me to tire of this little fellow.

"It went on for months. He would come in, pass the money to the care assistant— that's the one sitting with him. Then he'd choose another boy. We lived in terror from day to day. A few of us tried to run away, but we were always picked up by the police. They were told we were troublemakers and so they brought us back to the home. They were the worst years of my life. I was never chosen, but I lived in fear that I could be next. I had been abused before and knew what that was like, but to hear the screams of the boys he took has given me nightmares for years. I finally got away when I was fifteen, but I will remember his face until the day I die," he finished, with tears streaming down his face.

"What happened to the boys he took?" Harold asked softly.

"I don't know, they never came back to the home, it was like they disappeared off the face of the earth. When any of us built up the courage to ask about them, we were told they had been adopted and we needn't worry about them anymore. We knew it was a lie, but we couldn't do anything about it. Who would have believed us? Then I saw him here, I couldn't believe it, it's the first time I've felt safe and then he comes back into my life." He shuddered. "I haven't seen him in over six years, but I'll never forget him. What if he recognises me? Oh God!!" He started shaking again.

Harold put his hand on his shoulder saying, "Hush, Colin, he won't get near enough to see you, we will protect you, I promise."

Colin physically relaxed, and the others could see how much he trusted Harold.

"Who is he talking about?" John asked. "I was in such a rush to get in here I didn't take any notice of anyone in the bar."

Derek showed him the sketch of the two men he had made earlier. The colour drained from John's face.

"What's wrong?" Paul asked.

"Remember I told you about the incident in my previous parish?"

"Yes," they said in unison, still confused.

"Well, unless I'm very much mistaken, that's the man who orchestrated my removal from the parish. That's the man whose child I was accused of assaulting."

"Oh," said Paul, "what's going on? I thought we had caught all the men involved in the paedophile ring?" He was quite upset. He spoke to Adrian in his heart. *Why were we led to believe it was all over? How did this one get away? Did God not know about him?* Then he apologised, "I'm sorry, I didn't mean that, it's just such a shock to hear about someone who'd slipped under the radar completely."

"He hasn't," Adrian replied. "God knew that if you had known about him, you would have gone after him. That could have been very dangerous, remember these battles are not between flesh and blood but are in the spiritual realms. He has been in hiding. He heard about Tony Kerr and Peter Roles. He doesn't believe they or the police have anything on him, but he's kept a very low profile since the arrests. God was waiting for the perfect time. The time when he would show himself and here he is."

"Why here?" Paul asked.

"He thinks he's safe in a different parish. He's miles away from his usual stomping ground. He didn't know he would be identified by a former boy in care. Or by a previous pastor, God works in mysterious ways."

"What do we do now?" Mick asked. "We can't just go up to him and accuse him of abusing boys."

"No, but I could," Colin said.

Harold patted him on the shoulder, "You don't have to do that," he said.

Colin looked into Harold's eyes. Harold could see the fear in Colin's face, but it was nothing like it had been.

Colin turned to John, "You went after your abuser, didn't you? In the process brought down a whole ring of paedophiles. I can't stand by and let someone like him walk away. I couldn't live with myself. I need to do something."

Chapter 72

The six men and Alice looked at each other. "We need to pray for guidance in this." Paul turned to Colin, "We need to know what the Lord is asking us to do. We also need protection for you."

They bowed their heads in prayer asking the Holy Spirit to guide them. They knew that this man had been brought to their attention for a reason. If they ignored it, he could walk away and Colin would spend the rest of his life in fear and guilt. But they couldn't just walk up to him—or, could they?

They saw they had been letting doubt enter their minds again. They wanted to protect Colin, but how? If he confronted this man, then no matter what happened, at least he had done something, and they knew God was on their side. How could they lose???

When they finished praying, they had made a decision. They would encourage Colin to confront him. Then John interjected. "I will stand with him. I know this man and I can't let Colin face him alone."

They all agreed, but would be behind them in prayer.

"Are you ready?" John asked Colin.

"Yes," he replied. "It's time I took my life back."

They walked towards the two men at the bar. They were whispering, but loudly. The one, whom Colin had pointed out, was called Falconer. John remembered him very well.

Falconer was pointing his finger at the other man, poking him in the chest. Both John and Colin could overhear their conversation.

"I don't care where you want to go," Falconer told the other man. "I've paid you a lot of money over the years, you belong to me. You start running immediately after the arrests of Kerr and Roles, the police will be snooping around. You won't get another penny from me, just keep low and we can wait this out."

John tapped him on the shoulder. He jumped as if he'd been shot. He turned and recognised John immediately. "Oh, look who it is. The loser!! What are you doing hanging around here? Still trying to find a job?" He snickered.

"No offence, but this is a private conversation and you were not invited. So if you don't mind, I'm busy."

"Oh, but I do mind," John told him forcefully. "I know it was you who orchestrated my removal from the last parish. I'd like to ask you why? And don't insult my intelligence by telling me it was because I abused or accosted your son, we both know that was complete fabrication. But you would know all about abusing boys, wouldn't you?"

"What the hell are you talking about?" Falconer practically shouted. "Is it because I was a business colleague of Tony Kerr? Are you accusing me of having something to do with his and Roles' heinous deeds? Go away and bother someone else." Then he shouted to Robert, "Barman, two more beers here."

He turned his back on John, thinking he would slink away, defeated, but John just laughed. He turned quickly to see what was so amusing.

John said, "You can deny it, if you want, but if you're both so innocent, why is your friend here sweating? It's hardly a sauna in here!"

The other man tried to push past John and Colin. "I want no part of this," he said.

Colin stood in his path. "I think it's too late for that, don't you? Remember me?"

The man balked, "You were in the care home!" he whispered and tried harder to get away but couldn't get past Colin.

"Yes, I was," Colin told him. "You worked at the home. You were supposed to look after us. But I saw this man give you money to close your eyes as he abducted young boys. You turned a blind eye and a deaf ear to the screams of those little ones. But I remember, I will never forget. You're going down for it, the police are on their way, there's no escape."

Falconer turned around to look at Colin. "Don't be ridiculous, do you know who I am? I will stamp you into the ground, you're nothing. Who do you think the police or anybody else will believe? Your word, or mine?" Then he laughed, it wasn't a pleasant sound. "You haven't a chance, I can do anything I want and nobody can touch me."

"Oh, we'll see about that!" John told him. He had seen Robert call the police when Colin had said the police were on their way.

A few minutes later, as the four at the bar stared each other down, the door opened and Inspector Tate walked in. He walked over to John, ignoring Falconer and the other man.

"What's going on here, John?" he asked. "Are you okay?"

"Yes, thanks Inspector, I'm good. This is my friend Colin. I think you may want to hear what he has to say, especially about these two men here."

"I did nothing, I never hurt those boys," the care assistant shouted. "I'll tell you everything, it was him," he shouted, pointing at Falconer. "He forced me to do it."

"Okay, that's enough," Tate said. He turned to his officers and told them to handcuff the two at the bar. "Are you coming to the station with your friend?" he asked John.

The four men left the group and joined John saying "Yes!"

They could see Tate's face. They could practically read his mind. They knew he was scared, after what had happened earlier with Roles, they understood how he felt.

Falconer immediately insisted that he be allowed to phone his solicitor. He turned to John and Colin, his face blood red with rage. "Who do you think you're dealing with here? I'll be out in the morning, they can't hold me. I am rich and powerful. But know this, when I get out, I'll sort you two out, you can put money on that."

"Is that a threat I hear, Sir?" Tate asked.

"No," Falconer answered, "it's a promise."

The men looked at Colin, they could see him swallow nervously. John put his hand on his arm and said, "We're covered, don't be afraid. He won't touch you. That's a real promise!!!"

The two men were taken into custody. Tate spoke to John and the others. "Let's hope it's not a repeat of the incident with Roles," he said. "I don't think my officers could take another incident like that."

"We'll be covering you in prayer, and we'll wait to see what happens," John told him.

Inspector Tate didn't look all that confident. He asked John and Colin to come to the station with him in his car. They did and the four men turned to Alice and Craig. "We know you can't sit here praying all day and night, but pray as you go about your business please. Especially pray for Colin that he is brave throughout this ordeal," Harold asked them.

"Yes, of course!" They said in unison and the men left to follow John and Colin.

As soon as they reached the station, Falconer and the care assistant were separated. Falconer was put in one interrogation room and the assistant (who they found out was called Hughes) was taken to another. Falconer demanded they take off the handcuffs. The poor officer who was ushering him into the room was so intimidated he took the handcuffs off without asking a senior officer. He left the room as fast as he could and locked it.

Falconer immediately rang his solicitor. The officers could hear him shouting down the phone.

"Get here now," he was shouting. "I don't care how busy you are. I pay you a lot of money, so get yourself down here now!"

Two police officers stood outside the room. Falconer was shouting and swearing. He started threatening to sue the police department for unlawful arrest. The officers looked at each other, they knew Falconer hadn't been charged with anything, he wasn't under arrest, but they weren't going into the room to explain anything.

Tate, John and Colin arrived at the station, followed by the four men. Tate took a statement from Colin regarding his accusations against Falconer. Tate explained they needed dates and names of boys taken. Colin said a silent prayer before giving his statement. He really wanted to remember the names of the boys, but nothing was coming into his mind. "Please, Lord," he begged, "help me remember something."

Tate asked if he was ready to give the statement. Colin nodded. As he was relaying his story, the names of the boys came into his head. He could hardly believe it, it was as if someone was whispering each name into his ear.

When they were finished, Tate shook Colin's hand and thanked him for having the courage to go up against Falconer. He turned to John and said, "It will be hard to get a conviction, but we'll do everything in our power. I reckon the care home will have covered their backs and deleted these boys' names from their records. Falconer's solicitor will ask a jury whose word should they take—the rich and powerful man, or a previously homeless boy."

"What about that man Hughes?" John asked him.

"I'm on my way to interview him now. But to be honest, the same applies to him. We just don't know who Falconer has in his pocket. Will he get to the jury before the trial? Even if the trial goes ahead, how convincing does it sound that this Hughes would be honest enough to tell the whole truth, having taken bribes for years from the accused? You can see our predicament. Would you come with me when I interview him, please? I know you can't come into the room, but you could pray for me!" He bowed his head, embarrassed.

"Yes, of course," John told him. "Will you be okay?" he asked Colin, who looked quite uncomfortable in the police station.

"Eh, yes thanks," Colin whispered.

"I'll call Craig and get him to pick you up and take you back to the B & B. Is that okay with you?"

Colin nodded, looking very relieved. John called Craig immediately. Craig said he would be delighted to pick Colin up.

On their way, Tate saw the other four men and asked if they would join John in praying. They, of course, agreed.

Colin went to the waiting room. He wasn't used to helping the police, or being anywhere near a police station for that matter. So he bowed his head to pray. First, he thanked God for everything that had happened to him having met the four men on the road. Second, to ask God to make sure none of the police officers could identify him.

John and the four men went with Tate. They asked Tate if they could watch the proceedings through the two-way mirror. Tate agreed as he wanted their opinion of what exactly was going on in that room, spiritually.

Falconer was storming up and down. Paul turned towards the others and said in an astonished voice, "Can you see what I see?"

They all nodded their heads in agreement.

Chapter 73

The men stood stunned. The demons around Falconer were not fear or dread, or guilt. They were pride and arrogance. Pride looked like a beautiful woman. She flitted around Falconer, whispering things in his ear, touching his arm, his face and covering him with her arms. The men could hardly take their eyes off her, but the more they looked, the less attractive she became. Having looked at her for more than a few minutes, they could see just how ugly she was. She was actually one of the ugliest demons they'd seen, and they'd seen a lot of demons in their short time back on earth.

Then arrogance took over. It was huge, it nearly filled the room. It looked very powerful and there was no battle going on here. Arrogance had the upper hand and nothing seemed to be able to come against it.

Paul turned to Adrian, "Where is Falconer's angel?"

"This man," Adrian answered, "is too arrogant. He has let arrogance possess him. In doing so, he refuses to believe in God. He is not confused as some are at the existence of the Divine. He thinks he is more powerful than any God. He laughs at the idea of a guardian angel so he loses his angel's protection.

"He is left to the demons. His angel fought with arrogance and pride for years, but the more money Falconer made, the more arrogant and proud he became. Eventually, God called his angel back into heaven and Falconer gave himself completely over to evil and depravity."

The four men shook their heads in horror. Paul explained what they had seen to John and what Adrian had told him. John was shocked that he had actually known this man, though thankfully not very well.

Tate opened the door and said, "Let us see how Hughes is getting on. Shall we?"

They walked to the next interrogations room. They looked through the two-way mirror again. Hughes was completely covered by fear. It had totally engulfed him. It was hard to see any other demons around him, fear was so enormous.

"Is it safe to go in?" Tate asked the men.

"Well, he's covered by fear, so I don't think he will cause you any problems," Derek replied.

"Thank you," Tate said and walked into the room leaving the men outside praying.

"Name?" Tate asked.

"Matt Hughes," the man answered.

Tate noticed the beads of sweat on Hughes' face. His shirt showed rings of sweat around his armpits. *This man is really terrified,* Tate thought. He read him his rights, emphasising that he was entitled to a solicitor. He didn't want anything coming back at him in the trial.

Hughes refused a solicitor. He was so overcome with fear he just sat and answered the questions Tate fired at him.

What Tate heard, made his skin crawl. The total lack of sympathy that Hughes had shown for the young boys was sickening. Even now, as he was being questioned, all Hughes was concerned about was himself! He just wanted to know what would happen to him. Not once did he show the least bit of compassion for any of the young boys. He was worried that he would end up being blamed for everything. Tate learned that Hughes had kept a diary of all the boys Falconer had taken. He was willing to give evidence against Falconer and redeem himself so he told Tate everything.

"Where is the diary?" Tate demanded, he was becoming very angry with Hughes. *What are these men like?* He thought to himself, *Hughes and Roles keeping accounts of what was happening.* He understood Roles had a problem, a sickening one, but a problem anyway. But Hughes, it had been pure greed, he hadn't an ounce of compassion in his whole body.

"I want a deal first," Hughes shouted.

"Oh, do you?" Tate asked sarcastically. "What kind of deal were you thinking of?"

"I don't want to go to prison, they'll kill me there, I know. I know what other prisoners do to paedophiles. You need to ensure I don't go to prison."

"But I thought you weren't a paedophile. You said you did nothing to these boys?"

"I'm not, it had nothing to do with me. I was just obeying orders," Hughes whimpered.

"You just handed them over to a paedophile and a violent one at that. I've been told that none of them have ever been heard of since. Is that correct?" Tate snarled at him.

"I don't know what he did with them. I didn't want to know. If you go against Falconer, you end up dead."

"Oh, so you were afraid for your life. Afraid you'd end up dead, what about these young boys? What's happened to them? If I find that any of these young lads are dead, I will be charging you with first-degree murder, do you hear me? Where's the diary?"

"I won't tell you until I get a deal." Hughes dug his heels in, he was frightened, but he still wouldn't budge.

"I'll get back to you on that." Tate stood and slammed the door as he left the room.

He called one of his officers and asked if Falconer's solicitor had arrived yet. The officer informed him that he was on his way.

"Let me know as soon as he arrives," Tate instructed him.

He went to join the men. They had been standing, watching the interview with heads bowed. Tate knew they had been praying. This was all so new to him, praying about a case? What would his superiors think?

Tate and the men retired to the canteen. "Did you hear the whole interview?" he asked the men. "He has a diary with the names of all the boys in it. If they match up with what Colin has given us, we may actually have a case against Falconer. But he wants a deal. He doesn't want to go to prison."

"What happens now?" Paul asked.

"We're waiting for Falconer's solicitor to arrive. It's a different situation than Roles and Kerr. We were witnesses to the attempted abduction of a minor, that's how we could get a search warrant so quickly. But unless we offer Hughes a deal, which I'm very reluctant to do, I doubt we'll get a search warrant for his home or place of work. Without that, Falconer could walk, as the evidence is hearsay. We need something concrete."

As he was speaking, Paul was remembering the day at the church when Roles and Kerr had Aaron. His heart thumped and he thanked God that they had got there in time. He looked across at Tate and saw a new demon hovering over him. It seemed to flit from one side of him to the other. It looked like it was whispering in his ears. "What is it?" he asked Adrian.

"Doubt!" Adrian told him. "Doubt is clouding his judgment and he needs to be on the ball for this. He can't let it into his heart. This is the biggest battle he has ever had to fight. You need to tell him God is on his side. The victory is his, he just has to believe."

Paul reached over to Tate and put his hand on his shoulder. "You understand about us, don't you?" You know what we can see and hear?"

Tate nodded.

"Well, right now, doubt is clouding your mind. You may never have thought of doubt being a demon, but believe me it is. To be honest, I think next to fear, it is the most debilitating. It's robbing you of your usual sound mind and common sense. God will not let Falconer harm any more boys. I can promise you that. So work with what God has given you, and stop doubting yourself."

"Thank you," Tate said. "I feel quite helpless at the moment. I don't know where to go from here. I don't want to let young Colin down. He stood up to Falconer even though I could see the fear in his face, he didn't back down. So I don't want to do anything that might jeopardise the case and see Falconer walk."

"Then, may I make a suggestion?" Derek asked him. "We've been praying but I think you need to pray against the doubt and uncertainty that's going through your mind at the moment."

"I don't have to pray out loud, do I?" Tate asked, obviously embarrassed.

John laughed, "No, Ian, just tell God what's on your heart and ask Him to help you through it."

Tate nodded, easier said than done. He couldn't remember the last time he had prayed in the company of others before he had met these men. But to them, it was the most natural thing to do. So he bowed his head, he could feel the blood rushing to his face in embarrassment. In his heart, he prayed for wisdom and clarity. At first, his prayers were stilted as if he was just saying the words, but then he felt a peace settle on him. Something he had never felt before. It seemed to permeate his whole body, soul and spirit. Without thinking, he began to pray out loud. Asking for forgiveness for his unbelief and asking for guidance through the Holy Spirit. He then asked Jesus to be Lord of his life. When he finished, he looked at the five men, he had a broad smile on his face and his eyes lit up with a new confidence.

"I've never felt this good in my entire life," he told them. "Thank you and thank You God for introducing me to these men."

"Amen," they chorused.

Just then an officer came into the canteen and walked across to Inspector Tate. "Mr Falconer's solicitor has arrived, Sir," he said.

"Okay," said Tate, "show time, please keep praying for me."

Chapter 74

The inspector walked into the interrogation room occupied by Falconer and his solicitor. His Sergeant, Sergeant Philip Moore, looked up at him and looked again. Something had changed in his boss. He couldn't put his finger on it, but something was definitely different. He looked more confident. His boss never had lacked confidence really, but Sergeant Moore had seen a look of doubt on the Inspector's face when he went up against Falconer. Now all that doubt seemed to have disappeared.

He must have found some new evidence, he thought. He felt a bit disgruntled because normally his inspector would share any new evidence with him. *Maybe he just hasn't had the time,* he decided.

Inspector Tate smiled at Moore then turned his attention to Falconer and his solicitor. He noticed the solicitor was one of the top solicitors in the country. But that didn't bother him. He knew that his 'helper' was much more powerful.

"Good afternoon," he said smoothly. "Now that your solicitor has arrived, maybe you can answer a few questions for us, Mr Falconer."

"I don't have to put up with this rubbish!" Falconer shouted.

The Sergeant winced at the power and volume of Falconer's voice. He looked across at Tate and was amazed to see him smiling.

"Some very serious allegations have been made against you. And you must understand that we have to investigate these, whether true or false. So please calm down and answer the questions."

"You must be joking!" Falconer shouted again. "What allegations, from whom? A street kid, a drug addict? Surely, you're not going to waste your time on what that kid is saying. Is this what my taxes pay for? The police taking the word of a drug addict, running around wasting time. Why don't you get out there and solve some real crimes?"

"Actually, we have another witness who has informed me that he will produce evidence to back up these allegations. So please, can we get on?"

"What other witness?" Falconer asked. "No one has anything on me. Do you think I'm stupid that I'd allow someone to hold anything over me?"

"Well then, if these accusations are false, you will have no objection answering my questions, will you?" Tate was smiling broadly.

He looked straight into Falconer's eyes. He could feel the evil emanate from him, but something else was in his eyes. He hadn't seen it before. It was fear!!! Though he tried to cover it but Tate saw right through it.

"My client will answer your questions within reason," his solicitor said. "He is not under arrest I take it?"

"No, Mr Falconer is not under arrest at this time. He is helping the police with our enquiries."

Then he turned to Falconer again. "We have received information pertaining to the abuse and abduction of minors, Mr Falconer. Have you anything to say?" Tate looked straight at him.

"Ridiculous," shouted his solicitor. "How dare you accuse my client of such heinous acts?"

"No, Sir," Tate said. "I have not accused your client of anything. But we have taken statements from two eyewitnesses that put your client at the scene of these said abuses and abductions. Naturally, we have to follow up on these statements. I just wanted to hear your client's side of the story, before we set things in motion."

"What things?" asked Falconer agitated?

"On the word of two independent witnesses, we will proceed to request warrants for your business and home addresses. We will also be chasing up other witnesses, of which I'm told, there are several. So we will be following all leads. Now again, Mr Falconer, what have you to say to these accusations?"

"Show me your proof," Falconer sneered.

"I believe you are acquainted with a Mr Tony Kerr and a Mr Peter Roles?"

"Yes, so what? They are business colleagues of mine," Falconer replied.

"They have been recently arrested for the attempted abduction of a young boy. Mr Roles has been extremely helpful. We have yet to hear Mr Kerr's full story, but I'm sure it won't take us long to find out what he knows."

Falconer looked furious, but was that a bead of sweat running down the side of his face?

"If you had anything on me, you would have arrested me by now. I'm leaving." Falconer turned to his solicitor, "We're out of here," he said. His solicitor stood up, he wasn't looking very confident now.

Tate stood and opened the door for them. "Good day, gentlemen," he said smiling. "I'm sure I'll be seeing you both in the very near future."

Falconer grabbed the door, his confident attitude truly dented.

Tate knew they had him, but they would have to work fast. He watched as they left the building, then turned to his Sergeant Moore, "I want him followed," he told him. "He's seen your face, who do we have that's good at surveillance?"

"We can send Connors. He's done a few tails and he's just returned from holiday so Falconer won't have seen him."

"Ok, great, get on it now. I want to know his every move. Tell Connors to report back immediately if he sees Falconer going anywhere near any children's homes. I'm not having him near any kids if I can help it. Also, get someone to relieve Connors at four thirty and I want him watched through the night. I think he's rattled, but we need to be careful. He's not lying when he says he is a powerful man, we don't want him screaming police harassment. So Connors during the day, one other for the evening and get two for the night. They can keep each other awake. I don't want anyone sleeping on the job and missing something," Tate instructed him.

Sergeant Moore got right on it, he watched as Falconer and his solicitor stood talking outside the station. Falconer was pointing his finger at the solicitor, obviously shouting at him. *That's nice of them,* he thought, *giving me time to organise a tail.* He called Connors over and told him what he needed to do.

"Don't let him see you, but don't let him out of your sight either."

Connors left immediately. He turned his head away as he walked past Falconer and his solicitor. He caught snippets of their conversation. *If only I could hang around,* he thought. Falconer was speaking in a low voice, but it sounded threatening enough. Connors heard him say, "It's why I pay you the big bucks. If Tate gets anything on me, you make sure it disappears. I don't care how you do it, just make this go away."

Connors was itching to look back and see what the solicitor's reaction to this order was. *Better not,* he thought, *I could blow the whole thing. Better let the Sergeant know what Falconer's planning, so he can be prepared.*

Falconer got into to his Rolls. Connors gave him a few minutes lead and then started following him. He drove a few cars behind him through the city centre, making sure he couldn't be detected. The city streets gave way to more rural areas so Connors had to be extra vigilant not to be spotted. Eventually, the Rolls stopped at large gates leading to what only could be described as a country estate house. It was surrounded by eight-foot walls, topped with barbed wire. Connors continued down the road, watching Falconer in his rear view mirror. He watched as the gates opened, obviously Falconer had a remote control for them.

Chapter 75

Back at the station, Inspector Tate was sitting with the five men. "So," he said, "Falconer seems arrogant and powerful enough to get away with everything."

Then he apologised, "I'm thinking in human terms, forgetting that this is not a human battle but a spiritual one. I'm used to sorting things out myself, or with my men, it's hard to let it go and not worry what's going to happen. I'm struggling with how we're going to stop him. If he gets off, he will continue to be the abuser he is and hurt more children. I'm determined that that won't happen, but Sergeant Moore got a call from PC Connors saying he heard Falconer instructing his solicitor to 'make the evidence go away'."

Paul asked, "Where is Roles at this moment?"

"He's down in the cells," Tate answered, "why?"

John looked at Paul, he knew what he was thinking, "It might be a good idea to ask Roles about Falconer. See how much he knows," John told Tate.

"Okay," Tate answered, "I'll try anything at this stage. We've gone through all the evidence a few times. The lists that we got from the safety deposit box don't mention Falconer anywhere. It's like he's never had anything to do with Kerr and Roles. In fact, if it wasn't for Colin, we would be completely in the dark about him. I'm not as stressed as I was, somehow I know God will take care of things, and He won't let Falconer hurt another child."

"I would like to know what happened to the boys Falconer took," John said.

"Sergeant Moore has his people going through the records of the care home as we speak. Hughes says he has evidence against Falconer, but I'm loath to make a deal with him, he let those little lads be taken and he is showing no remorse. All he's worried about is what is going to happen to him, it makes me sick. We're checking the names of the boys from the facility. The men are concentrating on the ones that were supposedly adopted, or the 'run aways'. We're going back six years, it's a long process, but it has to be done. It would be easier just to get the list from Hughes, but I won't give him anything, he deserves everything that's coming to him. It means we won't have much information for at least a few days. But in the meantime, our lads are keeping a close eye on Falconer. I'll send for Roles now, see if he can enlighten us. I would like you all to watch through the two-way mirror, you can see things I can't," he said smiling.

They all agreed, and Inspector Tate rang down to the cells and instructed them to bring Roles up for interrogation.

"I'll get one of the PCs to take you to watch when I have him sitting comfortably."

Tate left the canteen and each of the men prayed that there would be a breakthrough soon.

John was hoping it wouldn't drag out indefinitely. He had a lot of things to arrange for his wedding and he was getting a bit impatient to get things done. But he knew in his heart, this was more important.

They walked with one of the officers to the room next to the interrogation room, where they could see Roles being led in handcuffs by two officers. He looked beaten. All the demons around him were mocking him. Guilt was all over him, overshadowed only by fear. John could only feel pity for him. He thought of all the years he had wasted being angry with Roles. All the times he imagined hitting him again and again in a rage, just disappeared. This man may be a monster, but he was defeated and he looked pathetic. Tate sat in the chair opposite him. Roles' head was bent in defeat. He lifted his head to look at Tate. His eyes were full of fear.

"We've called you from the cells to ask you a few more questions," Tate said to him.

Roles just nodded and Tate continued.

"We have reason to believe you have a relationship, or business ties with a man called Falconer. Is he a close friend of yours? Or is he a business partner?"

Roles physically shook at the mention of the name Falconer. Tate thought he had seen fear in Roles' eyes before, now he looked absolutely terrified.

"I, I, I don't know him," Roles stammered, clearly terrified.

How bad is this man, thought Tate, *putting this much fear in a grown man.*

"We know you know him," he said, "the question is, how well? Mr Kerr has been seen in his company and as you are a very special friend of Mr Kerr, it is logical for us to believe that he is a friend or business colleague of yours too. Don't lie to us, Mr Roles. That would be a very bad idea. There are a number of allegations against this man. These include abuse and numerous abductions. You were caught trying to abduct a child, maybe our witnesses got it wrong and the abuse and abductions are your doing? You see where I'm going with this? The court might believe that you were the one and only culprit in the abductions of these young boys."

Roles bent his head low, "How many boys did he abduct?" he asked quietly.

"We don't have that information at this present time, but we are certain that it has been going on for at least six years. If you've got anything to tell us about this man, now would be a good time. You confessed to your wrong doings and I believe the young man who pursued you, forgave you. You could be in a position to help a number of young boys, if they're not already dead!!!"

The blood drained from Roles' face, Tate could see the terror in his eyes. His hands shook and his knee bounced against the table in pure panic. "I, I can't," he said, dropping his head into his hands. "He'll kill me, or worse, he's so powerful, it would be easy for him to plant evidence against me. Then I would be convicted of all his crimes. He has friends and spies everywhere. You have no idea how powerful he really is."

Tate stood as if to leave, then he turned as if he had just thought of something. "He wouldn't know it came from you. We need to know if he has a place where he might be keeping the boys. I can't offer you a deal, but you know you will feel better for helping these young lads."

Roles kept his head down. "He owns a farm, it's quite rural. He has a large barn, but I've never known him to farm the land or keep livestock. There's also a small wood with a log cabin in the centre. That could be where he is keeping the boys."

"Where is this farm?" Tate tried not to sound excited.

"There's a country road, a few miles from his house, going in the direction of London, there's a turn off into a narrow lane called Dairy Lane. Half way down the lane there is a large gate. The sign on the gate says Falconer's Arms Farm. If he finds out I told you, I'll be dead by morning."

Tate nodded, he thought it was a bit melodramatic, but he couldn't be too sceptical, he didn't know everyone in the station. He knew he could trust Phil Moore and the young lad Connors was a good egg, but he'd need to bring more men into the investigation if they were to converge on the farm.

"Okay, Sergeant Moore, get one of your officers to check if Falconer has a farm on Dairy Lane, it should be easy enough to find out, then I think it's time to call Judge Lacy and request another warrant."

Within minutes, Sergeant Moore had a report of properties that were owned by Falconer. One of these properties was indeed a farm and it was situated on Dairy Lane. He reported this immediately to Tate.

Chapter 76

Connors rang Sergeant Moore, "He's on the move again. Do you want me to stick with him?"

"Yes, definitely. Don't let him out of your sight. Hold on Inspector Tate has just come into the office."

Tate asked, "Is that Connors you're speaking to?"

"Yes, Boss," Sergeant Moore said. "Falconer is on the move again, I've told Connors not to let him out of his sight."

"Okay, good, tell Connors about Falconer's farm. Let him know where it's located. If he loses him, he should be able to find the farm anyway. Tell him to head towards London and look out for a narrow country lane, the farm is on that actual lane."

"Okay, Boss, I'll keep you posted, he's just coming through the gates of his house now. I'm parked behind some bushes, he can't see me. I'll keep far enough away so I'm not spotted."

"Good luck, let us know where he's going, we need to keep him in our sights at all times."

Tate picked up the phone and called Judge Lacy. "Hi, Judge, it's me again, I'm asking for another search warrant."

"What is it for this time?" she asked.

"We have reason to believe that Mr Malcolm Falconer has abused and abducted young boys over a period of at least six years. Have you heard of him?" Tate asked.

"Yes, I know him. He's a very powerful man. You need to be very sure of your evidence to go up against him. Where do you want to search? And how did you gain your information?"

"He was identified by a young man, who had been in the care facility. He claims he came every so often and took young boys from the facility, they were never seen again. He owns a farm out on Dairy Lane. We think he might be holding the boys there. We're hoping they are there, if they're not already dead. We have Connors tailing him. He stopped at his house but is on the move again. We'll see if he goes straight to the farm."

"That's not a lot of evidence to secure a warrant," Judge Lacy told him. "We could both lose our jobs if this boy is wrong. Keep the tail, and let me know if your officer sees any suspicious activity at the farm. I'll have the warrant ready, but I won't do anything until we have more evidence."

"Thanks," said Tate, "keep it on standby. Connors will contact us as soon as Falconer reaches his destination. Hopefully that will be the farm."

"Just get me the evidence. If I go up against this man, I want to make sure we are covered."

Tate smiled to himself. "Yes, Judge," he said. He knew they were well-covered, but not the way she thought. It's time to speak to John and his friends.

He found them back in the canteen and walked towards them. "Please pray," he asked. "We have a tail on Falconer and we're hoping he'll lead us to his farm. Then

214

please God we can rescue the boys. I have a warrant waiting if I can find evidence of the boy's whereabouts."

Paul said, "We will be praying nonstop until we get this man off the streets and rescue these boys."

"Thanks," Tate sighed. "I feel better knowing we're covered in prayer." Then he chuckled and said, "Who would have thought I'd be relying on prayer to get the bad guy. I've always relied on myself and my instincts. I have to say, this feels very peculiar, but I like it. Thank you all, you've changed my life." He turned and walked towards his office.

A few officers sat in the canteen looked up when they heard him speaking. One of the officers turned towards his friend, "Is Inspector Tate actually smiling?" he asked.

The other nodded, "Never thought I'd see the day when we're up to our eyes in paedophiles and the Inspector has a smile on his face. He must know something we don't??"

Meanwhile, Sergeant Moore was supervising the online search for the missing, presumed adopted boys. He had a team of eight officers and civilians helping him. They were going through the care home records. Each boy that had been listed as adopted had to be checked out. It was tedious work—as Moore had insisted they go back ten years to be extra careful that no one was missed. He knew it would be a long process. Even given the eight people he had working with him, he knew he wouldn't get to the bottom of things for at least another three weeks. By that time, who knew where these boys would be. He sat with his team, "What progress have you made so far?"

"Slow," they told him.

"Give me the final two years, last year and this year. I'll work on that and you concentrate on the previous years."

Everyone was impressed that instead of supervising, Sergeant Moore was getting stuck in. This gave them new vitality. It was slow and required a lot of patience. Naturally, the adoptive parents were loath to give out information about their children over the phone. Each time the team reached an adoptive parent, they had to give their name and id. Most of the parents objected so they were asked to call the station to verify their identity. That made the process even longer, but the team knew the parents were being cautious and rightly so.

Most of the children adopted in the first three years of the search were found safe within a family environment. The names of the boys that were still missing were written up on a large white board in front of the squad room. Starting four years down the line, more boys were found not to have been adopted.

Sergeant Moore received a call from Officer Connors. "Something is going on at the farm. There is a van parked up outside a barn and I can see a lot of activity, but I can't get close enough without them seeing me."

Chapter 77

At the same time, Adrian touched Paul's shoulder, "You need to get to the farm now," he told him.

The others heard, they asked John to tell Inspector Tate that they had to leave immediately. John was learning to leave things with these men and not try to interfere. "I'll let him know," he said. "I'll continue praying."

They left in a hurry, they didn't know where they were going, but they knew the Holy Spirit would lead them. They arrived at the farm very quickly. They nodded to Officer Connors and walked through the small gate used for pedestrians. Connors was on the phone to his Sergeant and relayed the situation.

The men saw that Falconer was orchestrating the movement of a number of boys. The driver of the van was taking them from the barn and pushing them into the van that was parked next to it. The engine was still running, obviously they were in a big hurry.

Falconer noticed the men coming towards him. He walked towards them. "Can I help you gentlemen? You are on private property. I will ask you to leave immediately."

The men looked towards the van. "What's going on here?" Derek asked.

"This is none of your concern," Falconer sneered. "Get off my property, or I'll call the police."

"I don't think you'll do that," Mick laughed. "I imagine they would be very interested in this situation."

"I can have you arrested," he shouted at them. "Do you know who I am? No one can touch me and as I said, you're trespassing."

"Yes, we know exactly who you are but you're going to have to answer to a higher authority than the police," Harold told him.

"Oh please, no one, not even God can touch me. I am very powerful and everyone knows who I am. So be on your way, if you know what's good for you."

Adrian touched Paul's shoulder again. "Start praying in the spirit. Remember what happened at John's house, when you went against the fear? Start walking towards Falconer."

Paul looked at the others, they were already praying. All of a sudden there was light. It poured out of each man. It flowed through them as if it was water, living water. Then Paul remembered Jesus' words, 'if you knew the gift of God and who it is that asks you for a drink, you would have asked him and he would have given you living water' (John 4:10).

"We're not going anywhere," Harold told him.

Then the men started walking towards Falconer. He was ranting and shouting but they could see he was afraid.

He couldn't seem to take his eyes off them, it was as if he was mesmerised. He started shaking, then with great effort, turned and ran towards the barn.

He shouted at his driver to start the fire immediately.

The driver told Falconer, "One of the boys is missing. I can't find him anywhere."

"Don't worry, he'll soon run out when he smells the smoke," he snarled.

The driver shook his head, but started the fire, obviously more afraid of Falconer than killing a child. He'd seen Falconer in some strange moods, but this was the weirdest he'd ever seen. He didn't want to tackle him when he was like this. He couldn't tell what he'd do to him. Better just obey orders and get out of there fast.

The men kept walking towards them. The light streaming through them, Falconer couldn't get far enough away from them. "Light the fire," he screamed at the driver.

"I've started it, but what about the child inside?"

"Just do what you're told," he shouted again.

"I'm getting out of here now," the driver told Falconer.

Falconer grabbed him by the arm and pulled him back. "You're going nowhere unless I say so. If you're so worried about the boy in the barn, then get in and get him."

He tried to push the driver into the barn, but he fought back.

"I'm not going to burn to death for you, no matter what you say."

Chapter 78

The boys were crying and shaking, they looked terrified.

The four men looked at each other, "We can't let him take them."

Andrew whispered something in Mick's ear and Mick started running towards the van. He put his finger over his lips to the boys, "Shhh," he said. "You're safe now." He closed the rear door and jumped into the driver's seat. Then he drove the van towards the gates.

Falconer and his driver were struggling together. The driver was pushing him, trying to get away. By the time they noticed, Mick was already half way towards the gate.

"Get him," Falconer shouted at his driver. "Don't let him get away. We need to get rid of those kids. Do it now!!!"

The driver turned towards Falconer. This was his chance to get away, but he faltered. It was one thing to keep the kids locked up, but to let one die in the fire, that was a different ball game altogether. He turned and saw the men coming closer. There was something about them, they seemed to glow. It made him very uncomfortable. His skin began to crawl, he felt itchy and sore all over. Suddenly, the only thought in his head was to get as far away as possible from these men.

Falconer was screaming at him to get the van. He pulled away from him and started running, not in the direction of the van, but in the opposite direction. Falconer was alone. He turned and noticed how close the men were to him, he panicked. *I can get into the barn and out the back before they get near enough to me,* he decided.

He opened the barn door and ran inside. The draught caused by him opening the door accelerated the flames.

"What about the boy?" Harold shouted.

"He's at the back of the barn," Mark told him. "He's hiding under his bed, too terrified to move. But the fire hasn't reached that part of the barn yet, so he hasn't been injured."

"How do I get in?" Paul asked Adrian.

"Follow me," the angel replied.

The three men followed their angels to the back of the barn. There was a ladder up to an opening at the top of the barn. Paul didn't hesitate, he started up the ladder immediately. All he could think of was—what if this was Aaron?

Derek and Harold started praying in the spirit again. They asked for protection for Paul and the boy. They knew once they were praying in the spirit, their prayers were answered. They could hear banging and shouting inside the barn. It was Falconer, still screaming abuse as the fire continued to blaze.

Paul climbed through the small opening. He looked down to the lower level and there, behind a partition, were a number of beds. He had forgotten to ask the boy's name in his panic to save him. Adrian touched him and said, "I'm still with you, I haven't left you on your own. The boy's name is Brian. He's terrified, he will need coaxing."

218

Paul jumped down to the lower level. He looked back up from where he had come, how he was going to get back up there with a young boy was another thing.

"Brian," he whispered, "my name is Paul and I've been sent to help you."

He could hear the boy whimpering. He listened intently then started towards the beds. He got down on his hands and knees to look under the beds. He nearly cried when he saw the little bundle cowering in the corner. He put his hand out and touched the boy's hand.

"Brian," he said, "we need to leave this place. It's going to burn down so we need to move very fast. Can you do that?"

The boy tried to pull his hand away, but he was paralysed with fear. "I can't," he whispered, "he'll find me and hurt me again."

"No, he will never hurt you again, I promise," Paul told him. "Come towards me and I'll get you out of here. All your friends are safe, and listen, can you here the shouting? Well, that's the bad man. He's in the barn, so we need to get out."

"Are my friends really safe?" Brian asked.

"Yes," said Paul. "My friend saved them."

"I can hear Mr Falconer shouting," Brian said, "it's always worse when he shouts."

"Well, you'll never have to hear him shout again, but you need to come to me."

Paul could see the young boy trembling. He hadn't time to cajole him. He could feel the heat of the flames and knew they were coming closer. He caught Brian by his jumper and pulled him from under the bed. Brian was screaming but Paul wouldn't let go. He pulled him into his arms and hugged him. Brian went totally rigid with fear, but Paul held on to him. He picked him up and carried him to the edge of the loft. "Okay," he said, "if I lift you up high, do you think you can catch on to the edge of the loft and pull yourself up?"

Paul was sweating, if Brian hadn't the strength to pull himself up, and Paul doubted that he did, they wouldn't get out alive and he would have failed to save this boy's life. He started to get dispirited, just then Adrian touched his shoulder.

"Remember you were told you would see things you never thought possible? Well, now you will do something you never thought possible. Lift the boy high."

Paul did, the boy felt as light as a feather. He practically flew out of Paul's arms. Then he was standing on the upper level.

Brian looked down at Paul, he looked so far down. There was nothing to climb onto. He knew Paul wouldn't get out alive. His eyes were as big as saucers. The tears were pouring down his face.

Paul shouted at him to run towards the opening and climb down the ladder. Brian backed away, but he couldn't take his eyes off Paul. This man had saved him and now he was going to die. *Mr Falconer was right. Anyone who tried to save his boys would die.* He was so scared, he was hyper ventilating.

Then he heard a voice calling him. He turned around slowly, there was another man climbing through the opening. He took his hand and led him out of the barn onto the ladder. He made sure that Brian could climb down on his own.

Then he saw another man at the bottom of the ladder. He was an older man. He looked just like his granddad used to look. The older man was beckoning him to come down. He climbed down and the older man caught him in his arms. But these arms weren't rough, they were gentle and the man's voice was gentle. Brian looked up and the second man had gone back into the barn. Now he was going to die. He turned towards the older man and started crying.

"Everyone who helps me dies. Mr Falconer was right. You'll die too if you help me. Please don't help me. I don't want you to die too."

Harold said gently, "I'm not going to die, and neither are my friends whom you met in the barn. We were sent to help you, so keep looking up and wait, you'll see, they'll be okay."

Paul stood on the lower level, he wasn't afraid to die. 'Been there, done that.' He wasn't sure he fancied burning alive. He turned to Adrian, "Well, I guess this is the end of my mission," he said.

Adrian laughed and said, "Have faith, and look up."

Paul looked up and there was Derek standing on the upper ledge.

"How are you doing?" Derek asked him.

"I could do with a pair of wings about now," Paul replied.

"Jump!" Adrian told him.

Paul looked at him, "Pardon?" he asked.

"Just jump!" Adrian repeated.

"Okay," Paul said sceptically.

He jumped towards the upper level and his feet flew off the ground.

Derek had lain down with his hands towards Paul. Paul caught them. Then with strength that Derek never felt before, he hauled Paul up to the upper level.

They both lay on their backs in astonishment.

"How did that happen?" It was a rhetorical question, they both knew the answer.

Adrian urged them to hurry. The fire had taken hold and the barn was crumbling around them. They hurried to the ladder and started down.

Harold told Brian to look up again. When he saw the two men coming down the ladder, he just stood with his mouth open.

"Mr Falconer lied to you and all your friends, Brian," Harold said, "You see, my friends and I didn't die. And our other friend who saved the rest of the boys is alive too."

Brian's smile melted Harold's heart. Paul and Derek came over to them and Brian ran and threw his arms around Paul and then Derek. "Thank you for saving me."

The three men looked at each other smiling. "I thought I'd come to the end of the mission early," Paul told them.

"No chance," Derek said, "I think we're in this together to the end."

They heard a loud crash. Paul and Derek ran to the front of the barn.

Chapter 79

The front wall had collapsed, Falconer was trapped. There was a huge beam across his abdomen. He couldn't move. Derek and Paul's first reaction was to rush in and help him. But the fire was too hot and they couldn't get past the flames. Falconer was screaming, not for help, but he was still screaming abuse at them. He was shouting at them, calling them cowards for not running into the flames and saving him. He kept repeating, "Do you know who I am? This sort of thing can't happen to me. I'm too powerful. Get in here and get this beam off me. Your lives are worth nothing, I'm the important one, so do something!!!"

Paul shouted back at him, "We can't get past the flames, the fire engines will be here any minute, hold on."

Then Falconer started screaming and cursing God. Paul and Derek could see the demons dancing around him. He shouted that he couldn't possibly die, he was much too powerful. "I made a deal." He screamed. "I was promised a long and powerful life so God can't touch me!!"

He had just finished the sentence when the roof collapsed in on him. A beam fell straight down and pierced through his chest. Paul and Derek looked away in shock. The silence was worse than the shouting. When they looked back, they saw that the beam was in the shape of a cross.

Then they saw Falconer rise up. They both stepped back in fear. He looked as if he had risen from the dead and was completely alive in body and soul. He started laughing at them. "I told you, your God couldn't hurt me. You're both pathetic."

Paul and Derek stood speechless. Then Derek looked to where the beam had pierced Falconer's chest, his body was lying on the ground. He nudged Paul and pointed to the body. He looked back at Falconer. He looked more powerful than ever.

"Oh, now I can roam the earth free," Falconer sneered. "I can terrify children to my heart's content and nothing can stop me." He started laughing, it sounded so evil. They just stood in stunned silence. In their hearts, they knew God was all-powerful, but looking at this evil spirit, they were confused.

They noticed something moving in the fire. It was behind Falconer. It was the darkness. Inside it black shadows began to appear. They came from all different angles. They seemed to glide along the ground towards Falconer. Paul and Derek stood watching. The shadows seeped nearer and nearer to Falconer's spirit. Then, as if they had grown talons, they grabbed him. He tried to wrestle with them, but they were like smoke. They held on to him and dragged him backwards. "No, no, no, you can't, you promised. You can't take me yet!" he shouted.

Then Derek and Paul heard the most horrendous scream one they would never forget. It sent shivers down their backs and the hairs on their arms and necks stood to attention.

Falconer's spirit was gone. It had disappeared into the darkness. Harold came rushing around holding on to Brian.

"What on earth was that scream?" he asked them.

Brian looked confused, "What scream?" he asked.

They looked and saw his guardian angel with his hands covering the child's ears. What a blessing, and the boy would never know.

"It wasn't anything from this earth," Paul whispered to Harold. "Falconer is dead. He will never hurt another young boy again. We'll explain everything when we get back to the B & B."

Chapter 80

The fire engines began to arrive. The fire was put out quickly. The coroner came and removed the body.

Tate came over to the men. Mick was with him. "The boys are all safe and sound, thanks to Mick. Thank you all for your help saving this little lad. We've taken all the boys to the B & B until we can get them fostered. At least we know they'll be safe there. But obviously, it's not a permanent situation and these boys need stable homes."

"What about the driver?" Derek asked.

"We caught up with him, don't worry, he's not going anywhere except prison." Tate laughed.

Brian clung to Harold's hand. "Don't worry," Harold said, "no one will hurt you. You're going to stay at a very nice place with a lovely lady and her husband, until we can get you a mum and dad to look after you."

"Okay," Brian whispered, tears in his eyes, but he didn't let go of Harold's hand.

Tate bade them farewell and went back to the station. When he walked through the doors, all the officers and civilians stood and applauded him. Nothing like that had ever happened to him in his whole career. He shot a look at Sergeant Moore, "Job well done by all!!" he shouted.

The eight men and women who were going through the files smiled at him, knowing he appreciated all their hard work. They still had a lot of boys to check up on, but they were convinced that they'd found the majority of them, if not all of the missing ones.

"I think we can all relax tonight," Tate said. "Anyone fancy a pint? Drinks are on me."

There was a huge cheer and everyone volunteered to go to the pub after their shift had finished.

Chapter 81

Back at the B & B, Paul and Derek recounted events from the barn. They wanted to bring Mick up to date and explain the last horrible scream to Harold. They sat in silence, each trying to understand just what had happened. They'd never experienced anything quite like it before.

"Let's pray!" Mick said.

They bowed their heads and Mick led, thanking God for saving the boys, who were presently in the small sitting room, watching cartoons. Then, for all that had happened and for all they had seen.

A light shone over them. The Light of Jesus! It brought a perfect peace to each one of their souls, after such a horrible day. None of them wanted to move. They could only bask in His light. It brought a cleansing to them as well. All the evil they had encountered through the past couple of months and then the climax today left them feeling as if their souls had been contaminated. It was the only way Paul could explain it later when they met up again for the evening meal. Contamination that only the Light of Jesus could erase.

Alice came over to Harold. "The boys are all bathed and in bed now. We've put four boys in each room for comfort and for their security," she told him, "but Brian is insisting that you come and tuck him in, Harold. Will you please? He won't settle until you do!"

The others smiled. "Always the father figure," Paul said.

"Grandfather figure!" He laughed.

Alice smiled and said, "Oh no, Paul, he also wants to see you too, ha-ha, you don't get off that easily."

So both Harold and Paul went to speak to Brian. As they were nearing the room, they could hear Brian telling the other boys how Paul had lifted him high in the air, like he was superman. Paul and Harold looked at each other and laughed.

"I've been called many things," said Paul, "but superman?? Now that's special!!"

Harold clapped him on the back and whispered, "Well done."

They both walked into the room and found all the boys in the same room listening to Brian.

"Okay," said Harold. "Alice said you were all in bed. What's going on?"

"We just wanted to hear Brian's story. It's exciting," one of the boys told them.

"And we wanted to meet superman," another boy said.

"Whoa," Paul said, "I'm not superman, but sometimes when we pray and we need super strength, then God gives us super strength. You all have super strength," he added.

The boys all looked at each other, confused.

"How have we got super strength?" another boy asked.

"Well, you had a very bad time with Mr Falconer, hadn't you?" Paul asked.

They all nodded together.

"But look at you now. You're all safe and sound, you all survived and it takes super strength to survive all the bad things that happened to you."

"Wow," the boys said in unison. They all looked at each other in wonder.

"But," Harold told them, "you mustn't let what happened you make you hate people. You must pray and Jesus will help you forgive all the bad things people did to you. He'll heal you of all your bad memories and He'll help you forgive all the bad men as well."

"Even Mr Falconer?" Brian asked astonished.

"Even Mr Falconer!" Harold told him. "He's gone now, and he can never hurt anyone again. It's best to forgive him and forget all about him."

They nodded, but didn't look entirely convinced.

Harold said a short prayer asking God to protect the boys and give them a good night's rest. Then he ushered them into their own rooms.

Paul and Harold said goodnight to all the boys and then Harold tucked Brian in. The boys seemed quite peaceful, especially after what they'd been through.

When they returned to the table, Derek and Mick were having a serious conversation.

"What's going on?" Paul asked.

"We're just wondering what will happen to the boys after this," Derek said.

"They've been through a lot and I imagine some of them are quite traumatised," Mick added.

"What can we do for them? We can't expect Alice to keep them all here, especially as she's due her baby soon."

With that, the door opened and John and Jennifer walked in. They were both smiling and looked extremely happy.

"May we join you?" John asked.

"Of course," said Derek, "you don't need to ask."

"You both look very happy with yourselves," Mick said smiling.

"Ha-ha, we are." Jennifer laughed. "We've been speaking to Inspector Tate about the boys. He's agreed to put the full story in the local newspaper. We've spoken to the adoption authorities as well. You know, so much of this situation could have been avoided if the adoption society wasn't so picky with parents who want to adopt children."

Paul was about to disagree, but Jennifer held up her hand. "I don't mean 'picky', I know people have to be checked out, but some of the things they ask are nearly impossible to live up to. Anyway, we've had talks with them and they've agreed to let locals adopt these boys.

"We explained what they had gone through, knowing they may have a tough road ahead, we wanted to make sure that they can stay in touch with each other for moral support. And if they have problems, the parents can help each other. So our town will have an influx of boys needing counselling. But my man here is an excellent counsellor. I think he might be kept quite busy." She laughed.

"We've spoken to a few of the locals and they would love to adopt some of the boys. We think we can place them all, but any who can't be placed, Jennifer and I have agreed to adopt," John concluded, smiling at Jennifer.

"That's quite an undertaking for newlyweds," Harold said.

"Yes, we know," replied John, "but after what these boys have been through, it's the right thing to do. If the Lord wants us to have any of these boys, Jennifer and I are in agreement. We shall wait and see what the next few days bring. The best thing is these boys will be safe from here on in."

Chapter 82

Harold asked Alice where Colin was. "I haven't seen him since we got back."

"He's dining out with Craig and Mel and Mel's children," Alice told him. "He and Craig are getting along so well, I can hardly believe the change in him."

"Thank God," said Harold. "He really has worked His miracles on Colin."

They all said their goodnights and retired to their rooms. Each pair of men prayed before they got into bed. They needed a good night's sleep after the day they had just had. They woke the next morning completely refreshed.

They came downstairs to the dining room, it was chaos. The noise was deafening.

Harold strode in and wished everyone a good morning. The dining room went quiet. Should they say 'good morning' back, or would they be punished for all the noise?? Harold looked at their faces and laughed, "All I said was 'good morning'. Why do you all look so worried?"

"Good morning, Sir," they chimed.

"We are not in school now, boys," he told them. "My name is Harold and no one is going to hurt or punish you when I'm around."

They all sighed in relief. Brian ran to Harold and hugged him. Harold couldn't help but smile and remember his boys and all the hugs he'd received in his lifetime. Everyone sat down to breakfast and the boys were very well behaved. Then Colin came into the dining room. They hadn't seen him since the morning before. When he saw all the boys sitting around eating breakfast, he smiled but still had that haunted look on his face.

Harold called him to join them at their table. He walked towards them, but kept looking at all these young boys that were laughing and chatting as if nothing had happened to them.

Harold asked, "Are you okay, Colin?"

"Yes, thank you, I'm good. I just can't get my head around these boys. They look happy as if nothing had ever happened to them. Yet I remember everything as if it was yesterday. I feel so selfish harbouring this hatred for the men who hurt me."

"These boys are young and they've always had each other," Harold told him. "They were kept together and could help each other through the horrible times. Then yesterday, they were rescued and they know they are safe. This is just the beginning. There will be bad times ahead for some of them. But the fact that they were rescued while they were still young has played an important part. Don't beat yourself up, God will take the anger and hatred from you, all you need to do is ask."

"I know," Colin told him, "it's hard, but I know I have to learn to forgive and forget. But how do I do that?"

"Only by prayer, and letting the Holy Spirit work in you," Mick told him. "You're a brand new Christian, God is very patient, and He will work in you to give you forgiveness. Don't try to force it, let it come in God's time."

"Did the police get Falconer?" Colin asked warily. "Has he been arrested? I was out with Craig and Mel last night and haven't heard anything this morning."

So the men relayed the full story of the previous day's happenings. Colin just sat there shocked. They didn't tell him about the black spirits coming for Falconer's spirit. He was too new to this, and they didn't want to scare him. He would in time learn the full details, but it was enough that he knew that Falconer was dead and by nobody's hand but the Lord's. The look of relief on his face was wonderful. It was like he had been released from prison. They knew that he was relieved that he wouldn't have to go to court to testify and rightly so.

The men finished breakfast. Colin was meeting Craig and his team to carry on the painting in the church. He was really enjoying painting. The fact that he was also getting to know ordinary men, and working alongside them without fear, was a miracle in itself.

But the men had their work cut out for them, keeping the lads entertained and trying to help in the church at the same time. Time was moving on, and John and Jennifer's wedding was fast approaching.

Harold organised some of the boys to help him in the grounds of the church and in the garden at the B & B. Alice was quite big now and she couldn't bend to weed the garden. Robert was busy sorting the rooms the boys had slept in. He actually commented to Harold on the tidiness of the rooms. Each boy had made his own bed. "It's like they were in the army," he told him.

Chapter 83

The newspapers reported the story the following day. Shock ripped through the community. Though Falconer was not from their town, he hadn't lived that far away. To think all of this horror had been going on under their noses. It brought a lot of people down to earth. One spokesman said, "We've lived our lives as if we were privileged and no one else matters. Now we have to own up to our responsibilities."

The adoption agency was inundated with applications for the adoption of the boys. The ages ranged from six to twelve years old.

Craig and Mel spoke about the situation. Neither of them were in a position to adopt. Mel was doing okay financially, but just keeping her head above water, with three children to clothe and feed. Although since meeting Mick, her life had changed dramatically. Then meeting Craig was the icing on the cake.

I wonder if he feels the same as I do? she asked herself.

If he asked me to marry him, she thought, *I'd ask Mick to walk me down the aisle.* She smiled as she thought about it, it was a fantasy, but everyone should be allowed to have at least one fantasy in their lives. Craig had become a very important person in her life and the lives of her children. They adored him. They seemed to have a better relationship with him than they did with their dear, departed dad. He had always worried about money and worked so hard, they hardly ever saw him. She dropped the children off at school and arrived at work shortly before nine am.

When she went into the church, there seemed to be boys everywhere.

"What's going on?" she asked John.

"We're trying to keep them occupied," he told her. "Colin has stopped painting with the lads to show the boys how to help the women clean the floor. Once they know the drill, he will go back to his painting. Some of Craig's men are letting the older boys help with the painting. They are so delighted to be treated gently by other men, they are working very hard. I think they will all need new clothes before the day is out. There is more paint on them than on the walls," he said laughing.

"Why don't we try to get them into the local schools?" Mel asked.

"We haven't had a chance yet. The men brought them here to give Alice a break, though Harold left a few older lads looking after Alice's garden. Hopefully it won't be a complete disaster. Poor Harold, he is going from here to the B & B trying to keep an eye on them. Maybe you could get onto the schools? If you have time that is?"

"Yes, of course." She beamed. "I know the heads of both the primary and the high school. I'll get on to that now."

She rang both schools and spoke to the heads. They were only too delighted to have the boys attend. Next job was to have them fitted out with uniforms. Mel didn't want them standing out any more than they would, but getting the money was the problem.

John had a great idea. "Why don't we have a party on the church grounds this afternoon?"

"Better still," said Mel, "why not tomorrow, as its Saturday we can invite the whole town. We can call it 'bring and share'."

They both agreed it was a great idea. So the news went out through the people working at the church. Invite all your neighbours, they were told, let's get as many people to meet these young lads as we can.

The following day, practically the whole town turned up. Families came and old and young couples without children came. It was a great success. The plan worked, the boys were introduced to the townspeople, and in turn they were introduced to the boys. It also gave the boys back some of their trust in people.

Mel was arranging the food and drinks. Some women came to her with envelopes. "We'd like to give donations for the upkeep of the boys until they're adopted. They'll need clothes and Alice can't be expected to feed the lot of them for nothing. So please accept these donations," the spokeswoman said.

Mel was overwhelmed, once one lot of women handed over the envelopes, the rest of the town seemed to get the same idea. Every last man and woman gave towards the upkeep of the boys.

The boys had a wonderful time, they were exhausted by the time the party was over and practically fell into bed.

Sunday morning, Alice had them all up and dressed. "Where did you get the clean clothes?" Harold asked her.

"People have been coming and leaving clothes at reception all last evening and all this morning," she told him. "It's just another miracle," she said laughing with pure delight.

They all walked to the church for the service. Some of the boys had never been at church and were curious. Others, like Colin had been, were very reluctant. It was the first time the church was being used for the service in a long time. It wasn't quite finished, there were still bits of underlay that refused to come off, but all in all, it looked quite good. Inspector Tate arrived with his family, followed by some of his officers, including Sergeant Moore and PC Connors. It seemed the majority of the police force wanted to know more about this amazing God.

Derek approached John, "Please don't take offence at what I'm about to say."

"Of course not," John stuttered, completely flummoxed.

"You haven't had much time to work on your sermon this week. So let the Holy Spirit lead you today. Don't worry about what you're going to say, or how long it takes you to say it. You are an amazing preacher. I wish I'd had someone like you in my life. Please don't stifle the Holy Spirit, let Him lead you."

John was dumfounded, "Okay" was all he could say.

The thought had been running through his mind since Friday. Well, there was confirmation.

The service was brilliant, everything flowed as it should and people left the church with smiles and a lightness of spirit. Even the boys, who were scared of churches, came out smiling and laughing.

Monday morning, it was time for the boys to start school. Adoption papers were being received and processed with an urgency that was not usual.

Mel watched the boys going into school. They hadn't any uniforms yet, but they would have them within the week. Her eye caught a young boy. He was only about six. He looked up at her and she could see hope in his eyes. She knew there and then, he was for her. She could not explain it logically, but she knew God wanted this boy to be with her. She understood that she was just keeping her head above water at the moment, but what had John called God the day before? Yahweh Yireh—the God who provides. She went to one of the teachers and asked for the boy's name, it was Brian.

She was seeing Craig that evening. They were going for a meal at the B & B. He had wanted to take her to a special restaurant, but she never wanted to be far from her children, in case anything happened. She knew that was lack of faith, but she would work on it, now she was happy to be going for a meal with Craig and her babysitter knew exactly where she would be.

She spoke to her children and asked if they'd like a little brother? They were thrilled, especially her son, who had always wanted a brother to play with. *Well, that's that,* she thought. *Whatever happens, it's with God.*

Her and Craig sat in the main dining room and enjoyed a lovely meal. Afterwards, Craig became very serious. Mel was worried as this wasn't his usual manner. He took her hand in his and very seriously asked her to marry him. She was dumbfounded. She had not expected this so soon.

"I have loved you since the first time I laid eyes on you," he told her, "please say yes."

"Yes, yes," she said breathlessly.

They kissed and laughed and talked about when it would happen and what they needed to plan.

Then Mel remembered Brian. "I know I already have three children," she said. "But I saw one of the abused boys when I dropped the children off at school this morning. Brian is his name, I know God wants me to adopt him. You have no children, and taking on three will be hard enough, so if you don't think you can handle another, please tell me now. I'm already calling him my son in my head."

Craig laughed, "I've been praying about adopting one of the boys, but after what they've been through, I doubt they'd let a single man adopt. But we'll be a family, and we can give our children a good life. If your children agree, I would dearly like to adopt them as my own. What would you say to that?"

"I think that would be wonderful." Mel beamed.

They agreed to go to the adoption agency the following morning to apply to adopt little Brian.

They arrived at the agency first thing the next morning. They were the first to be seen. They told them their story and asked specifically to adopt Brian.

"This is very unorthodox," the lady said, "but we are in an unusual situation. We've had a number of applications for adopting the boys. A lot of the parents had specific ages in mind, but you have a specific boy? Brian?"

"Yes," said Mel, "he is about six years old. I saw him in the school yard yesterday and I knew he belonged in our family."

"Well, obviously, we will have to do searches on both of you. They will be rushed through, these boys need stability. It should be straight forward as you have a certain boy in mind. Normally, it would take at least six weeks for the CRB checks to come back but Inspector Tate has spoken to the department and they have agreed to rush everything through. He offered a few of his officers to help with the searches, the department has never had an offer like that before and they agreed immediately."

Epilogue

All the searches came back within a week. This was another miracle. Mel and Craig were granted adoption of Brian. No family was turned down. The people at the agency were very surprised, twenty-four different families applied. It should have worked out that at least three boys would not be adopted, but some of the applicants requested adoption of two boys. All the boys were adopted.

'With man this is impossible, but with God, everything is possible' (Matt. 19:26).

The following week was a bit of a blur. John and Jennifer were married. Alice did all the catering, helped by Mel and some of the women from the town. The sun shone brightly and the sky was a perfect blue on the morning of the wedding. John thought Jennifer looked radiant as she walked down the aisle, which had finally been finished two days before. Jennifer could see the love in John's eyes as he watched her come towards him.

Inspector Tate came to the service and so did many of his colleagues. It was a happy affair and both bride and groom never stopped smiling throughout the day and evening. John had a surprise for Jennifer.

"I've booked a fortnight in Crete for us. It's a five-star hotel, but I didn't know if you'd go along with the quick wedding plans, so I booked it for a week on Sunday. Is that okay with you?"

Jennifer was over the moon, "It's wonderful, now I can shop for summer clothes."

The day after the wedding, Alice looked exhausted.

"Are you okay?" Harold asked her.

She did love this man, he was like her dad. "Yes," she said, "just tired and I have a few twinges."

"Ahhh," said Harold, "when are you due?"

"Mmm anytime now," she said.

"How often are the pains coming?"

"About every ten minutes."

"Okay, we need to get you to the hospital. I'll get Robert, you have your bag packed?"

"Yes, Dad," Alice said laughing.

Harold made her sit down and went to get Robert. He shouted to the others and told them. Paul agreed to go with Harold and Robert.

They stayed outside the delivery room praising and worshipping God for all He had accomplished in these last months.

All of a sudden the doors burst open. Robert came out grinning from ear to ear. "He's arrived," he told them, "and he's beautiful. Come in, she wants to show him off."

They went through and Alice looked so serene and peaceful as she held her little son in her arms.

"Meet Harold the second," she said.

Harold blushed, but he was so proud, "Thank you," was all he could say.

Paul smiled at him and was sure he saw a tear in the older man's eyes.

Craig and Mel were married the following week. Mick proudly walked Mel down the aisle. Her two daughters were her bridesmaids and her two sons both held cushions, one with her wedding ring and one with Craig's wedding ring. She was so proud of them.

She looked at Craig, standing, waiting for her at the altar. He was so handsome, and the look of love in his eye nearly took her breath away. Colin stood by Craig's side as his best man. He looked fantastic and so happy. Mel was nearly overcome with gratitude to God for all he had done for her and her family and friends.

Craig couldn't stop smiling, he sent up a silent prayer. "Thank you Father, for my beautiful woman, You were right, she was well worth waiting for." He turned and smiled at Colin. He was so proud of this young man and what he had come through. They had become very good friends indeed.

Another wonderful wedding and all went as planned. This little town would never be the same. God had truly delivered the people from evil.

"Well, everything we were asked to accomplish has been accomplished." Paul said. "What now?"

Their angels touched their shoulders, and it was like each man had fallen into a deep sleep. With strong arms, the angels picked them up and flew out over the town and surrounding fields and into the city. They sat on the pinnacle of a church and woke the men up.

"Open your spiritual eyes," Adrian said. "Look around you. This is an ongoing battle for the souls of this city. This is just one city and the battle rages over every town and city throughout the earth."

The men looked mesmerised, sometimes it looked like the angels of God were winning, then in another spot Satan's demons seemed to have the upper hand. It was chaos, bloody and downright scary. They stood and watched speechless.

"In the previous months, you enabled us to win a major battle against Satan," said Adrian. "The paedophile ring you helped bring down was one of the biggest and least known throughout the entire country. Falconer had Satan's protection, but you, through your eagerness to help others like Colin, helped to bring him down. We won that battle, but the war goes on."

"Why are you showing us this?" Mick asked.

"Tonight, you have a choice." Andrew, Mick's angel told them. "You have obeyed the Father and completed the task He gave you. Now you have a choice, you can choose rest and the Father will accept you with open arms, or you can stay and help in our fight. Which will you choose?"

THE END